A Day Too Long

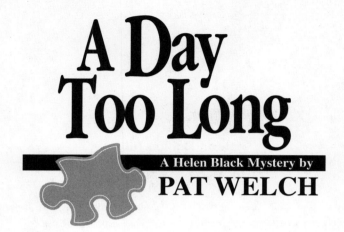

A Helen Black Mystery by

PAT WELCH

Bella
BOOKS

Ferndale, Michigan
2003

Bella Books, Inc.
P.O. Box 201007
Ferndale, MI 48220

Printed in the United States of America on acid-free paper
First Edition

Editor: J. M. Redmann
Cover designer: Bonnie Liss (Phoenix Graphics)

ISBN 1-931513-22-8

It ain't but the one thing I done wrong,
I stayed in Miss'ippi just a day too long . . .

— traditional prison blues

Chapter One

"I don't think I'm ever going to understand this stuff."

Sissy Greene bent over the notebook and chewed her pencil. Lank mouse-dull hair shielded her thin cheeks and hid her dark, worried eyes. "All this fraction stuff. It just doesn't make any sense." She spoke around the stub of pencil being chewed in her mouth and shifted on the porch swing to squint up at Helen in the morning sunlight.

Helen glanced down at the girl sitting beside her, then looked back at the two police officers at the edge of the front lawn. One of them spat onto the sidewalk, turning his gaze away from the pair on the porch swing. He said something to his partner, his grinning murmur drowned out by the squawking of the radio inside the black-and-white. Their

1

stares pierced through the morning heat as they took in every detail of Helen's appearance. And Sissy's, too. Shit, Helen tried to reassure herself, they're just bored. No one here has done anything wrong. Least of all me. But Helen could feel the inner protest wriggling through a maze of fear. It was just a routine call, right? Nothing to do with Helen. Probably Mrs. Mapple making one of her wild complaints about terrorists and aliens and any of the innumerable threats the old woman sensed around her. Or maybe this time it was a little closer to home. Maybe Mrs. Mapple had called about Helen, her newest boarder.

"Did you hear me?" Sissy nudged her ribs.

"What?" Helen tried to drag her mind away from the cops staring impassively in her direction. The back of her shirt stuck to her sweaty skin and she moved, irritated, making the swing creak. "I'm sorry. What did you say?"

"Is something wrong?"

"Not a thing." Jesus, even to her ears that sounded fake, perky, even. "What did you ask me?"

"Do you think I'll ever use any of this stuff anyway, Mrs. Black? My mom never does." Her dark serious gaze, calm and reserved, belied the strain that surfaced in her stubby little-kid fingers twisting the pencil around and around and around.

"It's just Helen, Sissy. And I'm not married." Helen smiled down at the nine-year-old sitting beside her on the swing. "Maybe you will use it and maybe you won't. But it sure can't hurt to get good grades, can it?" She peered down at the notebook. The kid had almost finished the problems — only two more to go. "Why don't you finish those two and we'll see how you did." Thank god fourth grade math wasn't beyond Helen's capacities yet.

Sissy sighed. "Okay." She took the pencil out of her mouth and started to write. "My mom doesn't really care if I get good grades or not, though."

Helen kept silent. Why lie and tell Sissy that wasn't true? Instead the two of them sat peaceably on the swing that moved gently, creaking in the early morning breeze. The cool breeze would soon die, of course. Already, at 7:00 A.M., the orange-yellow sun rising to their left bespoke another sweltering Mississippi morning. The porch of Mrs. Mapple's boarding house faced south. Behind them, a couple of miles to the north, Highway 20 stretched between Jackson and Vicksburg. Ahead of them lay the small town of Tynedale, the center of Purvis County. Situated on top of a hill at the north end of town, the boarding house porch offered a panoramic view of Tynedale just waking up and beginning to stretch its legs. Like most small towns there was a central core, just visible through the tops of trees, where stately old homes going to seed squatted ill at ease with strip malls and fast-food vendors. Mrs. Mapple's boarding house wedged the last respectable row of houses, not far from the trailer park. At the very center of Tynedale loomed the incongruous classical dome of the County Courthouse. Helen's appointment with her parole officer there was set for 10:00 A.M. As Sissy struggled with math beside her, Helen let her gaze travel from the courthouse to the hills beyond town.

Farther to the south Helen could see the top of Champion's Hill, where over a century ago the Federal and Confederate armies had tried to destroy each other in Grant's relentless drive to take Vicksburg. That accomplished, Tynedale and Champion's Hill had settled down to a few generations of obscurity, preferring to let the dead bury the dead. While Helen had never found a minie ball herself, local gossip held that those bits and pieces of spent ammunition could still be found in the dirt throughout Tynedale and the surrounding countryside. Also bones, from time to time, of the nameless soldiers who'd bled to death on the ground around the former Champion plantation. No telling now whether blue or gray had covered those bones when they'd walked the earth.

The sound of rap music thundering from Kyle Mapple's car as it backed down the steep driveway pulled Helen's thoughts back to the present. She could just make out his pimply teen-aged face, set in its usual sullen glare, through the car windows. Once on the street he revved the motor and straightened his skinny frame up from slumping at the wheel, speeding off and away from his mother's boarding house in a sound and fury that was sure to get the neighbors howling. Helen watched the car roar to the end of Gramm Street. Her view of Kyle turning the corner was blocked by the two police cars sitting in front of the boarding house. Actually, Helen reasoned, those cars would have the neighbors talking more than Kyle would. Their arrival at 6:30 this morning, lights flashing and uniformed officers bristling out onto the lawn, must have roused everyone on the block.

"Those cops aren't here about my mom and dad, are they?" Sissy asked, distracted yet again from her homework by the flashing red and blue lights.

"No, Mrs. Mapple called them because she thinks someone might have been trying to steal things from the house." Sissy's eyes got wide and her mouth fell open. "I think everything is okay, Sissy. They just want to talk to her about it."

"Do we have to tell them anything?"

"I don't know. I'm sure they'll talk to us if they want to."

"But —" Sissy chewed on the frayed ends of her dull brown hair. "The police would be here because something is wrong. So what's going on?"

Helen smiled and hoped her face was calm and cheerful. "I bet it's nothing bad. I bet Mrs. Mapple just got worried about things again."

"Helen, I don't like that one. The one with the sunglasses." Sissy scuffed worn tennis shoes on the weathered wood. "He keeps staring at you."

I don't like him either, kid. "We'll just go on about our business like he's not there. I bet he'll leave us alone."

"Okay." Sissy subsided, leaning against Helen with an easy familiarity that tugged at her heart — like they were sisters

4

or something. "I'm getting hungry. When is breakfast going to be ready?"

Helen cleared her throat. "Let's just try to get the homework done, okay? I have a feeling it will be ready in just a minute or two." Sissy subsided again, and Helen took another sip of coffee. Damn, it was cold. But she didn't want to go in for a refill and risk a meeting with Tynedale's finest.

Helen had overheard Mrs. Mapple's hysterical shrieks on the phone at 6 o'clock as she screamed over the phone that someone had tried to break in the back door again and this time she had the scratches around the lock to prove it, thank you very much, so the cops had just better earn all that tax money and get out there right away so folks wouldn't get murdered in their beds while they sat at the donut shop getting fat on the citizen's dime. Then a long silence, followed by Mrs. Mapple's angry statement that if she'd heard something the night before she would have called the night before, so she'd called as soon as she'd noticed the scratches when she'd gone out back to feed the cats this morning, and that if they didn't want the Tynedale police department to appear on Mike Wallace and Sixty Minutes next Sunday when she was killed dead by robbers they'd better get out there and take a look at the back door and that it would be God's own vengeance wreaked on their heads if they failed in their civic duty. Giving up on a morning to sleep in before meeting with her parole officer, Helen had slipped on jeans and t-shirt and gone outside with a cup of coffee from the endless supply Mrs. Mapple kept going in the kitchen. Absorbed as she was in her righteous tirade, the boarding house owner hadn't even noticed Helen slip out to the front porch.

Rubbing sleep from her eyes Helen had spied Sissy, clutching her notebook and pencil, crouched in a tight little ball on the porch swing. The big circles under the girl's eyes told of a sleepless night. Instead of asking questions, Helen had only said something about her homework, which had led to the unlikely situation of Helen as math tutor as the police arrived — two guys in dark blue uniforms and, strangely enough, one man in plain clothes. He'd stared at Helen briefly before following his comrades to the back yard, and Helen had a vague sense she'd seen him before. Maybe at the courthouse, she reasoned, on some previous visit to her parole officer. At least their disappearance had kept Sissy's distraction to a minimum, and math would keep both Helen and Sissy out of the way for a few minutes more.

She glanced down at Sissy now. "How's it going?"

Sissy looked up. "Almost done. Will you check it for me when I'm done, Helen?" Then she gave Helen one of those heart-breaking smiles.

"Sure." Weird, Helen thought, how this kid had latched onto her since she'd come to the boarding house a month ago. Who would have suspected an ex-con fresh out of two years in the Deasley Women's Facility outside Hattiesburg and a nine-year old waif might hit if off? And who would have suspected that Helen, after putting herself in a kind of emotional deep freeze to survive that patch of hell, would find herself warming to the kid? It must be outsiders recognizing each other, Helen decided, taking in Sissy's unwashed hair and wrinkled clothes, her unreadable dark eyes, her nail-biting and habit of hunching over her tender budding breasts. Did Nanette Greene even see that her daughter was at the dangerous and magical edge of womanhood? Maybe they just felt safe with each other. Sissy was in her own prison of neglect and clearly resigned to it.

As if conjured up by Helen's thoughts, Nanette came clattering out on the porch, cell phone to ear as usual. "Sissy? Oh, there you are. Is Sissy bothering you, uh —"

"Mom, the cops are here! Did you see them?"

"Hush, Sissy, I'm on the phone. Are you bothering, uh —"

Helen spared Nanette having to remember her name. "Not at all. We just thought we'd wait out here until Mrs. Mapple said breakfast was ready." Today Sissy's mother sported red

Capri pants so tight they showed her hip bones like handles. Thin arms and neck stuck out of her white pullover, and her white face strained tight and tense against the ponytail of long dark hair she'd yanked back. Helen could see a foreshadowing of Sissy's appearance in Nanette, but in the mother it was tied up in knots and pulled tight, ready to snap like a rubber band. Was she on something these days? Some kind of anti-depressant or stimulant that was getting her wired?

"Helen is helping me with math, Mom," Sissy piped up. Was that a note of accusation in the girl's voice? But Nanette was already talking into the cell phone. "No, Gary, I already told you. Your lawyer and my lawyer will have to work this out. I refuse to be in the same room with that bitch. No — no, excuse me but I'll call her anything I want to! I don't care if anyone in this dump hears me. As a matter of fact — what? Yes — well, it's your fault I'm staying at this boarding house to begin with. What — it's my fault? Who ran off with whose secretary, I'd like to know that?" The screen door slammed behind her before they could fathom Gary's response.

Helen glanced back down at Sissy, who crouched miserably over the scribbled page. "Let's take a look at those problems, okay?" Wordlessly Sissy handed over the notebook, then pulled her feet up on the swing and perched her chin on her knees, staring out over Gramm Street and Tynedale spread out before them in the morning sun.

"Yeah, these look right. All except that one." Helen pointed at the last problem. "Okay, you've got a five over a ten, right? So how many fives will make a ten?"

A few more minutes of coaxing and Sissy finally responded. She wrote the correct answer and then shut the notebook with a satisfied sigh. "Thanks a lot, Helen." Again with the winsome smile. She clambered off the swing. "Aren't you hungry yet, Helen?"

The thought of breaking bread in the presence of the police had dampened Helen's appetite, but she followed Sissy inside. Built around the turn of the century in a gloomy

Victorian style, the house was crammed with heavy oak and mahogany furniture that had endured several generations of Mapples. None of the rooms seemed to get much light, and the old striped wallpaper made everything seem even darker. Sissy and Helen made their way through the foyer, a narrow passage made narrower still by a collection of low shelves and tables holding everything from the tenants' mail to old magazines to stacks of the pamphlets from the First Nazarene Kingdom of God that Mrs. Mapple distributed at the shopping mall twice a week. Old dusty portraits of prior Mapples lined the walls at eye level, ending up at the end of the foyer with the present Mrs. Mapple's late husband. To the right, a steep staircase led the way to the bedrooms and bathrooms used by the boarders. The living room at the left rang with the sound of one of Mrs. Mapple's favorite television evangelists. Helen could smell bacon and eggs from the kitchen straight ahead. Mrs. Mapple stood at the stove, wearing a plaid robe and dark slippers, all five feet of her rigid with fury as she poked with angry jabs at the something in the pan. "I don't care if Chairman Mao himself walked through that yard last night," she was saying to someone. "I expect y'all to do something about this crime wave we got here."

"Ma'am, there is no crime wave. Like Officer Deets told you, we —"

She moved the pan off the burner, one small fist bunched in the small of her back when she straightened up again. Her cap of black hair, glossy with false color, shone almost blue under the harsh ceiling light. Legs swollen with edema and lined with varicose veins moved stiffly as she reached onto a shelf for seasoning. Her beaked nose, far too long for the rest of her tiny features, made her look like a duck when she walked with a rolling gait on her swollen legs. An angry duck, this morning. Mrs. Mapple didn't notice Helen and Sissy walk through to the dining room. She stirred scrambled eggs and continued talking to the handsome young cop who leaned on the counter. He spared a quick glance at the Helen, winked at

Sissy, then turned a bored face back to Mrs. Mapple. Apparently his job was just to listen. He didn't take down anything she said.

"And so I've told that Tommy Deets, over and over again, these young hoodlums just go wandering through without a thought to law and order, ready to take anything they can get." She turned away from the eggs and started buttering a platter full of toast, pointing her prominent beaked nose at the policeman. "After years of scraping and saving, it will be gone just like that, once they get in here and find that good silver I got put away. Not to mention cutting our throats."

Helen saw Sissy's eyes widen with fear. She steered the girl through the swinging doors into the dining room, where Nanette was perched on the edge of a chair and picking at a bowl of cereal. The cell phone lay on the table by her knife and fork, silent for the moment. Helen concentrated on pouring herself a cup of coffee and wished Mrs. Mapple would bring in the eggs so they'd all have something to do.

"Mom — Mrs. Mapple said we were all going to have our throats cut," Sissy whispered as she sat down next to Helen. "Mom! Did you hear me?"

"What?" Nanette didn't look up from the cereal bowl.

"Mom, there are cops here! Maybe they want to ask us questions," Sissy bubbled excitedly. "Mrs. Mapple said people are trying to break into the house."

Nanette looked up at that, her eyes barely focusing on her daughter. Helen wondered again what she was taking. Not even the mention of criminal activity under their noses seemed to rouse her — certainly her own daughter didn't seem worthy of her notice. Maybe that psychiatrist she'd talked about had prescribed something that left her only enough awareness to focus on her private misery. "Honey, don't pay any attention to what that old woman says. We're not going to be here much longer anyhow."

"We're going home?"

"I should say so. Once your bastard father gets his fat ass

out of the house. He knows this is only temporary." As she settled at the table Helen briefly wondered about Gary Greene and his fat ass. Had she ever met the man? She didn't think so. According to some of Sissy's mumbled comments this morning her father was out of town with his girlfriend this weekend — a weekend when he was supposed to take Sissy out. Helen stole a glance at the girl as Sissy contemplated her empty plate. Nice, having her mother rant and rave at every meal.

Mrs. Mapple pushed through the swinging doors and set the eggs down on the table, still talking to the young officer who walked in behind her. Helen helped herself to eggs and offered the plate to Sissy. "No, Sissy!" her mother protested. "What did I tell you about getting fat? Just have some toast."

Helen tried to chew her eggs and not look at Sissy's face while Mrs. Mapple rolled on. "And where is that Tommy Deets now? I know I saw him outside. He can do something about all this."

"Officer Deets is outside checking the area with Detective Ludy, ma'am. I'll see if they're about done," and he made his escape before any protest could be registered.

Mrs. Mapple set the toast down with a sniff. "Well it's about time we got a serious investigation into this ring of thieves. How long have I been calling them all about criminals prowling in my backyard, and only now do they bring out a real detective?" She sat down and reached for the coffee pot, mollified for the moment. For the first time she seemed to see her boarders at the table. "I'm so sorry that breakfast is late this morning," she said. "But as you heard we have had a little trouble this morning, and — where's Mr. Pemberton?"

"Do you want me to see if he's still asleep, Mrs. Mapple?" Sissy offered. "He sleeps a lot. And he snores really loud sometimes."

"Hush, Sissy," Nanette whispered.

"No, child, I'll do it myself. You eat some of those eggs, now. I made plenty. I expect Tommy Deets and that nice young officer will want some, too." With a martyred sigh Mrs. Mapple pushed her chair back, but at that moment Judge Pemberton slowly pushed through the doors. "There you are, Judge! I was just wondering what had happened to you. Now, just sit right down there and I'll fix you a plate."

The old man lowered himself into a chair, holding onto the table with one trembling hand. The other hand clutched at the worn leather briefcase that never left his side. In fact, Helen couldn't recall ever seeing him without this appendage of his former life as an officer of the court, like an atrophied limb that should have been amputated long ago. His jaws worked in a constant rolling motion as if chewing over some momentous pronouncement. His bald head, graced with a few stray white hairs here and there, bobbed in a palsied tremor as he let Mrs. Mapple arrange his fork and spoon around a plate of eggs. "There!" she said brightly. "How's that? And as soon as you're done that nice young boy of yours will be here to see you. Won't that be nice?" She bustled off, presumably in search of policemen, and left her boarders to themselves.

The judge lifted his leathery narrow face and seemed to smile open mouthed at the others. Helen doubted seriously that he knew anything of what happened around him anymore. He never spoke, never acknowledged anything going on around him, yet managed to get himself up and dressed and get down the stairs alone every day. Helen suspected he was in some stage of Alzheimer's disease that left him capable of tying his shoes but utterly helpless to understand where he was or who they were.

Sissy stared, fascinated, as he managed to get eggs into his mouth. The judge looked up and caught her watching him. He leered in her direction in what Helen surmised was an attempt at a grin. But she could see Sissy was scared by it. The girl finished her glass of milk and pushed away from the table. "I'm done, Mom."

"I'll be there in a minute. I'm expecting a call — hello?" She'd picked up the cell phone and started talking before the first ring ended. "No, I have to take Sissy to school now. Well, maybe you can see her this weekend and maybe you can't. How should I know?"

Then Sissy darted in again. "My notebook! I can't find it!"

Helen picked it up from the table. "You left it right here."

"Thanks, Helen!" She grabbed it and gave Helen another heartbreaking smile. "See ya later."

Helen turned back to find the old judge looking at her. His fork, held in trembling fingers, clattered on his plate. "Well, it's you and me, judge. What are you going to be doing today, sir?"

He said nothing as he blinked and stared. Helen wondered if he was trying to figure out who the heck these people were that hung around the house all the time. "I guess we both have a busy day lined up, then." She finished up her coffee and got up, but voices coming from the kitchen stopped her from heading out. The plainclothes detective and the other uniformed officer must have come back in. Helen heard a male voice in the kitchen.

"Mrs. Mapple, I don't know how many different ways to tell you this. We can't find any signs that anyone tried to force an entry. Those scratches could have been made years ago, by the look of them. No signs of footprints, no way we can lift any prints." Helen tried to place his accent. Not Mississippi. Maybe Louisiana, with that subtle flattening of some vowels. "And you say nothing seems to be missing. So there's really nothing we can do for you."

"What is your name again, young man? Detective Ludy? I don't care for your tone at all. Tommy Deets here will tell you I've been having trouble for months now, with gangs roaming the streets. Isn't that right, Tommy?"

Another male voice. "Yes, ma'am, you've been calling us for some time now with these complaints." This voice was older than the first — gruff with an undertone of patience, even gentleness. And for Mrs. Mapple to address him by his first name indicated that Tommy was a familiar fixture in

12

Tynedale. The older cop close to retirement that everyone knew and loved.

But Mrs. Mapple refused to be mollified. "Are you saying I'm a nuisance? Is that what's going on here? Tommy Deets, I've known you since you were in school. Have you ever known me to tell a lie?"

"No, ma'am." Helen could hear the misery in his voice and decided it was time to get dressed. As she edged past the judge, who was struggling with a piece of toast, Helen wondered again what a plainclothes detective was doing on a routine call like this. Tynedale wasn't exactly a hot-bed of gang activity. Maybe he'd just been bored this morning.

The doors to the kitchen swung open and Mrs. Mapple led the entourage of police into the dining room. "Why don't you just talk to my boarders, Detective Ludy? They'll tell you about all the problems I've been having." She stared, her shoulders dropping in disappointment. "Where is everyone?"

"Nanette had to take Sissy to school, Mrs. Mapple."

"And you are?" The detective stared at her over Mrs. Mapple's shiny black head. Helen took in his thick neck, cresting in folds of reddened flesh over his white shirt collar, his cold blue eyes set too close together over a short nose, the beefy shoulders bunched under his tight-fitting jacket. A lot of weight lifting a few years back, she decided, but he's slacked off lately. And definitely from Louisiana. Somehow, though, the passion and intensity in his voice and eyes over-rode the Black Irish pugnacity. She felt that intensity focused on her face and was surprised that she felt something more than wariness. Not attraction — no, maybe just recognition of a kindred spirit. Someone who just couldn't fit in, whose tenacity and severity matched her own. Didn't exactly make either one of them a hit at parties.

"Helen Black." She forced her face into calm — a skill she'd picked up fast inside. But already those scrambled eggs were churning in her stomach. It was like her guts associated any law enforcement uniform with the guards at Deasly and

13

reacted accordingly. Strange. Years ago Helen herself had worn a police officer's uniform. But that was in another life. Another Helen Black, who'd extricated herself from a messy youth in Mississippi to live in California and make of herself what she could. Now she was back here, starting over again in some weird cycle designed by a cackling set of Fates or Furies that must be having a great time at her expense.

"Helen Black." She didn't like the way Ludy said her name, his eyes narrowing. Sounded like it was a name he recognized. Shit. "You're a boarder here?"

"Yes." She fought back the urge to say "sir" to him. She wasn't at Deasly any more.

He nodded. "Did you hear anything unusual last night or early this morning, Ms. Black?"

She shook her head. "No, I didn't."

His gaze finally slid away from her face to take in the judge. "And you, sir? Did you hear anything unusual?"

The judge just stared and offered his leering grin.

"Judge Pemberton won't be able to help you, detective." The other uniformed officer Helen had seen earlier shuffled in behind Ludy. This must be Tommy. The dark blue shirt could barely contain his girth — one button looked about to pop. He ran a thick hand through his thinning brown hair, and he bent his big head forward to reach a pesky spot. Kind of like a worn-out Winston Churchill, she thought, with a few good years yet to protect and to serve. An elder statesman representing the law to the good citizens of Tynedale for a couple of generations now. His muddy brown eyes met Helen's briefly, then glanced over to Ludy. Hmm. Deference to the younger man? Maybe just trying to keep his bread buttered until retirement.

"Old gentleman is past knowing much these days," Deets offered in that deep gentle voice. "Has to be ninety if he's a day, and not in his right mind much now. I don't think —"

Ludy's face darkened. Without turning around he said, "Deets, when I require your assistance I assure you that I'll

14

ask for it. Until then allow me to question these folks, if you don't mind."

Deets froze in the doorway behind Mrs. Mapple, then backed off a couple of steps. Helen could see his round fair face pucker in embarrassment. One meaty paw dug a toothpick out of his shirt pocket, and he turned away as he slid it between his lips.

Ludy's tiny mouth twisted but he realized the obvious and didn't say anything else to the judge. With a nod and a piercing stare at Helen he left the dining room. Helen made her escape through the living room, hurrying past the sobbing evangelist, and got up the stairs to her own little room. Fortunately the room had been sparsely furnished, and Helen had refused offers of additional wardrobes and shelves and end tables from Mrs. Mapple. Just the bed and one small dresser and a set of shelves for a few books — that's all Helen needed now. Once she closed the door and turned on the ceiling fan she couldn't hear anything from downstairs, thank god. She looked out the bay window that gave her a view of the front yard. A light blue sedan turned into the driveway as she gazed down. It was Earl Pemberton, come to take his father to the doctor, just as Mrs. Mapple had promised the judge. As he got out, Helen saw him turn his pleasant bland face upwards. She ducked back before Earl could get a glimpse and go through his usual overly cheerful grin and wave. Like he was running for office, had to make sure everyone liked him. Today he was impeccably dressed, as always, his pudgy middle concealed by well cut slacks, his rounded almost feminine shoulders sloping under an expensive silk shirt. Soft and oily — that's what he seemed, always inspiring a shudder of revulsion when he tried to shake her hand with his soft paw.

She backed away from the window and started pulling clothes out of drawers. No need to get into the bathroom, either — she'd started the habit of showering at night. The boarding house had only two bathrooms, and Nanette took up most of the morning getting herself ready to face another day

15

of appointments with her psychiatrist, angry cell phone conversations, and staring at the walls absorbed in her own anger and hurt. Hold on, Helen ordered herself as she took a workshirt and pants out of the closet. Nanette and Sissy are none of your business. They'll be gone in a few weeks anyway. But her mind kept going back to Sissy's smile, that pleading look in her eyes whenever she spoke to Helen. Yeah, right, Helen thought. And what would Nanette say if she knew her daughter was getting attention from a convicted killer? It wouldn't matter that the death in question had been an accident, or that Helen had served her time without getting into any trouble inside. Just toss into the mix that Helen was a lesbian, and maybe Nanette would rouse herself from her little universe and notice that Sissy was a lovely and vulnerable young woman.

Just like Victoria Mason had been the night Helen killed her. Jesus. Helen caught her breath and sat down on the bed, reaching for her work boots. There wasn't any comparison, really, she assured herself. Sissy was certainly not alone in the world, despite Nanette's current behavior. And Victoria had been a young woman in her early twenties. Besides, Victoria was the one who'd brought the gun into the car that night, Victoria had turned it on Helen first. It was the struggle afterward that had killed Victoria. Even the jury agreed on that, coming down with a verdict of negligent homicide. The judge had given her the lightest sentence possible, and here she was out in the world at last.

Helen lay back on the bed, feeling the springs creak beneath her as she watched the ceiling fan cycle around and around and around. Sometimes it helped to go through the whole sequence in her head, as she'd done just now, from Victoria's face as she died, on through the trial, eventually getting to her hard-won freedom. Not today, though. Not with those fucking cops hanging around. When she was fairly sure she wouldn't throw up Helen slowly got off the bed and finished tying her shoes. Amazing, the way her mind and heart seemed to be as open and tender as a snail without its shell these days. Maybe this was normal for people getting out of prison. Maybe all of them went through emotional roller coasters like this once they were free to feel again. Or not.

At least these insignificant musings got her through the ritual of getting dressed and ready to go. She had time until her appointment, but the last thing Helen wanted was to hang around the house with Ludy and his pals. Maybe she'd grab a cup of coffee downtown, read the local paper —

Helen stopped. Yes, that was it. The local paper, the *Purvis County Clarion*. Ludy's face had been plastered all over it after he'd broken up the ring of car-jackers operating out of Tynedale. That was just after she'd gotten out of Deasly and was staying at her Aunt Edna's place on the other side of town. Ludy, so the paper said, had been a hot-shot cop in New Orleans until "re-assignment" to the fair state of Mississippi. Which probably meant he'd fucked up royally in the Big Easy, or pissed someone off so bad they'd gotten him dumped from the force. And now Ludy was a big fish in a very stagnant pond. He couldn't hope that Tynedale would provide him with a lot to do, now that he'd already busted the biggest crime syndicate the tiny town had ever seen. The poor bastard must be bored to death — that was why he'd shown up with Deets. Too bad he seemed to know Helen's name.

Finally dressed, Helen grabbed her backpack and headed down the stairs. She could hear Earl's appealing baritone responding to something Mrs. Mapple was saying — from the sympathetic noises Earl was making Helen assumed Mrs. Mapple was bemoaning the incredible behavior of the Tynedale police. Good time to make her escape, then. Helen walked quickly out of the house and met with Ludy lounging on the porch swing.

"We used to have one of these," he said. "Every night my daddy would sit out on that swing and drink his Jax beer and play his guitar. Too bad he wasn't any good at the blues. Momma just rolled her eyes and laughed." He got up and faced Helen, looking her up and down. "Yeah, he was awful. Dog would start howling whenever he tried to sing. He sure did love the blues, though. B. B. King, Howlin' Wolf, Muddy Waters, all them boys."

Fuck. The morning just got better and better. And what was up with this once-over he was giving her, right there on Mrs. Mapple's porch? For one eerie moment she felt his examination of her as something more than official interest. Even more amazing was the fact that she felt a response coming up from her gut towards this man. Bad, very bad. Better to consider her next words. "Did you want to ask me something else, Detective Ludy?"

"You in a big hurry? Going to be late to work?"

"I have an appointment downtown."

"Oh. That wouldn't be with your parole officer, would it?" He nodded, looking her up and down. "All dressed for work like that, I thought you were headed out to the warehouse. That's the SmartSave Warehouse, isn't it, just off the highway close to Vicksburg?"

"Can I help you with something?"

"You're in an awful big hurry, Helen. You don't mind if I call you Helen, do you? I feel like I know you so well."

"I don't believe we've met before this morning." She looked over his thick shoulders to the police car in front of the house. Tommy Deets had wedged his bulk behind the steering wheel, dark glasses blanking out his expression, toothpick sticking out of his mouth. He kept his face averted from Helen, although every few seconds he swiveled his head in Ludy's direction. Ludy must keep his guys on a very short lease. Bet poor old Tommy Deets didn't like that one bit.

"But I do know you, Helen. Don't you forget it." Ludy took a step closer. "I know who you are and where you come from. I'm not too sure Mrs. Mapple knows, though. When did you move in here, anyhow? Word is you were staying with your Aunt Edna McCormick when you got out."

Helen took a deep breath. She could smell the breath mint

Ludy used. It clashed unpleasantly with his fruity after-shave. "Then you know I've been here a month."

"Aunt kicked you out, huh? Poor old widow woman, didn't want you corrupting that son of hers, did she?" Ludy twisted his little mouth into a grin. "Guess she figured you'd be a bad influence."

Helen consciously loosened her hands from the fists they'd formed as Ludy breathed into her face. "My cousin Bobby has the brain of a six year old, detective. He had spinal meningitis as a child and was permanently brain damaged as a result. I don't think I'd be able to corrupt him even if I wanted to."

Ludy blinked in surprise. It was just enough. "Excuse me," she murmured as she walked quickly off the porch and down the sidewalk to her car. With hands shaking from rage she fumbled with her keys until she got the door open and slid inside. Already the interior of the old Rambler — an parting gift from Aunt Edna when she'd left for the boarding house, a guilty goodbye that managed to be an insult at the same time, given the car's age and decrepitude — was steaming hot. Helen rolled down the windows and waited for the steering wheel to cool off before attempting to start the engine. Deets and Ludy drove off as she sat there. When they were out of sight, Helen gingerly turned the key. The motor started at the first try this morning, for a change. She let the engine idle a few moments.

Gramm Street was now up and about, with plenty of people getting newspapers, walking to their cars, idling in flower beds, and peering at the Mapple house in curiosity. Terrific. How many of them had witnessed that exchange on the porch? Not only did she have a bored and angry cop on her ass, she had a whole fucking neighborhood sniffing at her like dogs.

Finally she felt the Rambler had been energized enough. The car huffed its way down Gramm, then seemed to jerk into life just before the stop sign. Helen pulled up to the intersection next to a dark green SUV of some kind or other — she couldn't really tell them apart — and the driver looked away quickly as she glanced his way. It wasn't until she'd made it through the intersection that Helen realized she'd seen that car almost every day for a couple of weeks. The driver, too. Maybe Mrs. Mapple was right. Maybe there was some terrible criminal scheme afoot in Tynedale, she thought, as the Rambler chugged downtown.

Chapter Two

"So how are things going over at the new place?"

"Fine."

Wanda Wylie glanced up as she scribbled a note in Helen's file. "I still don't get why you left your aunt's place, Helen. She seemed more than willing to have you stay indefinitely. And I know your cousin was delighted to have you there."

Helen watched her parole officer's slender dark fingers maneuvering the pen across the page. What was that nail polish — kind of a fuschia color. Looked good against her chocolate toned skin. Helen met Wanda's eyes when the pen quit moving. "It's not going against any conditions, though. We talked about that before. Right?"

Wanda sighed. "Right." She tossed the pen down and

leaned back in her chair, elbows planted on armrests. "Look, Helen, I just feel like there's something you aren't telling me. Remember what I told you? You have to be straight with me, from day one. Nothing else will work for us."

Wanda truly looked perplexed. Worry lines shirred her forehead, giving Helen a glimpse of the attractive older woman she'd become, with those huge soft brown eyes. Wanda couldn't be more than a year or two out of college. On previous visits Helen had already taken in the diploma gleaming new and wet like a coat of paint on the grimy wall, the photographs of Wanda smiling at the camera amidst other beaming young faces — most of them black like Wanda herself — the beautiful spiraling vase always full of fresh-cut flowers. Today daisies stood tall and bright yellow in a bed of fern cuttings. None of it, including the young parole officer assigned to her case, fit in with Tynedale County Courthouse. Helen found herself wondering what other cases Wanda had, and how they compared with her own. "I am being honest with you," Helen finally responded when it became clear Wanda was waiting for something. "Nothing's wrong. I just wanted to try being a little more independent."

"Nothing?"

Helen shook her head, hoping the smile she forced on her lips tempered her words. Wanda started making notes again and Helen glanced out the window so she wouldn't look at the clock again. She could hear cars on the main street, three stories below. Across from the courthouse she could see the Sno-Cone man doing brisk business in front of the park. A few kids were perched on top of the old Confederate cannon that pointed south. Colored chips of ice, rainbow slivers, dripped from their sno-cones onto the aged bronze. Helen had a fleeting desire to go out and join them, to get a strawberry sno-cone and suck the sweet juice that always meant summer. It would be good today especially, when the final heat wave Mississippi always offered as the last gasp of summer lay like a hot itchy blanket over Tynedale. She noted that no one stopped to read the plaque that told them how the courthouse had been built by slaves one hundred and fifty years ago. On the other side of the park a young couple laughed and lolled in the grass under the trees. A toddler stalked uncertainly on pudgy legs on the sidewalk beyond them, his mother watching with arms outstretched a few feet away. From the window far above it was like peering through a telescope, details strangely etched with painful clarity — the folds of baby-fat around the toddler's knees, sunlight sparkling on the sno-cones, the gleam of the girl's blond hair as her boyfriend pushed it back from her eyes. All vivid and real, all remote.

"And work? Tell me about that," Wanda was saying. Was that a note of desperation in her voice? Helen wondered. Maybe Wanda just wanted Helen to open up and pour out her soul into a messy pool on the desk full of manila folders and paper clips. Shit. Wanda Wylie was a nice person, Helen was certain of it. Maybe a few too many psych courses in college, though — Helen always had the feeling she was trying to fix her. Take her apart like a toaster oven, scrape out the burnt bits and scrub down the little grill, then screw her back together again ready for that next English muffin or slab of frozen pizza, firmly believing that she wasn't too fucked up to "work", somehow.

"Work is good. I just finished my ninety-day probation period." Helen could give her that much, at least, and spare Wanda details of the snide comments, the nervous glances and whispers she endured all day long. No problem. With a couple of notable exceptions, the other people in the warehouse were small potatoes next to some of the women Helen had seen every day at Deasley.

"Yes, I just talked to Bob Milson yesterday," Wanda said. She shuffled through some papers and singled out one sheet. "Your supervisor is very pleased with your performance, Helen. And no problems there with anyone, so he says."

"No, it's all going fine." Poor Wanda, so pleased with these nuggets of success scrabbled from the hard ground of her daily

23

work. Some of her charges would be only too happy to chew her up, spit her out, and pick their teeth with the bones left over. Helen gave her another couple of years, max, before burn-out hit and frizzled her into another career. Hopefully it wouldn't leave her soured beyond repair.

"All right, then, let's take a look at the calendar."

They arranged an appointment for next month. As Helen made a note of the date on one of Wanda's cards she wondered if the parole officer had met Detective Ludy yet. "By the way, Ms. Wylie —"

"Wanda."

"Wanda, there's something I should tell you about. It has nothing to do with me, really, but I think you should know about it." Briefly Helen described the events of the morning. Wanda's expression darkened from concern to alarm. "I'm sure Mrs. Mapple was imagining things — she seems to have a history of these calls to the police that turn out to be nothing."

"I appreciate your telling me, Helen. Detective Ludy, you said?"

"Right." Better safe than sorry, Helen thought as she made her way out of the courthouse. Wanda wouldn't be a match for Ludy, but no telling when this morning's little drama might come up. And it couldn't hurt to give a little something to Wanda, keep her happy and out of Helen's life as much as possible.

Helen blinked against the heat coming off the pavement. The Rambler was parked up the street, on the other side of the park. As she made her way across the grass she wondered if she'd have a chance to take a look at that back door tonight without attracting any attention from Mrs. Mapple or the others. Probably the old woman had watched too much television. Still, Deets and Ludy had seen something out there, even if they chose to dismiss it. Scratches on the door, they'd said, and —

Helen stopped, the Rambler door open. What the fuck was

24

she doing now? Her stomach clenched and her hands froze on the hot metal. The private investigator in her head should have been buried a long time ago — no more than a corpse that was starting to stink. She stared out at the park, not seeing the kids or young lovers passing back and forth. Maybe it was being in the courthouse, Helen tried to reason. Today, instead of locking her up like an arthritic joint it had jolted loose an old memory of how it felt to think, to act, to be — for just a moment — the Helen Black who had her own agency in Berkeley. Jesus fucking Christ on a crutch. She couldn't quite believe it, but maybe even little Wanda, with her soft eyes and overly sympathetic manner, had prodded that other Helen Black into life again. Or that confrontation with Ludy.

Helen felt her pulse subside and slid behind the wheel. The other Helen was, after all, just a ghost. It didn't matter what called her up. What mattered now was making sure it was dead.

"Helen Black? Is that Helen Black I see there?"

Helen rolled the window all the way down and leaned out. She kind of recognized the woman carrying a load of — was it towels? tablecloths? — and yelling at her from across the street. Tall, strongly built, with a voice to match. Her auburn hair was thick and cut close to her ears. By the time she'd made it across the street Helen recognized the woman who'd moved out of the boarding house leaving a spot vacant for Helen. She adjusted the stack of folded laundry in her arms when she reached Helen's car.

"Do you remember me?"

"Sure. It's Renee, right?"

"Very good! Renee Webster. Sorry, I can't shake hands just now. Thought that was you I saw walking up the street! How do you like the room?"

"It's great. No complaints."

"None, huh? Not even about Mrs. Mapple? Never mind, don't even answer that one."

"That reminds me." Glad of a distraction, Helen got out

25

of the car. "I found some stuff that I think must be yours in the closet after you left. I've been riding around with it in the trunk for a couple of weeks." Helen lugged a box out of the trunk and set it on the hood. "Not a lot of stuff. A pair of shoes, a jacket, a couple of shirts."

"No shit! They were in the closet?" Renee managed the stack of folded white towels in one arm and pawed through the box with the other hand. "I could swear I got every-thing —"

"These had gone down behind the back boards in the closet. You know these old houses, all kinds of weird hidden spaces." Helen found herself noticing the line of Renee's jaw, her strong neck and shoulders, the sheen of her hair in the sunlight. Then Renee looked up and Helen felt herself go red. "That's all I could find," she added lamely, fiddling with the lock on the trunk to keep her face averted. Damn. First noticing those long fingers of Wanda's, now appreciating Renee's neck. It had been a while since she'd felt the touch of another woman. Even counting those few times at Deasely when the loneliness had been too much, or some butch bigger and tougher than the rest needed to prove something with the fresh meat on her cell block those first few months.

A few seconds of silence told Helen that Renee had noticed her look. Maybe she was family, after all. There had been a moment or two when Helen was moving into the boarding house, as Renee had said goodbye to Mrs. Mapple, that Helen felt Renee's stare. Sometimes that's all it took to know — just that split second of eye contact.

Then Renee said, "My shop is right around the corner. If you have a minute, would you mind bringing it over?"

"No problem at all." Helen glanced at her watch. She'd just have time to get to the warehouse if they hurried. She picked up the box and followed Renee to a narrow storefront around the corner. Bougainvillea spilled out from flower boxes set waist high in front of the salon. The unmistakable scent of shampoo drifted out over the flowers. Over the door a sign read *Curl Up and Dye* in elaborate calligraphy.

Renee laughed at Helen's stare. "I know, it's crazy — but I promised myself when I had the money to buy this place I'd call it whatever I wanted and to hell with the neighbors. Hey, I'm back! Jeanette, come get these damn towels off me!" Another young woman scurried up to relieve Renee of her burden. "Thank the lord. One of these days I'll get a laundry service, I swear I will. Come on back with me, Helen."

The salon was small and bright and scrubbed. It reminded Helen of shotgun style houses she'd seen in Louisiana — long houses with room after room after room, constructed so you could fire off a shotgun, so it was said, straight through and out the back. A skylight overhead offset the dark linoleum and walls painted dull gold. Renee had kept to silk flowers and plastic ferns, but managed to keep them understated so they didn't look fake. Ceiling fans whirred on either side of the skylight. The only other decoration in the salon Helen noticed was an array of movie posters, mostly from the fifties and featuring very bosomy leading ladies draped over the arms of burly heroes. In the background, Helen heard Patsy Cline's heartrending voice piercing the sounds of blow-dryers and clippers, urging her lover to tell her now and get it over.

It was certainly a far cry from the hairdressers who had visited Deasley every other week or so. And an even farther cry from the salon she'd frequented in Berkeley, with its changing rooms, sunlamps, and maze of cubicles for waxing, massage, and skin therapy. Helen couldn't even remember the last time she'd gotten a haircut. She gave herself a glimpse in one of the mirrors over an empty chair. How did she look to others these days?

Helen saw a woman in her late thirties, thin but not skinny, with pale skin and dark sunken eyes. Her mouth was tight, an even line set like a scratch on stone. The beginnings of furrows dug around the edges of her mouth, making her

27

skin look drawn against her thick facial bones. She straightened her shoulders and the woman in the mirror didn't look quite so hunched and tense. And her hair — Helen didn't remember it turning gray. Most of the black was hidden behind silver now. As she walked on Helen saw another pair of eyes — an older woman under one of the dryers — looking at her. She probably wasn't the only one checking Helen out, either.

She made it through the gauntlet to Renee's tiny office — not much more than a big closet at the end of the building, sandwiched between the bathroom and a door that led to the alley out back. "Just set that box down anywhere, Helen. God, it's hotter than hell out today. Want a coke?" Renee sat down behind the desk and reached into a bar refrigerator behind her without looking. She stared at Helen's head as she handed her the soda. "You could use a haircut, I think. Come on by anytime — first one is on me."

Helen managed a smile and tried not to permit the image of a woman's hand running through her hair to overflow in her brain. "That's nice of you, Renee. I bet I could use a haircut."

"Not to say you don't have great hair. That gray looks really good on you, Helen. So, Mrs. Mapple's not driving you crazy yet? And how is Sissy? Jesus, I felt so sorry for her, with that nut-case mother of hers. Kyle's probably still moping around the house, being a teenage boy. Something wrong with that kid, though. But with Mrs. Mapple for a mom, who could blame him?"

"Judge Pemberton is still alive, too," Helen couldn't resist adding, letting herself play the game.

"Hell, he's older than dirt!" The phone on the desk rang. Renee rolled her eyes. "Forget that, honey, I'm on a break." She asked a few more questions about the boarders and Helen began to feel herself relax for the first time today — no, maybe the first time in weeks. Strange, just sitting in a hot little cubby-hole with a coke and harmless gossip made her feel better. All the while, though, Renee's gaze never left her face. Not hitting on me — no, that's not it — just trying to figure me out, is all.

"So how long have you had this place, Renee?" Helen asked. She was starting to get uncomfortable under that level stare. Time to bounce things back into Renee's court.

"Got it right before I left the boarding house. My divorce settlement came through and I finally talked old Louise Hardeen into selling. She'd only been moaning and groaning about getting too old to stand on her feet all day for the entire five years I worked here. I was the first chair up front, right by the windows. And she knows I brought in most of the business, too. I think that's why she didn't mind when I changed the name."

Helen wondered what had brought her to Mrs. Mapple. Maybe one day she'd find out. Renee had fallen silent and Helen glanced around the office. A picture of a young boy, maybe ten or eleven, hung on the wall. He had freckles and thick auburn hair. "Your son?"

"Yep. My pride and joy. Or my pain in the ass, depending. That was another reason I left the boarding house. I got custody of Sam, at long last, and I just couldn't see us staying there."

"He was with his dad?" Helen asked.

For the first time that morning Renee's warmth and expansiveness folded up like a door slamming in Helen's face. Shit — stepped on a land-mine there, she admonished herself. "Yeah. For three years I just got to see him every other weekend."

"That must have been tough for both of you."

Renee suddenly found the top of her soda can fascinating. A smile twitched briefly on her lips. "Skeeter's a strong little guy. Stronger than me, that's for sure. Uh-oh — he hates it when I call him that. 'It's Sam, mom!' Lately now he wants Samuel. Guess he's growing up." She looked up with a real smile then.

29

Helen thought of Sissy and Nanette. "It takes a toll on everyone, I guess. Divorce, I mean." This was getting a lot deeper than Helen had counted on, further than gossip. She looked down and saw her hands tightening around the can, creasing a dent on the metal. Enough intense talk for one day. "You didn't have Sam with you that day you moved, I guess — I don't remember seeing him."

"No, I never let him go to the boarding house." Renee blushed and laughed nervously. "I didn't mean the boarding house is a bad place to stay, Helen. It was just — there were other reasons."

"No, that's fine. I'm sure Nanette Greene feels the same way. A boarding house is tough on a kid," and she briefly thought of Sissy's pinched little face as she'd said goodbye to Helen.

Renee snorted. "I don't think Gary or Nanette Greene think of anything much beyond themselves. I heard she barely paid any attention to those cops this morning."

Helen smiled and set down the empty soda can. "So the grapevine is alive and well at the beauty salon."

"God, yes. That's old news by now." Renee took Helen's can and tossed it expertly into a bin by the back door. Helen felt the stare again and wondered what the grapevine had said about her.

"Gotta go. Thanks for the coke."

"Anytime. And I mean it about the haircut. Just stop by whenever you want." Helen gave her a final wave and hurried out past the women lined up in flowered smocks for their rinses and perms and dyes. Great. Now the word will go around the salon that a murdering pervert darkened their doors. Her thoughts stayed in that ditch until she was out on the highway speeding off toward Vicksburg and the Smart-Save Warehouse.

Then for some reason she heard herself humming that song — the Patsy Cline number that had been just barely audible at Renee's salon. What was that one? *Tell me now, get it over . . . Hurt me now, get it over . . .* Helen recalled crying over Patsy Cline with a bottle of something or other after a breakup when she'd first moved to California. Bourbon, in fact. Yes, that was a safe memory. A clean one, somehow, in spite of the booze. She'd been so much younger — everything ahead of her. Not a trace of gray in those days. Helen tested the memory, probing at it like a sore tooth. So why didn't that ghost disturb her like the others? Particularly the one she'd conjured up earlier, with thoughts of doing a little investigation into Mrs. Mapple's elusive master criminal? Maybe it had just been dead long enough, that's all. Maybe the other ghost would one day become a nice, safe little wraith. And maybe it helped to view some memories through a bourbon-soaked haze, as well.

She was still playing the song in her mind when she pulled up to the security gate. "Hi, Jim," she called out through the window. The aging security guard, the same one who let her in every single morning, went through the motions of inspecting her badge and peering into her face just like he did every single day. Did he do this for everyone, or just Helen? Apparently she passed muster. He pressed a button inside the guard post and the wooden rail creaked up to let Helen go on into the parking lot.

Things were pretty much the same when she walked into the building. Dottie was as usual perched in front of her monitor at the desk, her jaws working at her chewing gum. Helen saw Dottie's eyes, large behind the thick lenses, move briefly in her direction then fix their gaze back on the lines of text. Dottie had, Helen suspected, been a fixture at the SmartSave Warehouse since its inception — the kind of employee that knew every crack in the ugly green-painted walls, every fissure on the tiles floors, every rumor and whisper that traveled the buildings. Helen knew she'd been measured and found wanting by Dottie the moment she'd set foot in the place. And that wasn't likely to change just because Helen showed up on time, did her job and made no trouble. She simply was an offense, and that was that. Helen didn't attempt to speak to Dottie — she merely headed through the potted ferns and muted prints of placid Impressionist paintings that lined the walls to the time clock, hidden discreetly behind the water cooler.

Today Dottie surprised her. "I understand the police were out at your place today," she said.

Helen stopped at Dottie's desk and eyed her warily. No use denying it. Dottie probably had a pal at the local police station that kept her informed of interesting tidbits. "That's right, they were."

Dottie rolled her boiled looking eyes behind her glasses at Helen. "They come out to Mrs. Mapple's every once in a while." She even grinned. "Just so you know."

Okay, that was it. Between Ludy and the horrid little scenario with Nanette and Sissy, Helen had had enough for one day. She leaned against Dottie's desk with both hands and brought her face in close to the other woman's face. She could smell something fruity off of her. "Why, so I can be a little more cautious about my criminal activities? Or don't you know anything about that, Dottie?"

Dottie blinked and strained back in her chair. "I never said anything —"

"The hell you didn't. I know damn well you're the one who got the word out about me all over the warehouse." Helen stood up straight again, staring with satisfaction at the vein pulsing in Dottie's forehead. A cheap shot, terrorizing the old bag, but she couldn't resist. Helen shrugged. "Did you let them read my personnel file, too? I bet you sold tickets for that. Little extra pin money for the bingo parlor."

Oh, that last comment had gone too far. Dottie froze, pulling herself rigid behind her desk. Her cold eyes stared with frozen malevolence at Helen as she headed for the rack of time cards. "Bob wants to see you," Dottie said, snapping her gum as she spoke.

Startled, Helen's fingers slipped on her time card, making

it jerk under the stamp. Purple numbers smeared askew on the lined cardboard. She slid the card back into its slot in the metal tray before turning around. Now what? Helen had let her manager know she'd be in late. All the bravado she summoned up for Dottie boiled down to nothing as she saw how Dottie's eyes gleamed. Helen had no doubt Dottie registered that implied plea as weakness — yet another reason to despise the newest employee.

"He just said stop by sometime before you go home tonight." With that Dottie swiveled on her chair, presenting her broad back and bouffant hair to Helen. Clearly no conversation would be tolerated, so Helen turned away. As she walked down the short corridor leading to the warehouse, she gave a glance to Bob Milson's office. Door shut, lights off, no signs of life. The smiling plastic pig note holder fixed to the door sported a sheet of paper torn from a legal pad. OUT TO LUNCH, BACK AT 1:30, it read. Okay. Helen took a deep breath and continued through the heavy double doors into the warehouse, stopping by her locker at the end of the hallway to put away her backpack. It was probably just a pep talk, something Bob would do with any employee who reached the end of the probation period. And, Helen reassured herself, Wanda said this morning Bob had just told the probation officer she'd been doing well. Helen shook her head at herself as the doors swung shut behind her. Dammit, she was still acting like fresh meat on the cell block, constantly fighting down panic at the hint of authority noticing she existed. It's just a fucking job, she lectured herself sternly. No more and no less.

As always, the noise and harsh light and smell of the warehouse battered her senses the moment she stepped inside, and her taut nerves slowly relaxed. High ceilings and thick concrete walls reminded her of Deasley's central corridors, through which all prisoners tramped from cell block to every communal function in the facility. Every single day Helen had to fight off the disorienting impression that she was back in line, Ceecee in front and Rose behind her, queuing up for meals or recreation or chapel, their dull blue shirts a long stream flowing sluggishly by the khaki-clad guards. Then she heard catcalls, whistles, the distant thrum of the forklifts, tramping of work-boots, raucous hoarse shouts of the other SmartSave workers broke the spell. Underneath it all the drone of country music played counterpoint to the staccato of a day's work in the warehouse.

Breathing in the stale air, already hot and muggy, Helen took a moment to locate Marie Willis. Her supervisor stood surrounded by half a dozen men all twice her size. Helen slowly approached the group, wondering once again how the diminutive black woman had managed to achieve her position. Ability and talent, which Marie had in large supply, rarely secured anybody anything in the world of commerce. But Marie certainly didn't behave like someone who kissed ass or tolerated fools. Usually the Maries of the world ended up frustrated, furious and fired. As the only representatives of womanhood in the warehouse, Helen wished she could figure out how to befriend Marie, but she didn't know if that wish reflected honest desire for connection or a remnant of survival technique from Deasley. So far, though, Marie had demonstrated only cool distance bordering on contempt toward Helen.

And today was not going to be any different, Helen saw at once. Marie's gaze flicked in Helen's direction. "Good, you're back. This is a packing list of the latest shipment coming in. It's late again, folks, so let's all try to get it done right the first run-through and get out of here on time."

Helen took the sheaf of flimsy papers Marie held out to her. Apparently her job was to check off as others called out what the pallets contained when they were carried in on forklifts from the loading bays out back. Tedious work — and it put Helen into direct contact with the other warehouse workers. Always an uncomfortable spot, given the sullen stares and grudging release of basic information she always had to confront when dealing with "the guys." But apparently Helen had done a good enough job on inventory to be graduated to this slightly more important task. Fuck. Aware of the stares from the rest, Helen kept her face blank and scanned the packing list as she headed off to the section of the warehouse earmarked for this particular shipment of canned goods.

She heard a low grumble from one of the guys shuffling behind her but didn't turn around. Why bother? They disliked her and that wasn't going to change. Helen leaned against the cool concrete wall and waited for the others to get the forklifts positioned and begin unloading their contents. Her stomach growled, clenching down on emptiness. Shit, she hadn't had the time to grab any lunch after those few minutes with Renee at the salon. She idly watched as two men guided a pallet toward the immense, thick metal shelves, a pen ready in her hand. Tonight she was supposed to have dinner with Aunt Edna and Bobby, she remembered, hoping they'd have some of her aunt's meatloaf. It would make the evening tolerable, what with the inevitable silences and unspoken resentment they always swallowed down with these ritual meals. But Bobby's sincere devotion to his wayward cousin usually eased the tension for Helen. Maybe, Helen mused, she'd have time to stop by that toy store in downtown Tynedale right after work and pick up something for Bobby's electric train set. Another brightly painted train car, or section of track —

"You awake over there?" His hands encased in thick work gloves clenched at his sides. Helen couldn't remember his name but she definitely recognized him. The two guys lounging against the shelves behind him, too — they rarely ventured far from each other at the warehouse, forming a sort of ad-hoc gang. In response, Helen gave the men her best blank stare with one raised eyebrow. Usually her lack of reaction did the trick. Not today. They stared back, and their spokesman took a step closer to her.

"So start talking. What have you got?" Helen stood up from the wall, not sure where this bravado would lead. It occurred to her, as he approached, that they were quite alone in this section of the warehouse, in a corner close to the loading bays.

Jerry, so his name stitched on the SmartSave blue work-shirt read, got close enough so Helen could smell stale fried chicken from his lunch mingled with sweat and tobacco on his breath, so she could see the crooked nose that must have been broken once. Tiny blackheads scored his chin under the after-noon shadow coming in gray and brown. "Don't you worry about what we got, " he breathed. Behind him his comrades sniggered. "We want to know what you got."

Helen said nothing. What the fuck was this — some kind of double-dog-dare chicken shit game worthy of junior high? Her silence angered Jerry, who blinked and spat on the floor, spraying her boots. Without looking back he held up one hand. The five men on the crew quickly moved back. The forklift powered up, whining forward, and the pallet slid down onto the floor with a crumping sound. Shrink wrap tore under the weight of the load, sending its cargo hurtling down the rows. The dull sheen of fifty restaurant-sized cans of tomato sauce winked under the florescent light.

"Dammit, Jerry, the thing just fell right off! Right there on the floor! What we gonna do about that, you wonder?"

Helen kept her face impassive and her breath controlled, fighting the urge to kick Jerry in the balls right before dropping one of the dented cans on his head as he doubled over in pain. How would they like that response, she wondered? She could do it easily — for the first time she was grateful for all those hours pulling weeds at Deasley, her muscles hardening under the broiling sun. Glancing across the row of grinning men ranged behind Jerry she confirmed her suspicion that she was in a lot better shape than most of them. Too many Saturday night six-packs and corn-nuts had made her a match for any one of them.

But not all of them, all at once. And of course that wasn't what they were after, anyhow. She had to give Jerry that much credit. A steady stream of "accidents", of discrepancies in the checklists, of missing items — it wouldn't take long to get rid of her. Maybe Jerry had a bit more brains than she'd figured. But not by much.

Helen smiled and slipped the leash on her anger. She'd been a very good girl for a long time, but maybe Jerry needed to see the Helen Black that had made it through two years of maximum security. Helen felt her skin going cold and hot all at once. Jerry blinked again, a flicker of uncertainty passing across his eyes. "Having a good time, guys?" She made sure her voice was just loud enough to carry to the end of the row, so the others could hear. "Something to liven up the afternoon."

Jerry smiled and licked his lips. "This oughta get Marie lively, all right. Whyn't you just go on and tell her? She'll kick your ass right out to the highway."

"You think so?' Helen stepped closer, letting her smile fade. "That's what you're after?"

He stood his ground. "Fuck you," he muttered. "Cunt like you needs to get the hell out and go back to sellin' pussy."

"Selling pussy." She looked him up and down. His breath was coming faster now. "That's what you think I did, is it, Jerry?"

"Got too many pussies in this warehouse already, what with the nigger up front and now a whore back here." The words came out tight and awkward as Jerry registered that Helen wasn't buckling under his manly affront to her virtue or her abilities. The others, starting to get confused, looked at each other and shuffled feet.

Helen almost laughed. At least it was a game she understood and played quite well. "Let me ask you something, Jerry. Have you ever killed anyone?"

Everyone, Jerry included, froze and stared. Helen went on, "I mean, up front and personal. With your own hands. Ever

37

done that? Watched them die and know you did it? I didn't think so." She brushed past him, calling out over her shoulder, "Come talk to me once you can match that." Helen walked on surrounded by silence. "In the meantime let's get this all put away. You two, round up those cans. The rest of us will finish the load." Everyone stood and stared. Her empty gut twisted. Their confusion was somehow worse than their stupid pissing contest. And was she any better, bragging about Victoria Mason's death? She suddenly realized she was scratching her arms, just like back in Deasely after laundry day. The detergent they used had irritated her skin.

She never got the chance to find out if they would have listened. Bob Milson strolled up just as she reached the forklift. His round bespectacled face wrinkled in dismay at the confused sight before him. "What the — what's happened here, folks?" Hands resting on his ample hips, he hooked his fingers on the belt riding below his huge belly, waddling forward a step or two. Helen stood beside him, close enough to see the tiny gravy stain on the blue and red striped tie that flapped on the starched white shirt. Heavy jowls jiggled as he shook his head. Definitely a nice guy locked forever into middle management, and more than comfortable with his lot. Helen envied him — the ease with which he let his paunch flop over his belt, his total lack of concern about food stains. Would she ever relax that much with herself? "Somebody want to tell me how this came about?"

Jerry started to speak but Helen cut him off. "I think it's the forklift, Mr. Milson," she began. "He was starting to unload when the whole pallet just slid right off."

Milson's gaze traveled from face to face. Helen watched, hoping tension didn't show in her face. Then the guy sitting inside the forklift — another name she couldn't dredge up — cleared his throat and nodded. "Yeah. Yeah, this thing has been acting up for weeks."

Milson turned to look at him. After a moment's staring match he cleared his throat. "All right, let's take the damn thing outside and have Bud check it over. The rest of you round up this stuff. The damaged ones go to the food bank box, check in the rest. Jerry? Is Jerry here?"

"Yes, sir." He made the transformation from sand-lot thug to obsequious underling and trotted up to Helen and Milson.

"Finish checking this list and let's all go home and have a nice weekend."

No one else spoke, and Helen felt herself slowly relax. She must have taken them all by surprise just enough that she'd get away with it. This time. She seriously doubted that Milson believed he'd been told the truth, but he was going to let it go for now.

Or not. "Helen, come on back with me." She followed him back through the warehouse to his office, where he waved her to a seat. To Helen's relief he made no further reference to the incident he'd interrupted. "Now, where'd I put that file? I know Dottie gave it to me this morning." As he rummaged on his cluttered desk Helen looked around. She'd been in here only once before, when she was hired. At the time she was far too dazed by the whole process to notice much. Now, though, she could take in the scraggly ferns Dottie watered faithfully, the stained coffee-maker on top of the filing cabinet, the row of family photographs next to a calendar from the local super-market sporting views of the Natchez Trace. Milson had made up for the lack of windows by plastering available wall space with maps and charts of the SmartSave stores throughout the country. The office was kind of like the man, Helen decided — messy and overblown but basically harmless.

"Here we are!" Milson pulled out a file labeled with Helen's name from under the giant eight-ball he used as a paperweight. "Right in front of my nose, as usual. Let's see here." He pushed his glassed further up his nose and started talking. Helen lost the thread of his speech after a few words — it wasn't much more than she'd heard from Wanda that morning, an assurance that so far she was passing muster. Milson peppered his monologue with a few serious lines about SmartSave, working as a team, one big happy family, and other corporate platitudes to wind it all up.

"There you have it." He beamed and folded his hands on his desk, as if waiting for her to open a present. "Hope you feel the same and would like to stay with us."

Helen managed a smile. "Thanks, Mr. Milson. Yes, I'd like that." For now, she added to herself silently. She still couldn't decide if Aunt Edna had done her a favor by approaching Milson at church and asking him to give her errant niece a job, but certainly it was better than starving. Or having to stay on with Edna and Bobby.

"Good, good! Not that it's been too easy lately, what with all those computer supplies we lost a couple of weeks ago. Wish the cops would come up with a better answer for us." He sighed and scratched his head. "Still can't understand how a whole truckload of monitors and hard drives and the like could just disappear like this."

Without inside help, Helen thought. At least he had the grace not to give Helen, the certified ex-con, the evil eye. He sincerely seemed puzzled, just thinking out loud.

"And I hope we'll see you at the company picnic tomorrow," he went on.

Helen froze, her hand on the door. "Oh, is it tomorrow?" she stalled. Of course she wasn't coming, but she knew a brief performance for the boss was in order.

"Ten o'clock, Champion Park. Right close to where you live, I think."

"Yes, well, I'll see if I can fit it in."

He looked up at her somberly. "I think all of us — the executives who will be there tomorrow, and all of us here at the warehouse — would really like to see you there, Helen. It sure would make it feel like we're all one team, working together."

"Like a family." Helen nodded, swallowing down her anger. Sounded like Milson was counting on her presence. Maybe so he could show her off to the muckety-mucks who would apparently make an appearance to eat hot-dogs, tousle the kiddies' hair, throw a softball or two into the dirt. "Okay. I'll be there."

The smile came back. "Terrific! Why don't you just go on home, Helen? I know you've had a long day already."

That's right — he talked to Wanda earlier. Helen stabbed her time card into the clock and shoved it back in the tray, ignoring Dottie's stare as she headed out to the parking lot. Fuck all of them. Helen couldn't take much more of being everyone's pet project. Aunt Edna, with her church meetings and offers of prayer that finally motivated Helen to get out on her own. Wanda's youthful belief in her own ability to make a dent in the hardened crust her charges generally developed over pain and tragedy and evil. Even Mrs. Mapple, with her pamphlets and confrontations with the police. Now Milson.

Helen barely saw the security guard as he waved her through the gate. Her thoughts strayed back to that one moment that changed everything, when she herself thought she could help someone. But that someone lay dead in some isolated patch of earth. Helen didn't even know where Victoria Mason was buried. The image of Victoria dead in her arms haunted her all the way home.

The image quickly dissipated when Helen pulled up in front of the boarding house. The other woman stood leaning against a car across the street from Mrs. Mapple's front porch. She grinned, her flat face split almost in half by the spread of her lips. Helen hadn't seen her since they both shared a cell in Deasely. Reluctantly Helen rolled down the window.

Bertie Mullins leaned against the open window, her broad palms slapping on the hot metal. "Hey, Black! What's shakin?"

Chapter Three

Helen hung up the phone and took a moment to rest her head on the greasy glass of the door. It was stifling inside the booth, though, so she didn't stay that way for long. A movement caught her eye and she turned to see a tall skinny man wearing sunglasses taking a deep drag on a cigarette and staring at her through the smoke. Helen forced herself up and squeezed past him. The noise from the jukebox, something loud and twangy and doleful, almost drowned out the raucous laughter and shouts surging around the bar. Bertie was still sitting in a booth on the other side of the room. Two beers sat on the table before her. Helen braced herself and slowly made her way through the Friday night crowd. The *Tavern*, situated halfway between Tynedale and Jackson, did a brisk business at this time of the evening. Its patrons were generally working class, gathered from the combination of machine shops, gas stations and retail stores, with a sprinkling from the warehouses that lined the highway leading to Jackson. Helen saw a couple of faces from SmartSave up at the bar but she didn't think she'd been noticed yet. Several times she saw curious stares, from both male and female observers, as she made her progress. She noted, as she slid into the booth opposite Bertie, that it wasn't just two beers on the table. Bertie had already had one and was almost finished with her second.

Helen wondered again if this had been a good idea. When she'd gotten over the shock of seeing Bertie standing on Gramm street, her first thought had been to run like hell. But Helen knew her former cell mate would just keep after her, showing up all over town until she got what she wanted. Maybe, Helen had reasoned, a couple of drinks somewhere outside Tynedale — just listen to the kid's sob story then send her back home — use the same technique on her she'd used in Deasely — and Bertie would fade out of her life. Shit, she'd already backed down a half dozen men in the warehouse today. Bertie, with her childish temper and sudden bursts of vulnerability, would be out of her life again. Still, how the hell did she find Helen? Was the prison grapevine that good? Helen thought she'd covered her tracks but someone must have said something that had gotten through the guards on down to Bertie. Helen reached the booth and sat down, hoping the noise level would keep their conversation private.

"I went ahead and ordered one for you." Bertie swigged down the last few drops and clacked the empty glass on the scarred wood. "Did you talk to your aunt?"

Helen looked around for the waitress. "Not really in a mood for beer right now, Bertie. You shouldn't have bothered." Helen waved to the young woman carrying a tray who was expertly weaving a path through the muddle of tables nearby. She nodded and continued to take orders.

"Hey, this is so fucking good, being out on a Friday night! I surely did miss all this. You know, I think Sugar must have been here. She talked about a place called the *Tavern* where she met that guy once."

"Sugar? How is she?"

Bertie's smile never wavered as she answered Helen. "She's dead now. Killed herself, right after you left."

"Fuck." Helen felt all the air leave her body. She struggled to stay calm while Bertie stared, finally asking, "How?"

Bertie shrugged. "They think she got a knife somehow when she was working in the kitchen. She must have kept sharpening it for a while. Then one morning they found her wasted in the showers." Bertie suddenly gestured with her hands, and Helen realized she was aping how Sugar must have slashed her wrists.

"But how — they check everyone for that when they leave the kitchens. I don't get it."

"Who knows? Maybe it wasn't a knife, maybe it was something else. I always hated that little cunt. So she killed her old man 'cause he beat her every day? She should have just shut the fuck up about it. Whining all the time."

Helen closed her eyes against the memory of Sugar crying herself to sleep every night, of the bruises on her arms and legs from the beatings she endured in the showers, of her haunted eyes. Helen had known her for only two months — not long enough for the dull stare to replace the haunted look.

"So what did your aunt say, Helen? Am I invited over for dinner or what?"

Helen looked at Bertie. She still had a cherubic face, although she had to be, what, maybe thirty by now? — round and soft and glowing when she smiled, a wide grin under short curly blond hair. It was only when her face was at rest, or when she was angry, that you could see the hard little eyes like ice chips stained blue, or the narrow mouth stamped between those chubby cheeks. Her stubby fingers, round and soft-looking like a child's, tapped a drumbeat on the table.

Helen took a survey of Bertie's appearance. Expensive looking jacket, fresh hair cut swirling around her ears, and boots so new they practically squealed sticking out from under the table.

"What? Like what you see?" Bertie spread her arms wide and winked, leaned closer to Helen. "This is only a preview, baby. Hang around for the main feature."

"What can I get you gals?" The waitress was a lot older than she'd looked from across the room. The dark hair stretched tight into a ponytail was streaked with gray, and Helen saw liver spots on the hands poised over the notepad.

"Just a coke, please. And the bill."

Bertie waited for her to leave, then said, "Guess we have to get over to dinner, huh?"

Helen leaned back in the booth. Beyond Bertie's head two men shot a game of pool in the back room. The music on the juke switched to something a bit more blues but with a hard edge — maybe Stevie Ray Vaughan, or Robert Cray. One of the women watching the players started dancing to the relentless drive of the guitar in the background. She waved her beer in the air as she swung her hips in time to the sound. Helen watched through the thin gray cloud of smoke as she reached out and grabbed the shirt of one of the men bending over the table, cue balanced in both hands, landing a kiss on his bearded cheek to the applause and whistles of the crowd gathered there.

"If you're not going to drink that let me have it." Bertie slid the beer to her side of the table. "Don't worry, I'll be done by the time you finish yours and we can go on over to your aunt's place."

"We're not going."

Bertie stopped the glass before it reached her mouth. "Excuse me?"

Helen looked back at Bertie. "I just told my aunt I'd see them on Sunday instead. We're not going over there tonight."

"Here you are." The waitress set down the coke and laid

45

the bill next to it. Helen picked it up while Bertie stared back with hurt turning to anger in her little blue eyes.

"Thanks," Helen called, but the waitress had disappeared. Helen fiddled with the bill and took a sip of the drink. Bertie swallowed down half the beer, her blond head gleaming as it tilted back. Helen could see her fingers flex on the glass, a sure sign she was pissed off. "How did you find me, Bertie?"

Bertie's round little mouth curved into a bow but the smile didn't reach her eyes. "That cousin of yours is so sweet, Helen! All those pictures and stuff he used to send you. Remember?"

Helen sighed and shook her head. Helen flashed onto a memory of sitting on her bunk a couple of weeks before she'd gotten out. This was the last letter Bobby would have to send to Deasley. And he'd penciled in his address in Tynedale so carefully on the lined paper — "so you wont get losted when you come to my hous," he'd written. Aunt Edna had been very cautious about the mail they sent, but Bobby had been so proud of how he'd learned to write his own address all by himself. In the confused tension of preparing to leave, her cell-mate would have had a dozen chances to sneak the letter out and note down the address. "Still doesn't explain how you found me," Helen said.

In answer Bertie reached inside her jacket. "Brought you the mail. Aren't you going to thank me?"

Helen reached for the two envelopes. One was her bank statement, the other an ad for a singles' club opening in Jackson. Both were postmarked almost four weeks ago. Aunt Edna had put a rubber band around them and added a note asking the postal carrier to forward them to the boarding house. That meant Bertie would have been holding onto these for at least a couple of weeks, maybe longer. Otherwise her aunt would have just handed them to Helen this evening. For a moment everything Helen saw went red. With slow, controlled movements she tucked her mail into her backpack, then reached for her drink and took another sip. She couldn't

46

look directly at Bertie for fear of revealing her rage. "How long you been in town, Bertie?" she managed.

"Shit, I got out a month ago. Been staying with Daddy down in Biloxi mostly. But I thought I'd just come up here and see how my bitch Helen was doing." Bertie's stare traveled down Helen's throat to where her shirt was buttoned over her breasts. "She's looking pretty good to me."

"Cut it the fuck out, Bertie." Helen pulled money out of her wallet and let it drop on the table as she stood up. "We're leaving right now."

"You want to go so bad? Then why the hell did you come here with me in the first place?"

"To get you out of my neighborhood and away from what's left of my family. Christ, Bert, I live here now." Helen's voice dropped so that only Bertie could hear. "How could you even think I would want to see you again? We both left all that behind us."

"All what?" The sullen stare was back, the tiny smile fallen into a pout. This, Helen remembered, was when Bertie could be dangerous — when she looked like a naughty little kid. "You think you're all different now? You just stuck yourself in some ratty ass dump in the armpit of the world and made yourself the model citizen?" Her voice rose, garnering a couple of looks from the booths nearby. "You think the nice folks in Tynedale would like knowing who's shit on their doorstep?"

Helen sat back down again. This had been a terrible idea. For some stupid reason she'd thought she could control Bertie, just like she had inside. Bertie the kid, Bertie the runt, who would one moment seem so helpless and the next turn that horrible temper into violence. Helen saw her hands tremble and she put them on her knees under the table. Nausea churned her stomach as she saw Bertie's cute little smile return.

She took a deep breath and let it out slowly. Bertie had flagged the waitress and ordered something else. Helen shook her head as the waitress glanced her way. Everything was different now, out in the world that ate and slept and watched television and took their kids to school and got drunk on a Friday night. In their cell, those last few months they'd been tossed together like remains of yesterday's dinner, Helen had believed Bertie had looked to her for guidance and help and comfort. Now, in the space of a few moments, Helen doubted that conviction. Maybe all along Bertie had been in charge. Maybe Helen really had been her bitch.

There was a long silence. Bertie switched back to soulful little girl. "I'm sorry, Helen," she said, cocking her head to one side. "I guess — well, I've just been so lonely and all, down there in Biloxi." She twiddled her fingers around the empty glass and looked down, demure and docile. "Daddy keeps wanting me to work in his hardware store, and my grandma is after me all the time to come with her to church. There's — there's just no one I can talk to. And I thought, well, maybe you and me, Helen — you know?" Again the blue eyes glanced up, then down again.

It was a good performance. Helen might have bought it once, before she'd seen Bertie whale the shit out of another woman in the recreation yard right after such a display of hurt innocence. And that had been over Bertie's conviction that the other woman had cut in front of her deliberately. The ensuing fight had earned Bertie two weeks in lock down. "Cut the crap. I'm in no mood for it, especially after you stole my mail and fucked around my aunt's house. I want to know why you came to Tyedale. That's the only reason we're sitting here now."

"No bullshit, Helen! I just wanted to talk to you, that's all. You know, do some catching up and stuff."

"Uh-huh. What the fuck did you think that was, a summer camp? You don't 'catch up' with people from there, Bertie. And you sure as hell don't attempt to do it after you lie to them."

Bertie's face suddenly creased in a wide grin. She laughed

until tears spilled over her round cheeks. "Shit, girl, you are so damned cute! What the fuck are you gonna do, call a cop on me? That's a good one."

Helen thought of Ludy and shuddered. No way he was getting his paws on her life. In another second she came up with an alternative. "I don't have to tell the police, Bertie. All it takes is a call to my parole officer, letting them know I saw you in Tynedale."

"Go ahead. Daddy has enough money from the stores to take care of it."

"Daddy's money didn't keep you outside, though, did it? Come on, Bertie, it's been a long day for me. Cut to the chase so we can get out of here."

Bertie stopped smiling. "You work at that warehouse now." It was a statement, not a question. Helen realized Bertie was looking at the blue SmartSave work shirt.

Helen managed a smile. "What? You want a job there?"

"Maybe." She leaned forward again, pushing empty glasses aside. "What kind of stuff they got there?" She stopped as the waitress set down another glass, then jerked forward again. "What kind of jobs they got there?"

Helen shook her head. "Bertie, you've been in their stores. You know what they are. If Daddy's hardware doesn't interest you, I seriously doubt that a lot of groceries stacked in a warehouse will float your boat."

"Hey, I'm just like you, right? A reformed citizen. Besides, I'd look good in the blue shirt, don't you think?" Bertie winked. "Not as cute as you, though."

Helen rolled her eyes. "Come on, you're not after a job. You don't give a shit about working. What are you really after?"

She shrugged. "Just want to find out about you. What's your day like Helen? How do you like being at that place? Tell me everything."

Helen studied the too innocent face. What the fuck was she up to with all this? Certainly she knew Helen didn't have any money, any influence, anything Bertie could want. Not with Daddy's hard-earned wealth from his chain of hardware stores. Daddy, full of guilt and trying to raise Bertie single handed, would see that his baby girl didn't want a thing when it came to material needs. So what was going on?

"Speechless, Helen? Guess you always were the strong, silent type. Just what I like."

"Then why all the questions about my job?" Realization dawned on her like a cold fist in her gut. "It's the warehouse. That's it, right? You want — fuck, I don't know what you want from there. You can't be so stupid as to think of stealing anything in there."

Bertie's smile tightened. Helen got a glimpse of the older woman Bertie would become — round face thinned out with years of rage and violence, little mouth permanently hardened into a pucker, eyes dark with unspoken thoughts. Helen shivered, wondering if that's how she herself looked to other people now. Was she that full of repressed fury and pain, turning into what she saw sitting across from her in the booth?

This time Bertie let her eyes well with unshed tears. "And I thought you'd help me. Take care of me, like you did once." She wiped her cheeks convincingly. "Guess I didn't know you as well as I thought."

By now more than a few people were looking their way. Shit, one of the guys from SmartSave peered over a bunch of heads and seemed to recognize Helen. He turned to nudge his drinking buddy. Anger burned a hole in Helen's chest. "I'm leaving. Do what you want, Bertie. The drinks are paid for."

"Okay, okay, I'm coming." Helen hoped she didn't look like she was running away as she heard Bertie scrambling after her. Bertie stayed at her heels once they hit the parking lot. Fortunately it was empty at the moment. Helen looked up at the sky. Darkness seeped up over the hills to the south, and on the highway just ahead cars glinted as they rushed by beneath the setting sun. A pair of motorcycles pulled up to the *Tavern*. Helen kept walked swiftly around the building to the parking lot in back. Bertie's brand new sports car looked like a jewel next to Helen's battered Rambler.

"I'm really sorry, Helen. I didn't mean to make you so mad."

Helen turned around to see Bertie right behind her, breathing hard as if she'd been running to keep up. "Go home, Bertie. Take that job with your Dad's store for a while until something better comes along. And we have to stay away from each other. Period." She slammed the door of the Rambler behind her as she finished her speech. Bertie stood, hands on hips, looking more than ever like a petulant adolescent. Helen couldn't see her glare in the darkness but she kept watching until Bertie stomped off to get in her own car, her boots racketing the gravel with each angry step. Praying the Rambler would start up, she turned the key in the ignition. Fuck. Only a couple of clicks, then silence.

Helen was halfway to the bar when she heard Bertie running up behind her. "You going back in there, Helen?"

"Go home, Bertie."

"I have a car phone, Helen. And I can pay for the tow."

Helen hesitated. The red sky darkened as Bertie joined her. A few feet away, the noise in the bar picked up, as if sunset marked a turning point in the revels — music, shouting and laughter all went up a few decibels. Helen hated the idea of shoving her way back into the bar, through the crowds and smoke and smells. The longer they hung around, the more likely they'd be noticed. And if she asked around the bar for someone with jumper cables to help she'd merely ensure that the two of them would be remembered forever.

Helen swallowed down her frustration and tried to speak calmly. "I'd appreciate the help, Bertie."

"Hey, you can return the favor one day." As they walked back to their cars Helen felt the first drops of rain pelt her head. Great. She stayed outside Bertie's car as long as she could, getting colder and colder while she watched Bertie through a blur of rain sheeting the car window. Bertie finished the call and cracked the window. "Come on and sit in here with me, Helen. Can't have my best girl getting sick, can I?"

Helen shivered — the rain was cold and hard — then went around the car. The red leather interior smelled new, especially with heat blasting from the vents. Helen rubbed her arms and tried not to relax in the buttery-soft seat. "Don't you have jumper cables?"

Bertie shook her head as she lit a cigarette. "Want one? Suit yourself. No, no cables."

"That surprises me. Sounds like Daddy screwed up there just a little bit."

Bertie smiled through the wreath of blue smoke. "The cell phone is all I need, he says. Just stay inside the car and wait for help, he says." With one arm leaning on the steering wheel, the other reaching over the back of her seat, Bertie's breasts swelled up beneath her shirt, pressing their slight curves against the fabric. Helen got a glimpse of hardened nipples before she turned away, not wanting to see the other woman's lazy grin. "Besides," Bertie continued, "who knows but some asshole with his brains in his dick would try to help himself to more than jumper cables if I did the damsel in distress act?"

"Maybe Daddy knows you better than you think." The windows were getting fogged. Suddenly Helen craved a cigarette, but accepting one now felt like acknowledging some kind of petty defeat. Then she felt Bertie's hand caressing her arm.

"I think you know me better than Daddy does, anyhow." The hand moved, sure and firm, up Helen's arm to stroke the side of her neck. Then it was Bertie's warm voice, like hot oil sliding across her ear. "I know you remember. Your body does, if your mind won't."

Helen shoved Bertie's hand away. "Get the fuck off me. We're not doing this in the parking lot of some shit-kicker bar where they'd slice us as soon as look at us for this."

"Wanna bet?" The girlish giggle bubbled up in Bertie's voice. She was back at Helen's ear. "They might pay to watch us."

"That's enough, Bertie. I don't want to hurt you." Helen shifted until she could see Bertie's face, holding the other woman back with a grip on both her arms. "Let's not fuck this evening up any more than it already is."

But Bertie was laughing, pushing her chest forward slightly as she strained against Helen's grasp. In the dim red light from the *Tavern*'s neon signs her throat gleamed from rain and sweat. "That's the Helen I remember. The Helen I liked. You know I really liked you, don't you? Best of all the bitches I had in there. You were the sweetest, the best fuck on the block."

Then suddenly Helen felt fingers tracing over her thigh, a small hand edging its way toward her crotch. Maybe she was just tired, hungry, worn out from the emotional meat grinder she'd been through, what with Ludy, her meeting with Wanda, the visit to Renee's salon, and the confrontation at the warehouse. But she should have known — the way she'd looked at Wanda, her reaction to Renee — maybe Helen had just been alone too long. With a will of its own her body let Bertie's fingers touch her most sensitive spots, fingering expertly through the thick cloth of Helen's pants.

"Yes, yes, that's my little bitch, oh, getting so wet and soft for me. You're gonna come for me right here, aren't you? Gonna fuck you good and hard, little bitch, just like always."

Shaking with mixed feelings, Helen managed to push her away with one rough shove. Bertie's head bumped against the window. "It wasn't always, Bertie. Never that." Dammit, her voice was shaky. Helen took a couple of deep breaths before going on. "Once or twice we fucked. And that was that."

"You think so?" Bertie sounded calm and composed as she reached for another cigarette. The lighter glowed, a red eye in the darkness. "Maybe. Doesn't matter, does it, as long as we both liked it?"

Suddenly Bertie leaned forward. Helen could smell beer and nicotine. "And I know you liked it. You still want it, too. Don't try to lie to me about that, little cunt."

Helen stole a glance around the parking lot. Still empty. And at least the rain ensured that people going to and from the bar wouldn't linger to become witnesses to the scene she and Bertie had created. "So what? So what if we liked it? We were in a different place then. That's dead and gone. And I know you don't for one fucking minute believe that was anything like love or even like, what we did. That was just getting laid. A way to jerk off and pass the time until we could get out."

Lightning roiled the black sky. It must have been very close — thunder rattled the windows. Helen, startled by the sudden sound, wasn't fast enough to move out of Bertie's reach. Again the fingers played at her crotch. This time Bertie traced Helen's breast with her other hand. Now the girlish voice grated like a knife on stone. "You're just as much a whore as me, Helen. You want to think of yourself as so much better, Miss California Bitch, a cut above the rest of us whores at Deasely. Let me tell you something —" the gentle motion of her fingers grew rough. Helen held her breath against crying out in surprised pain that bled into intense pleasure — "you come just as hard and fast and creamy as every other whore I touched. No worse, and sure as fuck no better."

Beyond Bertie's curly hair Helen saw the tow truck lumber across the gravel. Bertie turned at the sound, loosing Helen from her grip. With relief washing over her Helen stepped back out of the car into the rain, waving her arms above her head. The next few minutes passed in a blur of rain and chill wind and hoarse conversation between Helen and the mechanic who got the car running again.

"Don't need no tow, ma'am. Just a jump was all." Helen couldn't make out his features beneath the yellow rain poncho but she was certain he smiled when Bertie stuffed a wad of bills in his greasy hands. Helen got into the Rambler as the truck ground back out of the parking lot.

"Helen?" She stood in the rain, her golden hair darkened and dripping.

Helen revved the motor. Should get her home safely enough. "Go home, Bertie. Thank you for your help with my car, but we need to both get home now." She backed up and drove off, rolling her window up tight against the sight of Bertie standing like a statue in the middle of the gravel lot. Helen kept peering nervously in the rearview mirror until she reached the highway. No sign of the sports car, as best she could make out in the rain.

The closer she got to Tynedale, the better she felt. Thank god the heater still seemed to be working. Helen let herself relax against the cracked vinyl of the seat as her clothes began to dry in the blast of hot air coming into the car. Unfortunately the damp between her thighs wasn't going away. Helen once again fought down nausea at the memory of how it felt when Bertie slid those fingers across her nipples, across the tender flesh rubbing against the seams of her pants. Shit, it had felt so good, even from Bertie. For the first time in months — no, years — Helen felt like crying. Dammit, she wasn't going to give in to this. She wasn't going to cry. She hadn't cried at her sentencing — not at any time during her parole hearings — not even the first time she'd been caught in the showers and introduced into the "family" at Deasely. And that one had hurt like hell, ending up more like a gang rape than a ritual beating. Tears were weakness, tears were the evidence you wouldn't survive this. Just think of Sugar, weeping her life out with tears as surely as the blood that had spilled from her body on the cold tile. Helen wasn't like that at all. She wasn't like Bertie, or Sugar, or Big Mary, or Dee Dee, or any of the others. Was she?

The anger of those thoughts carried her the rest of the distance to Gramm Street. By now the rain had eased. Still no sign of Bertie, thank god. She'd wait a bit before approaching Helen again. And Helen was certain Bertie wasn't through. It had to be the warehouse — no question. Bertie must have cooked up some scheme for stealing and expected Helen to fall right in with it. That little porno drama in Bertie's car was only a prelude to the set-up. But what the fuck would Bertie want with a lot of groceries? There wasn't any cash to speak of, not even on paydays. Unless for some weird reason Bertie was looking for a little excitement to liven up the hardware business. Still, she could do a lot better than SmartSave for that.

Helen's thoughts stopped abruptly as she parked the Rambler in front of the boarding house. She shivered, in spite of the heat inside the car, at the sight of the black and white parked in front of her. For one dreadful moment she wondered if someone had called Ludy to tell him she'd been talking to Bertie. That was unlikely, though. Helen waited a moment to calm herself before climbing out of the car. The rain had stopped completely, and she could see stars over Champion's Hill. A slight chill breeze scuffed clouds in front of the sliver of moon. Helen could see the sidewalk clearly in the pearl-gray light coming from the night sky.

Mrs. Mapple stood just inside the screen door, her black hair glossy and false under the porch light. She opened the screen door for Helen. "Thought I heard somebody park out front."

"What's going on, Mrs. Mapple? Did they find out something about the prowler?"

Once inside Helen saw Nanette Greene sitting in the living room, holding her head in her hands and sobbing uncontrollably. Officer — yes, Officer Deets, from this morning, the older cop with the silky voice, knelt beside her, patting her shoulder ineffectually.

Helen froze inside the door, unable to go further. Sissy. Something about Sissy.

As if reading her thoughts, Mrs. Mapple stepped beside her. "It's her daughter, little Sissy. She's gone."

Chapter Four

Helen lay awake before the sun came up the next morning. The ceiling fan whirred overhead, and that bird that never seemed to shut up was already at it on the tree outside her window. Everything else was silent, including Nanette Greene. She'd still been wailing after Helen had made a sandwich and taken it to her room. Helen had fallen asleep to the sounds of Nanette's loud display of grief —

Cut that out, Helen ordered herself as she sat up on the bed. The poor woman must be worried sick about Sissy. No wonder she was upset. Helen groped on the wall for the control switch and shut the fan off. It creaked to a stop and she pulled on her jeans and a clean tee shirt. "Thanks a lot," she muttered to the bird screeching in the darkness. No sense trying to go back to sleep now. Helen padded softly out of her room and went downstairs, stepping carefully over the stack of boxes that lined one side of the staircase. Mrs. Mapple must have gotten in a new shipment of pamphlets. The living room was dark, even the television silent for once. She ought to get up before dawn more often, Helen realized — the peace and quiet might actually soothe rattled nerves. She made it to the hallway and saw the kitchen light was on.

Shit. Oh well, maybe whoever it was made coffee. Helen pushed the door open and Kyle Mapple leaped up from the table as if he'd been shot.

"Sorry," Helen said in a low voice. "I didn't think anyone else was up at this hour."

Kyle jerked his head in what Helen guessed was a kind of greeting. "Got to go to work this morning. Early shift at the grocery store."

Helen almost smiled. That was the longest speech she'd ever heard from Kyle. He seemed embarrassed at his volubility, so Helen turned away and saw the coffee maker full on the counter, next to the sink. "Too bad. Mind if I get some coffee?"

Kyle shrugged. Helen took a cup from the cupboard, hoping she was interpreting Kyle's gestures correctly. He didn't object when she poured coffee and mixed in some cream. The window over the sink shone like a mirror against the black sky, reflecting the kitchen in a small square. She watched Kyle watching her while she doctored the coffee to a light brown. In the distorted reflection his pockmarked face smoothed, and the hawk nose he'd inherited from his mother blunted into something less prominent. His black hair, though, shone just like mom's. The orange shirt blazoned with the name of the grocery store didn't go too well with his sallow skin. She stood at the sink and took a sip of coffee as Kyle's double ran nervous fingers through that slicked back hair. And were those fingers trembling or was that just the wavery glass playing tricks on her eyes? Helen was startled when he spoke again. She dropped her spoon into the sink with a tinny rattle.

"So what did Deets have to say? About that kid, I mean?"

Helen turned around. He looked away but not before she could see the worry on his face. He was squirming in his seat as if he'd jump out of his skin. Why the hell should Kyle be so nervous? "Well —" Helen sat down at the table — "he didn't really say very much, Kyle. They've put out a missing persons report, they've got all kinds of information out about her. And they're trying to find her father, too." Kyle's eyes flickered at that but he didn't speak. "I don't suppose Sissy said anything to you about where her dad is right now, did she?" A shrug and a twist of the head. Helen guessed that meant "no." He kept staring at her, though, waiting for more. "They don't sit on missing kids, Kyle. Right now, all Deets or anyone else can do is keep an eye out for her. Given the problems her parents are having, it's not so surprising Sissy might feel like running away for a while."

"So he didn't search her room or anything? Look around the house and stuff."

Helen shook her head. "I don't know. Not while I was here, they didn't."

The relief that flooded Kyle's face was almost comical. "And he's not coming back?"

Helen shrugged. "Not yet."

"Okay." He made a show of looking at his watch and muttered something about being on time. Helen finished her coffee and went for more, staying in the kitchen until she heard Kyle's car thrumming down the street. He wasn't worried about Sissy — there was something else going on. He was certainly not happy with the idea of the police hanging around. For a moment she felt sick, thinking of possible connections between Kyle's nervousness and Sissy's disappearance, but she dismissed the thought before it had a chance to take shape. Kyle barely noticed the existence of anyone at the boarding house, as far as she could tell. Still, she filed away his behavior for future reference.

Helen took her second cup out to the porch and sat on the swing, thinking back over her own memories of Sissy from the day before. Her stomach started squirming as she recalled the way Deets stared down at her with those eyes the color of sludge from the Mississippi River, giving her a thorough grilling with his questions. Reminiscent of some of the Deasely guards, that flat dark empty stare that didn't see you as human. More like something in the way, a bug to wave aside or squash under a bootheel.

No, don't panic and don't get upset, she ordered herself. The man is just doing his job — it's always tougher when it's a kid. And don't even start to go to how you helped the kid with her math right here on the swing yesterday. Just think. The way you used to on a case. Helen sat upright at that thought. It felt awkward, wrong even, to let herself be "on a case" again. Not after the past few years.

After a few moments Helen could set aside the surge of emotion and stay in her head. Deets had asked all the right questions last night — what had Sissy been wearing, were there places she liked to go, did she ever talk about running away, who were her little friends at school.

Helen sipped her coffee and watched the sky begin to lighten. The bird, perhaps startled by her presence, had taken itself off to plague some other neighborhood. Come to think of it, Helen herself had actually answered most of the questions last night, with Mrs. Mapple playing Greek chorus here and there. Nanette had been too busy with her grief to think of anything but herself, crying out at the trials she had to endure, what with a philandering husband and impending divorce and now this. Deets had been gentle but persistent. Helen closed her eyes and let her mind travel over the painful territory of Sissy crouched on the swing with her notebook clutched tight to her chest. Did she ever talk about friends at school? Helen couldn't recall a single instance. Or places she liked? She talked a few times about trips with her father, camping mostly. Nanette despised camping. Nothing about running away, either.

Okay, then, on to clothes. Faded blue pullover, jeans with holes in the knees, scuffed white tennis shoes — Helen wasn't sure if they were Nikes or some other expensive kind or a knock-off from the local discount markets. Some kind of bracelet on her wrist, dark brown wooden or plastic beads, maybe. Long brown hair, parted in the center. A bit pudgy, and short for her age. Thin face, bags under her eyes, those sad bruised eyes —

"Excuse me. I'm looking for Nanette Greene. Does she live here?"

The woman stood uncertainly at the bottom of the steps. She slid her duffel bag off her shoulder and peered up at Helen. The first thing Helen noticed was the way her thick long black hair — pure black, not a glimmer of brown — gleamed in the faint early morning light. It flowed straight down her back like a dark river. Pale skin made her dark blue eyes look ever darker, despite their red-rimmed puffiness. Tears? Lack of sleep? Her khaki shorts and shirt were rumpled as though she'd slept in her clothes. Helen found herself taking in those plump pale thighs as the woman climbed up to the porch.

"Nanette Greene?" she repeated. "Is this —" she pulled a scrap of paper from a pocket — "is this 738 Gramm Street?"

"Yes, I'm sorry. Nanette Greene is here." Helen stood up, sloshing coffee onto the porch. Fortunately it missed the woman's sandaled feet. "You are —"

"Sorry. I'm Valerie Beausoleil, Nanette's sister. She called me last night."

"Helen Black. I live here with Sissy and Nanette." They shook hands. Helen finally saw the resemblance in the line of the jaw, the high cheekbones and deep set eyes. Sissy would probably resemble her aunt when she grew up, except for the hair.

"Have they heard anything else about Sissy?" Valerie went back down the steps to get the duffel bag.

"No, nothing yet."

"Guess no one was expecting me, huh? I wasn't going to come till tonight. But I just couldn't get back to sleep after Nanette called." Valerie yawned and stretched, straining backward. "Been on the road about three hours. God, what a horrible thing." Valerie rubbed her hand over her forehead and sat down on the swing. She leaned back and closed her eyes. "I just need a minute. Helen, did you say?"

"Right." Helen dragged her gaze away from that soft white hand, the long fingers resting on her knees. "Look, you want some coffee or something?"

"Might be a good idea." Valerie sighed and sat up straight. "I guess Nan is asleep?"

"I think so. Maybe I should go get her."

"No, I'll just go inside and get that coffee. I'm sure she needs to sleep."

Helen failed in her attempt to keep from watching Valerie walk down the hall, her hips swerving to avoid the cluttered furniture. Jesus Christ, she lectured herself, what the hell is wrong with you? "I wish we had something better to tell you," Helen heard herself say as she followed Valerie into the kitchen.

"Maybe she just ran away for a while. I know how Gary and Nanette can be, and Sissy's such a sensitive kid. Oh, thank you," she said, reaching for the cup Helen put on the table. "She talked about you, I think. Sissy, I mean."

"She did?" Helen felt a tremor in her mid section and wondered what the kid had said.

"Yeah." Valerie smiled and Helen felt her heart cracking. "She was crazy about you. Said you knew all kinds of things, helped her with homework, things like that." Suddenly

Valerie's face twisted and tears spilled onto the table. "Shit. I can't let Nanette see me like this. I'm sure she's already a wreck, anyhow," and she wiped her cheeks and drank down the coffee.

Helen was figuring out how to comfort Valerie appropriately when they heard footsteps in the hall. "Val? Is that you?" Nanette burst into the kitchen, crying out in a hoarse voice.

"Nan," Valerie whispered. Without another word she opened her arms and the other woman fell toward her.

"Oh, God, Val, along with everything else —" The words muffled against Valerie's neck.

"I know, I know, honey. It's going to be all right. Shh, now."

"Why the hell did she do this to me? Can't she tell what I'm going through, what with Gary and the divorce, and having to stay in this dump?" Nanette said through her sobs. "For her to run off like this, she had to know how hard this was going to be on me. And Gary still won't give us any cash, I'm using his credit cards for everything."

"Does Gary know? Maybe he has some idea of where she's run off to," Valerie said in a soft soothing voice.

But her sister would have none of it. "Oh, now you're sounding just like that old policeman, Beets or whatever his name is. Gary is far too busy with that little tramp to think of his only child. He's been gone since Thursday off at some cabin screwing his brains out through his dick. No one knows where the hell he is. And did I tell you he wouldn't even pay for Sissy's school clothes? My own daughter had to go to school in rags this year. I was never so embarrassed in my life."

The sisters stood near the entrance of the room, effectively blocking the doorway. Helen busied herself with the coffee pot, hoping they'd reposition soon so she could get the hell out. Particularly because she was angry at hearing Nanette's self-centered appraisal of the situation. Where was the worry and fear about Sissy in all of this? Helen bit her lip and rinsed her cup in the sink. Unfortunately the water running from the tap wasn't enough to hide the whispers behind her. She glanced up and saw them reflected in the window. Valerie's face turned away as she looked at them, and Helen was certain the other woman had been looking at her.

"Hush now, honey," she heard Valerie say. "Let's just sit down for a minute. Did you get any sleep at all?"

Helen turned around. Nanette and Valerie were sitting side by side at the table now. She tried not to watch Valerie's fingers as they kneaded her sister's shoulders, caressed her back, pushed Nanette's head gently down on her own shoulder. Irritated with herself and with both sisters, Helen left the room, well aware that neither Nanette or Valerie noticed her exit. Enough, she lectured herself as she climbed the stairs back to her room. Blue eyes and black hair and creamy white skin are no excuse for these thoughts. You have picnics to attend, anyhow. Helen paused on the landing. The door to Sissy's room was straight ahead. Helen heard Nanette complaining in the kitchen and decided to go in. Fuck them all, she thought, I'll take a look myself.

No need to turn on the lights — the sun was coming up and shone through the open windows. Helen stood in the doorway and looked around. Somehow it made the whole thing sadder to see just how little stuff Sissy had. Nothing on the walls besides a poster from a rock concert — a band Helen didn't recognize. The small bed was neatly made, no clothes lying around, and her schoolbooks were stacked in perfect alignment on top of the plain chest of drawers. Helen recalled Sissy's apparent lack of concern for her personal appearance. It was a strange contrast to the almost monastic look of the room — perhaps a mute testimony to the girl's desperate need for order in her disorderly life. She couldn't be bothered to take trouble with herself, but her belongings would at least be tidy. Helen swallowed hard past the lump in her throat and stepped further inside the room. The only thing even slightly askew was the closet door, which stood ajar. Nanette's voice rose in complaint from the kitchen — sounded like Helen would have a few minutes more, at least — and Helen went to the closet. Same military precision there. Shoes lined up on the floor, some nondescript clothes on hangers, jeans folded up on the shelf. With a sigh Helen gently pushed the closet door closed. As she turned to leave the room, her gaze was caught by a shoe box sitting next to the bed. Helen bent over and looked at the collection of rocks there, picking up a few of them for closer analysis in the growing light. Nothing here, really — just a hobby Sissy had taken up.

But now she heard Valerie and Nanette in the hallway beside the staircase. Helen moved quickly to the doorway with a final glance behind her — dammit, that closet door wouldn't stay shut, but it didn't really matter — and she was in the narrow hallway before the sisters appeared below. They were just climbing the stairs when Helen reached the sanctuary of her own room. By now the sun was up over Champion's Hill, and the bird was back. Okay, okay, Helen thought. I'm going already. She was showered and dressed and downstairs in fifteen minutes.

Now what? Helen asked herself as she headed to the front door. Valerie's duffel bag lay in the foyer. Helen carefully placed it out of harm's way, around the corner in the living room. It was surprisingly light. A woman who either didn't expect to stay long or who traveled light. Helen cut short her speculations about Valerie and went outside. Helen glanced up and down the block as she walked to her car — no sign of Bertie, thank god. Maybe that little melodrama in the rain had backed her off for the moment. Too many surprises yesterday, Helen thought. Unexpected visitors —

She slid into the Rambler. There was another unexpected visitor yesterday, Helen remembered. What about the man she'd noticed hanging around in the morning, the face that had seemed so familiar? She couldn't say for sure how long he might have been there yesterday, or when she'd begun to spot him. Deets ought to know about it, though. Helen cursed herself for letting that slip her mind last night. Too much happening yesterday. Well, that was one problem she could fix — she'd call Deets right away.

The closest gas station was at the other end of Gramm Street. Helen was rewarded for her efforts with the news that Deets had not called in yet, but she could leave a message. Helen curbed her temper and spoke with the sergeant on duty, putting in as much detail as she could.

"Did you get the license number, ma'am?"

Helen gritted her teeth. "No, I'm afraid not. Yes, I think I'd recognize the vehicle again, though." But would she? In all honesty Helen couldn't be sure. Hopefully this sergeant would take her seriously. Damn, she thought as she hung up, she would much rather have talked to Deets. Despite his age, and despite Ludy's apparent dislike, the aging police officer had struck Helen as capable and caring. As she revved up the Rambler Helen decided to try for Deets later, talk to him personally about it.

Having made that resolution, Helen belatedly gave her attention back to the road. Not that there was any traffic to worry about — not in a little town like Tynedale on a Saturday morning. Once she'd turned off Gramm Street and headed downtown, the trees grew more thickly around the well-kept old homes. Although most of them had been built after the Civil War, the residents of Tynedale had always maintained an ante-bellum ambience, right down to the wide and expensively-maintained front lawns dotted with enormous old oaks dripping with Spanish moss. The town matrons and local historical societies were no doubt bitterly disappointed not to be included in the annual tours of stately southern homes that took place every spring, but the sense of pride in the glorious lost cause of the Confederacy lingered here, as it did in most towns in this neck of the woods. There was even a commemoration of the battle on the hill just outside town, Helen remembered, every summer. This year it had coincided with her release from Deasely. Already disoriented by the swift and far-reaching changes going on in her life, she'd been further confused by the presence of scores of re-enactors in dress gray and fresh-faced debutantes in hoop skirts meandering the streets, sipping anachronistic and expensive Starbuck's lattes as they made their progress through history, oblivious to the obscenity of human chattel that had spawned their pageant in the first place.

Helen's stomach growled as she left the historic district and pointed the Rambler down an incline leading toward a row of small markets — including a coffee shop or two where she could get some breakfast, read the paper. She didn't eat out much these days, wanting to save her money for an apartment of her own. But she needed food and couldn't face Mrs. Mapple or Nanette or the judge this morning. And especially not Valerie of the black hair.

"What can I get you?" The waitress was very young, maybe Kyle's age, her face thick with heavy makeup and blank with boredom. Helen marveled at the way she clasped her pen between those impossibly long nails. "Special today is scrambled eggs with ham."

Relieved to face the anonymity of a sleepy-eyed waitress, Helen ordered eggs, grits and bacon. An abandoned newspaper lay in the booth next to hers. Helen grabbed it and scoured the pages of the *Purvis County Clarion* — nothing about Sissy, not that she'd really thought there would be, not yet. She tried to still her worries by glancing through the items found fit to print by the local editors. Garage sales, an accident out on Highway 20, the school board was having a meeting about the construction of the football stadium — shit, there was a notice about the damn SmartSave picnic, of all things, in the "What's Going On" section. Helen turned the page with a sigh. She'd almost forgotten. Looking up, Helen saw the local grocery store across the street. She'd pick up something — chips, a couple of six-packs, or cookies — before heading out to the park. And yes, that was Kyle's souped up Mustang parked at the back of the lot, hiked on its big rear tires. Helen stared out at the parking lot, seeing Kyle's worried face instead of the row of cars. Why the hell would Kyle be so freaked out about Deets being in the house?

"Here you go." The girl's nails clicked on the plate as she set it down. The grits looked good, better than anything Mrs. Mapple seemed to manage. Suddenly Helen felt enormously hungry.

"Do you have a pencil or pen I could use?"

The waitress looked only mildly curious when Helen thanked her. Helen waited until she disappeared behind the counter before turning the newspaper over to make notes, stopping now and then to take a few bites. Swept up in her own sudden sense of well-being, something she hadn't really felt in a long time, Helen was more inclined to go with it than question it. Okay, so the old dead wraith of Helen Black Private Investigator was lurking around. Fine — let's see what that damned ghost does with all this. She started to make notes between the lonely-hearts column and the astrological forecast.

By the time she'd eaten the last strip of bacon, Helen had to admit she'd often started on cases back in Berkeley with less to go on. Sissy was all too likely a run-away, given the situation between her parents, and most of the time kids like this ended up on the streets or staying with a close friend who would stall for a while before admitting they knew where she was. Even though the girl had never spoken as though she had girlfriends at school, there was still quite possibly someone she'd confided in, someone who knew where she was likely to hide. Then there was Gary Greene. Helen knew nothing about him beyond his apparent taste for cute secretaries, but he was the most likely person she'd go to. No doubt Deets and company were following that one up, checking out every romantic getaway shack in the state and beyond. And, despite the encroachment of a cold and unfeeling modern world, Tynedale was still a little country town. People still knew everyone else's business. In this case that would work in Sissy's favor. Someone may have seen something, even if it was the pitiable sight of a kid huddled in a doorway someplace. But it wouldn't do to discount the possibility of something much darker and uglier, of course. Helen thought again of the man in the SUV and looked around for a pay phone to call Deets. Ludy walked in just as she spotted one near the entrance.

Of course he saw her right away. Helen sat back in the booth and sipped water. The grits and eggs congealed in her stomach as her recent burst of energy drained off. "You're up awfully early today," he sighed as he slid into her booth. "Oh, you don't mind, do you?"

"Help yourself." She watched him as he made a show of reading the menu. At least he didn't appear to be dressed for work. A plain dark blue tee-shirt stretched over his muscled chest that was just beginning to turn to flab, and his jeans had seen better days. "I was just leaving."

"Oh, and just when I was hoping we could have a little chat, just the two of us. Just coffee and a doughnut, please."

"Right away."

The waitress twitched her little butt as she walked off. Helen pretended to ignore the glance he gave to the girl's hips. Once she was out of earshot, Helen asked, "What did you want to talk about?"

"Just a friendly chat. You know, get to know each other." He folded his hands on the table as if in prayer and turned his little eyes to look directly into her face. "I feel we got off on the wrong foot yesterday." A smile crinkled the corners of his eyes. "I have a feeling we'll be seeing a lot of each other, don't you?"

"I doubt we have a lot to talk about, detective. And as I said, I was just leaving." Helen reached for the paper but he was too quick for her. With a sinking in the pit of her stomach she watched him look over the notes she'd just made.

"Hot on the trail, I see." He handed the paper back to her and his grin widened. "Given your stunning record as an investigator I'm sure you'll be running rings around us good ol' boys. Have it all wrapped up in no time." He leaned forward and his grin vanished. "I expect you to stay the hell out of this unless you have information to tell my department. Understand?" Then those blue eyes darkened. Helen knew he was memorizing her face, all her features. Again the weird response came up inside her. As if she couldn't help being drawn to him, or somehow pulled into some dark scheme of his own. She closed her eyes and looked down at her plate, angry and confused.

His smile came back when the doughnut arrived. Ludy's eyes never left her face as he bit into the pastry. "So," he said as she got up, "what's this about an SUV in the neighborhood?"

Shit, he'd been in the station this morning after all. Helen sat down again and briefly told him. "I just remembered it this morning," she finished, realizing how lame that sounded. Any hint of a gray area around her own activities could only get Ludy on her scent like a fucking dog, slavering for the chance to create trouble for her. For some reason — maybe the sense of being a small creature chased down by a hunting pack — Helen thought briefly of Sugar, bleeding to death in the showers at Deasely. Ludy's presence at her table, his ability with a glance to bring the walls slowly sliding in on her, stripped away her tenuous grasp on calm. It was getting hard to breathe.

Ludy said nothing else as he swallowed the rest of the doughnut, leaving only a streak of jam on the plate. Helen got up again, tossing a few bucks on the table. "I have to go."

"Have a nice time at the picnic," Ludy called after her. Helen didn't turn around but hurried out into the sunlight. The heat and humidity were welcome as they enveloped her clammy skin. She leaned against her car a moment before getting inside. Her hands gripped the steering wheel so hard her fingers trembled as she tried to quiet her rage. No — not just rage. Fear, too. It was never going to be over, she thought.

Didn't matter if she had a piece of paper in her hand that promised Deasely was out of her life. She was always and forever wandering like a leper, ringing her bell with every step. And another ugly thought rose up in her head. How much of this was Ludy's homophobia? He'd made it his business to find out everything about her, it seemed. Yes, she was his personal project now. Fucking wonderful.

Finally it was getting too hot in the car, so Helen drove up the street and into the grocery store parking lot. Dixieland Supermarket was open for business at last. Helen roamed the aisles without really paying attention to her purchases, grabbing chips and dips and sodas and cookies and a bag of apples of the shelves. She knew she was getting too much but didn't really care. Nerves, maybe. By the time she checked out Helen had calmed down a bit. The ordinariness of the task, the simple act of purchasing groceries, helped to dispel her fear. It still struck her as something amazing — that you could go out of your own home and buy your own food and no one said a damn thing about it as long as you paid for it. She wondered how it felt for people who spent decades inside, how they dealt with the whole incredible process after years of having all their choices made for them. How would she have handled it?

Her thoughts were cut short when she saw Kyle sitting in his Mustang at the other end of the lot. Helen put her purchases in the trunk and tried to make out the features of the other person in the car. A young white man, she thought, but that was all she could see. She got behind the wheel again, and Kyle's companion climbed out of the Mustang. A bit older than Kyle, maybe early twenties. Heavier, too — blond and well-fed and well-satisfied with himself, if the smug grin on his face was any evidence. Well dressed, too, in his Banana Republic casual wear. The kind of guy who made homecoming king and football captain before heading off on a scholarship to Ole Miss up in Oxford. Why the hell would a guy like that be hanging around with Kyle, who was so clearly the type pegged as a loser? Helen watched the guy's back as he strolled

72

out of the lot and toward the side street running beside the grocery store. Something about him nagged at her mind. He turned his head briefly as he crossed the street, then she recognized him. Last night at the *Tavern* he'd turned his head just that way when he'd looked at her. Terrific, someone else from SmartSave killing time before the picnic. She wondered if there would be any gossip about her presence at the bar last night. These shitkickers really were hard up for news if that happened. Kyle got out of the Mustang a moment later and shuffled into the grocery store. Helen shrugged. Made no sense, but it wasn't any of her business. And the longer she sat in her car and stared off into space, the more likely it was Ludy would spot her and find some all new reason to be a pain in the ass.

Thinking of Ludy hanging around the coffee shop up the street was enough to get Helen out of the parking lot once she'd watched Kyle go back in to work. Damn, it was only nine o'clock. The picnic wouldn't get going until ten at the earliest. Anything was better than going back to the boarding house, though, so Helen went off toward Champion Park. She wondered how Valerie was faring — was she getting any sleep at all, or still letting Nanette cry on her shoulder? Had anyone heard anything about Sissy? Surely Ludy would have said something if he had any information, even if just to be mean or spiteful in some way. Where would they put Valerie up? Maybe she'd stay at a motel, although god knows what was available in Tynedale.

With her thoughts straying to Valerie's blue eyes, Helen almost missed the turnoff. Champion Park lay at the foot of the line of hills outside town. Pine trees lined the narrow graveled drive that widened when it emerged into the empty parking area. She had the park all to herself, apparently. Helen checked her watch as she pulled the Rambler into a slot near the entrance. Just nine-twenty- — the festivities weren't scheduled to begin until ten. Still, she hadn't bought any food that wouldn't keep for a bit, so she could just wander to her hearts' content, collect her thoughts and put on an appropriate persona.

Helen locked the car and walked through the opening in the split rail fence, glancing at the usual warnings about fires and unleashed pets and lurking after dark etched into a rough-cut wooden board. As soon as her feet hit the grass she felt some of her tension drain off. At this early hour the park could have been transported from some distant point in history, maybe even stretching its presence from the days right before the murderous bloodletting that haunted Mississippi, when victory had still been possible for the farm boys scraped together from the surrounding countryside — boys who had never owned a slave but still owned some vague sense of terrible offense committed against them by strangers — shouldering muskets and stumbling through thick pine groves toward death. The path meandered through old trees with spreading branches that stirred in the warm breeze and dropped twigs and needles and leaves before Helen's feet. She stopped for a moment and listened to the faint rustle of some tiny creature burrowing through pine needles. Given the geography of Tynedale and Champion's Hill, the soldiers sent out to meet Grant might well have made their way through this patch of ground. On mornings like this every footstep awakened some ghost, some wraith that flickered at the edge of vision then vanished when one turned to hear what they whispered.

The spell dissipated when Helen reached the end of the path and saw the barbecue pits and picnic tables. Another rim of pines laced the far end of the clearing, and beyond their thin trunks Helen made out the borders of a baseball diamond. The path picked up again after that. Wishing she'd brought her sunglasses from the car Helen kept walking until she came under the shelter of trees again. The top of Champion's Hill was visible through the branches, and Helen suddenly realized that she'd come full circle through Tynedale and wasn't far from the boarding house at all now. Maybe two miles, directly to her left through that brake of thorny shrubbery and over the hump of muddy clay that you could maybe call a small hill. If she was right, the trailer park would be a little over a mile past that. Helen kicked at a fallen log — seemed fairly solid — then sat down and stretched her legs out in front of her. She idly tried to remember what lay between here and the trailer park. Just past the trailers a couple of blocks of low-rent apartment buildings, then the old crumbling Catholic church, St. Bernadette with its abandoned old school. A vacant lot, maybe?

Something about picturing Tynedale in this way, like a map or like one of Bobby's electric train set towns, seemed to wipe her mind clean of the memory of Ludy sucking up a jelly doughnut. Like she held all of them in the palm of her hand, all the people trotting busily around doing daily things, from Renee clipping hair at the *Curl Up and Dye* to Mrs. Mapple screeching at the police to Dottie chewing her gum at the warehouse. Helen smiled at herself, remembering how she'd done the same thing at Deasely. Somehow envisioning even that particular shit-hole as a single entity had made it a little more tolerable. She'd often lay in her cot at night, stretching her senses as far as they would go to encompass first the glare of the light at the end of the cell block, from the guard station. Then the universe of sounds made by one hundred sixty three women tossing and turning in their sleep. The scratch of Warden Burr's pen on paper as he stayed up late at night fussing over files in his office high upstairs in the back wing. After that her thoughts traveled to the guard tower, where Hills and Boyle might be smoking and talking about the new arrivals or their wives or the ball game. Then the moon rising up over the trees, shining down on the barbed wire as well as the town three miles off.

Helen scuffed at the pebbles near her feet. No, that one wasn't a rock. Looked almost like some kind of shell or something. She picked it up and fingered the whorls and crevices, wiping away sand and dirt. Maybe some kind of fossil. Likely enough — god alone knows what might have been nestled in that red clay for centuries before the park was ever imagined. And maybe Mississippi had been buried under water and ice eons ago. It reminded her of Sissy's collection of rocks hidden in the shoebox under her bed, and Helen felt a swift pang. Surely the kid would come home soon, and Nanette would be able to enjoy her misery once again, and Aunt Valerie would go back to New Orleans.

Shit. Better not to go there. Helen tucked the fossil into her pocket and picked up a stone, a real one, to toss. People would be showing up soon. In fact Helen could hear high-pitched voices off in the distance, maybe at the edge of the baseball diamond. Just a couple of kids, probably, and the voices faded quickly as the kids moved on to another part of the park. She rolled the pebble in her fingers and aimed for the shrubbery. The rock arced up high, a black speck against the sun's gold, then landed without a sound on the tennis shoe that poked out from under the shrubs a few yards away.

Everything fell silent as Helen stood up, her hands and feet suddenly cold and numb. She stumbled once, looked down and saw that the sandy soil gave way to mud and pooled rainwater about six feet away from Sissy's body. Helen paused at the edge of mud, then knelt so that only the tops of her knees touched the wet earth. Sissy lay face down, her left hand caught in the brambles, her right arm buried beneath her torso. Her head was twisted so that she appeared to be looking back toward Helen with open eyes. Her lank brown hair, streaked with mud and plastered to her cheeks, didn't conceal the ugly purple-brown bruise on her forehead. Or the neat little hole, ringed with brownish red dried blood and traces of gray brain matter, drilled into Sissy's temple. Helen could smell how Sissy's bowels had let go in death, and the stench mingled with the mildewed odor of stagnant water. She couldn't tell how much of what she saw on the girl's body was blood or mud. The beaded bracelet hung broken and dangling from the hand that snagged in the bushes.

Helen realized she was slipping on her knees in the mud. She got up quickly and backed off the to thin rime of sandy soil, hoping that her brief survey hadn't destroyed any evidence. She scanned the ground quickly, unable to tell in the shadows if there were any tracks in the mud. Suddenly she felt the grits and eggs surging up in her chest. She made it to the clearing before she lost her breakfast. Through a haze of nausea she saw two kids — skinny tow-headed boys no more than eight or nine, probably — tossing a baseball back and forth at the other side of the diamond. They stared at her a moment before wandering off as she got up and tried to catch her breath. Strange, she thought as she wiped her mouth, to feel angry at these kids for being alive when Sissy lay dead in the mud. Helen took a breath and went slowly after them. Their parents must be around somewhere, she'd get them to keep the kids out of the way and call the cops. Then Helen would come back and wait with Sissy.

Chapter Five

Little Bro trotted on his plump four year old legs further away from Helen, then turned, beaming, tiny perfect white teeth brilliant in his black round face. "Fo' it, Hen! Fo' it dis way!"

Helen translated this to mean that the boy wanted her to throw the ball to him. She tossed the ball in the air first, once, then twice, and Little Bro hopped around excitedly. The light spongy surface of the bright green ball sported painted lines resembling the stitches on a baseball. Helen relented and pitched it high in the air. It sailed directly into Little Bro's arms. He squealed with glee and started back across the grass to Helen. Helen looked past his head. In the distance, on the other side of the baseball diamond, she could see the cops milling around in the wooded patch where Sissy's body lay. Their dark blue shirts wove a contrasting pattern with the browns and greens of the trees. Now and again a faint breeze, hinting at rain, ruffled the yellow crime scene tape that stretched around the area.

"Damn, when are they going to let us go?" Helen didn't have to turn around to know it was the plump woman in the pink shorts making the complaint. "We've been sitting here for almost an hour. We didn't do anything. And I don't want to be in this place one more minute. In fact, I'm never coming here again, if this kind of thing is going on." Her husband, the bald one who'd been lugging around a huge bag of charcoal briquettes, grunted as she voiced her opinion for perhaps the thirtieth time. The other hapless picnickers nodded and murmured. Helen wondered if she was imagining the stares pointed in her direction. After seeing her questioned by the cops they'd no doubt all figured out that she had found the body. Helen's refusal to engage in conversation with them had only made their resentment worse.

Little Bro twirled around on the grass, clutching the ball to his chest and giggling at some inner hilarity only he could fathom. At least playing with the child diverted Helen from the restlessness of the natives prowling behind her. She glanced away from the boy to look for his mother. Yes, Marie Willis was still talking to — was it Deets? It certainly was. His enormous bear-like body towered over the wiry black woman who stared up at him with the same look Helen had seen her give employees who wandered into the warehouse late on Monday mornings. Helen watched as Marie shifted on her feet, tight jeans molded to her slender legs and sleeveless red shirt stretched across narrow shoulders. Surely the cops wouldn't keep everyone here all day? This was no place for Little Bro to hang around. And if the murmurs in the background were any evidence, the other patrons of Champion Park were on the verge of mutiny.

"Little Bro! Settle down!" Marie turned away from Deets

to watch as her son flopped down on the grass next to Helen. She looks pretty pissed off, Helen thought, just like every day at work. Can't see a damned bit of difference. Marie glowered in their direction, then turned her glare back to Deets after ascertaining that Helen wasn't murdering her first-born. She stood stiffly, her back ramrod straight, arms folded tight across her narrow frame. Then Deets nodded, stuck his pen in his notebook and walked back to the others, leaving Marie free to stomp across the grass to gather up her son and leave.

"Jesus," Marie sighed as she reached down for the boy. "What a morning."

"I know. Sorry." As soon as she'd spoken Helen realized that was a dumb remark. Why did she need to apologize for the situation? It was the police, not Helen, who'd blocked off the entrances and exits to the park, who'd rounded up everyone they could find on the grounds and refused to let them leave.

Fortunately Marie hadn't been paying attention. "Just five more minutes," she muttered as she took her son's hand. "Just five more minutes and we wouldn't even have been here. But this monster here —" she tugged gently at his hand, and he turned to gaze adoringly up at his mother — "He just couldn't wait to get to the park and hit those swings." To Helen's amazement Marie plopped down on the grass next to her. She let her elbows rest on her knees and looked at the cops. Helen glanced at her profile, noting how the chiseled delicate features softened as she pulled her son close and cradled him in her arms, kissing the top of his head as he bent over the ball and sang to himself. Helen was touched by the transformation from stern martinet to affectionate mother. This was a side Marie never displayed at work — but why should she? Surrounded by good ol' boys, some of whom would be even more disturbed by color of her skin than by her gender, Marie had no doubt learned the hard way how to keep up a tough exterior. The change was disconcerting. Helen had to work at keeping her face blank when Marie turned to her.

"Hope this little guy hasn't been driving you crazy."

"Actually he's been keeping me sane for the past hour." Helen forced herself to meet those dark eyes. "Thanks, Marie. I enjoyed playing with him. What's his name, anyhow?"

Marie smiled again. "Charles. After his dad, so Charles Jr., really. But everybody calls Charlie Bro, so this demon got to be called Little Bro."

Charles settled into his mother's arms with a sigh, all energy spent at last, heavy eyelids drooping. "I just wish we could go home."

"I'm sure it won't be long now," Helen said. "They just want to account for everyone in the park."

Marie looked at her again. "Are you okay, Helen? You knew her, didn't you?" This time her piercing gaze held no anger, just intense concern. Was it the presence of her own child? The death of another child, bringing home to Marie the terrible responsibility she had for the fragile tiny being that slept in her arms? Helen had never imagined Marie cared a rat's ass about her. She had to glance down at the ground as her eyes blurred. In all this terrible morning, no one had offered a hint of sympathy. Of course, she'd expected none from Ludy or Deets — they weren't there to comfort, and they certainly weren't about to show any quarter to a convicted killer who'd come across yet another body. And none of the disgruntled barbecuers and ball-players corralled and questioned by the police had anything but morbid fascination with her, spiced with contempt once they'd figured out Helen wasn't going to talk about it.

Helen swallowed hard before speaking. "Yes, I knew her. And yes, I'll be okay." Dammit, she didn't need to crumple up like this. And she didn't need to let loose and start babbling about Sissy, not here and not now, and certainly not until she had a clue what Ludy cleared with the media. "Thanks, Marie."

Deets ambled up to the crowd, diverting everyone's attention from Helen. Marie scrambled to her feet without rousing Little Bro. The angry whispers died away as Deets cleared his throat.

"Okay, folks, sorry y'all had to wait. We need everybody to leave the park now so we can get to work on this thing, all right? And don't hesitate to give us a call if anyone remembers anything — anything at all that might help us." Helen barely listened to his brief speech thanking the good folks for their cooperation as he walked slowly forward, herding everyone in the general direction of the parking lot.

"Helen —" Marie's touch on her arm was gentle. Little Bro muttered, his head lolling on her shoulder. "Maybe you need to take a couple days off next week. I'll call Bob tonight, if you like."

"No. I'll be fine, Marie, thanks." It occurred to Helen that Marie had done a lot more than just offer a moment of compassion when she'd allowed Little Bro to run off some steam with Helen. Her eyes blurred again and she reached out to stroke the boy's head to cover her confusion. Why was Marie being so kind to her, showing such trust in her? It didn't jibe with the Marie Willis that barked out orders in the warehouse and had more than a couple of the guys there quaking when she walked around — and who barely acknowledged the existence of Helen Black.

"You sure?" Marie glanced at Deets, who stood waiting behind Helen.

Helen allowed herself a heavy sigh. Apparently Deets — more likely Ludy — wasn't quite finished with her yet. "I'm sure. It's probably better, anyway, to come on in and keep busy."

"If you're certain." Marie finally left, trailing behind the last of the crowd.

Helen waited until she'd walked behind the fence sur-

82

rounding the baseball diamond before turning around to face Deets. She saw that the apple-cheeked congenial cop on the edge of retirement had aged in the last few hours. Now his full round face, drained of all color, displayed every line and wrinkle around his eyes and mouth. Helen glanced down at his hands as he folded up his notebook and slid it into his shirt pocket. He saw her looking at his fingers and immediately they stopped trembling. "I'm afraid we still have a few questions for you. Detective Ludy would like to speak to you," he said. The words came out hard and clipped, the tone an icy contrast to how he'd spoken to the good citizens moments ago.

"Right." Helen nodded, not trusting herself to speak. As they got closer to the trees Helen felt her stomach clench. Now she could make out the white and red of the ambulance parked on the grass on the far side of the shrubbery. Close to the stretch of muddy ground Ludy stood with two other men, both in plain clothes. All three men wore their badges clipped to their belts. The gold-plated shields caught the sunlight and sent beams out across the shadowy copse. Helen couldn't hear his words but she could see his hands moving in short chopping gestures as he spoke. Deets and Helen waited at the edge of tree line as Sissy's body was carried out. One pale arm, damp with dew and streaked with mud, stuck out thin and gray and stiff from under the cheap blanket. Helen fought down nausea, breathing deeply and willing the shudders to stop. She didn't want to get the dry heaves in front of Ludy and company. As if he'd sensed her thought Ludy moved away from his colleagues and peeled off his rubber gloves as he headed in their direction. He slid in the mud a little as he walked, and Helen was certain he heard the snigger made by one of the other detectives. They moved quickly to join the crime scene investigators gathered at the other end of the shrubs near the fence. Ludy didn't seem to notice them as he walked up to Helen. She could see the sweat darkening his shirt around the chest and armpits, the ashen taut skin of his face, the anger burning in his eyes.

"Fancy meeting you here. We just can't seem to stay away from each other," he started. Helen met his stare for a few moments, then looked beyond him to the shrubbery ringed with yellow warning tape. Helen unsuccessfully tried to blank out the image of Sissy's arms splayed across the thorns, then looked back at Ludy. She could feel Deets shifting around behind her, and a moment later Ludy reached out to take the notebook Deets held out. He flipped through the pages, his stare lingering in Helen, then glanced down at what Deets had written. "So — you showed up an hour early at the park? Why is that?"

Helen stifled a sigh and wished there were someplace to sit down. Memories rose up as she mechanically answered Ludy's questions, none of them pleasant. How many times, when she was a cop in Berkeley or during her years as a private investigator, had she done exactly what Ludy was doing now? The home movies of that other Helen Black now coursing through her mind mingled with the nightmare images of the investigation that had put her in prison. She felt panic sweep through her body and hoped that Ludy couldn't tell.

Finally he looked up from the notebook and flipped it shut. Without looking away from Helen, he said, "Deets, you boys are on that SUV description?"

"Yes sir, did that first thing."

Ludy took a step closer to Helen. She smelled his sweat, saw the barely-controlled rage in his eyes. She had to will herself not to take a step backward. "Good thing you're not going to be leaving for a while, isn't it?" he said softly. "Not if you don't want to break parole." When she didn't respond he turned and spat onto the grass.

"Is there anything else, Detective?" she asked in what she hoped was a calm voice.

"Yeah, there is." He got even closer, his faces only inches away from hers. "This doesn't happen on my watch, do you understand me?" Ludy blinked hard, and the skin around his

84

left eye twitched as the vein at his temple pulsed. "I will not accept this."

Helen's patience broke. She felt her control, so rigidly maintained for hours, slip off like snake skin. "Sounds like you're holding me responsible for something here. I mean, beyond disturbing your day off."

Ludy stared back in surprise. His face darkened to a dull red. "You think this is something to make jokes about? I can assure you I'm not laughing."

"Good. Neither am I. So unless you want to charge me with something I should get out of your way and let you get to work." She heard the words rolling out of her mouth without quite believing it. Jesus fucking Christ, she might as well just haul off and slap Ludy right across that angry little face of his. Even Deets nervously shuffled his feet around in the grass, ready to jump in and prevent this little tete-a-tete from evolving into something bigger. The other men — Helen had noticed right away that no women were present — kept sending furtive glances in their direction as they went about their tasks.

"Of course you're not being charged with anything, Ms. Black. You are merely helping us with our investigation." His mouth twisted into a grin. "I'm sure you want to do everything possible to cooperate, don't you? It's just an interesting coincidence. You come into town and somehow another girl ends up dead. What was her name — Victoria Mason. Yeah, that's it."

The air thickened, seemed to turn red. Helen's rage trembled through her body and she took a couple of deep breaths, forcing her mind to work. This had to be deliberate, she managed to think — Ludy trying to needle her into admitting something, Ludy playing on a very slippery slope between harassment and tactics. She'd done this kind of thing herself as a cop, years ago in Berkeley, when it seemed warranted. You never knew what might set someone off, needle them into revealing more than they knew. What good would it do to respond? Anyway, Ludy wasn't really pissed off at Helen, she was sure of that. Something else was writhing inside him.

Once she had her voice under control again, she said, "I've told you everything, detective. If there's nothing else I would like to leave now." Great, a staring match again. Helen realized suddenly that Ludy didn't seem to see her, or hear her. Instead his breath grew ragged and his eyes glazed over.

Helen felt her own fury fade. Fascinated in spite of her revulsion, Helen watched as his hands knotted into fists. Deets moved forward to stand beside Helen. Something ugly here, Helen thought, buried down deep and surfacing like a shark. This was not the reaction she'd expected from a seasoned homicide detective who'd earned his scars in a city like New Orleans. Not even when the murder involved a child. For a moment she wondered again about his descent from the big city to the small potatoes of Tynedale, Mississippi. Maybe he feared the killer would elude the police of Tynedale — more specifically, elude Detective Ludy. And maybe that would be a replay of something that took place in New Orleans. Some failure so horrible that leaving town was the only option?

Deets coughed, breaking the silence that swathed them like the humidity. Ludy shrugged and folded his arms across his chest. His face smoothed to blank mask. "Just so we understand one another," he said.

Helen nodded. She said again, "Is there anything else, detective?"

He looked her up and down, a strange expression moving across his face. "Get the hell out of here."

Knowing that Ludy's face contorted with rage would haunt her dreams for some time, Helen walked away. Apparently the police had finished talking to everyone and decided the good citizens could go about their business. Only a handful of stragglers remained in the park, gathered in groups around the picnic tables. Most turned their heads to watch Helen as she strode across the grass, then turned back to their companions to mutter either imprecations or curious questions regarding the person responsible for their ruined Saturday. Helen had almost reached the grove of old trees near the entrance when two boys, somewhere around eight or nine, sprinted in the direction of the taped-off crime scene, laughing as they dared one another to get up close. They circled around Helen and took off for the baseball diamond.

"Jeff! Jeffrey Hamblin! You get your butt back here!" shrilled Jeff's mom from a picnic table at the edge of the clearing. The boys, still giggling, turned and loped back to their families to plop down on the soft grass. They didn't spare a glance for Helen, who made her way into the welcome shade of the trees. She blinked as her eyes struggled to adjust to the relative gloom of the thick foliage. Something stirred to her right. At first she thought it was just the two boys, then a glimpse of vivid color flicked at the edge of her awareness. Orange. Bright ugly orange.

Kyle Mapple darted through the trees just ahead of her, his uniform making a garish display against the muted grays and greens of the trees. Helen remembered the fear in his eyes this morning and moved quickly after him. Why the hell would he run away from a scene that would grant the whole town ghoulish delight?

"Fuck!" Helen hissed. The branch she'd stumbled over left a painful sliver in her arm. Blood welled up and made a thin trickle moving toward her hand. She thought of Sissy's arm caught in the thorns and moved faster, anger and sorrow and a vague sense of guilt pushing her forward. Couldn't hurt to find out where Kyle was off to in such a hurry.

She reached the parking lot in time to see him run past the last row of cars. Then he disappeared. Helen reached the final car on the lot, panting and sweating from the unaccustomed exertion. Where the hell — then she saw the narrow paved path that led from the parking lot. It snaked through a stand of pines and curved out of sight a few yards ahead.

Helen took a deep breath and kept going on the path as it circled around the parking lot and finally ended at the end of a street she didn't recognize. Helen wiped sweat off her face and realized her dizziness came from lack of food. She leaned against a tree and looked up and down the street. More of an alley, really. She recognized it as part of the warren of auto repair shops and appliance warehouses that formed a boundary at the south end of town, separating the park and Champion's Hill from the residential sections of Tynedale. From the silence punctuated only by her ragged breaths, Helen decided that all the workers must be out enjoying their weekend. Nothing stirred amongst the rows of Dumpsters and stacks of oil-stained wood pallets.

Dizzy from hunger, weak from shock, and thoroughly overcome by the heat, Helen slumped down onto the ground and waited for her breath to come back. In the silence and heavy air laden with the scent of machine oil Helen's grip finally slipped off. She didn't realize she was crying until salt tears fell from her face and stung the bloody scratch on her arm. For some reason she thought of Sissy's math problems and wondered if she'd gotten the answers right. Helen's sobs eased after a few minutes. Then she heard the noise from the other end of the alley. Not much of a noise, really. Just a rustle, like something being dragged across the ground.

Helen got to her feet and moved slowly away from the pines. Now she could hear other things. Feet shuffling on the pavement. The murmur of voices rising in anger. Shit, how much had she missed already? Her own tears, her efforts to catch her breath, must have covered up any other sounds for the last few minutes. She felt her heart begin to pound again — not from exhaustion or sorrow this time, but from tension that coiled like a spring inside her chest. Glancing around the alley, she saw that there were several narrow passages between the buildings that could provide cover if she felt the need for it. And of course the path leading back to the parking lot. Helen kept creeping forward, deliberately pushing aside the sense that she must look like an idiot, like something out of a bad television series. She didn't even know if Kyle's voice was one of those echoing at the end of the alley. Probably she'd round the corner only to find a bunch of workmen from the surrounding businesses breaking for lunch or a cold beer or even a game of craps. And this fucking around in the alley would prove to be just a way of avoiding thinking about Sissy, after all. A way to block out the image of that little bead bracelet, the muddy sneakers splayed pigeon-toed in the mud —

"So what the fuck are you doing back here, asshole?"

"I just — I didn't know — maybe you were still here." That was Kyle, the feeble response. Helen didn't recognize the first voice. She froze at the sound. It came from the dingy gray building marked ABBOT AND SONS. A metal door wide enough to accommodate a small delivery truck was rolled up. The voices echoed on the dirty concrete walls. Helen edged herself into a shallow doorway two buildings up the alley and waited for more. Behind her a worn wooden door with loose slats gave her a flimsy support as she cautiously leaned back. Good, she was just out of sight if they poked their heads out. She took slow, deep, silent breaths and tried not to think of how stupid it was to chase Kyle down on the slender hope he knew something about Sissy's death. Too late now, of course — better just to sit it out a few minutes until she could get away.

She didn't have long to wait. The first voice started in again. "What did I just tell you this morning, shit-brain? To stay the fuck away from me. Guess you didn't hear me too good." The high-pitched voice pierced the silence. Another kid? Helen didn't think so — sounded too hard, somehow, for youth.

"But I didn't know you was gonna kill anybody, Dave." Kyle's voice wheedled and cracked, his words spilling out in a stammer. "You didn't say nothin' about that shit."

"Aw, fuck, you are so full of shit you squeak. Don't he squeak every time he opens his damn mouth, Curtis?"

A snigger — must be Curtis. So at least three of them. Maybe more. "What the hell are you talking about?" That was yet another voice. "We didn't kill anyone."

"That little slut in your house? Shit, why would we do her? You got shit for brains, fucker."

"Look, peckerwood —" Helen heard a weird dull thump. Someone hit something? Or someone. "He just asked you a question."

"Forget it, Curtis. Shit face here doesn't have anything in his head but what I tell him to, right?" Another thump. Jesus. Helen didn't think she could handle a lot more today, but if Kyle was being slugged a few feet away she was going to have to do something. Even if it was just run.

"Damn, I didn't mean anything by it." Kyle's voice sounded thick, the words barely distinguishable, like he was talking around a mouthful of rocks. "Why'd you do that?"

Then she heard the first voice again, just barely above a whisper. Helen strained to make out the words. "So you won't go running your fucking mouth off. So you'll remember what happens when you talk a bunch of shit. I will own you, fucker." This time she heard a cough, deep and wet and shuddering. Kyle. It had to be. Helen flattened herself against the wall in her effort to fight off nausea that threatened to have her retching. Her head hit the door, and the subsequent rattle echoed along the alley.

"Hey. Thought I heard something."

Sudden and total silence. Everyone must be listening. Dammit, Helen cursed herself.

"Curtis, Mackie. Get out there and see if we got company."

"Right, Dave."

Fuck. No way out of this but to walk right through it.

Helen pushed herself from the door and got into the alley just as two men emerged from the garage. Curtis and Mackie might be brothers, given their similar dark coloring, lank mousy hair, and weak chins. Unfortunately they both looked pretty muscular, like they'd worked out quite a bit and made it a habit. One wore a black baseball cap with faded lettering that might have read NEW ORLEANS SAINTS once. Both had dull brown eyes. They gazed at her suspiciously, looking her up and down. One of them spit a long stream onto the asphalt. That was the one without the hat.

Helen tried on a smile and hoped it didn't look as awkward as it felt. Could she pull off the image of dithery female wandering off lost without a big strong male to help her out? Now was definitely not the time to play helpless southern belle who counted on the kindness of strangers. "Oh, hey there. I'm sorry, I thought I saw my friend come back here. Maybe you've seen him — about my height, black hair? He was wearing his shirt from work, you know, from the grocery store?" She kept the smile on her face and took a step closer, fighting off every instinct that told her she should be running her ass off out of the alley. Right now. She fiddled with her hair and cocked her head to one side. "His name is Kyle. You haven't seen him, have you?"

"What the hell is going on?" Dave emerged from the garage and joined his comrades, Kyle trailing close behind. He'd changed clothes since Helen had last seen him getting out of Kyle's car in the parking lot of the grocery store. Now he wore a black tee-shirt and black jeans. It didn't go as well with his blond coloring as the SmartSave blue workshirt he'd worn at the *Tavern* the night before. Helen suppressed a sigh. Damn these tiny little towns. You couldn't get away from anyone in a place like this.

"Helen Black." The soft high voice went flat as Dave gazed at Helen and moved past his pals to stand in front of her. "What brings you back here?"

"Oh, Kyle, there you are. I thought I saw you in the park

a few minutes ago. I was — I was just coming to see if you could come home and help your mother. She's going to have her hands full, what with Nanette and all," Helen babbled, wincing inwardly at the flimsy story.

"You live in the boarding house with Kyle." Dave didn't make it a question — more like pulling a piece of information from a file, reviewing it then storing it away again. To Helen's surprise he didn't refer to the warehouse, although she was certain he knew she worked there. What did that mean? Nothing? Everything? Shit, they couldn't just stare at each other waiting for someone to pull a gun or a knife or a fist. She swallowed and started again.

"Yes, that's right. It's just terrible, isn't it? That poor little girl found dead. Kyle — don't you think you'd better come on home with me?" Helen tried hard not to notice as Kyle wiped a smear of blood from his lip and hunched protectively over his stomach. He stepped forward, then hesitated, glancing at Dave.

A slow smile played across Dave's features. "Yeah, Kyle. Why don't you go on home with your, uh, friend?"

"Okay." Kyle brushed past Dave with a grimace of pain. Helen let her gaze flicker toward the boy for a moment but knew it wouldn't help anything to remark on his physical condition. "C'mon, let's go," Kyle muttered when he reached Helen. She saw sweat beading on his face. That little walk must have cost him. Just how bad did they punch him around in there?

"Everything okay, Kyle? You're not hurt or anything, are you?" Dave said, never taking his eyes off Helen as he spoke.

"Yeah. Fine." Helen touched Kyle lightly on the arm to steer him away. Curtis and Mackie both moved forward as if to follow, but Dave lifted his hand in a sharp gesture. It worked as well as a command to well-trained dogs. The other men stood still and all three watched as Helen and Kyle walked slowly up the alley. As soon as they reached the path leading to the park, Kyle pushed her hand away. Helen glanced over her shoulder. Apparently Dave and company weren't coming after them, probably only because there was a possibility one of them would get away and make trouble. She took one last look at them, standing like a trio of statues lined up in the alley. She breathed a little easier as they moved closer to the parking lot, where other people were still visible packing up cars and gathering up kids. Safety. As soon as they emerged from the path Helen turned to Kyle.

"What the fuck was that all about?" Helen didn't mean for the words to come out so harsh and sharp. Kyle turned away, still hunched over his sore stomach. "I'm sorry, Kyle. I'm not angry. It's just been — well, bad day doesn't begin to describe it."

"Leave me alone." He coughed again, gasped at the pain, wiped his mouth. "It's none of your fucking business."

"Those assholes just tried to beat the shit out of you. Looks like they almost did it, too. Hey, I'm talking to you." Frustrated and exhausted, still battling with horror from the image of Sissy in the park, Helen lost the last bit of control and grabbed Kyle's arm.

"Get your hand off me, you fucking — you fucking queer!" Kyle batted her hand away. That wasn't sweat that poured down his cheeks now. He wiped at his tears with both hands balled in fists, like a frightened child, and managed a trot down the path away from Helen.

Helen put her hands on her hips and watched him drive off in the usual thunderous rumble, leaving a thick gray cloud of exhaust to dissipate in the parking lot. She made her way to her own car, overcome by a sudden wave of exhaustion. She was just too damned tired to figure anything out now. Helen let her mind mutter aimlessly as she guided the Rambler back to the road, odd thoughts spilling over each other in a jumble of images. Strange to think that she had to drive in a wide circle to get back to Gramm Street, when a quick walk through the park would get her home faster. Kyle and Dave and whatever the hell they'd been doing might or might not be relevant to Sissy's death. Obviously Kyle thought it was. Dave wasn't averse to beating Kyle but he didn't want to make a scene with Helen. Kyle had been nervous about Deets coming around last night. Sissy's bracelet had stayed on her arm. No one seemed to know where Sissy's dad was. A green SUV had been haunting the neighborhood for a week before Sissy's disappearance. The park was located between a bunch of warehouses and an abandoned church. And Sissy may or may not have been raped.

Helen pulled the car over on the side of the road and wept — great racking sobs that tore at her chest in huge aching heaves, that left her gasping for breath. She cried until her eyes burned, swollen and streaming. She cried until her whole body trembled with grief and despair. Cars flashed by in swift succession. No one slowed or stopped. Gradually Helen was able to breathe. Her sides ached and her face felt boiled. She looked up, her hands in a death grip on the steering wheel. The sun had moved down to the top of Champion's Hill. She saw the golden green shimmer of the trees that covered the land, the deep red of the sky hovering over Tynedale. Although she couldn't see it, the boarding house was less than a mile away.

For a moment she thought about Valerie and Nanette. Was it an awful thing that she'd not really thought of Sissy's family until just now? Maybe that was because Sissy had seemed so alone and forgotten. Maybe Valerie had cared. Sounded like it, if she had been hearing regularly from her niece. Helen couldn't imagine what awaited her at Mrs. Mapple's house right now. Shit, that was so selfish, to be thinking of her own feelings in the midst of this. The memory of Valerie weeping at the kitchen table this morning — just this morning — solidified Helen's resolve to get her ass in gear. There might be something helpful Helen could do to put a little oil on the troubled waters at the boarding house. If nothing else, she could help Mrs. Mapple cope with the confusion in some way. Better that than sitting her by the highway thinking alternately about Sissy and Valerie's black hair.

Helen turned the key and the Rambler growled to life. Helen drove home. She had no place else to go.

Chapter Six

At first Helen couldn't tell what the noise was. It certainly didn't sound like that damned bird. More like a soft rustling, somewhere outside in the front yard. Helen turned over on her side, trying and failing to find a comfortable spot in the mattress. Her body kept rolling back into the well hollowed out in the center. She lay there, wide awake, staring up at the blank black ceiling. But the rustling continued, just loud enough to be annoying and keep her from going back to sleep. Helen sighed and gave up. She switched on the lamp by her bed and saw that the clock on the dresser read eight-thirty. The sun should be up by now, but the window over her bed showed a gray cloudy sky. More rain ahead.

She rolled up and swung her legs over the side of the bed, surprised at how alert she felt.

Last night she slept better than she had in weeks. Not a single nightmare, no restless tossing that tore sheets off the mattress, not a trace of her usual early morning bleary eyed confusion. Didn't make a lot of sense, she puzzled as she pulled together jeans, shirt, socks, shoes. Maybe just sheer exhaustion, after weeks of tension about every detail of her life. It had finally caught up with her and knocked her flat. Helen turned off her lamp and padded to the bathroom. When she came out she went back to her bedroom for shoes and stood still, listening for a few moments. The rustling continued, and now she could identify it. The question was who sat on the porch swing, moving slowly back and forth — Nanette? Not likely at this hour, given the sedatives the doctor had prescribed last night. Mrs. Mapple never sat there, as far as Helen could recall. And Kyle just didn't seem like the porch swing type. It couldn't be Judge Pemberton, who got up every Sunday at nine and waited for his son to take him to church.

That left Valerie Beausoleil. Helen deliberately shoved aside her desire to go down and talk to Valerie. The poor woman probably just wanted some peace, she reasoned as she crept quietly down the stairs and into the kitchen. Suddenly overcome with hunger, Helen cautiously took a bowl and spoon and helped herself to the cereal and milk Mrs. Mapple kept in stock. There was just enough light from the gray morning sky for Helen to see what she was doing. She took the bowl out to the screened-in back porch and watched birds flying across the pink streaked sky over the pines. Helen crunched at the cold cereal, marveling at how awake and alive she felt. Just like her wonder at the good sleep she'd had last night. What the hell did it mean that she could feel so well after the day she had yesterday? It was as if some valve had been released, or a spring snapped inside her. All the anger and fear and strain of the past couple of months, struggling to build some kind of new life and cope with hostility coming from all sides — something about Sissy's death had granted her a gruesome reprieve, both from others and from herself. Helen ate the last bite of cereal and wondered what her therapist back in California would have said about it. Although she hadn't seen or heard from Ms. Gruenbach in years, Helen easily conjured up her image. She could almost see her, gray haired and tweedy, perched on the rattan chair at the other end of Mrs. Mapple's back porch, turning those owlish light-blue eyes on her and asking Helen what she thought it all meant. Did Sissy's death represent a death in Helen herself, in some part of her that identified with the girl? Was it a distraction from Helen's own troubles that provided a welcome means to stay in denial about the mess she'd made of her own life? Or maybe it was an opportunity for Helen to play detective again, to somehow prove to herself she could still do it. And of course let's not forget that I might be doing some kind of compensation thing, using Sissy's death to make up for the other death I caused — the one that landed me in prison.

Helen got up with her empty bowl. Enough of that shit, she lectured herself. Ms. Gruenbach would never have treated the death of a child in such a facile manner — she was selling the therapist short and she knew it. I was exhausted and I got some badly needed rest and food. And that's all.

"Is that Helen?" Valerie leaned against the wall just inside the kitchen. Helen dropped her bowl with a clatter in the sink. "God, I'm sorry. I thought you heard me come in." Her voice came out in a husky whisper. "I didn't mean to startle you."

"It's okay. I just didn't know anyone else was up." Helen looked at her. Pale and taut, Valerie's face stood out in sharp contrast to her dark hair. She blinked as Helen turned on the lights, turning swollen eyes away from its glare and pushing her hair back. With her arm she cradled a shoebox against her side. "Come on in and sit down."

Valerie stood, hesitant. "I don't want to disturb you."

"You aren't. Please, sit down. I was just going to get some orange juice. Would you like some?" Helen rummaged in the refrigerator as Valerie sat down. Usually Mrs. Mapple ran to pitchers full of the stuff, courtesy of Kyle and the grocery store. Yes, there was some left back behind the milk. Helen kept busy at the counter, pouring juice into glasses, to let Valerie compose herself a bit.

Valerie managed a smile of thanks. "I guess I should try to eat something," she said after a few sips. "I just don't feel hungry." Her fingers trembled around the glass and she pursed her lips. The skin of her face was stretched taut and fine, like thin delicate parchment likely to break at the least pressure. "I won't be much good to Nan if I pass out, will I?"

"How is your sister?"

Valerie sighed and closed her eyes, leaning back in the chair. "Sound asleep. I wanted to get her out of here last night, especially when the cops came to look through Sissy's room, but as soon as she took those pills the doctor gave her she was out like a light. I'll take her over to my hotel as soon as she wakes up."

"How about you? Did you get any sleep?" Helen couldn't help asking, knowing she was only opening a door to her own grief by expressing concern. She picked up her own glass so as to keep herself from reaching out and taking Valerie's hands between her own, massaging those long slender fingers and pressing those palms against her own face. Walk away, she counseled herself, get up and walk away now. Don't care. She's never going to care about you.

Valerie shrugged. "I think I dozed off for a bit in a chair in Nanette's room. There's this damn bird, I don't what kind it is, whistling and calling right outside — it woke me up for good a few hours ago."

"Would you like to use my room?" Helen blurted out. When Valerie stared back at her Helen babbled on, "I'm leaving in a little while, I'll be gone all day long. Maybe you

can get a couple of hours sleep before your sister wakes up."
Great. A whole new image of Valerie curled up safe and sound
in her bed, that black hair spread like an exotic fan over the
pillow. What the fuck was she doing? Sissy was dead, Valerie
was grieving, Helen had no business interfering. Or lusting.

"Maybe. Thank you for the offer." Valerie's gaze dropped
and she reached out for the shoe box, making its contents
rattle. Helen recognized the box full of strange rocks she'd
seen in Sissy's room yesterday morning. "Funny, I just wanted
something of hers today. I know I shouldn't have gone in
there, but the cops went through it pretty thoroughly last
night. I'll put it back." She sorted through the pebbles aimlessly, and Helen saw tears on her face. "Can you imagine, a
little kid like Sissy having a damn box of rocks in her room?
No radio, no phone, no costume jewelry, no clothes everywhere, shoes all over the floor. No toys or stuffed animals.
Just a bunch of rocks."

"Valerie —" This time Helen did reach out, grasped
Valerie's wrist in a loose clasp, felt the tremors coursing
through her body. "Valerie, if there's any way I can help you,
anything at all." Helen stopped. Get a fucking grip, she lectured herself again. She doesn't need you maundering at her.
Still, Valerie didn't pull away or brush Helen's hand off.
Instead she looked up and seemed suddenly calm. No, not
calm — eager. Determined.

"There is something."

"Name it."

"Tell me how Sissy died. I mean, tell me what you saw. I
know you found her, and I know Nanette will want to hear
this once she gets past the shock."

"Valerie, I'm sure the police —"

"No, not the police. I want to hear it from you. You were
there. Helen, I'm begging you." Her voice broke with her plea.
Helen released the other woman's hand with a sigh. Did
Valerie really and truly want this?

Of course Helen told her. Not without a certain amount of

judicious editing, but fortunately Helen hadn't seen a whole lot before calling the police. As she told her story to Valerie, Helen felt herself slipping back into cool observer, delineating details as succinctly as if she were writing a report back in her office in Berkeley during better times. And she realized that while she hadn't had the chance to closely examine Sissy's body, she'd noted plenty about the location. The park itself was a lot closer to the boarding house than one would think. Because there were no direct streets between Gramm and the park, anyone driving a car would need to take a roundabout route circling the town and ending up at the park after driving past the row of warehouses where she'd seen Kyle yesterday. But on foot, if one cared to wander through the morass of condemned buildings on the old Catholic school grounds, one could very quickly walk to the end of Gramm street, push through a broken door to get into the school, climb up a muddy hill to the fence that bordered the shrubs where Helen found Sissy.

"The police said it didn't look like she'd been — molested," Valerie said, pulling Helen back to the present. "But they don't know for sure yet."

"I see." Not until the autopsy. But Helen refrained from saying those words, not wanting to add imagery to Valerie's nightmares.

"So some bastard shot her." She choked on the word but managed to get it out and keep talking. "Nothing else yet. Is — is that true? I mean, you saw her. She was shot, like they said." Valerie turned away abruptly, leaning her elbow on the table and holding her head in her hands. Helen watched as she fought back shuddering sobs. "Fucking bastards," she said finally. "Why would he do that? I'll kill that monster if I get anywhere near him."

"He?"

Valerie looked up and wiped her eyes, drew in a shaky breath. "Gary Greene. Who else would it be?"

"You think her father did it?"

"The cops haven't found him yet. At least when they left last night they were still looking for him." Talking about her theory seemed to bring her a sense of calm and purpose — at least it gave her something to hang onto. "He must have taken her, she tried to get away, and he chased her down. Shit, he never cared about her since the day she was born. He only cares about his own prick. It's the only thing that makes sense, Helen. Kidnapping Sissy would get back at Nanette like nothing else. And it all went wrong." She looked at Helen eagerly, as if willing the other woman to believe along with her.

"Maybe so. I'm sure the police will find him soon." According to Nanette's statement Friday night, Gary drove a red sports car. Not a green SUV. Still she was sure Ludy would have Gary high on his own list. Maybe right up there with Helen.

"Helen? You've thought of something else. What is it?"

"Nothing." Helen regarded Valerie, who turned to her with such a trusting, anxious face, her cheeks still wet. How long would it be until Valerie learned about Helen's own past — about her involvement in the death of another woman, her status as graduate of Mississippi's notorious Deasely women's facility? Then maybe Valerie would have another pet theory starring Helen as murderer.

Someone was shuffling around in the hall outside the kitchen, breaking into Helen's thoughts. Valerie and Helen both sat up straight, and Helen shook off the vague sense of guilt. She hadn't done anything besides talk to Valerie — nothing to be ashamed of. A moment later old Judge Pemberton creaked his way into the kitchen. Helen smiled at him. He gave her a blank stare as he lowered himself down into a chair. Once he'd safely landed he looked around in wonderment, as if he'd never seen the room before.

"Can I get you something?" Helen asked him. He swiveled around to look at her. "Some juice?" No response. Helen noted that he'd dressed in a fresh suit today — it was a bit moth-eaten on the cuffs and lapels, and the knot of his tie was crooked. A thin streak of blood lined his chin, evidence that he'd managed to shave himself today. With a gesture that seemed to drain him of energy he heaved his briefcase onto the table. Helen had to look away from the spittle forming a blob at the corner of his mouth. "Here, I'll pour you a glass of juice." She set the glass in front of him and remembered it was Sunday morning. Of course. He got up early on Sundays because his son Earl took him to church every week. So why was the old man still here? It didn't seem likely Earl would forget. Maybe Helen should stick around and make sure the judge didn't get into any mischief. Which reminded Helen — she wanted to stop by Earl's toy shop downtown and pick up something for Bobby's train set before setting out for Aunt Edna's. They ought to be home from church around eleven-thirty. It seemed strange to be thinking along the lines of a daily schedule, after what happened yesterday, but Helen couldn't bear the thought of hanging around the boarding house today. Even Aunt Edna's meatloaf was not too high a price to pay. Besides, she missed Bobby. It would feel good to spend time with someone who gave a damn about her.

Valerie took a long look at the judge, then said, "Maybe I should take you up on that offer, Helen. About getting some rest." Fortunately Helen could hear Mrs. Mapple stirring around in the room over the kitchen, which meant she'd be down in the kitchen and able to look after the judge in a few minutes. They left the old man sitting at the table and staring down into his glass of juice with a puzzled expression on his face.

Mrs. Mapple, strapped into her faded paisley robe, passed them on the stairs, muttering something about Earl Pemberton and a phone call and emergencies. "I think I should tell that young man I'm raising my fees for his daddy, what with all the extra work I do for him," she said as she flopped her way toward the kitchen. "What with having to take him to church and clean up his messes and spend all day fetching and carrying, it's a wonder I haven't dropped dead from the overwork, not to mention visits from the police which I don't hold with for a minute, I have more than enough to do, Lord knows I don't complain . . ." Her voice trailed off as she went into the kitchen. Valerie exchanged a silent smile with Helen, and once again Helen resisted the impulse to touch the other woman, pull her into an embrace. No fucking way, she told herself sternly. Just keep moving.

They tiptoed past Nanette's room. Helen paused long enough to listen, felt Valerie standing close behind her. Not a sound. Shit, Helen thought, here I am leading a beautiful woman to my bedroom. First time that's happened in years, and not a fucking thing I can do about it. Thank God she'd followed her impulse to make the bed before leaving the room earlier this morning. "Here we are," Helen said in a low voice. She closed the door gently and did her best not to look at Valerie.

"This is so nice of you, Helen. Jesus, I guess I'm a lot more tired than I thought," and Valerie stretched and yawned, leaning backward so that Helen could see the graceful line of her neck curving over her breasts and down her stomach to her legs. Helen moved away and located her backpack as Valerie sat down on the bed. "Maybe I should leave a note somewhere in case Nanette wakes up and looks for me."

"Here, you can write one with this and I'll slip it under her door." Valerie took the pen and notepad from Helen and started to write as Helen turned on the ceiling fan. "Still looks cloudy out there. I think we're going to get some rain."

"Oh, I'm sorry — I think I wrote on something important. Did you want to keep this?"

Helen took the sheet of paper Valerie held out and saw Sissy's scribbled math problems. She looked up at Valerie as she folded the note over. "Maybe I should. Here's another one." She tucked it into her backpack without any idea what she ought to do with it, but somehow it just seemed wrong to use it like scrap-paper. Valerie wrote a second note.

"There. Hopefully Nanette will sleep a little longer," and she lay down and closed her eyes. Helen puttered around the room a few minutes longer, wondering if she ought to do anything else. By the time she turned at the door to say goodbye Valerie was already sound asleep. Dammit, Helen thought as she slipped the note under Nanette's door and hurried down the stairs, she looks just as beautiful in bed as I thought she would.

It had now become a habit for Helen to check Gramm Street for cars familiar and unfamiliar. She backed out the Rambler and noted that Kyle's Mustang was wedged between a neighbor's station wagon and another neighbor's pickup. When did he get home and what the hell was he doing all night? No sign of the green SUV, or of any kind of red sports car that she didn't recognize as belonging to other residents of the block. A few drops of rain spattered her windshield as she turned off Gramm and headed downtown. Now what? Helen felt at loose ends as she halted at a red light. Earl's shop wouldn't open until ten at the earliest, maybe later on Sundays. And Valerie had definitely rattled her cage. Not to mention the soreness inside every time Sissy rose up in her thoughts. Valerie had kept her distracted for a few minutes, but alone in the car plenty of disturbing thoughts boiled up to the surface of her consciousness. And dammit if she wasn't still hungry. While she waited for green, Helen turned on the radio. Between preachers and static she picked up a local news broadcast. "Our top story today is the murder of a child over in Tynedale . . ."

"Shit," Helen muttered as she switched off the radio. The skies chose that moment to unleash a downpour and the Rambler stuttered its way through the intersection. The streets of Tynedale yawed empty and gray and damp this Sunday morning. Most good citizens were probably in church right now. Wait — there was some kind of neon light shining through the murk at the end of the street, past the darkened doors of the pizza parlor. *Rosie's*, the sign blinked on and off

in fire-engine red. Good, Helen thought as she pulled up —
coffee and the other not-so-good citizens of Tynedale.

It took a few minutes for Helen to shake off the rain, catch
her breath and glance at a menu. A waitress walked up and
poured out coffee for her. "Another ugly day out there, huh?"

"Afraid so." Helen glanced up and saw the appraising
glance, the short-cropped hair, the firm jaw, the muscular
hands gripping the coffee pot. Her gaze traveled past the
waitress and took in the posters of Rosie the Riveter lined up
with photographs of WW II era women bent over machinery
in factories. Jesus fucking Christ, she thought as she spied the
stack of alternative papers piled high next to the cash register.
Or maybe, she changed her mind, I should say "eureka." A
dyke hangout in Tynedale? Not possible. Hurriedly she
glanced around the room. Yep — almost all women, a few
black faces dotted amongst the white, and a woman at the
expresso machine sporting a buzz-cut and a snake-like tatoo
on her upper arm.

"Special today is tofu scramble and grits." That clinched
it — that and the smile on the waitress' face. What were the
odds of tofu and grits in any other establishment in this neck
of the woods?

"I'll just have some toast."

"Whole wheat, wheat-berry, sourdough, cinnamon-raisin,
white, herb bread?"

Helen settled for wheat and got up to grab a paper from
the stack by the cash register. She didn't harbor any illusions
about being a hot commodity, but just because she was the
new kid on the block she was certain she'd at least get
checked out by the staff, maybe some of the patrons. With a
sigh she turned to the front page of the Sunday paper. Yes,
Sissy had made a big headline. Nothing new there beyond the
fact that she had in fact been killed by a blow to the head.
Helen leaned back, staring at the poster of Rosie on the wall
without seeing it. No mention of sexual assault, although of
course that didn't mean it didn't happen — maybe the cops

were keeping that one quiet. Had she been killed somewhere else and then placed in the bushes later? Without a chance to examine the area Helen couldn't tell. The mud had looked pretty well trampled, she remembered. And Sissy's hair and clothes had been mud-streaked. No rocks she'd noticed near the bushes. Fuck, if only she'd been able to pay closer attention, or had a little time to look around before Ludy showed up —

"What a surprise!" Renee had another woman in tow. They stood staring down at Helen. Renee was the only one smiling. "I don't think I've ever seen you in here before."

Helen managed a weak smile. "First time. It's the only place in town open on Sunday morning, I think."

"Just for us sinners. Helen, this is Gwen."

"Hi." Gwen took Helen's hand reluctantly and dropped it as fast as she could as Renee made explained how she and Helen knew one another. Gwen would have been very pretty if she'd cracked a smile, Helen decided. Her hair reminded Helen of Valerie's, except Gwen cut hers shoulder length. She was thinner than Valerie, too, and slouched over a bit. Gwen stalked off in search of a table, giving Renee a glance over her shoulder as she left. Jealousy? Helen thought with a jolt. My god.

Renee stood there and grinned. "We come in here a lot on weekends, especially when my son is with his dad. So when you gonna let me do something with your hair?"

"Oh. Well. Maybe when I'm in town next week?" When I go to see my parole officer, Helen thought. "Friday. In the morning, about the same time I saw you this week?" It might do her some good to take Marie up on that offer of a couple of days off. She'd try for Thursday and Friday, give herself a long weekend. A thought buzzed around in the back of her mind, something about doing a little investigating, but she pushed it aside and tried to pay attention to Renee.

"Great. Oh, Jesus," Renee said as she saw the front page of the paper spread across the table. Helen handed the paper

107

to her. "Listen, we heard that on the news last night. That poor sweet kid! It just makes me sick." Her pleasant round face creased in sadness as she skimmed the story. "I can't believe it."

Helen watched her carefully as she said, "Did you know her very well?"

Renee shrugged. "About as well as any other customer at the salon. Actually hairdressers and bartenders and shrinks all hear about everyone's problems." She handed the paper back to Helen and glanced around, then leaned forward and spoke in a low voice. "I'm the one who suggested she try the boarding house for a while. You know, just temporary."

Helen found it hard to imagine Nanette going to Renee's salon for a haircut. She'd figured her more for the country club type. Renee smiled at the look of surprise on Helen's face. "No, she wasn't my client. Nanette has Melanie take care of her — did you see her the other day in the salon? Tall red-head? Anyhow, I told her about Mrs. Mapple a couple of months ago when she came in for her usual visit. Just as a temporary thing, you know. Of course I didn't know that Kyle — well, I had only been there a few months myself."

Helen, alert now, studied Renee's face. What the hell was this about Kyle? Something about the way Renee shut up convinced her not to follow that line of conversation. Not yet, anyhow. "So a lot of people knew about Nanette's personal problems, then."

"Who didn't? You've been around here long enough to know all Nanette's dirty laundry by now — she'd talk to the dog next door if she thought he'd listen. Besides, adultery is a hot topic at the salon these days."

"Did you know Gary, her husband?"

"Little mister country club, you mean?" Renee snorted. "He hits forty, gets a sports car and a floozie. Word is she found hubby screwing his secretary on the living room sofa and bolted out of the house with Sissy."

"Yeah." Helen noticed that Gwen was glaring in their

direction, arms folded across her chest. Renee followed Helen's gaze and with a quick muttered farewell beat a hasty retreat as Helen's toast arrived. She paged through the paper think- ing hard. Renee might be a good source of information on Sissy. Besides, she needed a haircut. And anyhow she liked Renee, Helen realized as she finished her toast. It felt strange, after such a long stretch of not liking anyone. Rather, of not letting herself like anyone. And she'd liked Sissy, too, she thought, fighting back tears as she signalled the waitress for her check.

Helen paid the cashier, who checked her out as thoroughly as the waitress had, and darted back to her car in the rain. As she drove off toward Earl Pemberton's toy shop, the sun began to break through the clouds gnarled overhead, sending waves of heat through the car windows. The rain had completely stopped by the time she got to *Cabbages and Kings*. It took Helen a moment to place the name of the store, but as soon as she did the entire poem by Lewis Carroll flooded through her mind, along with the classic drawings of the Walrus and the Carpenter. Pemberton had taken decorating cues from the Alice books, as well — lots of reproductions in life-size cardboard of the various magical creatures from both books situated in Victorian window dressing. The sun beat down hot and steady on her back as she reached for the door. Damn, they opened at 10:30 on Sundays, she read from the stenciled notice hanging by the entrance. Another few minutes to wait. Helen glanced idly up and down the street, wondering where she could wander for a few minutes — wasn't there a bookstore nearby? — and then she noticed the green SUV parked a few yards ahead.

Was it the same one? Helen cursed herself for not noticing more about the vehicle before. She took a few steps toward it but the voices coming from inside the shop froze her in her tracks. "They think it was me, dammit," one raised male voice wailed. "How could I do that to my own little baby?" Then the voice hushed down to a murmur. Another male voice responded, pitched too low for Helen to make out the words. Without hesitation Helen went back to the door and pushed. She was in luck. The door swung open noiselessly. Helen got inside quickly, thankful that no bells or alarms announced her presence. Maybe Earl had forgotten to turn them on? Or maybe if she stepped further inside the door she'd set off some system designed to alert clerks in the store that patrons had arrived?

She took a moment to look around while she caught her breath. Everything was still dark, but Helen made out long low shelves, about kid high, crammed with brightly wrapped packages. The Power Ranger stuff was closest to the door, followed by rows of comic books — no, they were called graphic novels now. Straight ahead a cash register, surrounded by displays of neon colored pens and toy key-chains and wind-up trinkets, gleamed in the rays of sun filtering in through the blinds. As her eyes grew accustomed to the gloom Helen saw a group of miniature chairs set in an alcove around a long table placed at the back of the store to her left. An assortment of blocks and books covered the table and Earl had tacked up posters on the surrounding walls. Helen turned to her right. That must be Earl's office, behind the glass wall covered by floor-length blinds. Harsh white light glowed from the half-open door.

"Gary, you should go talk to the police right now, dammit! Do you want them to think you're running away?" Helen recognized Earl's thin, slightly whiny voice.

Gary Greene sobbed. Was he drunk? Maybe. His words came out slurred but that could be grief and exhaustion. "Jesus Christ, Earl," he got out, "my little baby girl is dead. Who do you think they'll be chasing down? That bitch Nanette —" here his voice toughened into a growl — "she'll convince them I did it. I can't fucking believe it. First my wife runs away and ruins everything, now this. A man shouldn't have to take this, not from his own family. I could kill her, I swear it."

Then she heard a heavy sigh. "I mean it, Gary. I'm sorry for you, God knows I am, sorrier than I can say. But you have got to get out of here and go to the police. Goddammit, I told you not to be creeping around the house like that. I told you I'd let you know how she was."

Gary had stopped crying. Heavy silence. Helen stiffened, hand on the door ready to escape. Had they heard her? The next words dispelled that fear. "Yeah, and you did a terrific job, Earl." Gary's voice hardened into icy calm. "You and that cunt mother of hers. I should kill both of you, worthless shit-heads."

"My God, Gary," Earl said, his voice breaking with tension. "You're acting like you think I did it." Straining to pick up the words Helen was surprised at the wariness she could hear coming from Earl. "You're just out of your mind with grief, son, and I don't blame you. But you gotta get out of here and talk to the police, right now." It came out wheedling, fearful.

Earl's plea apparently served only to anger Gary further. "How do I know you didn't?" Gary responded. "How do I know you and Nanette didn't plan this whole thing, right under my nose, just to spite me? You been fucking my wife, too, along with everything else? Took my money, now you're taking everything else."

"Come on, Gary, just take it easy now. Why do you imagine I'd hurt Sissy?"

"You'd have the best chance of anyone. Just where the hell were you, anyway, you son of a bitch? What were you doing Friday night? Taking more money out for that damn church fund you keep talking about? That fund you won't explain to me? What is that fund, you son of a bitch?"

"Just take it easy," Earl repeated. Helen didn't think she imagined his change of tone. The money, maybe — the mention of money had done that. But why? She tried harder to listen as Earl's voice faded to just above a murmur. Trying to keep Gary calm, probably. "I was right here closing up the shop, Gary. Like every Friday night. And I have witnesses who can prove it — my cashier, Linda, and her boyfriend. Then I went to *Rosie's* for dinner, like I do every Friday night."

Strange, Helen thought. He didn't sound right. Too cautious, not nearly angry or appalled enough. And methodical in his recitation of his whereabouts. Like he'd known he would need an alibi. Or was he just trying to keep Gary calm? That was probably it. But she couldn't help remembering how Earl had always brought things to Sissy when he visited his father. What had they been? Helen couldn't really remember. Books, she thought. Nothing memorable. It hadn't seemed important at the time, and certainly Sissy had never shown a lot of interest in Earl or his gifts. From what she was hearing now, though, it sounded as if Gary had somehow talked Earl into keeping an eye on Sissy — possibly Nanette, too — as an unofficial spy for the errant father and husband. Until Gary had taken matters into his own hands by hanging around the boarding house in his brand new car. None of it sounded good to Helen, and Ludy would certainly take an even dimmer view than hers. And why the hell would Earl agree to it? Sounded like money had changed hands here. Maybe Earl was a cheap substitute for a private detective. He had the advantage of being right on the spot. She'd have to do some quiet checking. Did Gary Greene's firm do the books for Earl and his toy shop? He'd be in a position to know if Earl needed cash. And given his penchant for secretaries and new cars, not to mention the drain on finances a divorce could bring, Gary wouldn't have much money to throw away on expensive professional surveillance. Helen glanced around the shop again. Certainly Earl looked nothing if not prosperous, but looks didn't count.

Helen tensed, listening to feet shuffling and heavy breathing. She'd gotten lost in her musings, quit paying attention to Earl and Gary once their voices grew quiet. Was a fight in preparation back there? Maybe she should call the police herself — but she stopped in mid-motion. Not yet. Two

112

brawls in two days was a bit much, even for her. Only if she heard something beyond angry words. Besides, Ludy and Deets would have a field day if Helen kept showing up at all the wrong times and places. She breathed a silent sigh of relief as someone — no doubt Gary — dissolved into tears.

"Ah, fuck, I just don't know what to do. You gotta help me out here, Earl. Let me stay at your place. I just can't face the cops yet, can't face seeing my baby gone."

"Now Gary you know you can't do that. You have to just relax and go on downtown and ask for Deets. He'll take care of everything. Why don't you let me call them for you?"

"I guess you're right. God, nothing ever works for me, Earl. I should never have left them. I knew Nanette could never take care of herself or our little girl on her own. Earl, do you — do you think she'd have me back now? Maybe she really needs me there, to comfort her. Should I go talk to her now, do you think?"

Shit. Helen could hear them moving around, maybe getting ready to emerge from the back office and make their way out front. She backed out quickly and hurried to her car. Nothing helpful she could do here now, and it sounded like Earl had the situation under control. Helen moved the Rambler to a different parking slot, further down the street in front of a convenience store. It was a busy spot, lots of cars coming and going on quick errands. She didn't think she'd be noticed, and it afforded her a good view of the front of *Cabbages and Kings*.

Sure enough, a black-and-white followed by a plain green sedan pulled up in front of Earl's shop. Helen watched Deets clamber out of the police car. Ludy emerged from the sedan. Together they disappeared inside the store. A delivery van then parked next to Helen, and for several minutes she couldn't see the front of the toy store. When the van's driver finally took off both Earl and Gary stood on the sidewalk, talking to Ludy. Another woman had joined them. Young and pretty, with a soft mass of curly blond hair falling across her

113

shoulders, she looked dazed and helpless as she witnessed the scene. This might be Linda, the cashier, Helen reasoned as she turned her attention back to Gary. Yes, she could just see a faint resemblance to Sissy. Something about the way he held himself, even now as he stooped under the weight of grief and confusion, reminded Helen of Sissy's strong sturdy body. Helen swallowed down the surge of emotion as Gary ducked his head down and folded himself into the back seat of the sedan. Then it was Helen's turn to look puzzled as she saw Earl climb into the back seat of Ludy's car. Made perfect sense for Gary, of course. But why the hell was Earl going, too? The toy shop owner refused to look at Linda, who called something after him. Was it moral support? Helen wondered, watching as the car sped off with Deets close behind. No handcuffs. Probably just questioning. Earl shouldn't have been tagging along. They must want to question him as well.

Linda stared after them until both cars were out of sight, then went shaking her head into the store. A moment later Helen saw lights go on, and a hand turned around the "closed" sign. Helen left the Rambler where it was and hurried up to the shop, making it inside just ahead of a harried looking mom with three noisy kids in tow. Helen quickly found what she wanted — the bright red caboose was just what Bobby needed for his train set. It was the last one, too. She grabbed it off the shelf and looked for Linda.

Poor Linda. She'd certainly not expected this. Her pretty face was still marred by puzzlement as she punched keys in the cash register. "That'll be twenty-nine ninety-five."

"Really? I thought it was only nineteen dollars."

"Oh, my goodness! You're right." Linda sighed and shook her head. "I'm so sorry. Guess I'm just not myself this morning."

"I — I saw the police outside as I was coming in. Did y'all get robbed or something?"

Linda looked at her with a wary expression. "No, ma'am."

She fiddled with the cash register tape. Behind her Helen could hear the three boys jumping up and down, their mother shushing them in vain. Linda's gaze moved past Helen to take in the presence of other customers, and she bent to her task.

Helen tried again. "I thought I saw Earl with them, too. Is everything okay here?"

But Linda refused to be baited. "That's twenty-one fifty-seven, ma'am," she told Helen in a chill voice. Helen waited patiently while the girl made the wrong change and minutes later she was on the freeway heading toward Aunt Edna's house. She wasn't sure whether Linda was scared or if maybe that was a display of loyalty to Earl. Was there any way, she wondered, she could do some digging without getting caught? Renee might be a good place to begin, but the grapevine was all too public. Maybe she could befriend Nanette. Or Valerie. Helen almost laughed out loud. There she went again, trying to rationalize ways of getting closer to the woman.

Suddenly, despite everything that had happened the past two days, Helen felt good again. The car sped along, windows open to the air and sun, bright green fields rushing past in a blur of color. Whatever the reason, it felt good to use her mind again. Good to think like a detective, good to do something besides ponder her navel and her past up in that tiny bedroom. Good to see the world free of gates and locks and bars and grim-faced women gone gray with boredom and despair. Good to imagine, even for just a moment, that maybe she could help find out what had happened to Sissy. Helen found a station on the car radio that played something besides ranting preachers and listened to Willie Dixon play the blues on the short drive to Edna's place.

As soon as she stepped out of the car Helen's mood died. Bertie sat next to Bobby on the front porch of her aunt's house. She grinned up at Helen. "Hey. Long time no see."

Chapter Seven

"Are you just about ready for lunch, honey?" Edna McCormick appeared at Bobby's bedroom door. She hadn't changed yet from the clothes she'd worn to church that morning. Dark blue dress in a flattering design, real pearls at her neck, fresh coral nail polish — and she'd had her hair done recently. Helen had never seen her aunt's face so carefully made up, with just a hint of rouge and a pale pink lip gloss that flattered her skin. Helen looked away, hoping her aunt hadn't seen the expression on her face. She missed the Aunt Edna of the ugly flowered house-dresses moving slowly and painfully in the trailer outside Tupelo. The Aunt Edna without money or tasteful clothes, who had always had to make do with home permanents and who would certainly not be wearing nail polish. The Aunt Edna who hadn't come into money by promising to keep her mouth shut about the past.

At least her cousin, permanently frozen in time, was behaving exactly the way he always did. Bobby looked up from his train set. "Look, mommy! Helen got me this. I really like this a lot," and he grinned and held up the caboose for her to see. "She said she got it in a toy store downtown."

"That's real nice, honey. And wasn't that nice of Helen to bring it to you? Did you say thank you to cousin Helen?" Edna sat down on Bobby's bed and watched him as he struggled to attach the caboose to a section of his electric train. "I think that meat-loaf is just about done now." Edna patted Bobby's shoulder to get his attention. "Momma's talking to you, son."

"Mommy, I can't make it work right." Bobby's face turned pink with exertion, then deepened into the red of anger. His thick hands fumbled with the toy. Any moment now, Helen knew, he'd completely lose his temper and start to flail out at the offending toys. Breathing hard through his nose Bobby gripped the caboose and shook it. "I can't make it work right," he repeated.

"Here, Bobby. I bet if I hold this part and you hold that part we can get it to stick together like you want. How about that?" Helen took the engine off the tracks and guided Bobby's hand in her own. He plucked at his tee-shirt and his mouth twisted in a pout but he let Helen fit the caboose into the grooves at the end of the engine. He had to be — how old was it? Thirty-six? No, it was thirty eight. He'd had his thirty-sixth birthday right after she was transferred to Deasely. Almost completely bald now, Bobby had the pasty skin and flabby body of a middle-aged couch potato whose idea of exercise was reaching for a can from the six-pack in the cooler. Squatting on the floor in his jeans and sneakers, he looked exactly what he was — a big overgrown baby. And was he more prone to anger now than before? Helen couldn't imagine the frustration of Bobby's life. Somehow he seemed to sense that he wasn't all there, but there wasn't a damn thing he could do about it. "See? Now we got it!" The caboose snapped into place and Helen laid the train back on its tracks.

Bobby eagerly reached over for the remote controls. Lips pursed in concentration, he carefully pressed a button and the train began to move. "Now we got it!" he crowed. A big grin wiped out all trace of the rage he'd displayed moments before, and he pressed another button. "Listen," he whispered as a horn tooted. "I like that the best of all!"

"It's very cool, Bobby," Helen smiled at him.

"Cool!" Then, Helen and Edna forgotten, he lay down on his stomach until his face was level with the train circling around and around, through the plastic trees and cardboard buildings.

Helen leaned back against the bed, stretching her legs out in front of her. She kept her eyes on the train's journey as she asked, "So how did you meet Bertie, Aunt Edna?"

"Bertie? Who do you mean?" Helen twisted around to look at her aunt's face. The only thing she saw there was puzzlement.

"The woman playing with Bobby on the front porch when I got here."

Edna shook her head. "I don't know any Bertie, Helen. Are you sure it wasn't one of the neighbors? They've been so nice to us here, so friendly. Oh, you must mean that nice Roberta. You remember, don't you, Bobby?" She got up from the bed, her movements slow and careful. Helen realized her arthritis must be bothering her a lot lately. She couldn't help glancing at her Aunt's gnarled hands twisted in the apron. "Unless you're talking about Mrs. Tillman from next door."

"How do you know Roberta, Aunt Edna?"

"We met her in the park a couple of weeks ago. A sweet girl, from Jackson, I think. She's been so sweet to Bobby. Brought him games and books. Even took him for a ride once. Didn't she, sweetheart?" She stroked her son's balding head affectionately. "And I think she has a younger brother back home just like Bobby. She sort of tears up whenever she talks about him." Edna shook her head sadly. "So nice and respectful, too. You don't often see young people so polite these days. Ya'll put the toys away now and come on down to dinner. Bobby, you hear me?"

"Okay."

"Now, honey, what do you say?"

"Yes, ma'am."

"All right, then." She leaned slightly to the right as she left the room, favoring that leg. Helen bit her lip. Shit. Now what? She couldn't imagine Bertie being sweet and gentle. What the fuck was that bitch up to? She even took Bobby for a ride. It chilled Helen's blood to imagine it.

Of course, Aunt Edna was lonely, too. Anyone who treated Bobby well would be a saint in her eyes. And Aunt Edna had aged considerably in the past two years. Who the hell was she to throw stones at her aunt for wanting a bit of peace and comfort? Then there was the whole question of Bobby. He had so few connections to anything resembling a life — how could his aging mother not be won over by such a nice young woman as Roberta?

It had to be money, somehow. Surely Bertie wouldn't go to all this trouble just to give Helen a little grief. Edna had that nice new car, the big house, the tasteful clothes, the means to provide Bobby with a comfortable life. Once again Helen cursed the day her aunt had left the trailer park and moved up in the world. But if Aunt Edna hadn't taken the money offered by her husband's former employer to keep her mouth shut about the company's shady behavior, Bobby would no doubt be locked up somewhere once Edna died. There simply wouldn't be enough money for anything else — certainly not from Helen, earning just above minimum wage at a warehouse and not likely to do much better for a long time.

Helen watched the train circling endlessly around the perfect little town with its tidy rows of houses and trees, its plastic policemen, its neatly labeled SCHOOL and HOSPITAL and TRAIN DEPOT. Too bad life hadn't been like this train set for any of them, Edna or her late husband or even poor Bobby. It might be nice to know your life would only stretch as far as the confines of the artificial universe where the trains always ran on time.

"Come on, time for dinner." Helen picked up the remote and played with the controls until everything shut down.

Bobby heaved a huge sigh and struggled up to his knees. "Okay."

"Here, let's put this under the bed so Momma won't get mad. Listen, Bobby —" She sat down cross legged on the floor and put her hand on Bobby's arm. "Let's talk about Bertie. What kind of stuff did she give you?"

He put one plump finger to his lips, his eyes wide and serious. "It's a secret. I'm not s'pozed to tell nobody. Cross my heart and hope to die." He leaned in closer. "We don't tell Momma about the game."

"What game?"

"You know, the one where I listen if Momma is comin' outside and Bertie goes back down the street and we pretend she didn't come over. Like secret ages."

"Secret ages. You mean secret agents."

"Yeah, them." His brow wrinkled. "How come you made her go away like that?"

"Well, Bertie had someplace else to go. She couldn't stay for lunch, now, could she? Momma would see her." Helen bit her lip, wondering if that had been wise to warn her away. Bertie had gone off willingly enough, with a friendly clap on the back for Bobby and a grin for Helen the moment Edna called out the front door. Anyhow, what the fuck was she doing here? It had taken all Helen's will to keep from slapping Bertie's face into the next county when she saw her sitting next to Bobby. Was it some half-assed plan cooked up to get Helen to be pals again? A weird kind of apology?

"Hey, Bobby. Roberta gave you some stuff, huh? Books and toys?"

He nodded vigorously. "Wanna see 'em?" Without any further urging he shoved the train set to one side and lumbered over to the brightly painted trunk that held his toys and favorite items. He rummaged a couple of moments then turned around with full hands and a big smile. "See? She gave me all this stuff."

"In the park."

"Uh huh." They looked innocent enough to Helen. She turned the pages of the biggest volume — a large illustrated book of fairy tales — and found nothing worse than the seven dwarves. Coloring books, a popular children's book on animals babies around the world, even a photo album.

"See, that's her!" Bobby pointed his stubby finger at the black and white photographs of Bertie at the beach, dressed for her school pictures in progressive years, one or two from some birthday party long ago.

"She gave you this, too?"

Bobby's face grew red. "She won't mind! Honest! It was sitting in her car one day. I just wanted pichers of her to look at. She won't care, Helen!" His face puckered with anxiety. "I'm gonna give it back."

"So you just borrowed this, huh?" Helen opened the old album cautiously, cradling the cracked spine in her palm. Bertie would never miss it. Although it was odd she'd had it in her car. Not like her, to cart around such sentimental stuff.

Bobby sighed with relief at his absolution. "Yeah, borrowed it."

Chilled at the sight of the cherub who'd grown into Bertie, Helen flipped through quickly. "There's lots of empty spaces here at the end, Bobby."

"I know. She's gonna take pictures of me to put in there." Bobby grinned and took the album back, reverently examining each picture. "She says this is her special book. I'll take good care of it, honest." Suddenly his face folded in fear. "You gonna tell on me? I'll take good care of it."

"It's okay, Bobby. What about these?" Helen took the two tape cassettes from Bobby's stack of treasures. No markings, nothing written on them to indicate their contents.

"Songs and stuff. Like about the farmer and the cows, the spider, stuff like that." Still absorbed in the photo album, Bobby barely noticed the tapes.

"Mind if I borrow these? I'd like to hear these songs."

"Okay." Helen slipped both cassettes into her bag near the door. Maybe if she played them backward she'd hear some strange subliminal message. Next, Helen chided herself, it would be death rays. If Bertie hoped to get into Edna's good graces, Bobby was the perfect route. But what possible motive could she have? No, it had to be some complicated plot to persuade Helen to go along with whatever strange and no doubt twisted ideas Bertie had about their connection. Bertie had to figure on Helen wanting to protect Bobby and Aunt Edna at all costs. Helen sighed, closed her eyes and rubbed her forehead. She wasn't up to this, any more than she was up to her aunt's underdone meat loaf. "So this is like secret agents again, with you and me, Bobby. Right?" she said, putting as much lightness in her voice as she could manage.

"Right!" Bobby giggled, both hands to his mouth. Edna called up the stairs and Helen followed Bobby as he shambled ahead across the thick piled expensive carpet, through the dining room with its imposing table and chandelier into the bright cheerful kitchen. She still couldn't get over the contrast to the trailer where she'd watched her Uncle Loy die — where she'd sought refuge from her parents enraged at her sexual perversions during teenage years — where she'd finally been unwelcome once she'd disgraced Aunt Edna by dragging Loy's name through the mud. This house at the edge of Tynedale's newest suburb was a palace compared to the trailer. Funny, Helen thought as she sat down to soggy meat loaf and watery vegetables and the ubiquitous white bread, how her relatives lived as though they were still in that trailer. The dining room had never been used, as far as Helen knew. And the living room had a just-unwrapped feel to it, as though the movers had only minutes ago put the sectional sofa down in front of the glass-topped coffee table. The homiest room in the whole place was the kitchen — and even it was a little too white and bright and charming. Had they really lived here for almost two years? Helen piled meat and vegetables on her plate knowing she'd never get it all down.

"So, how is the warehouse these days? Did you get a promotion yet?" Helen mumbled answers at her aunt's questions, growing more irritated by the minute at Edna's deliberately perky tone of voice. Of course the other woman was full to bursting with the news about Sissy Greene. But this was the new and improved Aunt Edna, who avoided ugly truths and refused to look reality in the face.

But there was one truth Helen couldn't let slide, not this time. "So, you met Bobby's new friend at the park? Which park was that?"

Aunt Edna looked up, startled. "Oh, you mean Roberta. She was in the park up the road a few weeks ago, just started playing with Bobby over by that little pond where all the goldfish are." Aunt Edna's face softened at the memory of Bertie's kindness to her first born. "So rare these days to find nice young people, you know? Especially such a pretty girl like that. She's even talking about bringing Bobby to Sunday school one of these days. I don't know where she goes, of course — but I'm sure it would be just fine."

The meat loaf sat like lead on Helen's stomach, and her answers got shorter and more abrupt. She refused dessert, finally, offering to clean up the kitchen while Bobby raced back upstairs to his train set. She let her aunt's chatter roll over her like the water flowed over the plates, wondering how the hell to let her aunt know that the last place they'd ever find Bertie was in a church.

Finally Helen had had enough. She scraped leftovers into plastic containers and said, "You know about what happened yesterday, don't you?"

Edna sighed and bent over the kitchen table, scrubbing furiously at some invisible flaw with a dishcloth. "That young girl. The one who lived at that boarding house. Helen, you could have stayed here with us. I just don't understand why —"

"Aunt Edna, I'm the one who found her." Helen set the plates down on the counter and turned around to see her aunt grasping the back of a chair and hanging on for dear life, her round wrinkled face stretched taut in horror. "It just happened, I was in the park yesterday morning, and she was there." For the first time since finding Sissy, Helen dredged up into her mind the full image of the girl's body, in glorious technicolor, stretched out in the mud, arms tangled in the thorny shrubs. She hesitated, wondering why she hadn't been haunted by nightmares last night, why the memory hadn't pursued her every waking moment. Maybe because somehow her mind and body had needed a safe place, a refuge where it was okay to remember. And maybe she'd hoped that refuge would be here, with her only living relatives.

Wrong. God, she was so fucking wrong, again. Edna drew in a deep breath and bent back over the table. Her voice trembled as she said, "The police didn't think you did it, did they?"

"Jesus." Helen felt the wind go out of her and she sat down clumsily at the table, drained of all feeling. "My God, Aunt Edna, are you asking me if I killed her?"

Her aunt, face twisted in fear, refused to look at Helen as she sat down beside her. She picked up a fork and fiddled with it, tapping it against a dirty plate in an annoying staccato of clinks until Helen was tempted to grab it away and stab her arm with it. "I know you didn't kill her, honey," Edna said in the same tone of voice she used with Bobby. "It's not that."

"Well, then, I guess I just offend your sensibilities. Is that it?" Helen grabbed her aunt by the shoulder and forced her to turn so they faced each other. The fear in Edna's face said it all. "Maybe you're just upset that I keep having dead bodies turn up around me. You can dress me up but you sure as hell can't take me anywhere, is that it?"

Her aunt's face went from white to pink, lips trembling and breath coming in ragged gasps. "You — you do not touch me that way, Helen! I won't have it in my own house!"

Helen leaned back and regarded her aunt as the ice of calm detachment swept over her body. "I guess you don't want me in your house, then. Right?"

Edna shook her head and stood up. "We will not have this discussion. I will not tolerate —"

"As I recall, you just don't want any discussions, Aunt Edna. You didn't want to discuss what Uncle Loy did that got you all this money you have now — no, listen to me, dammit!" Helen stood up and wedged herself between Edna and the table, effectively trapping the older woman against the kitchen counter. "You didn't want to talk about the past, you didn't want to know I'm a lesbian, and you didn't even want to know what happened to Victoria Mason."

Somehow the terror in Edna's watery eyes just served to spur Helen on. Her mouth worked as if she was trying to speak but no sounds came out. "Fine. You're going to listen now." Helen leaned in closer until she could smell her aunt's talcum powder laced with the flowery old-lady cologne she wore these days. "I killed Victoria Mason. It was an accident. I was trying to save us both from being killed — trying to get us away from two men sent to kill us — and Victoria pulled a gun on me. She was scared, a kid, no more than a kid. She didn't know what she was doing. All she could think about was getting away, and I stood between her and escape." Once again Helen saw Victoria's small white face, huge frightened eyes. The girl's features had begun to fade from Helen's memory, bleared by the passage of time, but that moment before her death was incised in Helen's mind. "And I was trying to save both of us."

Suddenly Helen wasn't in the huge white kitchen in her aunt's house. She was back in the rented car, in the middle of the night, driving like hell to get out of Mississippi. Then instead of Aunt Edna's pale face she saw the gun. She heard Victoria's voice demanding that Helen let her go. Saw her own hands, trembling, reaching for the gun. Touched the cold hard steel of the weapon as it shook in Victoria's hands. Saw the flash and smelled the awful acrid tang, heard the swift, sharp explosion. Looked into Victoria's eyes as the light faded from them. Felt the girl's body go limp as sticky blood surged in a bolus of heat and pulsing life between them.

Something broke through the shreds of image seething in Helen's mind — Aunt Edna sobbing, her wrinkled spotted hands held before her eyes. Gently, anger spent now, Helen pulled the old woman's hands away. She had no idea what she'd just said, but she could bet her aunt had gotten the gist of it. "And I want you to know what it was like in prison, too," Helen said. Her voice sounded dead to her own ears. She let go of her aunt's hands.

"No, Helen, please — I can't hear this — I don't want to know — oh God —" But was she really all that terrified? A glint in the older woman's eyes, a kind of calm stealing over her face. Maybe some part of Edna did want most desperately to hear the truth. Certainly she made no move to get away, now that she had the chance.

Helen leaned back against the table. Oddly she felt more light and free than she had in months. In fact, since her exodus from Deasley. And then all at once, like something out of a story she vaguely recalled — a children's story, where bad little girls had toads and lizards spitting out of their mouths every time they spoke — it came tumbling out. She told Edna about the heat and stench of two hundred women crammed into a squat series of ugly concrete buildings meant to house sixty prisoners. Then she told her about the guards, the way some of them toyed with their charges like boys pulling wings off flies. Next came the endless humiliation of every bodily function subject to observation and comment. "Can you imagine what that's like, Aunt Edna?"

"Helen, please —"

"Or what it feels like to know you're buried so deep inside the heart of the world that no one knows or sees or hears? It's being dead, that's what it is. Two fucking years of death. And now you expect me to keep being dead by shutting my mouth and pretending none of it happened." Helen took a deep breath. Jesus, she was sitting down again and she didn't even know how she got there. "I can't play that game. Never again. This happened to me, all of it. And I won't swallow it down like you want me to."

A few moments went by and Helen realized she literally couldn't speak any more. She had no words left. Completely emptied of everything — memories, emotions, thoughts — she looked up at her aunt. Edna stared straight ahead, her face immobile and white like carved ivory, her hands alabaster sculptures among the detritus of dinner. As Helen watched her aunt swallowed, with a visible movement of her ropy neck muscles. "All right, Helen. You've had your say. Now you will leave."

"Yes. It's time to go." Helen got up, nearly sat down again. How the hell did she get so light headed?

"You are not to come back to this house, Helen. And you are not to be around Bobby any longer." Edna's eyes were dark and unreadable but there was no mistaking the chill in her voice. "I don't want you around my child."

Helen almost laughed as she made her way slowly around the table to the door. "You think I can corrupt Bobby? For God's sake, at least accept reality about your own son."

The slap was totally unexpected — a much harder blow than Helen ever imagined her aunt could have mustered. "Don't you dare talk to me about my son, you ungrateful little tramp!" Aunt Edna hissed, her calm broken and her eyes flashing with fury. "What do you know about any of it? Did you have to change his diapers when he became a grown man? Did you ever worry about how to take care of him when his momma and daddy were gone? Did you ever think of anything

127

or anyone but yourself? And you don't even think enough of yourself to keep from going to hell. Because that's exactly where you're headed, living the way you do."

Helen rubbed her cheek and was amazed to feel her eyes well up with tears. "You mean because I love women. Funny — you make it sound like being gay was worse than killing someone."

"The Bible condemns you and your kind to hell, and you know it. I know you haven't forgotten that, even if you've forgotten everything else about the way you were raised."

Helen shook her head and smiled. "Oh, no, don't worry about that. I remember everything about how I was raised. I have nightmares about it all the time." She pushed her way out of the kitchen and stumbled out of the house. She was already on the highway before she realized she hadn't said goodbye to Bobby. But what did that matter? Poor Bobby would never know the difference — his universe was only big enough for himself, through no fault of his own. Then Helen remembered all the drawings he'd sent to her when she was in Deasely. And there was Bertie. Fuck, why had she let her emotions get the better of her like that? How the hell was she going to protect Bobby from Bertie? Screw Aunt Edna, she thought, she can take care of herself from now on. As if I ever made a difference in her life anyhow. But Bobby was a different story. She'd have to find a way to keep Bertie out of all their lives.

Thinking of Bertie reminded Helen of the tapes. She dug around in her bag and pulled one out, popped it into the ancient tape player on the dashboard. A syrupy female voice, accompanied by a plinking electronic keyboard, chimed into Helen's car. Yep, the farmer in the dell. Nothing too evil there, last time Helen had heard. Okay, what about the other one? It was worse than the first — a children's choir singing "Jesus Loves Me" followed by "A Closer Walk With Thee." Helen turned it off after she heard the opening bars of "I Come to the Garden Alone." Damn, this weird game of Bertie's was like something out of Grimm's fairy tales. The fact that Helen couldn't figure it out just made it all the more infuriating.

Her anger carried her back to the boarding house, as if she'd switched into automatic. She buried the tapes back in her bag as she approached her neighborhood. Before she knew it Gramm Street in all its decaying urban ugliness loomed into view. At the end of the street she saw the inevitable black and white of police cars, the dull green of Ludy's unmarked vehicle. Great. The perfect end to a perfect afternoon. Helen parked the Rambler across the street from Mrs. Mapple's house and trudged up the front lawn. The sun slammed heat into her back, and she felt sweat forming pools all over her body.

Valerie Beausoleil and Ludy stood talking on the front porch. The detective turned away and headed toward his car as Helen approached them. Deets wasn't far behind. "Been to church, Ms. Black?" Ludy asked, his face impassive and un-readable behind the reflecting sunglasses. Should Helen tell him that those sunglasses were outré now? Maybe not today.

"I doubt my religious beliefs are of any concern to the police, detective," Helen said, immediately regretting the words. It wasn't smart to let Ludy goad her. Her best defense against him was simply not to respond. But this time Ludy just stalked off. Perhaps he just couldn't resist needling some-body who wasn't able to reciprocate. Helen joined Valerie on the porch and they watched the police drive off.

"Are you okay?" Helen took off her sunglasses to look at the other woman. It had been a stupid question. Bleached with exhaustion, taut with grief, Valerie looked like hell. No, Helen decided reluctantly, she looked beautiful. Shit. "Did they have any news?"

Valerie shook her head. "No, not yet. Just more questions, mostly about Gary. He turned up today. I guess they've been questioning him for a while, now, but they don't seem to think he did it."

So at least Helen didn't have to decide whether or not to

talk about the appearance of Sissy's father on the scene. "Where's Nanette?" She should be answering questions, not Valerie, Helen thought indignantly. She was Sissy's mother, for Christ's sake. Okay, enough — cut that out. Valerie doesn't need you to defend her.

"Nan is asleep over at the motel. I got her a separate room so I wouldn't wake her up with my own coming and going. She woke up for a while around — oh, I don't know — maybe noon?" Valerie slumped down on the porch swing. After a moment's hesitation Helen sat beside her. "She sent me back for some of her stuff." Valerie nudged an overnight case with her foot. "I'm supposed to take her downtown for a statement tomorrow morning."

"Did you get some sleep yourself?" In my bed, no less.

"Yeah, a little. Jesus, I'll be so glad to get us out of this house. I guess — I guess I'll have to hang around long enough to pick up Sissy's things —" Valerie's voice broke off. She closed her eyes and leaned against the back of the swing.

"Maybe you want to be by yourself." Helen started to get up but Valerie pulled her back down again. The grip of her fingers, long and slender and strong, burned on Helen's skin like flames. She shivered, unable to help herself.

"No. Helen — I hate to ask you this. I shouldn't impose."

God, please impose on me. "I'll do anything I can to help," Helen responded, her tone cautious.

"I know it sounds awful, but could you take me for a drink somewhere? I have got to get away from this house for a while. Nanette is out, and I don't think I can take this." Valerie gave her a wan smile. "You must think I'm terrible. I'm sorry. I shouldn't have asked you."

Helen couldn't help smiling back. "To tell you the truth, I could use a drink myself. Come on, we'll find something." So an hour later they were in the *Tavern*. It wasn't Helen's first choice, but she knew no other places to go. Besides, she was certain Valerie wouldn't want to stray too far from Tynedale and Nanette. Fortunately, Helen's guess that the place would be almost deserted was correct. Just a few people sipping at beer and listening to country music on the juke box. They were both into their second drinks when Valerie got around to her life in New Orleans. Of course Helen noticed immediately that Valerie was being extremely careful about pronouns.

"So when my partner left me last year, I just stuck it out there in the same apartment. Have you ever been to New Orleans, Helen?"

"Once, a long time ago." That had been with a lover, during one wild Mardi Gras. Helen smiled at the memory of how she'd bared a bit more than her tits that night. "Does your partner still live in New Orleans?"

"Hell if I know. She and I weren't exactly on speaking terms, not after I found out she'd been playing around with my best friend." Valerie looked up sharply as soon as she realized what she'd said. "Oh well, that's one little family skeleton out of the closet now."

Helen couldn't take her eyes off Valerie — she was even more beautiful when she blushed. "Not a problem. You're among friends here."

"I wondered, the first time I saw you the other night. In fact —" now a genuine smile stole across her face for the first time — "I even wondered from Sissy's letters. The way she described you."

"God, I don't even want to know what she said."

"It was all good, Helen. Made me want to meet you. Christ, did that sound stupid or what? Guess I'm just not acting like a sane person right now."

"You could hardly be expected to. Not with what you've been through." Oh, shit, that look in Valerie's eyes — it was too easy to get lost there. And if Valerie was acting interested it had more to do with the need for comfort than the need for Helen herself. They couldn't do this, they just couldn't.

But even as she scolded herself, Helen could feel the old sinking sensation, the vertigo of body needing body, as they looked at each other. "Maybe we should get out of here. I've had all I need to drink." Valerie tossed money on the table before Helen could protest, and a few minutes later they were back on the road. Helen took off in the direction of Tynedale, and they sat silent together, both staring out at the road. Now what?

"Do you want to get back to the boarding house?"

"No. Helen — I just need — fuck, I don't know what I need anymore. God, I'm just not used to this. I've always been the tough one, and Nanette always leaned on me. Always."

"So, who do you get to lean on, Valerie?"

"No one, I guess. Myself."

Helen smiled. "You sound just like me."

Valerie shifted in the seat so she could look at Helen. "I don't really know anything about you, Helen. I've been babbling about myself and my troubles for hours. Tell me about you."

Great. That takes care of that. "Not much to tell, Valerie."

"I doubt that. Jesus, how did I get drunk on a couple of beers?"

Helen glanced over to see Valerie curling up on the seat like a child. Dammit, she needs to get to her hotel and get some rest. "No big deal. You haven't eaten or slept for a couple of days, not to mention all the stress." It was no use — it didn't matter that Helen knew Valerie was grieving and exhausted. It still hurt that she didn't really give a damn about Helen. What the fuck did she expect?

"Where's your hotel? Valerie — where is your hotel?"

"Huh? Oh, it's called the River View Inn. On Jackson Street. No, not Jackson — James?"

"James. I know where that is." Of course there was no view of a river anywhere near the motel. Helen parked near unit six and helped Valerie out of the car. "Come on, you've got to get some sleep."

"No, I have to get my car. It's still at the boarding house."

"You're in no condition to be driving right now. We can

worry about that later, after you've sobered up." Helen could feel Valerie's breast as she leaned into Helen for support. Christ, she felt good — sturdy, strong, solid. Better than anything Helen had felt near her in years. And her hair smelled like vanilla. Something light and fresh and sweet. "You won't be much good to Nanette if you haven't had any rest."

Valerie sat down on the bed and Helen stood uncertainly by the door. "Helen. Don't leave." Her face was cast in shadow by the uncertain light of the bedside lamp. "Please?"

Gingerly Helen sat down on the bed as far away from Valerie as possible. "Okay. You still need to talk?"

"No. No, that's not what I need," and before Helen could stop her Valerie's hands were on her face. Helen couldn't work up the will to resist as Valerie kissed her, hard, her tongue lightly teasing Helen's lips.

Christ. Helen forced herself to remain still, willed her body not to respond to those pale long fingers stroking her neck and shoulders. "Valerie —"

"Val." The word came in a soft warm sigh, teasing Helen's skin.

"Okay, Val. Listen. Maybe I should just check on Nanette and you can lie down now." Helen gently pulled Val's arms from around her neck and carefully lowered the woman to her back. Val gripped Helen's arms with surprising strength, preventing her from rising off the bed. "Please. I know you're going to regret this once you've slept it off."

"No, I won't." She pulled herself up again and kissed Helen, leaning hard into the kiss, her lips soft and insistent on Helen's mouth. Then she leaned back and looked at Helen seriously. "Do you think I'm awful?"

"What do you mean?" Helen managed to say as she tried not to breathe too heavily.

"For — for doing this. For kissing you." Suddenly Val crumpled, and Helen caught her, holding her up in her arms. She could feel the other woman's body trembling. "It hurts so bad, Helen. I can't really look to Nanette right now — she's worse off than I am. Her own daughter." Val pushed away from Helen and sat on the edge of the bed, fighting back sobs.

"Valerie, you're in a lot of pain right now. No one could blame you for looking for a little comfort. I certainly don't." Helen took Valerie's chin in her fingertips, turned her face so they were looking at each other. "I just don't want you to feel worse about yourself later."

"Let me worry about that, Helen." And before Helen could get away, Valerie was holding her tight. Somehow Helen was lying down, and then Valerie was unbuttoning her shirt, rubbing her breasts with flattened palms, gently applying pressure until Helen heard moans coming out of her own mouth.

It was all so much like a dream that Helen could never piece it all together later. That afternoon remained a series of broken, confusing images. First Helen's clothes were on the floor. Then she was helping Valerie slip out of her jeans. Then Valerie's fingers strayed between her legs, probing and teasing. Hands cupping her crotch, absorbing heat and moisture. Helen's hips shifted, moving up against those hands. The tension spreading and glowing, something hard that melted deep inside her body, as Valerie lowered her face to Helen's thighs. Her tongue flickering like flame across sensitive skin until Helen's body surged in release.

"Now you," Valerie breathed as she straddled Helen, moving swiftly up to position herself over Helen's face. The scent of her, hot and musky, as she moved back and forth. Helen watched her own hands reaching up to Valerie's breasts, saw the pleasure stealing over Valerie's face as Helen's fingers explored the rich full weight there. The bedside lamp cast soft yellow light over them both as Valerie reared her head back, her breath catching in a harsh gasp. Then Valerie's whole body trembled as Helen took one hand to the slick soft flesh between Valerie's thighs. And Valerie shuddered, finally, spent and silent as she eased herself down into the bed.

Helen watched Valerie's profile a moment, then closed her eyes. She drifted into a light doze, lulled by the rhythm of the other woman's breathing and the overpowering smell of sex lingering on the sheets. When she woke a few minutes later, Valerie was sitting in a chair beside the bed, wearing a robe and brushing her hair.

"You took a shower?" Helen asked, lost in studying the way the dark wet hair gleamed in the soft light.

"Yes." Valerie smiled and continued, keeping her eyes on Helen. "I think I smelled like beer."

"I don't remember noticing that particular smell." Helen sighed and stretched, luxuriating in the spacious hotel bed. Somewhere inside her head a tiny alarm sounded. This little scene had all the earmarks of a painful goodbye. She cringed away from that thought and sat upright, rubbing her face, catching a familiar scent on her fingers. "Maybe I should get cleaned up, too."

"Go right ahead. There are plenty of towels." Helen picked up her clothes and walked quickly into the bathroom, acutely aware of her nakedness in front of Valerie and of the way Valerie very carefully didn't look at her. She was only mildly disappointed when Valerie didn't follow her into the shower and offer to rub her back along with a few other areas of her anatomy. Better this way, she thought as she toweled off. Short and sweet, no muss or fuss. Just a quickie and we're both out of here. Helen caught the bitterness in her own mind and cut it off. Enough, she lectured herself as she got into her clothes. You knew it would be like this. Behave.

Valerie was fully dressed when Helen came out of the bathroom. She prowled nervously around the room as Helen stood uncertainly by the bed. Now what? "Maybe Nanette is awake now," Helen finally said.

"Oh, yes," Valerie said. Helen winced inwardly at the relief in the other woman's voice. Was she that eager to be rid of Helen? Valerie fumbled with keys at the dresser while Helen made an awkward and shuffling exit. "I do need to go get my car, though." She bit her lip and glanced at Helen.

"Well, why don't I take you back to get your car before you check on Nanette?" Helen offered. Jesus, she was acting like a teenager at the prom, Helen scolded herself as they got into the Rambler. Grow up. We're both adults, we can deal with this. All the drive back to Gramm Street Valerie and Helen remained silent. It was only when they pulled up in front of the boarding house that Valerie spoke.

"Look, Helen, I don't quite know what to say."

"You don't have to say anything." Helen turned off the engine. It was getting dark now. Please, please, Val, don't say a word. Don't look at me.

"I mean, saying thank you isn't right. I feel —"

That's enough. "Don't say a word. I completely understand what happened today. I was there, remember?" Helen smiled, hoping there wasn't any reproach in her words, hoping Valerie wouldn't speak any more. Hoping Valerie would touch her again.

"I wonder if you do understand." Valerie sighed and opened the car door. "I'll be back tomorrow to see about getting Sissy's things packed up. The police are through with them now."

"Why don't I do that for you?" Helen said. Anything, she'd do anything to help take that frozen look off Valerie's face. Damn, they never should have given in to this. Now Valerie couldn't wait to get away from her. "I still have all my boxes from when I moved in, stuck away someplace. Let me pack things up."

"If you're sure." They stood by Valerie's rented car a moment longer, unable to read each other's expressions in the failing light. Then Valerie planted a swift kiss on Helen's cheek — no more than a light touch — and she was gone as

Helen trudged wearily up the steps onto the porch. She remained there, motionless on the swing, as the moon rose like a big blank eye up over Champion's Hill. A cool breeze stirred her hair, and she began to think about going inside. From the living room she could hear the dull murmur of the television. Cars drove by, the glow of headlights breaking through the gathering darkness. When she heard Mrs. Mapple's high-pitched whine echoing through the house she got up and went inside.

Of course it was the local evening news, and of course it was all about Sissy Greene. Helen moved quietly through the foyer, hoping to escape detection as Mrs. Mapple leaned in toward the set. "My God, my God," Mrs. Mapple murmured, clapping her hands to her face. "What is the world coming to now? Oh, is that you, Helen?"

Helen sighed and gritted her teeth, turning back on the stairs. "Yes, ma'am," she called out.

"Just come in here a minute and listen to this! You see — I was right to call the police, to be worried about everything going on. I mean, it's just too much for a body to deal with, I know these things are sent to try us like the good book says, I just don't understand how this has all come about, and now I suppose I'll have to figure out just what to do with that poor old man who won't even know his only child has done this."

Helen stood next to Mrs. Mapple and listened as the news announcer proclaimed that a second tragedy had befallen Tynedale. Earl Pemberton's body had been found swinging from the rafters of his home that afternoon.

Chapter Eight

The door to Sissy's room stood ajar, revealing a dim sliver of its interior. Helen pulled down the yellow crime scene tape. The black lettering stretched beneath her fingers as it gave way with a snap that echoed down the hall. Memories, memories, Helen thought with a pang as the sticky surface clung to her skin, like it always did. Yes, did. Past tense. She finally got it off her hands. Bright fragments fluttered to the floor as she pushed the door open wide.

First things first — open the window and let in some air. A cool breeze touched Helen's face, stirring up dust motes as it seeped into the room. This window overlooked the side of the house. She couldn't see the rising sun but its rays were visible on the scraggly rose bushes below. Either Mrs. Mapple neglected this portion of her yard or the Mississippi sun was just too much for them. Overblown blooms drooped brown-edged petals to the hard-baked clay soil, and Helen idly wondered if they needed water, or just needed to go ahead and die and get it over with.

"You're still here?"

"Shit." Too late to stop the word coming out. Helen stared sheepishly at Mrs. Mapple, framed in the doorway. "Sorry. You startled me."

Mrs. Mapple pursed her lips and tugged at the belt of her plaid robe, pulling it tight over her plump tummy. Helen kept staring, wondering what was different. It was the bun of black hair, she decided. Usually a smooth cap, so even and neat it might have been lacquered onto her head, this morning Mrs. Mapple's hair floated in spidery strands crawling across her head. "I thought I heard someone in here," the older woman muttered.

"I'm sorry if I woke you. I promised Valerie — Ms. Beausoleil — I'd help get these things packed up."

"Hmm." Mrs. Mapple reached up to pat her hair in place. Helen got a glimpse of the crepe-like skin on her neck, the liver spots on her hands, the slight trembling in her fingers. Helen turned away and reached for the light switch, not wanting to see the damage any longer. Did they all look this bad, two days after the fact? And how the hell could she explain her own sense of well-being, in the aftermath of Sissy's death? Like a fucking vampire, battening on suffering while everyone else sustained wounds that would perhaps last a lifetime. She surveyed the mess the police had left on Sissy's narrow cot. School books, clothes, bits of paper. Vampires never die, she thought. Just everyone around them.

"Don't know how you can stand being in here." Mrs. Mapple stayed at the doorway while Helen moved aimlessly around the room. "Don't know how anyone will want to stay in this house now." Helen turned around at the quaver in the other woman's voice. "It's a curse, that's what it is. My Lord,

I just don't know what I'm to do, what with that poor little girl, now Earl, it's the judgment of God on me and mine." She paused in her religious rhapsody to peer at Helen. "Are you going to be leaving, too?"

"Not unless you ask me to." How could she tell her that this boarding house was the last stop on the line? That she didn't have anywhere else to go?

"And now I'll be losing the rent from Nanette Greene. No doubt the judge too, although I have no idea what will happen. Maybe the state will take him on — I surely don't know if Earl had any other relatives."

Helen gripped the tennis shoe she held, fighting down anger. Was everyone involved with Sissy worried only about themselves, how this horrible death reflected upon them? Even me, she realized as she let the shoe drop. Here I am, playing detective for a while to relieve my own frustrations. How much of this is about Valerie? No, Valerie isn't out for herself. Valerie cared. Valerie hurts. It's the only reason she let me touch her yesterday. Which says what exactly about both of us?

Mrs. Mapple's grating squeal broke in on her thoughts. "So I really should get downtown to take care of things. And since you'll be here I could just let him stay with you."

"I'm sorry, I didn't catch what you were saying." Jesus, what had she missed? Who was staying here?

"The police should be around this afternoon." Mrs. Mapple's voice echoed against the walls as she scurried back to her own room. "And you won't have to do a thing. He's already had his breakfast, and he's all dressed and everything." As she bustled out toward her own room Mrs. Mapple said something else about letting the old man sit outside in the sun every morning.

Helen sighed and sat down on the bed. Fine. Babysitting a senile old man, then the police to deal with after lunch, no doubt including Ludy. And from the eagerness she'd heard in Mrs. Mapple's voice Helen knew she was bursting to talk about the events of the weekend with anyone who would listen. Helen lay back on the cot and stared at the ceiling. Sissy had probably done this, too — she'd probably known every crack and ripple in the aging plaster, seen strange patterns of faces, buildings, mythical beasts — maybe even drawn some of them in that notebook of hers.

Helen got up abruptly, sending some books stacked on the bed crashing to the floor. Where the hell were those boxes? She went into the hallway and bumped into Judge Pemberton, dressed in his usual rusty black suit and clutching the worn leather briefcase in trembling hands. Helen decided Mrs. Mapple had hurried him through his morning shave when she saw the bloody scrape on his chin.

"I was just about to take him outside to his lawn chair so he could get some sunshine and fresh air." Mrs. Mapple peeked out from behind the judge and patted her black hair into place. The sparkle in her eyes and flush on her cheeks told Helen that this break in her dreary routine was a real treat for her, and Helen felt guilty about being so judgmental a few minutes ago. Besides, who the hell was Helen to throw stones at anyone for lack of sensitivity? "And his sandwich for lunch is fixed already, sitting in the fridge."

"What about the police? You said they'd be by to talk to him?"

Mrs. Mapple guided the old man down the stairs and Helen tagged along. "Oh, Officer Deets already knows it isn't any good trying to talk to the judge. It's that nasty detective, that man Lucy —"

"Ludy."

"Now, I ask you, what kind of a name is that? Sounds a little bit off, if you ask me. And you know how people from New Orleans are — always thinking they're better than the rest of us. Not polite at all, not like Tommy Deets."

Helen thought of her own recent experience with someone from New Orleans. Valerie hadn't been exactly polite, but she certainly hadn't put on any airs while they'd been fucking.

141

She watched while Mrs. Mapple settled the judge into one of the rickety plastic chairs overlooking the scraggled vegetable garden. The judge glanced up at the woman, a flicker of confusion mottling his pale face, then turned to stare at the back fence. He pulled his briefcase closer to his chest and his features settled into the usual blank mask. "He'll be fine like this for a while. And I generally don't take him to the bathroom until right before lunch."

"Uh — the bathroom —" Helen began.

"Oh, you don't have to worry about that one little bit! He's just fine by himself, thank the lord above." She kept up a cheerful chatter as she sped up the back steps and into the house. A couple of minutes later Helen heard Mrs. Mapple's car tearing off down the street.

"You'd think she was afraid I'd change my mind and she'd be left here all day after all," Helen mused out loud to the judge. Pemberton shifted in his chair as she spoke. Now he faced the back door. "Do you want to go back inside? No?" Helen crouched on her heels beside him. His lips were working and his gaze settled on her face. No words came out. Helen sighed and stood. "Well, we're stuck with each other for a while. I'm going to go back inside, but I'll be out to check on you in just a little while. We'll figure it out together today, all right?"

He was in the same position when she came back out an hour later. To her surprise the sorting and arranging hadn't taken very long. Almost everything — books, clothes, trinkets — the whole pitifully small assortment of Sissy's earthly possessions lay ready for boxes. All that remained were some things on the shelf in the closet. As she sat on the grass beside Judge Pemberton, Helen realized that her worry about the old man sitting alone out here had kept her from getting too caught up in emotional straits while she went through the dead girl's belongings. She actually felt a bit of gratitude to Mrs. Mapple and the old man. Stretching her legs out in the grass she leaned back on her elbows and peered up at the sun. "Almost lunchtime, sir. Does she bring you your sandwich outside or take you back to the kitchen? Oh, I almost forgot — we have a potty trip now, don't we?"

So, how the hell did Mrs. Mapple do it? Helen got up and gently touched the judge's elbow. He looked at her, his mouth moving as though he would speak, then leaned forward in the chair. "Here, can I hold that for you?" To her amazement he managed to bat at her hands as she reached for the briefcase. Something like anger passed rapidly over his features. "Okay, we'll just work around it then," Helen said. What was in there, anyhow?

He rose slowly, unfolding himself a little at a time and making small grunting sounds with the effort. It took them several minutes to get inside and up the stairs. When they reached the bathroom, Helen closed the door behind him and stood waiting in the hallway. Unwilling to stay and listen to the judge taking care of his bodily functions, Helen moved toward Sissy's room and looked inside. Just the closet, then she'd better figure out where those damn boxes had gone. Oh, hell, she could do it while Pemberton stayed in the bathroom. Helen pulled the closet door open and groped on the shelf.

For a few moments she stood frozen, looking down at the stack of student notebooks. The top one bore a thin layer of dust. She brushed it off, then perched on the stripped bed. She knew what she would find in these notebooks.

And every one was filled with drawings. All the drawings Sissy hadn't wanted her mother to see, to ridicule — her secret life of observation. This must be the Greene family house, where Sissy had lived before the sordid melodrama of the secretary had played out. And perhaps this was the back-yard, lined with old trees and a wooden fence. Helen turned the pages and found a sketch of Nanette, followed by one of Nanette and Gary — at least, it looked like the man Helen had seen in the distance yesterday morning. Had Sissy known she was capturing her mother's perpetual moue of anxiety in the lines around her mouth and eyes?

Then the drawings changed in subject matter with the next notebook. Startled, Helen looked down at sketches of Mrs. Mapple, of the porch swing, of the rose bushes below Sissy's window. Her fingers trembled as she saw her own face limned on the cheap paper. Did she really look like that? Worn, haggard, old. Haunted dark eyes, too deep set to make out any expression. Something wet fell from her face to the page, smudging the ink. Helen swallowed hard a couple of times and stacked the notebooks on the bed. She had no idea if Nanette would want them. Surely Valerie would. Maybe Valerie would let her have one. Maybe that would be a terrible idea, though. Could she ever stand to look through the drawings?

Startled by a sound at the doorway Helen looked up to see the judge standing there. He shuffled into the room and sat next to Helen. She kept her face turned away from him as she struggled to control herself. Who knew what the fuck he was capable of understanding at this point? No reason to upset him. "Everything okay?" Helen's voice broke. She couldn't hold back any more, and with the senile old man as witness she sobbed for the second time in two days. Once she got her breath back she felt something on her arm. It was the judge — he was patting her awkwardly. For the first time in their lopsided acquaintance Helen saw something like the light of awareness in his faded colorless eyes.

Helen wiped her cheeks. "You know exactly what happened to your son, don't you? Everyone thinks you're incapable of understanding, but you do. Somewhere in there, you get it." She covered the judge's hand with her own, her skin absorbing the sensation of thin brittle bones beneath papery flesh. Like bird wings.

Ludy chose that moment to show up. Helen felt Judge Pemberton jump at the sound of the doorbell. "I guess we have to go," she said, smiling an apology as she helped him to his feet. "You wait here, sir. I'll let them in and bring you down in a minute."

Ludy looked as though he hadn't slept in a week. Puffed and swollen, his eyes fixed on Helen with ill-disguised contempt. "Aren't you supposed to be at work?"

Helen steered Deets and Ludy into the living room. "My supervisor suggested I take a couple of days off after what happened this weekend. I took her up on it."

"That was very understanding of him."

"Her."

Deets cleared his throat and walked around them into the living room. Helen tried to think of him as Tommy Deets, Mrs. Mapple's childhood pal, and failed. She'd known cops like him before — wearing the uniform like a second skin, their entire lives revolving around their work, no room for relationships with people who weren't victims and perpetrators. Did Deets have any family? Any friends? Any life outside of his role as protector and defender of the good folk of Tynedale? He looked back at her and cleared his throat again.

"You're here to talk to Judge Pemberton. He's upstairs." She left the room, well aware that Ludy was watching her every move. To her relief the old man had maneuvered the stairs just fine on his own. Helen could see that his eyes were still awake and alive. Despite all evidence to the contrary, she was now convinced he knew what was going on. Ludy and Deets silently watched her settle the judge in a chair. "Do you need me here, detective?"

Again those hard little dark eyes focused on her. Helen recognized that look. Ludy wore his self-control like a bad fitting suit — beneath that demeanor he was just as maddened as he'd been Saturday afternoon. Eaten up from the inside out, and unfortunately Helen was in the way this time.

"I can't imagine we would. Deets?" Like a well-trained dog, the other man pulled a notebook and pen out of his pocket. Helen caught his smoldering glance at Ludy. Great — Ludy and Deets weren't getting along either. At the sight of him flipping the pages, Helen glanced at her own hands and realized she was still holding Sissy's book of drawings. She

145

edged toward the hallway until she heard sounds coming from the judge.

"Nn — nn — nn —"

"What was that, sir?"

Just more mumbles, accompanied by futile waving gestures. Deets followed the old man's stare. "Ma'am, I think he wants you to stay." He glanced again at Ludy, his face carefully blank this time. "Maybe if she just sat in on this, sir?"

Ludy refused to look at Helen as she sat down on a sofa off to the side. Helen could tell, though, that this time he wasn't mad at her. Deets had spoken out of turn, that was all. Ludy didn't take kindly to anyone even hinting that they had ideas about how to run an investigation. Nice for Deets. Helen stole a glance at the older cop as she settled down on the sofa. They must have an absolutely lovely time working together, she thought with a flicker of amusement. Deets would probably always work more quietly, slowly, cautiously than Ludy — a combination of experience and knowledge about the community Ludy couldn't possibly have yet. And Ludy must feel the weight of Deets and his years like a ball and chain to be dragged all over Tynedale. Lovely. She hoped they'd kill each other one of these days.

At least if she sat this way Pemberton could see her and she didn't have to look at Ludy or Deets. The judge calmed down right away and leaned back on the sofa.

"Sir, we know this is a very bad time for you," Ludy began. "Mrs. Mapple tells me that you learned last night about your son's death." Ludy waited for a response. Nothing but silence. Helen looked back at Sissy's notebook, turned the pages, tried to figure out where she'd taken the sketches. Anything but witness this awful scene. Okay, here we were back at the boarding house. Now — was this the park? Yes, it looked like the entrance to Champion Park. Her blood chilled. It didn't necessarily mean a fucking thing, she lectured herself. She'd probably gone there quite a few times, there didn't have to be a connection. Then came a series of awkward sketches that didn't make sense, as if Sissy had been trying a study of one particular building. What was it? Helen knew she'd seen it before. Something big, institutional? Her school, maybe? No, that wasn't it. And that thing on top of the building, like an antenna or weathervane. Jesus, where had she seen it?

Ludy tried a couple more times, never getting anything but wheezing from the old man. Deets stayed silent. Out of the corner of her eye Helen saw that his pen wasn't moving. "So we're wondering if you could tell us anything, anything at all, about your son's activities. We know, for example, that Earl and Gary Greene —"

Suddenly Judge Pemberton moved on the sofa. Helen looked up to see him holding out the briefcase to Ludy. "You want me to take a look at this, sir?" the detective asked. "Deets, you getting this down?"

"Sir, I don't think this is —"

"Dammit, Deets!" Helen jumped at the fury in his voice. Even in the dim light of the living room she could see the red creeping up Ludy's neck. "Did I ask you for your opinion?"

Deets shut up and crossed his ankle over his knee, bending over the notebook. Bad, very bad, Helen thought. You don't do that to your subordinates in public. Ludy must be a lot closer to breaking than Helen had guessed. And what did that say about the lack of significance both she and Judge Pemberton had in the detective's eyes? He was losing sight of what mattered here. Deets and Helen exchanged a glance. The look in the other cop's eyes unnerved her. Was that actually fear? Or was it just he didn't want dirty laundry aired in the boarding house?

The spell of silence broke when the briefcase fell to the floor. Papers splashed the worn carpet, splaying out in front of Helen's feet. Suddenly Ludy was next to her, helping gather up the assortment of documents. Helen could almost taste Ludy's frustration as they sorted through the pile. Two letters from his long-dead wife. A black and white photograph in a plastic bag that showed a group of robed judges sitting primly for the camera. Possibly Pemberton was among them? A yellowed document of several pages stapled together that proved to be the deed to the judge's house in Biloxi. A small pile of receipts, all handwritten and dated thirty years ago, showing purchases from a variety of liquor stores. And the bulkiest item was a folded newspaper for Biloxi, dated April 13, 1975.

"Deets." Ludy fished the newspaper out and handed it to the other man. They looked at each other, then at the judge. "Sir —" Ludy crouched down and looked into the judge's face. He sighed. "We won't take up any more of your time." He took the newspaper and the other papers, stuffed them back in the briefcase and then lay the briefcase on the sofa.

Helen followed them out. Deets went to start the car while Ludy lingered on the porch. "I doubt he even really knows his son killed himself," Ludy said conversationally, resting his foot on the porch swing and gazing out over the tranquil neighborhood.

"Probably not. What — what happens to him now? Mrs. Mapple says he doesn't have any more family." Helen couldn't seem to stop herself asking — not after this morning, when she'd seen a glimmer of intelligence behind the wall of insanity. Yet another one lost through the cracks — like Sissy, like Helen herself.

"None that will own him, that's for sure." Ludy shoved away from the porch swing, setting it in motion with a jerk. "Then again, maybe he knows more than we think. Like most people who think they can lie to the police."

Shit, here we go again. "I haven't lied to you about anything, detective."

"We'll see."

Helen went back inside while Deets was driving down Gramm Street. The old man waited for her in the living room. "Think you can eat your lunch now?" she asked. Whatever had possessed the old man to come to life a few minutes ago had now subsided, and he let her lead him into the dining room. As he ate, Helen sat and stared again at Sissy's drawings. That was when she figured out where she'd seen that mysterious building before. Saturday afternoon — while Ludy was building up a head of steam when they carried Sissy's body away. The broken cross on top of the abandoned church had poked up into the hot blue sky, crooked and black over the tops of pine trees.

But this was different. It took her only a few seconds to figure it out. Helen had seen that broken cross from a distance, from the park. Sissy had drawn it from a completely different perspective — from somewhere on the church grounds. And drawn it over and over and over. What the hell had she been doing there? In her mind Helen traveled across the muddy slope behind the park to the abandoned church. Was it just an interesting set of buildings? Or maybe it had been Sissy's secret getaway, where she wouldn't hear her mother's perpetual whine or have to smell the distinctive blend of disinfectant and old grease that permeated the boarding house. Maybe that's actually where she was killed —

Dammit, she should have said something to the police. Then she remembered Ludy's red face, the way he was barely keeping himself in check. No, it wouldn't do her any good to bring it up to him. Not yet. Better to go there on her own and see what she could see. "Yeah, right," she muttered to no one as she took Judge Pemberton's sandwich plate to the kitchen. At least she'd say something to Deets. She'd contact him before the day was out.

When she got back to the dining room, the judge was trying to push himself away from the table. "Okay, want to go outside again?" Helen asked. "Or how about helping me find those boxes? No? Maybe you need a nap. I don't like the look of that sky. I think it's going to rain." She kept up her end of the conversation until he was safely settled in the living room again. Hopefully the afternoon talk shows would keep him occupied. Yes, she thought as she watched him watch the TV. I'll go find Deets as soon as Mrs. Mapple gets back, show him these drawings. Chances are they'll just brush it off, but I have to give it a shot.

As she switched the channel on the television, Helen glanced over her shoulder. Maybe Mrs. Mapple had put the boxes in the crawl- space under the stairs. Couldn't harm anything to take a look could it?

The sound of applause from the studio audience covered her struggles with the door. Maybe it was just jammed. Helen took the doorknob in both hands and tugged. Shit, this was really stuck. After staring glumly at the door Helen got down on her hands and knees to examine it more closely. Would Mrs. Mapple really lock it? Or was it just jammed. From her kneeling position Helen yanked at the door again. She felt sweat break out on her face and back as she kept pulling.

"What are you doing home?" Kyle slammed his way into the hallway. Helen started. She hadn't heard him come in through the kitchen. "Aren't you supposed to be at the warehouse."

"I took a day off." Something was different about Kyle. What the hell was it? Same ugly shirt from the grocery store, same loose jeans hanging on his thin frame, same acne-scarred face. No, wait. His expression. Usually a smirk played across his mouth, and his dark sullen eyes would move quickly away from visual contact longer than a few seconds. Today, however, he just kept staring at Helen. She suddenly became very aware of her own sweat and heavy breathing. Kyle shoved his lank dark hair out of his eyes and looked her over, his gaze traveling up her body lingering on her breasts. Feeling an icy knot form in her gut, Helen turned back to the door. "Do you have the key to the crawlspace, Kyle?" she asked, giving the door another tug. "I need to get some empty boxes out of here."

"Where's Mom?"

Christ, he'd moved up behind her without making a sound. Something weird going on here. Helen's body tightened, began to feel itchy. "She's out doing a few errands. Judge Pemberton is in the living room," she added, as if that might make a difference.

It didn't. Kyle snickered, and Helen heard a rustling behind her. She turned around to face Kyle. "Yeah, I got the key. Whyn't you come over here and get it?"

Helen barely registered the words. All her attention focused on the gun barrel in front of her face.

Chapter Nine

Strange, to suddenly feel your body go cold all at once. Helen had felt it before but forgotten about that odd stillness. Cold and light, as if she could float up from the floor. As if she weren't really here.

Kyle's sweat dropped in fat plops on the wood beside her. His eyes glistened in the dim light. She could hear his breath rasping like an old accordion. His orange work shirt, stained and wrinkled, stretched taut over his shoulders as he clamped down on the gun. He held it as far away from his body as he could. Its dull gray metal gave off a gleam as he waved it in a gesture pointing to the stairs. "I don't think the judge will mind if we let him alone with his TV for a while. You just go on upstairs, now."

Helen kept her eyes on the gun. If he fired it now, her face would be pulverized. A part of her mind ground on mercilessly, wondering how and where he'd gotten the weapon — and whether or not he knew how to use it. Didn't make her situation any better, in fact made it worse, if this was just a new toy for him. He'd be too quick to shoot at shadows.

Then she heard her own voice echoing in the hall. "Kyle, you don't want to use that thing."

She'd never seen his eyes light up this way — not that she'd paid a lot of attention to his eyes before. But now she could see he was sweating almost as much as she was, and his breath came in quick pants. Jesus. Rape in the middle of the afternoon, with some game show whining in the background. She'd known Kyle was a bit fucked up, but his absolute insanity shocked her. What the fuck was he thinking? Stupid question — he wasn't thinking. Not with his brains, anyhow. Kyle grinned, moved one arm to wipe sweat off his brow. The gun wavered and Helen flinched. "You don't want me to use it? Then you just haul your ass upstairs and we'll find out what's underneath those clothes."

"Kyle, you don't need a gun to do this. One of us is going to get hurt. Put the gun down, Kyle." Maybe if she kept saying his name she'd get through to him. Nope, he was enjoying his brief stint of power over her far too much. She actually heard him giggling. "Come on, Kyle, this is crazy. Your mother might walk in any second, and —"

Uh oh. Big mistake, to mention Mrs. Mapple. An angry snarl replaced his eager grin. "That's enough talking, bitch. You're gonna get up those fucking stairs now. Time for you to find out what you been missing while you been licking pussy." Her heart stopped for a moment as he gestured with the gun. "I know all about you. The guys at SmartSave, they all say you fuck women. Well — we'll see about that after today, right?" His eyes gleamed and he started to giggle. Nerves? Excitement? Didn't matter, as long as that fucking gun was waving around in front of her.

Helen kept her hands out in front of her and fought to keep her voice calm as she got up from her knees. She moved very slowly to the stairs. She could see the judge sitting on the sofa, his face turned to the television set. God, she was going to upchuck all over the floor. "Kyle. Listen to me. This is getting out of hand. You're in control here, you say what's going to happen. You don't have to let this go any further." He was staring at her chest. Good. Maybe he wouldn't notice as she tried to maneuver into better position if he stayed focused on her tits. If she could edge just a little closer to him, she might be able to kick his legs hard enough for him to lose balance. No, that was stupid. He'd fire down at her right away. And what the fuck did he propose to do to her after raping her? Kill her? Get her to promise not to talk about it? Or had he somehow convinced himself that sex with him would be the turning point in her perverted life, that she'd even be grateful to him?

"Kyle, I'm going up the stairs now. Okay? Nice and slow, see?" Her heart pounded in her chest so hard she thought she could see it. Jesus, the barrel was right in front of her face now. "Take it easy, Kyle. See, I'm just going to move past you." She did, holding her hands out wide. Good, she was only a couple of feet away from him now. "Let's just settle down and figure this thing out. Okay?" Somehow she'd managed to sound calm all this time. Inside her body geared up for what was coming. The sense of lightness drained away, replaced by a rush of adrenaline that set her head spinning. "Relax. Everything is going to be fine." The hall closed in on her like a box and suddenly it was hard to breathe. Christ, there wasn't much room here for maneuvering. Merely by stretching her arms wide she could touch the walls on both sides. Kyle, too, no doubt felt trapped, which didn't help.

Then Judge Pemberton appeared in the hallway behind Kyle. Shit, she had actually forgotten about the old man. She stole a moment to look at him. He leaned against the doorway, briefcase hugged to his chest, mouth moving noiselessly. Could

154

he tell what was going on? Kyle followed her gaze as it darted out over his shoulder. That was all Helen needed.

First she grabbed his hands and shoved them hard into the wall. The gun fell down at their feet, bouncing once on the wood. Helen had a heart-stopping half moment wondering if it would fire as it jolted on the floor. It didn't. It spun around and stopped against the door to the crawlspace. Kyle yelped in pain. Helen felt his hands twitch beneath hers. Surprise wasn't going to be her ally for more than a couple of seconds.

Kyle struggled to wrench himself free. Helen brought her knee up into his crotch as fast and hard as she could. Kyle bounced backward with the force of the blow, his face white, his eyes bugged out. The yelps stopped as he gasped in hoarse ragged breaths. He crouched over himself as if cradling the pain that spread out from his loins.

Helen leaned over and picked up the gun. A thirty eight. Safety still on. Jesus fucking Christ. A flood of relief mingled with the hot spice of anger washed over her. She watched herself slapping Kyle's face against the wall, leaving a thin smear of blood on the grimed wood. "You fucking idiot," she heard herself say through gritted teeth. Saliva bubbled at the corners of her mouth and mixed with sweat on her cheeks. "Fucking son of a bitch." Then something tore inside her, some inner fabric split down the center from top to bottom. One part of her retained the emptiness, the other part boiled with rage as she hit Kyle again and again and again. "Little asshole, what the fuck were you doing?"

Then for a moment Kyle's face — whimpering and bloody, mouth twisted in a piteous wail — faded into another face. The hall in the boarding house swirled and narrowed into a smaller, darker space. The rental car. A long dark stretch of road in the middle of nowhere. And a girl looked up at Helen in the car, eyes wide in pain and surprise, eyes fading into the glaze of death, eyes staring at Helen, staring at nothing. Nothing. "Why did you die, you little bitch? Why?" She felt the words tear out of her like bloody rags hanging in the air hot with terror.

Helen let Kyle slump to the floor. Someone was crying. It was Kyle. No, it was her. Sobs racked her chest as she took bullets out of the gun and placed them in her pocket with trembling fingers. Kyle lay in a huddled sweaty mess in the corner by the living room, his whole body shuddering with each breath. Helen leaned against the wall and looked up at the judge. He stayed in the doorway, staring down at Kyle. Slowly her vision cleared and she could make out the brief-case, the stained and badly knotted tie. Shit, she felt like she'd had a personal visit from an eighteen wheeler. "It's okay, Judge. It's done now." Aching in every bone and muscle, Helen heaved herself up and stuffed the gun in her waistband. "All right, Kyle. Get up."

For a second she worried she'd seriously injured him. A sharp splinter of terror pierced her heart. Then he turned his face to her. Yes, he'd have a few bruises but he'd live. His eyes weren't swollen shut yet, but he needed ice on his face right away. Helen forced grit into her voice. She'd have to keep this up a while longer. "Get the fuck up, asshole. Your mother will be home any minute."

That was enough for Kyle. He crawled his hands up the wall, wincing at the soreness in his groin, then cautiously walked down the length of the hallway to the kitchen. Helen paused by the judge. "Look, I have to talk to this butthead for a little bit. I think you should stay out here. We're going to be all right. Got it?"

The judge didn't make a sound. He turned around and sat on the sofa facing the television. "Good idea." Helen glanced at Kyle, who was looking back at them. "Keep going. We have to put something on your face. I'll be right there." She followed Kyle into the kitchen.

A few minutes later Kyle had an ice pack clutched to one eye. Helen leaned against the wall, shaking all over. Then she looked at the phone on the wall. A black and white could be

156

here in just a few minutes if she called 911. At the very least Kyle would get the fear of God put into him, maybe a lot more. He was what — seventeen? Juvie hall, or maybe tried as an adult. Then years of being sent through the system like so much raw meat through a sausage grinder. Therapy? Maybe not. She vividly recalled her own battles with the chimera of going cold turkey off the bottle during her first weeks behind bars. Nobody had given a shit about rehab for her. Kyle might not get the help he needed once he got stuck in the legal maze.

"You gonna kill me, or what?" It might have been funny under other circumstances — one sullen eyeball staring at her around the ice-pack he held to his swollen face. "Whyn't you just get it over with? I'm getting tired of looking at you, stupid queer."

Jesus, one more whine and she'd go ahead and make that call. Helen felt a grim pleasure when he cringed at the sound of her voice. "I don't know yet, shithead. Might be more fun to call the police and make sure you get to be fresh meat in jail. Didn't think of that, did you? I guarantee you, Kyle, once you get in there you'll be grabbing your ankles for a while."

That image shut him up for a bit, and Helen tried to think. First she'd get him to tell her where the gun came from, then she'd decide. If she heard Mrs. Mapple drive up she'd tuck the gun in her pants again and take Kyle to the police station. For now, they had the house to themselves. Kyle stared down at the kitchen table. The sullen glare was back in his face. Helen resisted the urge to knock him through the wall. Instead she pulled the gun out and slammed it hard on the counter, savoring the pleasure of seeing the little prick jump. "Good. I have your attention now, right?"

"Now what? You still gonna shoot me?"

"Keep up that whine and I just might do it." She dug for the bullets, lay them out one by one on the counter next to the gun. Kyle stared at the shiny metal, fear darkening his eyes as she put them one by one into the gun. "Now. You can start by telling me what the fuck a little ass wipe like you is doing with a real live gun like this one."

He made one last try at a good pout. "You gonna beat me up if I don't talk?"

The gun was loaded. "No, Kyle," Helen said, turning around with a smile. "I'll just shoot your knee caps off. Or maybe your dick. If you have one, that is. After all, you were awfully eager for me to see it just a few minutes ago."

The suggestion of damage to his male member helped Kyle to start talking. He couldn't get the words out fast enough after that — about the guys from the SmartSave warehouse, about the computer supplies and small appliances stolen from the shipments last month, about how they'd just given him a gun a few days ago. "He didn't want to, but I kept on telling him I needed one. So Dave —"

"Dave. From the warehouse. Dave Abbot?" she interrupted, remembering the name on the shop in the alley.

"Dave let me have this. I thought, okay, finally I'm in with the rest of them."

"When was this?"

"Huh?"

Jesus, she was going to slap him into Vicksburg in a minute. "When did Dave give you this gun?"

"Saturday." He glanced up, puzzled now, the ice pack slipping down his cheek.

Okay. The day after Sissy disappeared. Most likely unconnected. "Go ahead. They gave you this thing. Then what?"

"Well —" Here Kyle slumped down and went into his usual mumble. Helen strained to pick up the words, but she finally picked out that she herself had been a big topic of discussion over the weekend. "All I kept hearing was Helen Black this, Helen Black that, like you had it all figured out or something. Like they hated your guts. So I thought maybe if I could show them you weren't so fucking perfect, they'd quit shoving me around." He glared up at her and tossed the ice pack to the table. "I'm not a big baby. I'm a man, just like them."

"Oh, I get it." Helen sat down and deliberately started examining the gun. Kyle went still, his gaze fixed on the weapon. Apparently something could still get through his thick skull. Besides a bullet. "You get two for the price of one by raping me — proving your manhood to them and getting me out of the way, is that it?" She made sure the safety was on before pointing the gun into his face. It would have been comical, seeing his eyes almost crossed as he focused on the barrel, if he hadn't been so clearly terrified. "Plus you get to show a dyke all they've been missing out on. With your little prick being the star attraction."

"I don't know, I never did it — I mean, I don't have girl-friends —"

Helen eased up, pointing the gun toward the ceiling. Wouldn't do to have the idiot wet his pants in Mrs. Mapple's nice clean kitchen. "I'm not surprised, if this is the best technique you can come up with. And just what the fuck were you going to do with me when you were finished, cocksucker? Throw me into the bushes like Sissy?"

"But she said you liked it rough — that you used to love it when she hurt you." Openly sobbing now, Kyle's nose dripped mucus onto his chin. He wiped at it with a trembling hand. "She said you'd do anything to get laid. So I thought you might, I mean with me. And you might like the gun and all," he finished lamely. His eyes went wary, clearly not sure she'd buy such a ridiculous piece of shit.

Then it hit her. She. Oh, fuck. "You mean Bertie Mullins."

Kyle looked up at the name. He picked up the ice pack and covered the brown-purple welts on his cheeks. "She said she would get you to help us. She told me —" He closed his eyes and leaned back in the chair. He started to shake his head, stopped with a grimace at the pain.

"Told you what? Something about me?"

"How you killed that girl." He fingered his swollen lip as he stared at Helen. "Shot her in cold blood. Like the way you almost shot me today."

"I see. What else did Bertie say?"

"Just that she'd talk you into helping us. She could play you, she said. Do things to tease you and get you crazy, then make you do whatever she wanted. Like in prison, when she was your girlfriend." Despite all the terrors Kyle had experienced during the past hour, his face could still light up in sleazy delight at the thought of women fucking women.

"My girlfriend. Christ, Kyle. You are such a dumb fuck. No, I'm not going to shoot you, asshole," she sighed as his face froze in fear again. "You're definitely not worth a bullet. Besides, your mother would probably increase my rent."

"Huh?"

"Never mind. What else did Bertie say? Anything about my family?"

Kyle looked genuinely puzzled. "No, she didn't. Just about Sissy."

Helen's blood froze. "What about Sissy?" she asked in a quiet voice. "Goddammit, Kyle, answer me."

"She said you killed her, all right? That you liked killing people." The words burst out in a wail and Kyle began to cry again.

"For God's sake, cut it out." She watched him while his tears subsided. "Do you really believe that, Kyle?"

He shrugged. "I don't know. I don't think so. Not till today, anyhow." That sullen look was back on his face, the expression that made Helen want to spank him or shoot him, she wasn't sure which would be the most pleasurable. "If it helps you come to a conclusion about me, Kyle, I would have shot you by now if I enjoyed killing people."

"Yeah, well, you still got the gun, don't you?" Kyle pouted. Helen suppressed a smile at his wince. Good, it would hurt him a while to make that smirk. "What am I going to tell Dave about the gun?" He was whining.

"That's your problem. The gun stays with me." Even as she spoke Helen knew she couldn't keep the damn thing. Guns were certainly easy to come by in Mississippi — Dave wouldn't have had much trouble obtaining one either legally or illegally in this sportsman's paradise — but her ass would be hauled off to God knows what if this gun were found in her possession, Wanda or no Wanda. She had to get rid of it, quick, preferably where Dave and Bertie would never find it. Deets? Helen couldn't shake the idea that he'd be receptive to her approach, especially if it would mean he'd get to spite Ludy somehow. Yes, as soon as Mrs. Mapple got here they could go over to the police station. Helen had no doubt she'd be in for a difficult afternoon, but it was better than sitting on the damned thing. Still, there was one other question she had to get answered.

"So are you telling me the truth about when you got this gun, Kyle? Come on, talk!" She started to move closer to him, more from fear than impatience. Once again she saw the hole in Sissy's head.

It must have showed in her expression. Suddenly Kyle got a look on his face as if he'd wet his pants.

"Saturday! I got it Saturday, okay? When you came in and fucked everything up."

"I fucked everything up? You little asshole, they would have painted the floor with you."

"You don't know anything! They know I'm one of them, they wouldn't do that to me!" he whined.

She looked at his weaselly face, smeared with tears and knotted with bruises. He deserved punishment in the worst way. Kyle couldn't be more than nineteen. Maybe if someone beat the shit out of him a few times he'd get off this stupid trail and get his life straightened out. Helen glanced down at the gun. A thirty-eight. She forced herself to remember Sissy's head in the mud, the tiny hole over her right ear. Someone with excellent aim, then. Not Kyle. And this gun in her hands would have blown her head off, made more of a mess.

161

Yeah, and who died and made Helen a coroner? Years of experience had its value, though. And this was one big fucker. Enough to make Kyle feel like a big man. God knows what else the gun had been used for, before winding its way into his pathetic paws. She looked up again at Kyle.

"What? What're you looking at now?"

"Not very much. Come on, we're taking a little trip."

"Where?" He stood up when she did, his eyes wavering back and forth between her face and the gun.

"Downtown." Too risky to wait until Mrs. Mapple came home, Helen decided. They'd just pack the judge into the car and all go to the police station, like a little family outing. "Go get Judge Pemberton and take him up to the bathroom."

"Huh?" Now Kyle had an all new expression for his face — dumb.

"You heard me. We'll make sure the old guy is all emptied out, then take a trip to find Deets."

"No fucking way!" Kyle wailed, the ice pack dropping with a soggy plop to the floor. "You're gonna get me thrown in jail, all because I — I mean, nothing happened. What are you so mad about?" he stammered.

Helen shook her head, almost laughing. "Kyle, your best bet with me is to keep your damn mouth shut and do what I say. Now, let's go."

And he'd actually made it to the living room to gather up the judge when the front door burst open. Instinctively Helen stuffed the gun into her waistband at the back and pulled her tee-shirt out, blousing the fabric until it completely covered the weapon. Nanette Greene flew to Helen in a swirl of flowery cologne and dark-toned silk. "Oh, my God, it's her!" Thank god the woman's embrace kept her hands around Helen's neck and not straying toward her waist where the gun was hidden. "You found my little girl, my baby —"

The rest of her words faded into a muffle as she buried her head in Helen's neck. Was she drunk? Helen looked past

Nanette's skinny shoulder and saw Gary Greene standing in the doorway. Someone else stood on the front porch, in the early afternoon shadows. Helen got a glimpse of Valerie's face and flashed back on the memory of how she'd looked yesterday, her head tossed back in climax, eyes fluttering shut.

• "Ms. Greene —" She gently disengaged from Nanette's clutches and held her off at arms' length. "I haven't had a chance to tell you, I'm so sorry for your loss."

But Nanette kept babbling. Helen got a quick look at her eyes. No, not drunk, but definitely on something again. Gary stepped up behind his wife and awkwardly patted her shoulder. "Honey, just calm down, now. Remember what you promised me and the doctor?" Nanette made a mighty effort to calm herself, taking in deep shuddering breaths as she collapsed into her husband's arms.

Gary Greene turned to face Helen. Despite the gray exhaustion marking his face, Helen could see Sissy in his dark eyes, his smooth dark hair, the firm line of his jaw. At the moment even the shadows under his eyes reminded Helen of Sissy the last time she'd seen her alive. Fortunately a rustling noise from the living room reminded her of the task at hand. Kyle stood poised at the end of the hall, Judge Pemberton in tow.

Helen extended her hand to Gary, keeping her attention fixed on Kyle. "I'm so sorry to meet you under these circumstances, sir." Valerie stepped inside and Helen felt her heart stop beating for a moment. Terrific. She couldn't even look at the woman.

"Helen offered to help get Sissy's things put together." Valerie stepped into the light and Helen finally looked at her. "Nanette wanted to come by herself to pick them up," she said to Helen.

"I see. Well, yes, they're just about ready." Today her eyes looked gray. Maybe just an effect of the dark clothes, or the dim light in the hallway. Violet blue, yesterday. Okay, enough of that. "Maybe you folks would like to be alone for a bit? Kyle and the judge and I were going out on a little errand. Weren't we, Kyle?"

Then Nanette flung herself at Helen again. "Gary, darling, if only we'd known!" Nanette wailed in Helen's ear. "If we'd known that Friday night would be the last night our little baby doll had on this earth, you wouldn't have been with that tramp, gambling in Biloxi — you would have been here with us, a happy family again!"

A wave of anger moved quickly across Gary's features. Helen couldn't keep her eyes from straying to his nether regions. Yep, he did have a fat ass, after all — despite the expensive clothes, his hips flared out like a woman's beneath a slender waist. "Nanette, you promised me, now. You have to try to stay calm. Let's just get through all this." His grip on his wife's shoulders tightened, and Helen saw that the reins he held tight on his anger slipped a bit with every moan Nanette uttered. "Why don't you just sit and take it easy in the living room, sweetheart, and Val and I will go on upstairs."

"No!" Nanette screamed. Arms flailing, she shoved away from her husband and stood on the bottom step. Her hair, tousled from all the nuzzling and flinging, whipped loose and caught Helen right in the eye. With tears blurring her vision, Helen saw movement by the living room. Shit. Kyle.

"You can't keep me away from my baby doll, my little Sissy," Nanette yelled. "I refuse to sit down in there while the rest of you maul over her things!"

"Nan, please, just relax." Valerie moved forward, brushing past Helen to reach her sister. "We're all here to help."

Helen managed to break free of them and, wiping her eyes, got to the front door in time to see Kyle's souped up car speeding in a roar down Gramm Street. Suddenly drained of energy and emotion, Helen leaned back against the screen door. She felt cold metal pressing on the skin at her waist. Jesus fucking Christ. How could she go downtown and tell the

police a damned thing without Kyle? The only witness she had
to it all was a senile old man. The same senile old man Ludy
and Deets had dismissed as a waste of time only an hour ago.

"Helen?" Valerie stood just behind her, voice pitched low
so Nanette and Gary couldn't hear. "What happened?"

Helen turned around. "What happened?" How the hell
was she supposed to answer that? Sissy's death happened.
Kyle's rape attempt happened. Two fucking years of prison
happened. The final severance of her family happened. Valerie
happened. Valerie.

"Helen, please say something. You're scaring me."

"You should be scared. You should be running for your life
right now."

"What are you talking about?" Drawn and pale and exhausted, Valerie's face showed the strain of the past four days.
She looked awful. She looked beautiful.

"Nothing." Helen left.

Chapter Ten

Maybe another drink would help drown out the noise, Helen thought. The juke box howled some whiny crap about a woman deserted by her man like it was headline news. Whoop de fucking do. Her bleary eyes stared down at the assembly of empty glasses lined up on the scratched and stained table. Yep, she could still count — a total of three shot glasses and three bottles. Was that all it took these days to knock her on her ass? Not drunk enough yet, then. Time to summon the bartender? No, wait, in this place she had to go get it herself. Helen stirred in the booth, then decided it would be better to let the room settle down first. The bar had this weird tendency to shift and shimmy at the moment. What the hell was up with that?

Helen leaned back against the padded seat, felt the vinyl split a little more under her weight. The Monday night crowd, such as it was, huddled near the big-screen television set where the football game battled on in vivid color. Mostly guys, a couple of women hanging on muscular arms and shouting at the screen. Helen watched through the cigarette smoke as one of the men detached himself from the crowd and made his way, beer bottle in hand, to her table.

He wasn't too bad looking, actually, with his broad shoulders and thick blond hair. Nicely dressed, too — pristine white shirt, tight jeans, shiny boots. His eyes, though. Small and dark and blank. No, not blank. Kind of flat, as if nothing flowed underneath that perfect surface. Or was it just that she was well on her way to being shitfaced?

"Well, looks like you got a pretty good view of the game from over here," he started, smiling and leaning over the table. "You can see better from a distance, I think, with those big screen things."

Not too bad, Helen thought. A bit more intelligent than the last guy, who'd sauntered up a few minutes ago and started talking about the wet tee-shirt contest next week. "Yeah, you can see a lot of things better from a distance. A big distance." See, the words didn't come out all slurred yet.

He wasn't taking the hint, though. "Not everything," he responded, giving her a meaningful look with those tiny eyes. "For instance, now that I'm close up to you I'm wondering what a pretty lady like yourself is doing alone." Then came the smile, all those perfect teeth shining at her. Christ, he looked like a commercial for some hygiene product, with his white shirt and matching teeth. He nodded at her assortment of glassware. "Looks like you need another one."

"No, thanks." Maybe she ought to get out of here. Find the next bar so she could continue her project of discovering the perfect state of inebriation. This bar was far enough from Tynedale that she wasn't too concerned about spending a little time and money pretending to herself that her life

167

hadn't turned to complete shit again. Pretending she wasn't scared out of her mind about that fucking gun, about Kyle and his comrades, about what Bertie was up to, about the police and her parole. Vicksburg was close by — maybe one more spot, a couple more drinks, and she'd know what to do about everything. Helen almost laughed out loud as she struggled for her wallet. She almost believed her own bullshit, she realized, almost believed that she could think her way out of this one. The sight of her recently acquired friend peering at her with those flat little eyes suddenly seemed hilarious.

There, she managed to stand up and fumbled for her wallet. "Looks like half time is over. You'd better get back to your friends."

"We're not friends?" Jesus, he actually reached out and took her arm. Helen gazed at him, anger rising in her mildly soaked thoughts. "I thought I could make a new friend tonight."

Helen flipped his hand off as if it were a bug. Maybe she should just tell him she was toting an illegally acquired weapon in her car and was probably headed back to Deasely. That ought to do the trick. Instead, she said, "Let's not play this one out. Okay?" Something in her tone must have told him to back the fuck off. The little eyes turned mean and opaque as he backed off, his back ramrod straight. Helen steadied herself against the booth and watched him walk up to a blond woman who wasn't much more sober than herself. The woman smiled and giggled at something he said. Good. Everyone's happy now. Helen pulled out a couple of twenties and laid them on the table, then realized she'd better make a pit stop before leaving. She didn't see Valerie until she emerged from the bathroom.

Valerie stood uncertainly at the edge of the crowd gathered in front of the television. Even in her impaired condition Helen could read the lines of tension in the other woman's body as she scanned the faces. Of course she looked beautiful, dammit. Not tall, not slim, certainly not very happy at the moment — Valerie's long dark hair gleamed in the dim light through the smoke, her blue eyes widened as she looked through the knot of people. She spotted Helen just as Helen was trying to decide the best way to exit without being seen.

Shit. Helen froze in front of the corridor leading to the restroom. Valerie made her way unnoticed across the room as the football fans shouted in unison at some spectacular event unfolding in the game. As she got closer Helen saw a lot more than tension in those dark eyes, in the way she tossed her hair over her shoulders. She was angry. Well, that was her problem. Helen had enough problems of her own right now. Including a terrible desire to melt into a pool at Valerie's feet, dissolving under the gaze of Valerie's dark blue eyes. Just one look would be enough. Shit. "What are you doing here?" Helen asked in what she hoped was a neutral voice.

"I need to talk to you." Valerie kept her own voice pitched low but the emotional edge cut through the words. "Not in here, though. Can we get out of this place?"

Helen almost shook her head then decided she didn't want the room spinning. "Maybe it's not such a good idea to have that conversation just now. Maybe tomorrow."

Then Valerie peered closely at Helen, recognition stealing into her expression. "You're loaded, right? Great. Why the hell did you leave that way?" Something besides anger passed across Valerie's eyes as she spoke — something dark and sad. Now what? "I really need to talk to you."

Helen glanced over Valerie's shoulder. Sure enough, two women talking in intense whispers was enough to gather attention from a few guys in the crowd. And that included Helen's mean-eyed pal, who had apparently decided the blond wasn't enough for him. "Okay. Let's go." Helen followed Valerie through the room, conscious that she was walking very, very carefully around the tables and stools. Valerie glanced back a couple of times as if aware that Helen might not make it without assistance.

Then Valerie pushed the door open. Cool air brushed

Helen's face. While Helen had been getting reacquainted with the effects of drinking, the skies had grown dark. Not a hint of rain, for once — and a full bright moon glowing in a black sky dotted with stars. Distant from city lights, the view from the little roadhouse showed a full display of constellations whose names Helen had long forgotten. She stared up at the sky, and she could feel Valerie staring at her. "Why did you follow me?"

She looked at Valerie when the other woman didn't answer immediately. "I didn't, exactly," Valerie finally said. "When you ran off like that, I knew something was wrong. Something had happened. I got Gary to help me put Sissy's things in his car, then he took Nan back home. That's when I decided I should try to find you."

"Back home? You mean to the hotel?" Helen asked, hoping to stave off further questions just a minute longer.

"No, back to their house." Valerie wiped a hand across her face, a gesture of weariness. "They decided it's time for a reunion. I guess that's a good thing. Look —" She grimaced and ran her hands through her hair. "I really think we ought to talk."

"So what makes you think it's okay to follow me?" Helen asked. She wasn't too drunk to get mad, and she had only a tenuous hold on her emotions right now. Something softer and more dangerous than anger threatened to break through when she looked at Valerie, and the only way she could stay in control was to go ahead and be pissed off. It might get rid of Valerie, too, if she let loose. That irritating little voice in her head whispered a plea to not run the woman off, but Helen ignored it.

"Can we talk about this in the car?" Even in the gathering darkness Helen could tell Valerie was nervous, fidgeting and looking over her shoulder. "Look, let's get out of here, okay? This is no place to get into anything."

Helen sighed. All she wanted right now was to go to the next bar up the road, not get into a long and intense emotional conversation with a woman who didn't really know anything about her. "I'm not exactly good company at the moment, Valerie. Maybe some other time." She walked across the graveled lot to her car and heard Valerie crunching along on the rocks behind her.

"You are in no condition to be driving, Helen," Valerie said in a low voice. "If you get stopped they'll take you in for sure."

Helen stood, hand on her car door, envisioning the whole scene. A khaki-clothed Mississippi highway patrol officer pulling her over, ordering her to walk a straight line, finding Kyle's gun in her backpack, a quick check of her record. Right back to Deasely before you could say "busted." Valerie was right, dammit. "Look, why don't you bring your car around here? I've just got to get my stuff out and I'll go with you." She watched Valerie walk away, her back to Helen's car, before going for the gun.

A torrent of mixed feelings washed over Helen as she opened the trunk. She didn't know if she should be enraged at Valerie taking up babysitting duties or relieved at finding an ally. But for Valerie to suddenly go tearing off around town looking for her, a one night stand in the midst of grief — what was this about? Not about Helen, unfortunately. The recognition gave her a cold feeling in the pit of her stomach. Okay. Analysis later, she scolded herself. Right now you have a big problem to figure out.

Helen prayed her backpack was still there. In the parking lot of a place like this you could never be too sure what would happen. Yes, thank god. The battered canvas still sat next to the spare tire. She made sure the unloaded weapon nestled down in the bottom of her backpack and had it zipped by the time Valerie drove up beside her. Neither woman spoke as Valerie took them quickly out of the parking lot and turned toward Tynedale. Helen let the bag rest on her lap, the outline of the gun marking her thighs. She couldn't feel them but she knew the bullets were nestled in a different pocket in the bag. It made her skin itch, to think of what she carried with her.

What the fuck was she going to do now? She had to get rid of the gun, preferably to the police, and somehow keep herself out of trouble. And what about Kyle? Where had he gone? She stared out at the blur of stars. No answers there.

Helen turned to look at the other woman. Valerie's profile etched a delicate line against the black sky. Right now her white face looked hard and cold in the moonlight. What would Valerie say if she knew about the gun? About the kind of woman who was sitting beside her? Helen sat still and tried to get mad at Valerie, but she just couldn't get any more anger worked up. Maybe she'd wanted Valerie to come find her. Maybe she was just too tired. Maybe Valerie would marry her and take her away from all of this. Maybe Valerie was even more fucked up than Helen was. Scary thought.

Valerie sighed. "Okay, Helen," she finally said, keeping her gaze fixed on the road ahead. "You have every right to be mad at me. I'm sorry. I just couldn't watch you do what she —" She broke off. Tears welled up and spilled from her eyes, bright glistening tracks on her ivory skin. Like a child, with a balled fist Valerie wiped them dry. "I knew you would be heading to the nearest bar and getting loaded. And I couldn't stand it. So go ahead and hate me if you want."

Helen kept her voice quiet. "I don't hate you at all. I just don't get it."

Valerie shrugged, a grim smile stealing across her face. "Doesn't matter. I'll take you home."

"Not until you tell me who 'she' is." Helen rolled her window all the way down. Cold air with a hint of rain flowed across her skin, breaking through the haze of alcohol. Helen took a couple of deep breaths. Still carrying a buzz, but better. Valerie had gotten to her just in time. "You said 'she' a minute ago," Helen prodded when the silence continued. "I want you to tell me who 'she' is."

"My ex." The car slowed down. Helen recognized the stretch of road leading off the highway — in another couple of minutes they'd be at the boarding house. "Julie would get that look on her face — exactly like the one you had right before you took off — sort of cold and hard and determined, nothing was going to stop her. Then she'd disappear, sometimes for days on end." The car passed under a street lamp and Helen glimpsed the pain carved into Valerie's face. "I can't tell you how many times I had to go through the Quarter looking for her. God knows there are plenty of places in New Orleans to get drunk, too." Valerie gave Helen a glance, looked away quickly when she met Helen's eyes. "I can't explain it, Helen. It was kind of a reflex, I guess. I sort of went into automatic when you ran off like that." She made a laughing noise and shook her head. "Guess I'm still pretty fucked up myself. Still acting like a co-dependent. Thought I was over that shit."

Helen's body congealed into ice, and the temporary relief provided by alcohol drained away. The flat yellow glow of street lamps blurred in a stream of uneven light that created a gloomy backdrop for her thoughts. So it was this Julie that gave Valerie that haunted look. She hadn't even thought of Helen as she'd driven around Tynedale on her quest for watering holes. Okay, fine. Valerie Beausoleil had arrived only three days ago. In that time she'd lost her much-loved niece and shepherded her somewhat screwed up sister through a terrible time. Helen was just a bump in the road to her. What else did she expect? She'd been an idiot to imagine anything further. Stupid, stupid, stupid.

"Helen, please say something." The car halted at a stop sign and Helen turned to look at Valerie. "Do you hate me now?"

"No, of course not." Helen reached out to touch her arm, stroking the smooth white skin as a glacier closed around her heart. She was able to gaze at Valerie with apparent tenderness while pain twisted her guts. Helen marveled at her own foolishness while her fingers traced a teasing pattern on Valerie's arm. One quick fuck and she'd forgotten all the lessons she'd learned at Deasely. And not just at Deasely. Her whole frigging life had been a long and painful education in isolation. The hot knife of shame and sorrow pierced her with exquisite agony, cauterized the wound and formed another interior scar. Why fight the prison in her mind any longer? It was part of her now, a deep presence stronger than any locked cell.

"I'm grateful you showed up tonight, Valerie." Dammit. Helen closed her eyes. She didn't want to see Valerie looking at her. A beautiful woman appears in her life, and it had to be like this. Helen sliding down a well-greased slope toward destruction, Valerie still under the spell of a twisted relationship with an alcoholic. "How did you find me, anyhow? I didn't say anything about where I was going." Already her mind was working out a plan — how to use this to her advantage, how to get Valerie to go along with it all. Christ, it was disgusting. No, Valerie tearing off on a mission to save her was even worse. Better this way. It would cure her of the dark-eyed woman forever to go through with the plan taking shape in her mind.

Valerie made a sound like a laugh. "Like I said, I got to be an expert in tracking down Julie in New Orleans. Tynedale isn't all that big. Not too many places you could run, Helen. Just a couple of bars. Everything else shuts down as soon as it gets dark. And your car is, shall we say, distinctive."

"Too bad there aren't any women's bars around here. At least the scenery would have been better." Helen opened her eyes and stared straight ahead. She recognized the streets. They were getting closer to Valerie's hotel. The idea solidified in her mind and she glanced quickly at the other woman. "God, I don't know if I can handle going back to the boarding house tonight," she said with a heavy sigh. "After going through Sissy's things — I'm not sure I can take it." Helen heard her voice break. Jesus, was she laying it on too thick? Surely Valerie wouldn't buy it. "Did Kyle or Mrs. Mapple come home after I left?"

"Yes, Mrs. Mapple showed up. And Kyle is her son, right? No, he didn't come back."

Was this what it had been like with Julie, her ex-partner? First the agonized search, then the brief union replete with tears and apologies, followed up with innocuous conversation during the ride back home to their charming little flat in the Quarter. Maybe sex for a chaser. "I don't know if I can handle it," Helen repeated, sinking back into the seat as if exhausted. "Maybe I could come over to the hotel with you? Just for a while. You know, get some coffee, talk for a while. Doesn't have to be anything more."

Later Helen figured she'd still been pretty drunk. She couldn't remember how they'd ended up in Valerie's room again, both sitting awkwardly in uncomfortable chairs, sipping bad coffee out of styrofoam cups. Helen tried not to remember the previous night as Valerie leaned back in the chair and closed her eyes. "So," Valerie continued, "there was a tearful reunion at the boarding house. Gary and Nan just sort of collapsed into each others' arms, crying their eyes out, and claiming they'd always loved each other. That Sissy would have wanted them back together."

"Sounds like you don't believe that." Maybe she should just take the gun back to the boarding house, put it back in Kyle's room — no, that wouldn't work. Bertie and her squad of thugs would already have some nasty little plan in place to involve her. The police? Yeah, right. With Ludy looking for blood, he'd be sure to find some way to nail her. What about Wanda? Could she trust the young parole officer with the truth?

"You're not listening to me at all, are you?" Valerie looked disgusted. She set her cup down and got up to prowl around the room. "Okay. Sorry if I'm boring you."

"No, no, that's not it." Jesus, she had to stay away from that damn boarding house tonight. She had to get some space to figure out what to do. "I'm sorry, Valerie. It's just been an awful day, and there's a lot going on you don't know about."

"So tell me." Oh, it was tempting — to open up, let Valerie inside, let her see all the rough patches in her life. Especially when those blue eyes looked through her. "You don't trust me, do you?" Valerie hung her head, her black hair shielding her face. "Can't blame you. What do you know about me, after all? And after what I just told you, about Julie — well, I'm not exactly a prize, am I?" She shrugged, keeping her face averted from Helen. "Look, I already had a room ready for Nan and Gary. You can sleep there tonight. You don't have to stay in here with me." She grabbed a key from the desk and held it out to Helen.

Later Helen knew everything would have been different if she'd taken the key from Valerie's hand, if she'd said good-night and taken herself off to the other room. Instead of taking the key Valerie offered, Helen reached out to take Valerie into her arms.

Valerie made a show of protest. "No, Helen, you're drunk and I'm exhausted." She pushed gently away and searched Helen's face, both hands stroking Helen's cheeks. "Now is not the time for this."

But Helen persisted. Leaning into Valerie's neck, breathing in her scent, Helen's hands moved slowly up her back, remembering every curve and line and ridge of flesh and muscle. "I can't think of a better time," she murmured. "I need this. I need you." God, was she really saying this out loud? And really meaning it? Impossible. But this was happening, right here in this seedy hotel room. As if she had eyes outside her body, Helen watched herself trembling at Valerie's touch. Each stroke of her fingers stirred up flames in Helen's skin. Heat rose up below her belly, spreading out like a fan in her body. And she could feel the response in Valerie, in her rapid hot breath and the pulse at her wrist. Helen laved her tongue over Valerie's palms, then placed those palms flat on her own breasts so Valerie could feel the stiffened nipples.

Then somehow they were on the bed. Helen shoved her backpack out of the way and a moment later Valerie's clothes were on the floor. Valerie tried one more time. "This isn't right, Helen," she said between gasps. "We really should think about this first."

Helen shut her up with a kiss, letting her hands travel across Valerie's back as they lay down together. "Okay," she murmured. "Start thinking."

"It's just that — that —" She stopped talking as Helen stroked between her legs, lying back on the pillow with a sigh. Helen watched her hair flowing across the white sheets, watched her face as her eyelids fluttered and closed. As if from a distance, Helen observed her own motions on the bed. Valerie trembled in her arms, lost in the flood of feeling, unaware that Helen stared down at her seeing a stranger. A few moments later, still flushed from climax, Valerie pushed Helen flat on the bed and lay on top of her. She began to lave Helen's body with her tongue, moving closer and closer to Helen's thighs. Helen stared up at the ceiling, still in that place of disconnect between body and brain and heart. Yes, sensation still coursed along her skin, muscles still tightened in response to Valerie's touch, body still contracted in pleasure. But who was it that lay there watching it all? That had carefully orchestrated this moment, playing on Valerie's need and sorrow so Helen would have a chance to do whatever she wanted? Even as her back arched with the final release Helen marveled at the way she'd neatly severed herself from herself. Should she be disgusted? Horrified? Relieved? She didn't know anymore.

"Hey, where did you go?" Valerie leaned on one elbow and smiled at her. "You okay?"

"Yeah. Think I just had a lot to drink tonight." Helen looked back at the ceiling as the throbbing in her loins subsided. She'd stay here tonight, maybe just go ahead and ditch the gun. Drive over early in the morning to Vicksburg, throw it in the river maybe. Even if it had been the gun that killed Sissy. For a moment the dead girl's body, tangled in the muddy thorns, imposed itself on the cheap plaster as she stared. All over again Helen saw the dark brown stain that spread across Sissy's shirt across her stomach. Suddenly nausea rose up inside her.

"Sorry, Valerie," she muttered, making it to the bathroom in time. As she fled Helen stumbled over something that almost tripped her up. Her backpack, she thought — her last conscious thought before reaching the safety of the john.

A few minutes later, wiping her face with a towel, Helen emerged from the bathroom. "God, I am so sorry, Valerie," she said. "Believe it or not, I haven't had so much to drink in a long, long time. It's just been a hell of a day, and —"

She stopped, towel in hand. Valerie sat on the bed with her back to Helen, her shirt flung loose across her shoulders. Helen's backpack still lay on the floor, all its contents scattered across the cheap carpet. Well, almost all. The flimsy plastic grocery bag, the one she'd stuffed with bullets, was still safely zipped inside the pocket. And only the muzzle of the gun showed, poking its shiny snout out of the dirty canvas.

Helen tossed the towel back into the bathroom. "Like I was saying, I don't usually do this sort of thing. Drink like that, I mean." Jesus, now she'd start babbling? She grabbed her shirt and jeans and perched gingerly on the bed. Maybe Valerie hadn't seen it. Helen nudged the backpack with her foot, concealing the gun, then turned to face Valerie.

There went that theory. Valerie stared at her with a hard, cold look, her delicate face as grim and solid as an alabaster carving. "You always carry a gun with you?"

"No." Okay, she'd get her clothes on and get out. She was pretty sobered up, she could get to Vicksburg and the river on her own. Then come back and sort out living arrangements. Helen slowed her thoughts down, tried to think of what she could say to Valerie. "I don't always carry one. Don't worry, I know how to use it."

"Is that so?" Helen stood up. Valerie had switched on the bedside lamp, and Helen could see the expression on her face, noting vaguely that already she was getting a sense of the other woman's expressions, how to interpret them. No, it wasn't anger. It wasn't disgust or revulsion. Valerie feared her now.

"Christ." Helen sank down on the bed, all ideas drained from her. Anger she could have dealt with. And even disgust. Lord knows she'd had plenty of lessons in handling those feelings lately. But that Valerie should be afraid of her — Helen winced as Valerie cringed away, pushing back further on the bed in a reflexive motion.

"Valerie, the gun —" Now what the fuck should she do? "It isn't what you think."

"How the hell do you know what I think?" Valerie's voice shook. Helen looked up to see tears in the other woman's blue eyes. A shadowy resemblance of Sissy's sad, tense features haunted Valerie's face. Helen quickly looked down at her hands. "You want to know what I think?" Valerie finally continued. "I think that my niece got shot and died. I think a woman who was close to my niece is carrying around a gun. I think this woman went out and tried to get drunk because she's hiding something."

"Valerie." God. Helen sighed and put her head in her hands. "Sweetheart, it really isn't what you think. Just let me —"

"I guess I already let you, didn't I? More than once." Valerie shoved off the bed and started gathering her clothes. "What the hell have I been doing? I don't know you, I don't know anything about you except that Sissy liked you. And now Sissy is dead."

"Please sit down. I can explain everything." Yeah, right. Anything to get Valerie calmed down. "Please. Do you really think I killed her? That I would shoot that sad little girl? Is that what this is about?"

Valerie stopped prowling and sat down in the chair facing Helen. "I don't know." She met Helen's eyes. At least the tears were gone. "Helen, I don't know what the hell is going on here. I don't know anything about you except that Sissy loved you. I don't even know myself right now."

Helen gave up. The same old cold dead feeling spread over her. "I have to go. I'll get a cab back to my car." Better to leave before Valerie found out the truth. She couldn't bear the idea of those blue eyes looking at her with revulsion when she found out.

"I won't bother you again."

"Yes, you will. I'm never going to know what happened to Sissy, am I, Helen?"

Her hand on the door, Helen froze. Valerie's voice did the dirty work — that sad, resigned, quiet voice, full of pain and struggling to accept it. Helen stood there and felt fury mix with desire. How dare Valerie come into her life and fuck everything up? It was all too much. Sissy, her aunt, her past coming up to bedevil her in the shape of Bertie, and two nights spent in Valerie's arms. Two nights that split her world into shards.

"Okay." Helen threw the bag down and stood directly in front of Valerie. "Okay. You really want to hear this? You really want me to tell you everything?"

"Yes."

Helen told her.

Chapter Eleven

An angry red eye, the sun rose over the abandoned pier
with a harsh light that reflected off the water and hurt
Helen's eyes. The weeds wavered like skeletal hands in the
warm breeze that brought the distinct tang of rotting vege-
tation across the Mississippi River. Helen glanced back at
Valerie sitting in the car, then beyond the car along the access
road leading back to the highway. Their illegal entrance had
so far eluded the observation of state troopers. Valerie stared
out the window across the empty field, gaze turned away from
the sun and the river and Helen.

Helen's head hurt. Her body felt hollow, drained of everything, sitting flat in a state of inertia. Not so much a hang-
over — she really hadn't drunk enough last night. No, more a

lack of sleep. And delayed reaction, maybe, to the unaccustomed effects of talking so much about herself. Helen stared down at the gun in her hand. Wrapped in several layers of grocery bag plastic, it should keep all right for a couple of days. Her thoughts strayed from the weapon back to the woman in the car, who'd found it in the hotel room. Was she going insane, to be worrying about Valerie while she tried to save her own ass from going back to Deasely for something she didn't do? Helen knew she'd lost the knack of intimacy, if she'd ever possessed it. The role of penitent in the confessional fit her about as well as a teddy from Victoria's Secret.

There was a sound from behind. Valerie climbed out of the rental car and leaned against its side, her back to Helen. With a sigh Helen bent down to the muddy banks of the river. Awkwardly she dug away at the loose dirt around the bottom of the stone pillar that extended deep into the earth. She had no idea when — or if — she'd come back for it. She could only take that risk once she'd figured out a way to do it safely, some way to get the gun to the police without implicating herself. Maybe just a simple anonymous phone call would do. Helen's gaze swept the area one last time. No one else lurked behind the sere brown shrubs, she was positive. Still, they'd waited too late. Should have done this at night. But headlights from the car might have alerted people in the neighboring areas that someone cruised the access road. This was probably the best they could do — folks would be just waking up, getting the coffee-maker revved, rubbing sleep from their eyes. And this was a shortcut between Port Gibson and the main road. Lots of people probably cut through here illegally on their way to work or school or whatever. Nobody would care.

Helen folded the washcloth taken from the hotel she'd used to wipe down the gun and put it into her pocket as she headed for the car. Valerie got in and started up when she saw Helen marching through the weeds. Helen lay the cloth down on the seat between them as Valerie drove slowly over the gravel. "Be sure the maids at the hotel take this for washing," Helen said, merely for the comfort of having something to say.

"Right." Valerie glanced over her shoulder as she merged into the highway. "What did you do with the bullets?"

Helen looked down at the mud on her hands. No one would find them beneath that rock in the midst of the tangled thorns. She reached for the cloth to try getting some of the dirt off her fingers. "It's okay, they're taken care of."

"In other words, the less I know the better." Helen watched Valerie's grim smile. She looked as exhausted as Helen did. Worse, with those ugly lines etched on her pale skin. "After everything else why not tell me that, Helen?"

"Okay. Doesn't matter. I buried them under a rock out there." Helen tossed the cloth down and opened the window. Pine trees moved in the breeze. The air felt cold, soothing on her face, drying the sweat beaded on her forehead and cheeks. Another storm on the way, and autumn setting in. "And that is absolutely everything I have to tell you, Valerie. You've got it all now." Jesus, why was she snapping at the poor woman? Just tired, maybe. "I'm sorry. You don't deserve that."

"We're both exhausted," Valerie sighed as she leaned her arm on the window. "And we have to figure out what to do next."

"No, we don't."

"What do you mean?"

"It's not we, Valerie. It's me. I'm the one who has to figure this out. I've dragged you in as deep as you need to go." Helen glanced at the other woman — God, she was already starting to know Valerie's gestures and expressions — and saw the grim set of her jaw. In spite of everything Helen relaxed into amusement at herself for sliding so swiftly into the habits of coupledom. Sure enough, Valerie made that little grimace again before speaking.

"Helen, you haven't done anything wrong here. No, just forget about the fucking gun a minute and listen to me.

Getting rid of it was just survival, okay? I understand that. There was no easy way to explain the gun to the police. Especially to this character Ludy."

"So what are you saying here, Valerie?" Helen said through the gathering tightness in her gut. "You're going to go with me to the wall, support me through thick and thin? Stand by your woman, like that old song?" Uh oh. That came out all wrong — like a whip cracking over their heads. Helen listened to the echo of her words circling in the silence of the car, looking out through the window as if the landscape was broken by the bars of her cell.

"That's not what I meant. I'm just saying you aren't guilty of anything."

"Who are you trying to convince, me or yourself?" There, that should help a lot, Helen thought. Just as she'd observed herself making love to Valerie, like watching a movie, Helen watched her own anger and fear lashing out at the other woman. "Didn't you hear anything I said last night? I killed that girl two years ago. Shot her dead in the middle of nowhere."

"Helen, you've paid for that already. There's no point in —"

"I have a psycho bitch on my case who's trying to get me involved in her ridiculous little crime ring she created just because she's bored. I have a teenage would-be rapist on the loose. I have a frustrated big-city cop on my ass just because he can. I have my last bit of family telling me go to hell. But according to Valerie Beausoleil everything is hunky dory. Just a big fucking bed of roses, never mind all those thorns with blood all over them." Her anger was spent almost as soon as the words were out of her mouth. Too late. At least she'd stopped herself before saying something about the ex-girlfriend, and how Valerie must be looking for some new basket case to fix up. Anyway, it wasn't really anger, was it? Just another layer of armor against getting hurt.

Valerie's face, set in stone, looked across the highway and

into the rising sun. She stayed silent until they reached the parking lot of the bar where Helen's car sat. Helen gathered her bag and her courage and opened the door. Might as well try one more time to say it right. "Look, Valerie. I'm a fucked up mess right now. I can't even begin to tell you how grateful I am to you, but the best thing you can do for yourself — and for me, too — is stay away. I'm poison. You don't need it."

Valerie turned to face her at last. Helen's gut wrenched at the sight of her sad smile, a smile she'd probably never see again. "Sissy didn't think you were poison, Helen. And I don't, either." She didn't even say goodbye before driving off.

Now what? Helen managed to get the car started. She sat there for a couple of minutes, letting the engine idle. No way she felt like going back to the boarding house, meeting God knows what on her arrival. And as far as work — she wanted to avoid that one more day, take advantage of Marie's good graces before facing either the warehouse or the guys who'd thrown their lot in with Bertie Mullins. Faced with the brilliant morning sun as she pulled slowly out of the parking lot, Helen fell back on the old stand by of food. She hadn't eaten anything since breakfast yesterday, she realized. Maybe she could manage some toast at *Rosie's* before dealing with the wreck of her life.

Oddly, Helen felt light and empty and calm as she nudged the aging car into Tynedale. She sat at a red light and pondered in amazement. It wasn't lightheadedness from hunger. Why the hell should she feel this way? She parked in front of the café — the only place open in town, as far as she could tell — and sighed with relief to see only a couple of other diners there. And they were too absorbed in the consumption of caffeine to bother about Helen.

While waiting for toast she glanced idly through the paper she'd grabbed from the front counter. Valerie's face superimposed itself over the newsprint, followed by images of the gun dropping into the water, Sissy's body curled on the ground —

Sissy. Helen sat up straight, then dug into her pockets. A couple of moments' search turned up the crumpled scrap of Sissy's math problems. She turned the paper over and stared down at the drawing of the ruined church. Why had Sissy been lurking around the condemned property? Maybe she'd just liked the look of the broken cross against the sky, or the elegant lines of the old building. Maybe an escape from people and noise and confusion — a place where she wouldn't be bothered, a breathing space. But it was awfully convenient to the park. Helen's mind started to form an idea about going there herself today. Why not? Couldn't hurt, no one would know, maybe it would help her put Sissy to rest. Studying the simple lines on the ruled page Helen didn't notice the other woman walking up to her booth.

"People are going to talk if we keep meeting like this," Renee smiled.

"You're getting an early start," Helen said, matching Renee's smile with one of her own, surprised by how pleased she was to see the hairdresser. "Don't tell me someone is waiting desperately for a haircut." Valerie must have shaken her up more than she realized — was Helen actually starting to like people again?

"No, thank god. This is just the best time for getting paperwork done, when all normal people are still asleep." Damn it, the woman looked refreshed and relaxed, Helen groused to herself, eyes clear and bright, smile genuine, thick auburn hair glossy in the early morning light. Helen remembered Renee's partner — what was her name, Gwen? Yes, Gwen — who'd glowered at her Sunday morning. Valerie, she thought with a pang. Renee hesitated, then asked, "Mind if I join you?"

"Please do." Renee glanced down at the paper as she slid into the booth. "How's your week going?"

"Oh, the usual. Hair everywhere. Anything new?"

"You mean about Sissy? Nothing I know of."

The waitress took Renee's order of grits. When she left, Renee said, "So were the police onto him?"

Helen's heart dropped to the floor. Jesus, how the hell did she know about Kyle? No, wait. She must mean Earl. From the way Renee stared at her, Helen realized her face must have blanched. She meant Earl Pemberton. That's what Renee was talking about, not about Kyle or Bertie or the rest of it. Helen took a deep breath and said, "I don't know. They wouldn't say anything to me."

Renee stared down at the plate set in front of her, biting her lips as she thought. Helen watched a shadow pass over her pleasant face. "Wonder if the son of a bitch left a note," she muttered.

"You mean a suicide note." What was this about? Something spiked through Helen's awareness. This was possibly important. She needed to keep Renee talking. "Did the papers say something about that?"

"Just hints." Renee poked at her grits, took a bite. "Best thing that asshole ever did was to check out." She met Helen's stare and forced another bright smile on her face. "I guess the old judge is completely out of it, right? I mean, he doesn't talk or anything."

Helen shook her head and pushed her toast aside. "The judge can't take care of himself at all. He does have his moments, though — I think he picks up a lot more than people realize."

"Huh. Poor old guy." Renee gave up on the grits and sipped bitter coffee. "Too bad."

Too bad he was senile, or too bad he was still cognizant of the world around him? This deserved further probing. The arrival of fresh coffee broke the spell, and Renee began to chat about her shop. "Before you know it the little old ladies who need their hair permed will show up, so I try to get the bills paid early in the day," she was saying.

"I don't suppose you'd have time for me today? I know we

said Friday, but I have the day off, so I wondered if you could fit me in."

Apparently it was casual enough for Renee. "I just need an hour or so," she said as she put money on the table and glanced at her watch. "That'll make it eight o'clock. My first little old lady is at nine." She left with a smile and instructions for Helen to knock on the door around eight. Helen added a few bills to the table and hurried to her car.

Her luck held at the boarding house. Her eagerness to find out what Renee knew kept her from being tense about confronting the Mapple clan as she quietly went up the stairs to the bathroom. No signs of activity while she showered and changed and made a rapid escape, stopping long enough to leave a brief message on Marie Willis' voice mail at the warehouse — hopefully Marie would be satisfied with that. On her way out, she went back into Sissy's room. The piles of clothes and books were gone, but a few sheets of paper peeked out from the floor under the cot stripped of bedclothes. Helen took them, trying not to notice how barren the room felt. One afternoon and all trace of Sissy's life husked off.

She got to *Curl Up and Dye* just before eight. The street seemed deserted. She parked the Rambler next to a silver pick-up — Renee's, probably — and looked for signs of life from the salon. Renee peered through the closed blinds at her knock, quickly letting her in. "Hurry, before Leticia sees us."

"Leticia?"

"Leticia Musgrove. She's my first appointment today. I swear she always sits like a damn spider out there in her car, waiting for me to open the door so she can crawl in." Renee led the way to the sinks in the back, nattering away like a pro as she soaped and rinsed Helen's hair. Helen squinted up through suds scented with coconut. She would have to forcibly take the conversation toward Earl. "So I think I'll check out this new hair coloring. It looked really good on the model at the conference up in Memphis."

"Yeah, maybe I should consider getting my hair dyed."

"But you have such beautiful hair, Helen! I wouldn't change a thing," and Renee aimed the hose at her scalp.

Helen relaxed into the warm water, into Renee's fingers massaging her head. Thoughts of Valerie floated through her mind. Cut it out, she lectured herself. "Well, maybe I'm just looking for a change. God knows after all the terrible things going on lately I could use one. First Sissy, now Earl — and nobody knows what to do about the Judge."

Renee silently wrapped Helen's hair in a towel, giving the terry cloth a sharp tug. Her expression, so animated a moment ago, froze into something flat and unreadable. But Helen persisted as she followed Renee to a chair at the front of the salon. "Mrs. Mapple says she doesn't think Judge Pemberton has any other relatives. No one seems to know anything about the family, except that Earl came from some other town a few years back. Kind of a mystery."

Renee picked up shears, took a deep breath, gazed back at Helen in the mirror. For a brief crazy moment Helen wondered if she'd been wise to press Renee when she had so many sharp objects at her fingertips. Finally Renee said, "I feel sorry for that old man. I'll bet he's had more than his share of grief with Earl."

"Really?" Helen watched her hair falling down to the dark linoleum in small clumps. "Seems like Earl took really good care of him. He came to visit a lot, took his father to church on Sundays. He even brought presents to Sissy from the store."

Renee snorted and kept cutting with little jabs of the scissors. When she didn't respond Helen glanced at her face, surprised to see Renee's eyes bright with tears. "Sorry," Renee said, setting the shears down and wiping her eyes. She picked up clippers but didn't switch them on.

"Hey. What happened?"

"Nothing, really. Just a fight with my other half this weekend. You know, the knock-down drag-out kind where we say lots of things we have to apologize for over and over again."

She put down the clippers, picked up the shears and resumed the haircut.

"Guess all this stuff with Sissy and Earl Pemberton got the whole town upset. I know people are worked up at the boarding house, too."

"Worked up. You could say that. Damn bastard, with his toy shop, everyone thinking he's a model citizen —" She bit her lip and went for the blow dryer. Helen endured a few minutes of hot air whining over her head, watching Renee as her hair fluffed out. Why would they be fighting about Earl Pemberton? Maybe she could offer a sympathetic ear about the girlfriend, gently tease out the connection while Renee cried on her shoulder. Helen gave herself a quick mental slap for using a very nice person yet again for her own ends — then Renee took the towel from her shoulders.

A few moments later Renee was sitting in the chair next to Helen's, leaning her chin on her hand and talking about the weekend battle at home. "Gwen gets so mad at me for wanting to talk to people, be around people. I mean, she got upset when I tried to talk to Sissy, for God's sake. Like somehow they'd find out our dirty little secret. I can barely persuade her to go into *Rosie's* with me once in a while, she's that paranoid." Renee shook her head and fiddled with a comb from the workstation. "You should have heard her on Sunday afternoon, after we bumped into you at the diner. You'd think I'd taken out a full page ad in the *New York Times* just by saying hello to you."

"Jesus, I'm sorry. I mean, I'm sorry if I was the cause of anything —"

Renee waved her hand. "It's not your fault. You didn't start this. We've been fighting our way back into the closet ever since my ex-husband tried to get custody of our son a few years ago. She's just scared, I know that." Renee flipped the comb back onto the counter. "It got really bad when I started worrying about Earl Pemberton. He was in the same house as Sissy, for Christ's sake. What was I supposed to do, keep my

190

mouth shut and risk the poor kid's safety?" Renee shuddered, closing her eyes against whatever awful image she'd conjured up. "It was all I could do to keep from kicking his sorry ass into the Gulf of Mexico, I can tell you that. Especially when he started bringing those toys to her."

Realization dawned slowly on Helen. "Earl was trying to get his hands on Sissy? Seduce her or something?"

"Or something." Renee's mouth twisted in disgust. "Look, I probably shouldn't be saying this to you."

Oh, God, please say it to me. Helen kept her gaze fixed on her reflection in the mirror, carefully avoiding staring at Renee.

"It was the way he'd look at Skeeter — Sam, my boy. Made me squirm." She paused, clippers in the air, took a deep breath and went on. "I don't know anything at all, not for sure. I just didn't like it. I mean, he just shows up out of nowhere with his senile father. You have to understand, Helen, he has no wife or kids, no friends, no one who knows a thing about him. And this is still a small town. People talk about strangers. Especially people like Leticia Musgrove, and half the other old ladies who come tottering in here once a week." Renee cast a guilty look in Helen's direction, which Helen translated as a hint that she herself had been the object of heated discussion more than once.

"Did your son ever tell you anything?"

Renee shrugged. "They just talked about school, sports, stuff like that. It wasn't that. It was the way Earl would give him this little secret smile whenever I took Skeeter back to his dad. Like they shared some deep dark secret." She shook herself and bent over Helen's head again. "Nobody ever knew anything about him, though not for want of trying. Or of talking about it, either."

"So you must know about me, then." Helen made herself stare at Renee, convincing herself she was ready for anything the other woman might say or do. To her own surprise, it mattered very much what Renee thought of her. Not just

191

because whatever got discussed in the salon became common knowledge — but because she realized she wanted Renee to like her, to include Helen in her circle of friends. Helen kept her face impassive while the inner turmoil waged inside her, breaking a crack in the crust that had up until now kept everything and everyone out. Up until Valerie, maybe.

Renee met her stare evenly. "That was different, Helen. Your situation was an accident, no matter what anybody says about it. But Earl Pemberton —" even saying the name seemed difficult for Renee, her mouth grimacing over the words — "he comes into town and has the nerve to open up a toy shop. A toy shop, for God's sake. All those little kids coming into the store, and him staring at them. Made me sick."

She fiddled with the combs and scissors at the work-station. Helen watched her fidget. Renee must be getting nervous by now, uneasy about all she'd revealed to a stranger in the past hour. "Look, just forget about it, okay? I don't know anything and I'm just talking bullshit here. Guess I got more upset about Gwen than I realized." She offered Helen a half smile of apology and reached for a broom.

Helen watched her, knowing that any expression of faith in Renee's instinct would be unwelcome just now. But Helen was certain that years of dealing with people had in fact given the hairdresser an extra edge of instinct. At least she wouldn't dismiss the notion out of hand. Besides, there was that weird conversation between Earl and Gary. Lots of hints tossed around, about something not quite kosher taking place on both sides. The silence between Helen and Renee became unbearable when there was a loud clattering at the door. A fleeting expression of relief moved across Renee's face as she sprang up from the chair. "That's Leticia Musgrove," she muttered. Helen got up with a final glance at the mirror, pleased with Renee's handiwork.

"And how are you today, Leticia? It's already getting hot out there, isn't it?" The elderly woman, balanced on her cane like a clutch of sticks, peered curiously at Helen as she murmured a response.

"Thanks, Renee. What do I owe you?" Helen asked, reaching for her wallet.

But Renee waved her offer aside. "On the house. I consider it a public service, getting your hair into shape." And that refusal was trying to cover her awkwardness, Helen realized as she let herself out. Or a plea for silence. She got into her car and, after a moments' hesitation, headed back to the boarding house.

Mrs. Mapple's voice rang through the stuffy foyer. "Now, I need you to find that son of mine, Tommy Deets!" she shouted over the telephone. "No excuses! I've had about enough of — what? No, he's not at his job. Don't you think I have sense enough to look there first? They don't have the slightest notion — well, I don't care. What with all the mayhem and murder happening around here, I can't sit by and let my only child be taken by killers and thieves."

Back to normal — and no need to worry about Kyle for the moment. Helen crept quickly up the stairs. The judge was not in his room. Outside, perhaps? Maybe she should take advantage of his absence to check out his room. Mrs. Mapple's voice floated through the hall. Helen spared a moment to worry about what had happened with Kyle — more time for that later — then slipped into Judge Pemberton's room.

Damn, no sign of that briefcase. Maybe there was something else. She stood in the doorway, surveying the bare dresser, the walls empty of decoration, the single bed under the window. No trace of personality here, worse than in Sissy's room. Same for the closet — just a couple of suits and a few white shirts lined up neatly over the second pair of shoes.

Okay, she'd have to go see if she could coax the briefcase away from the old man. Helen got out through the garage while Mrs. Mapple burst into tears on the kitchen phone. A pang of guilt and sympathy twisted her guts. The poor woman

193

didn't have a clue about her son. Would it help for Helen to fill her in? What if Bertie and company had done something to him? No. Helen hardened her emotions. Kyle had brought all this shit on himself. What could she say or do that would help? Okay. First, the judge. Then she'd figure out what to do about Kyle.

Sure enough, the old man sat in the same lawn chair, staring out over the same sere grass as yesterday. And the same battered briefcase clutched on his lap. Helen sat down cross legged on the ground, the dead grass crackling beneath her body. "Okay," she sighed, peering up into Judge Pemberton's face. "We both know you're a lot more in tune than anyone thinks. Right?"

He turned milky eyes at her, his mouth working soundlessly.

"And I'm sure you remember everything about Earl, too — what he did, how he died a couple of days ago. That's why the cops were out here. So —" Helen reached for the briefcase, met the expected resistance from the old man. It took only a couple of moments to wrest it free. "This will only take a minute," she said as she started rummaging through the papers. "The way Ludy and Deets looked at each other when they saw that newspaper — yes, here it is."

A thin whining pierced the air as Pemberton beat at the air with his trembling hands. Feeling like a monster, Helen finally dug out the yellowed newspaper. The whining cries built up into a crescendo as she turned through the fragile pages. She found the story on page seven — not quite hot enough for the first page, but still big enough for the main news section. And maybe buried this deep due to the judge's influence?

The old man's whimpers died out as she read. Yes, Earl had been tried and convicted for child molestation, sentenced to fifteen years. So he would have gotten out about ten years ago if he'd served the full time, maybe sooner. Helen noted again the date of the paper, resolving to see if she could get her own copy through a library. Then she replaced it in the briefcase. Getting up to her knees she settled the cracked leather case into the judge's hands and looked him in the eye. "I'm really sorry, sir. Honestly. I hope you can forgive me for that rude behavior. Especially after you were so good to me yesterday." She kept talking, certain there must be some spark of intelligence hidden behind the filmy gray oblivion in his eyes. "But I have to find out what happened. Both to Earl, and to Sissy. You remember her, don't you? I know you do."

Judge Pemberton squinted at her, his head cocked to one side as if struggling to drag up memory from the dim depths of his mind. He blinked, opened his mouth, closed his mouth and stared. "Okay, look. I know how hard it must have been, all those years, trying to live with what your son did —" Helen stopped, stood up straight. Was that a lie? How could she know how this old man felt, watching his mind, his capacity to think and act and participate in the world, crumble and slip away like earth dredged by inevitable currents? Watching his son punished for despicable crimes, crimes for which there was no forgiveness anywhere?

But she did know, Helen thought as she went back to the house. Judge Pemberton knew as well as Helen did what it was like to be imprisoned. That, at least, they could share. And as for Earl — it was hard to believe that this little ugly secret had stayed a secret in Tynedale for so long. Unless someone were deliberately working to keep it as quiet as possible. Maybe. She glanced down at the judge, who had subsided back into whatever world of gray vagueness he normally inhabited. Helen left him, doubting he'd heard anything she'd said.

Helen went in through the kitchen, determined to say something to Mrs. Mapple. Then she could contact Deets, try to urge them to find Bertie —

But the phone rang as Helen walked in the door. "Yes?

Yes? Where is he? Oh, my God!" Helen watched as Mrs. Mapple went through a few more exchanges. She finally hung up the phone, turning to look at Helen with horror on her face.

"My baby boy," she managed to get out. "He's been in an accident."

Chapter Twelve

The social worker tugged at her tight-fitting blue suit and peered past Helen's shoulder into the living room where Judge Pemberton sat on the sofa, his eyes fixed on the local evening news. "This is all highly irregular," she said. "I specifically said last night, when I made the initial call, that I expected to be here this afternoon." She heaved a sigh and gave Helen a baleful look. "You don't know when Mrs. Mapple will be back?"

"No, I'm afraid not. She's — she's had a family emergency." Helen took in the woman's irritated expression, the way she fiddled with the buttons of her jacket. Ms. Quigley — was it Quigley? Something like that — whatever her name was, she didn't like being kept waiting and she certainly didn't like not having everything all neat and tidy. Great. She was in for a really good time with the old judge. "I don't know when she'll be back."

"I see." Ms. Quigley pursed her lips, then jerked a cell phone from her voluminous shoulder bag. Helen stepped into the living room as she angrily prodded the number pad on the phone. Judge Pemberton looked in her direction as she entered the room. Behind her Helen could hear the social worker hissing on the phone. "No, she isn't. I know, she told me last night she would be here. Well, we could place him there for now. Yes, we tried that but we can't locate any other family members."

Helen hoped the judge couldn't tell his future was being determined by a testy stranger. She sat down beside him on the sofa, speaking loud enough to cover the other woman's words. "There's someone here to see you," she started. "You remember Ms. Quigley? She says she stopped by to meet you yesterday. That lady out in the hall — see?"

Of course he doesn't, Helen scolded herself. He kept his gaze on Helen's face and she kept talking. "Well, she's going to take you to visit another house tonight. Maybe for a long visit. I'm sure Mrs. Mapple told you all about it last night."

Helen tried for a few more minutes, then gave up. Ms. Quigley snapped her cell phone shut and pranced with sharp clicking steps into the living room. "We'll take him over to the home in Jackson tonight," she said. "Did he have a suitcase or anything?" She looked expectantly at Helen.

Instead of talking Helen decided it would be better to go look for a suitcase. Sure enough, a small one sat in a corner of the Judge's room, tucked behind the chair. Helen had missed it before. Had Mrs. Mapple tucked it out of sight in case it stirred some kind of reaction in the judge? She hurried back down the stairs, suitcase in hand, to see the social worker herding the elderly man in front of her. Helen handed over the suitcase and watched Ms. Quigley tuck the judge into the waiting car. "Where are you taking him?" Helen asked as the door shut on the judge.

The other woman looked startled — she must not have been expecting anyone to want to know that information. "St. Martin's Rest Home in Jackson."

"I might come visit him later. If that's okay." Ms. Quigley gave her a doubtful glance before climbing behind the wheel and driving off. Helen got one last glimpse of the old man's face, a pale creased moon behind the wavery window glass. Helen rubbed her arms against the chilly autumn wind as she watched the car turn off Gramm Street. It wasn't dark yet, but shadows lengthened across the front lawn as Helen went back into the house.

Empty house, now. Helen stood just inside the front door and realized that for the first time in months — no, in years — she was completely alone in her own home. No one else behind the closed doors, no dull susurration of sound signaling the presence of another human being, no immanent threat of interruption by anyone else. It took Helen several minutes, and several deep breaths, to realize that it felt good to be alone. No need to control her expressions or voice or gestures. No tensing of muscles at the sound of approaching footsteps. No deep-seated current of fear or worry about who was watching and what they might see.

Helen moved slowly through the silent house, making her way up the stairs to her bedroom. She looked out at the darkening sky. Below her, neighbors were coming home from work and school, cars coming to a halt in driveways or kids on bikes wheeling up to the front doors. Helen felt a now familiar grief tug at her heart. Sissy should have been walking up the steps now, maybe settling on the porch swing with her books, tucking her feet under her legs while she pulled out her notebook —

Helen took the folded sheet of paper from her back pocket. She looked up from Sissy's sketch of the church to study the horizon. Yes, she could just make out the top of the abandoned building from her window. The park would be a few feet beyond. Helen folded the paper and tapped the creased edge against the windowsill. Okay. She had a couple of daylight hours left. Better to go check out the deserted grounds of the church than sit here waiting for Mrs. Mapple or Kyle or Bertie or Ludy or any of the other people who might not like her very much right now.

Just as she'd hoped — no one in sight on the narrow street that fronted the fenced-in church grounds. St. Bernadette's loomed like a ragged edged mountain, the surrounding gloom unrelieved by street lamps. If anyone was at home in the ramshackle houses facing the church, they must be sitting down to dinner or the evening news right now. Helen drove slowly past the church and found a small, paved turn-around at the end of the street past a handful of small one story homes slightly crumbled at the edges. Lawns littered with tricycles and plastic chairs fronted the street. Helen spied some room to park between a pair of pickups in front of a house strung with Christmas lights. Fortunately the battered Rambler fit these surroundings, increasing her chances of escaping notice. Helen walked slowly back to the opening she'd seen in the fence, hearing only the distant barking of dogs and the dull murmur of televisions coming from half a dozen living rooms.

Was this how Sissy had gotten in? she asked herself as she squeezed past the rusted edge of the chain link fence. Or did she have a different way in? Maybe some secret passage, balm to her child's heart, safe from mothers and boarding houses and the harsh world of school. Helen stepped carefully over broken pavement and jagged piles of rotting wood. Shadows stretched deep and dark here, and only a crescent of the red-yellow sun arced over the slanted roof, glinting on shards of metal and purple glass from the cracked stained windows. Various things crunched under her shoes, and Helen saw something small and black scurry further into the darkness. Terrific.

She made it intact to the front doors of the church. Hanging limp from the door handle, a broken chain swung once in the faint breeze coming in off Champion's Hill. Helen pushed the door — thank heavens it didn't creak, that would have been too much — and slipped inside, pulling a flashlight from her back pocket. She stood still, just inside the door, for a few moments, trying to put herself into the position of an adolescent girl. What would Sissy have liked about this place? Helen switched off the flashlight and watched dust motes drift in the thick golden light piercing through the ceiling. She forcibly put aside her nerves at the rickety structure hanging over her head and moved forward through stale air. Nothing moved. She got up to the front near what would have been the altar. No crucifix, now — no mute and bloody god suspended overhead. No wine or bread. No candles or glowing red presence of holiness. Just silence. No wonder Sissy had loved this place. Helen dredged through her vague memories as her eyes adjusted to the light. Catholics must have a ritual for emptying a church, for leaching out all trace of the holy upon vacating a sacred site. And it worked. She felt nothing more than emptiness here.

Helen pulled out her flashlight again and circled the light around the cavernous room. She glanced overhead once again and moved closer to the side of the room, next to a pedestal split along the front in an even seam. Yes, Sissy stood or sat or knelt here, leaning back against the dusty pedestal. After making a quick check of the floor for sharp edges Helen let herself slide down to the floor and peered up through the cracked ceiling to the broken cross. It didn't match the sketches perfectly. Helen scooted cautiously around the pedestal. Okay, this was better. Maybe over by that door she'd have the right view.

Helen settled against the door, resting her head on the

frame. She felt the door give under her weight and moved forward as it opened into the room beyond. Helen got up and turned her flashlight into the interior. Close to the altar, off to one side — maybe the vestry, where the priests housed their robes and dressed for services? Narrow and dark, it would have been claustrophobic when filled with robes and implements of priesthood. Helen turned away, switching off the flashlight. She stared up at the cross and watched birds, dark points against the deep red sunset, fly over the church. She was almost ready to explore the rest of the building when the footsteps echoed out in the foyer.

Possibly over by the cracked stone bowl just inside the front door, now drained of holy water. Helen breathed slowly and told herself to calm down. A glance over her shoulder confirmed that she could slip out through the vestry if she needed to. Better to just sit tight and see who the hell had decided to get religion tonight. Besides her, of course. Thank god she'd turned off the flashlight.

He — or she — stepped slow and careful through the arched entrance into the church. It was too dark to make out features. Helen crouched low between the pedestal and the first row of pews. The footsteps continued, no breaks in the slow pace, so she probably hadn't been spotted. Straining to see better, Helen realized that the interior of the church had been gradually edging toward complete darkness. She could make out movement, a moment of pale color sliding across the back of the room, as the silent figure painstakingly worked its way toward the front. Toward the altar. And toward the pedestal.

Enough. Helen slid back, feeling her way cautiously with every inch. The door to the vestry was right behind her, and she wanted to be a lot closer to escape in case she was seen. There, just another couple of inches — if she could just keep her shoes from scraping across that one rough spot — okay, the door was at her shoulder now. Squeeze past without any more noise and she'd be home free.

In her relief Helen didn't feel the boards beneath her right leg give under her weight. Without a warning creak or groan, the rotted wood strained and broke with an echoing snap. Helen couldn't help crying out in shock, but everything happened too fast — splinters slicing into her thigh, hip slithering across the floor into a jagged-edged emptiness, foot suddenly dangling in a big black nothing. With the rest of her threatening to follow.

"Shit!" Helen yelled before she could stop herself. She clawed out to grab the pedestal. One remote part of her mind registered the complete lack of supporting foundation beneath the wood floor. Yeah, they condemned the building, remember? For a reason, apparently. She felt her nails tearing on wood and stone as she slipped further into whatever disgusting debris lay below the church, felt her foot flailing around waiting for some kind of purchase on something. Felt her hip wrench painfully, impale on a stave of wood, move closer to the black hole that now swallowed her leg.

"Dammit," Helen muttered through clenched teeth. She heard her flashlight roll across the floor out of reach. A sharp stab of pain flew through her leg into her side, seizing her arm so that she loosened her grip on the floor. The pedestal moved a few inches further, the hole a few inches closer.

Then light dazzled her eyes. She tried to stare up past it, into the face of whoever stood over her, but failed. Helen turned her head away, eyes watering. The light descended to the floor, throwing the altar into eerie relief. Helen twisted to look again, trying not to scream as she slipped deeper, her hips following her legs. Suddenly the floor moved away from her hands. Something — someone — gripped her forearms. With a final twist of her hip that she'd pay dearly for later, Helen felt herself lifted free of the floor.

A moment later Ludy lowered her to the front pew. Helen eased her leg out in front of her as far as the kneeler would allow. Was anything bleeding? Not as far as she could tell. Ludy aimed the light at Helen, sweeping it across her torso and down her legs. "How bad?" he asked.

"Can't tell." Helen tested her knee, looked at her hands. Just a few scratches on what she could see. No blood on her jeans. "It doesn't look like I'm bleeding. Nothing broken. Just bruises, I think."

"You sure?"

"Pretty sure." Helen leaned back in the pew. Her heart seemed to be slowing down now. She turned to face Ludy, whose expression was completely unreadable in the darkness. So maybe his voice would tell her what kind of shit she was in now. Once again, under his blue-eyed scrutiny, she felt that glimmer of intensity between them. Helen turned away and started to rub her leg. "But of course the real damage is coming now, isn't it?"

Ludy shifted on the seat. "Meaning?"

Helen couldn't help it. She started to laugh. "Fuck, just come out with it, Ludy. You think I'm just shit, and we both know it. So cut the crap and do whatever it is you feel like doing. Get it over with."

The detective set his flashlight down on the pew between them. Its light bounced off dark dusty wood and sent shadows at odd angles across the room. Ludy's flat face gleamed, vivid in the gloom, as if hanging severed in the air. "You are trespassing, aren't you?"

Helen sat up, pain forgotten, startled at his mild tone. What was going on now? "Surely that's good for a fine, at least," she said, studying his face.

He shrugged. "Let's just say you owe me one."

"Okay, Ludy. I don't get it. Here's your chance to ream me and you're just sitting there like you're waiting for communion. What happened? Where's Deets and all the rest of your little boy scout troop?" Shit, she was talking too much — covering her strange reaction to him and hoping to scoff her way out of this.

Ludy looked at her. "We're all alone here, Helen. It's just you and me tonight. I'm trespassing too. Nobody knows I'm here." In the play of light and shadows his face remained impassive. Her pain finally fading, Helen felt tension tremble through her exhausted arms and legs. She wasn't sure what the man was about to dish out but it couldn't be good. She actually flinched when he stood up, leaning forward on the wooden railing. He gazed up at the empty altar. "This reminds me of my old church in Louisiana," he finally said, his words echoing up into the broken ceiling. "I like these old ones, you know? Not all plain wood and flat walls, like in the new modern ones. I like 'em like this, with all kinds of niches and corners and little statues in the corners. They don't build churches like this now. No room for all those painted statues and holy pictures."

Helen decided not to comment that she wasn't a Catholic — had in fact been brought up in a stridently fundamentalist church that thought Catholics and communists were both sliding down the slippery path of damnation. Not to mention lesbians. Ludy turned around slowly, folded his arms across his chest and cocked his head to look at her. At least, that's what it looked like — she couldn't see his face at all now. When he spoke again the venom was creeping back into his voice. "It's the drawings, right? You wanted a look at the church same time Sissy might have been here."

Helen kept waiting silently, not sure how to proceed. Ludy apparently took her silence for surprise. "Yeah, I know you think all us cops down here are just shoveling in doughnuts and chewing tobacco, picking our overalls out of our crotches."

"Don't tell me what I think, Ludy," Helen said, stung into responding. "A shield in your pocket doesn't turn you into a super hero. We both know you pulled me out of that hole just to fuck with me a little longer." Fuck, she cursed herself. That had to be shock from the fall, to make her snap that way at Ludy. Now she'd pay for those angry words.

To her astonishment he just sat down. Yeah, he was mad, but not at her. It was almost as though he hadn't even heard her. His next words confirmed that suspicion. "I haven't been back in a Catholic church for six years," he said. "Not since Theresa's funeral."

His wife? Daughter? Lover? Helen stayed rigidly silent, not wishing to compound her previous error. She could see Ludy's face again. Not anger, exactly — grim and determined. A kind of cold and empty hate, maybe. Without passion, but grown from a foundation of steely rage that had hardened over time into a permanently fixed mask. "She was twelve, about Sissy Greene's age. We know who it was, the asshole who worked in park maintenance. He'd done the same thing to three other girls — kept 'em all for about a week before he finally killed 'em. We even know where he did it, one of the maintenance sheds in the park. But he got to walk. Fucking lawyers." Ludy's mouth worked, his jaws clenching and relaxing, then a big sigh. "I keep track of him, though. Right now he's in Alabama, working on a garbage truck. Piece of shit learned his lesson. He won't start up again for a good long while. Theresa was the last."

"Is that why you left New Orleans?" Helen ventured.

He didn't seem to mind the question. He almost laughed. "It was leave or be asked to leave, in the end. After Theresa, my wife took off. Then things just — it was time to go." Better not to pursue that history. Ludy stared at the bare wall over the altar, seeing — what? Scenes of his own shattered life, maybe. Helen gazed with him, wondering what nightmares played out in Ludy's mind every night. In glorious technicolor, no doubt. Just like hers. "And this is a lot closer to Alabama, anyhow."

An ugly thought flashed through Helen's mind. "It's not the same guy this time, though, right?" Her thoughts flew back through the few details from the scene she could recall. No, it had certainly appeared Sissy had been on the run when she was killed. And she'd disappeared only the previous afternoon.

"Nothing like his m.o.," Ludy said. His tone remained almost conversational, like he was shooting the shit with a colleague over a beer. An act? Maybe. Dammit, she couldn't see his face. "I can see why the kid liked it here, though — especially after a day in that boarding house. But what the hell happened?"

"She runs off after listening to her mother ranting at Gary Greene on the phone," Helen said. "You think she came here — her special hiding place. Then — what? Somebody kills her here? No, she sees something here. Something that she wasn't supposed to see. Runs away, whoever was here first runs after her." Jesus. Kyle and Bertie. That auto repair shop was only a couple of blocks away. And the gun Helen had dropped into the river? "How did she die, Ludy?" God, she had to know. Had to risk that question. "The papers didn't say anything, and I couldn't see —"

"Shot." He gestured in the darkness, maybe pointing to his own head. Helen slumped back in the pew, grief flooding her body in a painful rush. "Someone must have shot her while she was running."

"So who was in here? What were they doing?" Helen knew as soon as she spoke that she'd gone too far with the shop talk. Perhaps the image of Sissy running from her murderer shook his willingness to confide, or maybe it was Helen's pointed questions. She sensed him freezing up beside her. Great. Now he'd always regret that he'd revealed so much of his past, shown his weakness, and to a lesbian at that. "You have some idea who it was?" she finished lamely.

Ludy shook his head with a pained expression. "You know better than that. Quit being stupid. You haven't been stupid until tonight. I fucking hate stupid."

"So coming in here was stupid?"

"Then we were both stupid, I guess." Ludy stood up again, taking the flashlight. Helen looked at him and saw his face settle into the same pattern of irritation she'd become accustomed to. "By the way, an old friend of yours has been hanging around with Kyle Mapple lately."

"Really?" Shit. Bertie Mullins. Which meant Kyle must have talked. "How is Kyle? All I know is Mrs. Mapple ran out of the house to go to the hospital." She'd have to be very, very careful what questions she asked right now. There was no telling what story Kyle might have given the police.

"He'll live. The car was totaled. Kyle came out of it with a concussion and a broken leg. Maybe you and Bertie would like to send him some flowers," Ludy went on, looming over her in the darkness.

Okay, she could play a little dumb for a few minutes. "The only Bertie I know is Bertie Mullins," Helen said slowly. "I know she's out now, but we're not exactly bosom buddies."

"Oh, I thought that's exactly what you were." Was he grinning? Leering? Helen wasn't sure, given the shadows. "Surely she'd want to look up her old girlfriends."

Helen took a deep breath. She would have to make the truth work for her — at least, some of the truth. Besides, Ludy apparently already knew Bertie had been poking around Tynedale, maybe even knew she'd come to harass Helen the night Sissy died. "Yes, she did. But it was a very short visit. I sent her back home and haven't seen her since. Just like I told Wanda."

"Your parole officer."

"That's right." Helen fought to keep her face blank. She bent over her injured leg, flexed the muscles, willed the darkness to work in her favor. For something to work in her favor, for once. When Ludy didn't move, she added, "Listen, detective. I know Bertie Mullins is bad news, all right? I don't plan on having anything to do with her, ever. You'll be the first to know if she shows up again."

Helen must have caught just the right mixture of belligerence and fear in her tone. Ludy turned away and slowly edged across the front of the church. He paused near the pedestal by the vestry, leaned down and picked something up from the floor. "Your flashlight," he called out. "You might need it." He stood there, clearly not willing to leave without Helen.

Helen sighed and got up — thank god, nothing seemed broken or sprained — and made her way to Ludy. She took the flashlight from him and let him lead her outside. Once free of the ruined building, they both stood breathing deeply of the cool night air. Stars gleamed in a spray of light across the clear sky. Autumn had settled in, Helen realized with surprise. She reached out to touch the chain link fence, her fingers laced around the cold metal. Her hand jerked on the fence, sending a rattling echo through the silence, when Ludy spoke. "You haven't asked me about Kyle and Bertie."

Helen let her hand drop to her side and faced him. He stood like a black pillar against the deeper blackness of the church. "I figured you already told me everything you want me to know about them," Helen countered.

"So you only saw Bertie once? Never went along for a little party with Kyle and Bertie? You're sticking to that?"

Helen felt the last of her patience drain away. She leaned against the church door, her entire body aching with exhaustion. "Ludy, you're in control here. You can do what you want. I've told you the truth — I have all along. So go ahead and make what you want of it. No? Nothing else to say? Then I'm going home. I've had all the excitement I need for one night."

Helen went back across the gravel, her footsteps grating in the dark silence of the churchyard. Ludy stayed behind, his flashlight dark. Helen had no doubt he stared at her retreating back with contempt. She only stumbled a little on her way to the Rambler, her right leg threatening to buckle when she put all her weight on it. Hell, it was probably one big purple bruise, from ankle to thigh. She made it inside the car without falling down, and as she drove off she got one last look at Ludy standing outside the church, like some alien plaster saint fixed to the condemned building.

Helen steered the car through the narrow streets lined with old houses. Yellow lights from front windows beamed warm gold across the battered hood as she circled back towards the church. This time she took a side street that ran behind the church and came up on the other end of the alley where the auto shop stood. Helen turned off the engine, waited. No sign of Ludy anywhere. Quiet and dark, just like it should be. Yes, that stretch up ahead — that was the path leading to the park. And the church a couple of blocks beyond. Now that she had a good idea of the layout, she could even map out how Sissy might have run from the condemned building to the muddy hill a few yards away.

She sat there in the car, lights and engine off, drumming her fingertips on the steering wheel. What the fuck did she think she was doing now? Waiting for some kind of clue to pop up, bright and shiny and plain as Ludy's nose? Something pretty to take to the cops, prove she was a good little reformed girl after all. Idiot.

The line of light under the auto shop's door sliced a thin edge of white brilliance across the oil stains and cracks in the aging asphalt of the alley. Okay, now what? Helen felt an ache in her palms from gripping the steering wheel. Get out of the car? Try to listen? Go back and see if Ludy was still at the church?

She opened the car door, easing it past that point where it always creaked. For the first time she felt grateful that the ancient Rambler's inner lights didn't work. The chill wind blew across her face, making her eyes water. How the fuck did it get so cold so fast? Chips of light from stars and the moon floated in the puddles. Helen stepped carefully across the alley, her body tense with the strain of listening through the breeze that gusted through the narrow street. Nothing — just black and silent and cold. She felt her way to the niche between the auto shop and the warehouse, where she'd waited and listened Saturday afternoon as Kyle had barely escaped a beating.

Too late Helen heard the muffled sound of footsteps beside her. Bertie Mullins' perfect teeth showed in a happy grin. "Just in time for the party," she chuckled.

Chapter Thirteen

Yep, the whole gang was there — Dave, Curtis and Mackie stood behind Bertie, leaning on an assortment of cars that waited for attention in the bays. A quick glance at their faces showed Helen that all three men looked to Bertie for guidance. Their eyes moved in their otherwise impassive faces, continuously following Bertie as she paced edgily around the room, only briefly shifting to focus on Helen. Helen gripped the crate she perched on, her right leg sending a vague message of pain she hardly noticed. It was getting hard to breathe. The fumes mingled in close stale air gave her the beginnings of a serious headache.

Bertie paused in front of Helen. Helen forced herself to breathe the foul air, forced herself to study Bertie's face closely. Her mind shied away from the potential outcome. If they'd been responsible for Sissy's death, why would they hesitate to do the same — or worse — to Helen? And Bertie had that eerie expression Helen remembered from Deasely. Like there was something else sheathed in Bertie's small, sturdy body, fangs and fur breaking through the human façade.

Bertie's little grinning face shoved in close to Helen's. The smell of cigarettes and alcohol blurred on her breath. Helen froze so she wouldn't appear to be cringing from the other woman. A tiny vein pulsed in Bertie's throat. Then without warning Bertie placed gentle hands on Helen's cheeks and drew her in for a kiss.

The hands may have been gentle, but her kiss was not. Bertie's tongue shoved its way in past Helen's teeth, sucking her own tongue hard. Through the pounding in her ears Helen heard a snigger from the guys. She tried to focus her gaze past Bertie's golden curls, into the room, to see what the three mouseketeers might be doing. Bertie released her, finally, with a bruising twist of lips that left Helen gasping for air. And not just from shock or fear, either. Even in the midst of her terror Helen could feel a faint pulse of response, deep in her guts, that only added to the overwhelming sense of despair at the situation. No time, though, to ponder her twisted state of mind. Helen stayed silent and dragged her palm across her lips, her eyes staying on Bertie's weirdly triumphant expression. Then she spat on the floor. Specks of saliva spattered Bertie's expensive boots, but Bertie didn't seem to notice.

"Bet that got you wet. Want me to find out?" Bertie's tiny childlike hand moved close to Helen's crotch, and one of the guys — Dave, Helen thought — let out his breath in a wavery sigh. Great. A gang-bang along with everything else, and Bertie running the show. It doesn't get any better.

Helen shrugged, said nothing. Somehow she must have managed to keep her face blank. Bertie paused, a wave of confusion passing over her delicate features. Helen decided to ignore the men. Bertie was obviously running this show, so Bertie was the key to controlling this situation. Helen stood still, unflinching as Bertie's fingers played with the zipper tab of Helen's jeans. Another second, and her fly was open, those slim fingers poking at her thatch of pubic hair. Suddenly an image flashed through Helen's mind — bare gray walls and ugly green linoleum lit by harsh light. No, not this place, although the walls were similar. Deasely shimmered in her mind's eye, her memory of the stink of its antiseptic-bathed halls mingling with the nauseating fumes of the auto repair shop. The stares of Bertie's pals blended with Helen's re-collection of the flat indifferent glances of the other inmates at the facility. And Bertie's little hand, pawing at her crotch — that was familiar enough. With painful clarity Helen recalled night after night of Bertie's amorous advances, all surprisingly similar. On her very first night in the cell Helen shared with Bertie, Helen had felt the younger woman's gaze on her back, her legs, her ass.

"I always take the top."

Helen froze in the act of stowing her few belongings on an empty shelf. She turned around to see Bertie's grin stretched across her little white teeth. Helen shrugged, felt her face settle into the blank mask she'd adopted for her new self.

Apparently that hadn't been good enough for Bertie. "I'm not just talking about the bunk, either," and she'd hopped lightly down onto the floor. Helen fiddled a few moments longer as she sensed Bertie prowling behind her. She gave up at last and turned to face Bertie. The girl was leaning against the wall, eyes narrowed as she stared into Helen's face.

Great. "Whatever," Helen had said. The overhead lights flashed once, twice to signal lights out, casting eerie shadows through the bars. The small cell seemed to close in on Helen, and for a moment she couldn't breathe.

Then as the lights stayed on for another few minutes,

Helen turned away from her new roommate and tried not to think of those bright little eyes watching her as she struggled into the blue shift issued to all inmates for sleep wear. It bagged out loosely over her knees. She felt small and helpless in her ugly garb, standing in the middle of a tiny room. The cell plunged into darkness as the lights shut off, and Helen went to bed, stifling a sigh. The weeks she'd already spent behind bars hadn't inured her to the constant sound of other people. Snores, sneezes and coughs, mutters and cries from the dreams and nightmares of two hundred sixty five other women penetrated her mind and chased away any hopes of rest.

Tonight, though — this first night in her new cell — something else broke through her efforts to find enough peace to sleep. Helen's last cell-mate, a tall thin woman with skin as black as ebony and the beautifully sculpted face of a queen, had thankfully been a silent sleeper. Bertie, on the other hand, tossed and turned and tumbled around on the bunk, heaving big sighs and worrying at the sheets. When all the noise subsided, Helen allowed herself a deep breath of relief. Finally. But then she saw Bertie's legs on the rungs leading down to the floor, followed by her sturdy little body. Bertie stood looking down at Helen in the darkness, then leaned over and put her face close to Helen's.

First came the hot breath on her neck, often rousing her from an uneasy sleep after tossing on the narrow bunk for a couple of hours. Then a whispered word or two, something short and sweet like "let's fuck." Silence meant consent for Bertie, and at this point she would slide noiselessly under the sheet and wrap her leg over Helen's thigh.

In the beginning it had just seemed easier to let it happen. Still in that weird frame of mind that had carried Helen through her trial and conviction — a distancing from her surroundings, from events, from her own life flowing by — Helen would lie with legs open to Bertie's probing, barely twitching in response as the other woman thrust and sighed and slid sweaty skin over her body. Then there would be the final grunt, a jarring shift of skimpy mattress as Bertie vacated Helen's bunk and crept up to her own again.

"Hey! I'm talking to you!" The slap stung Helen's cheek. In reflex Helen's hand moved toward her face, her fingers tracing the marks left by Bertie's palm. The scenes from Deasely blurred, edges melding into the auto shop and the three men leering at her from the mangled hulks of cars that weren't going anywhere. Helen felt the wall pressing into her back, the grit under her shoes, breathed in the thick smell of motor oil. For a moment she stared out across the room. Helen realized with a start that she hadn't remembered that first night since she'd left Deasely. And now here it was, flooding her consciousness with immediate clarity.

"That's better." Bertie's hot breath, redolent of liquor, blew across Helen's face. She could feel Bertie's hand playing with her crotch again. The younger woman leaned in closer. Her erect nipples prodded Helen's chest, and she rubbed them gently back and forth to arouse a similar response in Helen. "We'd better get down to business," she murmured as her fingers again slithered deeper between Helen's legs. "These boys tend to get impatient."

Sniggers from the audience. Helen let her gaze move out across Bertie's narrow shoulders, past the men hunched in the background, trying to pin down what she felt. Anger? Sort of. No, not really that. More like a sense of liberation. Like she'd cast something off her shoulders that had been weighing her down for a long time. What the hell was this? Helen puzzled at it for a moment but was quickly drawn back to the present when Bertie slapped her again.

Bertie paused, reared back, turned those childlike blue eyes back to Helen's face. "You might as well get into it, bitch," she muttered. Her heart wasn't in it though. Helen met her stare and saw the confusion coursing through Bertie's eyes. Good. The sense of weightlessness grew and filled her

216

body. Helen felt herself smile. More confusion for Bertie, who started to pull away.

"Not so fast," Helen whispered. She grabbed Bertie's hand and pulled it back below her waist. "You didn't finish what you started."

Now Bertie was completely freaked out. Fear passed over her face as she failed to pull away from Helen's grip. Then the fear was replaced with pain. Helen's grin widened as she felt Bertie's hand twist in her own. Helen tightened her clasp around Bertie's wrist, forcing the other woman's hand to bend backward. Painfully. Bertie's fingers twitched but Helen kept her grasp firm. Her face creased in astonishment, Bertie let out a small high-pitched whine. Helen glanced over Bertie's shoulder as she hunched forward. Good, the men were confused, too — if that vacant look in their faces was anything besides their usual expression. The three of them moved uncertainly, shifting from foot to foot between the cars, stealing glances at each other.

Bertie finally pulled free and cradled her injured hand close to her body. Helen kept smiling as she zipped her fly, enjoying the ugly red flush that crept up the other woman's face. Time for taunts? No, maintain a grim silence, stay neutral, Helen thought. Another quick look at the men told Helen they would stand their ground until they saw what Bertie was going to do — although that situation could change at any moment. Were they really that brainless? Maybe that's the only kind of men Bertie allowed in her life. A weird suspicion half-formed in Helen's mind, that possibly Bertie had slept with them and used sex to pull the strings. Could be. Certainly control laid the foundation for the way she'd raped Helen their first night together. Bertie had recognized Helen as the perfect victim. Defeated, no will, no energy to fight what was happening to her — she would have spotted Helen a mile away. Probably had, in fact, and then gleefully enjoyed the luck that had tossed Helen into her cell.

Bertie's eyes, brimming with unshed tears, glared up at

Helen. "Cute," she muttered as she stood up straight. "Just not cute enough, bitch." Her gaze faltered as she met Helen's eyes, and she turned to glance over her shoulder. The men, alive to Bertie's every gesture, moved forward a couple of steps. Shit. In reflex Helen tried to move back, only to meet the wall. She looked down. Not a fucking thing in the vicinity to help her. Not even a damn crowbar, or chain, or any of the stuff auto repair shops were supposed to have lying around. Just some shiny patches of oil puddling in the uneven floor.

"I think we should fuck you before we kill you. What do you say, boys?"

The goons smiled. Terrific. Order had been restored in their little world, and their happy faces loomed up in the shadows as they approached the two women. Helen heard someone's zipper slide open. "Whyn't you get her ready, Bertie?"

"Suits me just fine." Her calm somewhat restored, Bertie raised her arms and perched her hands on the wall beside Helen's head. A gleam of metal near Bertie's waist caught Helen's eye, and she glanced down to see a gun tucked in the belt. Helen tried to concentrate on the gun as one of the men pinned her own arms up over her head. Like a vague memory Helen's right leg, still sore from being twisted at the abandoned church, reminded Helen with a scissor of pain that she'd already been through one wrenching experience this evening — and might not be able to drum up the energy for more. Bertie's hands slid down the wall and moved across Helen's shoulders to her breasts. She kneaded the tender flesh with brute abandon, staring into Helen's eyes as if searching for signs of distress.

All righty, then. Maybe the death she'd managed to avoid this far, despite all the events of the past decade of her life, had finally caught up with her, as solid and flat and sure as the bricks pressing into her back. Again that sense of liberation flooded Helen's body. Irritated, she set aside the strange feeling. Now was not the time for analysis. She had to figure out how to get out of there alive. Alive. Unlike Sissy. Sissy, who'd desperately struggled up the muddy slope behind the park to get away from her killers.

That was just the inspiration Helen needed. With a light clean sense of detachment Helen let herself free-fall, depending on the man holding her by the wrists to keep her from dropping to the floor altogether. Sure enough, he grunted, startled, but held on tight. Bertie took Helen's apparent faltering as an encouraging sign. She smiled again, moved her face in close, licked Helen's throat. Then she slid both hands down Helen's torso. "Give me a hand here, guys," she said in a hoarse whisper. Helen felt her jeans give way as the other two men jerked the pant legs down. Helen forced her legs to remain weak and floppy, fighting the urge to stiffen and kick back. She then urged a whimper out of her throat. The sound excited Bertie, whose breath was hot and stinking in Helen's face. Helen shut off the nausea that rose up when Bertie shoved her fingers into Helen's crotch and concentrated instead on getting at least one hand free. Good. The guy keeping her pinned to the wall had taken away one hand so as to stroke himself, and with his continuing distraction his grip on her wrists had loosened. Helen moaned again, twisting her head from side to side in a faked display of fear. With each gyration she eased her right hand closer to freedom. Then in one jerky motion the hand flailed out, flopping down onto Bertie's shoulder.

Deep in her own heated fantasy of violence, trusting her pals to assist her, Bertie barely seemed to notice when Helen cautiously moved her free hand. With rising anger Helen noted that she herself had indeed gotten hot and wet between the legs. Jesus. Even this horror couldn't freeze her up, apparently. In some background crevice of her mind Helen filed away this current outrage to be dealt with later. At least her wet cunt gave her the advantage of keeping Bertie distracted.

Helen reached for the gun just as Bertie plunged fingers deep in a painful thrust. At the same moment she clamped her teeth down hard on Bertie's earlobe. A gratifying screech of agonized shock greeted Helen's ears. Bertie recoiled, tried to pull away, then realized she'd leave a portion of ear behind if she jerked back too fast. Helen felt her fingers close around the gun and she grunted with the effort of pulling it out while keeping her hold on the other woman. In the background the three men stood in varying stages of stupefied arousal, a bit slow on the uptake. Was this some new and exciting lesbian love rite? They started to move only as Helen began to pull the gun free of Bertie's clothes.

She wasn't fast enough, though. Too late Helen realized that Bertie had figured it out and now held the gun firmly in one hand. The other hand clamped down on her bleeding ear. Trickles of red dripped through her little fingers onto her shirt. Bertie took the hand away from her ear and looked down at her own blood. Both arms now free, Helen relaxed against the wall, her bare legs shivering in the cold dank air. Then Bertie slapped her. Three times the bloody palm stung on Helen's face, leaving sticky red smears on her skin. Helen registered the blows from some vast distance, a chasm that had formed in her mind and body between inner and outer reality. Yes, this would be it, she thought. Now. It's finished. Shouldn't she be feeling something? Not just this sense of being drained. As if a valve had opened in her toes and emptied her of feeling, of will, of reason. Her eyes followed the small round opening of the gun barrel as it traced the cleavage between her breasts and lodged at her sternum. Helen looked up again. Bertie smiled. Thin streams of blood webbed in the cross-hatch of wrinkles forming at the corners of her mouth and eyes. Helen felt a sudden and surely inappropriate curiosity. Bertie had always seemed so childlike in appearance, so small and dainty and deceptively fragile. How could those age lines show up on her cherubic little face?

A muted click told Helen the safety was off, the gun was

ready to fire, her life was over. "I think we're done playing now, don't you?" Silence. The guys, silent and still, watched and breathed and waited. Helen heard someone loudly licking their lips. The cold hard metal etched a circle on her chest. Helen knew how it felt to be shot. First the surprise as body and mind rebelling against the invasion. Then intense hot pain, slivering from the point of entry to spread outward like fire, also a big puzzling surprise. Then, if you were lucky — as she'd been lucky the first time she'd been gut-shot — oblivion. Bertie should get her in the heart if she kept the gun pointed at her chest. Fast and clean and painless. Strange, how the only thing she seemed able to keep in her mind was the memory of Valerie's long thick black hair on a white pillow. Her blue eyes alight with pleasure from Helen's hands and mouth. Would Valerie ever know what had happened to her?

"Can't say it's been a pleasure, Helen. Now you're just another piece of shit to wipe up." Was that a wistful smile playing at Bertie's mouth? "It could have been a lot of fun, too."

"Bertie — I dunno —"

"Shut the fuck up." Whoever had spoken subsided. In the silence Helen heard Bertie's breath moving in and out of her small sturdy body. Other things cracked through Helen's consciousness as she waited for death. The rustle of some small animal, probably a rat, scurrying to safety in the shadows. Something dripping from one of the cars on the racks. Wind creaking at the grimed windows. The gleam of Bertie's gun under the fluorescent light. Crunching sounds on the gravel outside.

Wait. The gravel outside. Bertie heard it, too. With one glance from her the men sprang into action. One of them killed the overhead lights, and suddenly the room filled with shadows, gray and darker gray under the thin stream of moonlight filtered in through the skylight over the bays. Another man wove a path through the cars to the window at the front of the shop, peering out through the accumulated oily dirt to get a look at who was out there. Helen felt Bertie's gun move away from her chest. She stayed against the wall, not sure if she ought to move. As she watched the three men darting in confusion around the shop, Helen realized that Bertie was the only one armed. Jesus. What the hell was going on? Maybe Bertie had gotten a little too big for her britches this time, surrounding herself with shit-brained wannbes while she got to play queen bee. Maybe Bertie wouldn't have killed her after all. Maybe they hadn't killed Sissy. Maybe it would turn out to be some big stupid game. Bertie's game, fueled by her skewed desire for power and the willingness of idiots like these three — and Kyle — to play along so they could prove their own manhood. Given their panicked scurrying it made sense. Helen slumped on the wall in confusion, noticing belatedly that Bertie had deserted her.

Fuck. It was time to quit playing philosopher and try to get the hell out of here. Helen managed to tug her pants back up over her legs, then crouched down as low as she could. More footsteps outside — several sets of them, in fact. Cars pulled up. The squawk of a radio. The police? Impossible. This was no movie.

But the shouted demand for those inside the shop to come out and surrender confirmed her misgivings. Talk about the fucking cavalry. Helen took a deep breath and crawled away from the wall toward the uncertain shelter of an old Buick. Good solid old vehicle, manufactured in the U S of A at some point in the distant past. Surely its metal hide would protect her from flying bullets. Helen slowly shook her head, trying to chase down a thread of thought that didn't quite fit the pattern weaving across her mind. This just wasn't right, somehow. A gun-toting Bertie and the three mouseketeers out for a gang bang didn't have a niche in the relatively small-potatoes operation Kyle would have been caught up in. It was some stolen computers, for Christ's sake, not a Machiavellian master criminal mind bent on world domination. A shoot out with the cops felt all wrong, like the Keystones meet Freddie Kruger or something.

A whiny voice broke through Helen's fuddled thoughts. "Now what, Bertie? It ain't supposed to be like this. You said —"

"Just shut the fuck up, all right?" Helen knew that undertone of fear. Around the front tire of the Buick Helen saw Bertie squatting next to a partly dismantled pickup, blood still gleaming at her earlobe. Bertie looked over at Helen, opened her mouth as if to speak, then suddenly light flooded the building.

Apparently they'd not been able to stand the suspense any longer. Two of Bertie's comrades stood framed in silhouette at the entrance to the shop, hands stretched up over their heads. The glare of headlights from the cars lined up outside set off their capture in high relief as hands pulled them aside and out of view, presumably off to handcuffs and police cars and the local jail.

Helen glanced at Bertie again. The other woman's face was blank with shock at the desertion of her two hand-picked associates. The shock hardened to fury at the sound of weeping from across the room. "I'll rip you a new asshole if you don't shut the fuck up," she hissed.

"They're gonna kill us, Bertie — those cops are gonna kill us."

"I'm gonna kill you! You need to be scared of me more than them!"

Helen debated the wisdom of trying to advance from the Buick to the pickup truck just beyond. Right past the truck the door stood wide open. Bertie frowned at the floor, her forehead wrinkled in thought. Maybe it would work. Helen got down on hands and knees and started the crawl. Bertie's voice sounded quietly at her back.

"Not so fast, cunt." She turned to see Bertie's dead stare,

the one that meant she was past any kind of reason. It was a look Helen remembered very well from Deasely. "You and me are going together."

"Bertie, don't be an idiot. Taking me hostage isn't going to help you at all, and it might even make things worse for you." Helen mouthed the words, knowing they wouldn't even register with Bertie, while she noted the patches of oil right next to the other woman's boots. Good. If she could get her to side step into the oil, she might be able to throw Bertie off balance and get out. Just a little closer, she willed Bertie. For a second or two, as Bertie crept between the cars toward the Buick, Helen thought she had a chance. One more inch — now.

Ludy chose that moment to make his dramatic entrance. Later Helen couldn't recall a single word he said. His yelled demand echoed across the rows of cars, startling both women. Helen jerked forward in a final lunge to reach Bertie's gun, slipping on the oil as she pitched forward. The next thing she knew the concrete floor had somehow gotten on her face. A piercing pain stitched through her eyes and she screwed her eyelids tight shut against it. A muffled moan came out of nowhere — no, it must be out of her mouth — and Helen turned her head to get away from the pain. She could see Bertie sitting on the floor, her ass smack in the middle of a pool of grease, her back pressed to a stack of tires.

At the edge of her blurred vision Helen saw a man approach. More shouts in the distance. Flashlights bobbing and weaving strange patterns on the ceiling, on the cars, on the floor. Who the hell was this guy? Through streaming eyes and a veil of pain that threatened to plunge her into unconsciousness, Helen made out a wide girth straining at the official uniform of the Tynedale police. Deets. So it really was John Wayne and the cavalry after all.

Bertie panted, sweated, turned to look at Helen. Her

mouth gaped open. Shock? Fear? Surprise? Delight? What the hell was it? Helen's gaze moved painfully from Bertie's baffled face to the gun lying on the floor next to the pickup, about a foot away from Bertie's hand.

Deets murmured something, gave Helen a quick glance right before Helen closed her eyes in the futile fight against the knot on her head. "Over here!" Deets shouted. "We need an ambulance, she's out cold."

But I'm not. Helen finally unglued her eyelids and realized she hadn't said the words — just thought them. I'm awake, I'm ready to get the bad guys, I'm with you. Her mouth kept trying to open but nothing came out. She focused her eyes on Deets walking closer to Bertie. The other woman silently shook her head, the odd look of puzzlement still fixed on her blood-streaked features. As Deets came closer, his gun steadily pointed out in front of him, Bertie shook her head and threw her hands up over her eyes.

The next few seconds went by in a montage of disconnected images in Helen's mind during her final moments of awareness. Was she back at Deasely? No, the smells were all wrong. It was just the concrete under her back. No, that was wrong. And whose shoes were those off to the side? Sissy's? Hers were worn and dirty, just like those — no, the shoes Helen saw now were just too big for Sissy. And wasn't Sissy gone somewhere? Wait. Wait.

Then someone said something. A woman's voice. Oh, God, maybe it was Valerie with her. But the words were all wrong. Like something out of a different language. Then she couldn't feel the concrete beneath her any longer. That meant something important, but Helen couldn't remember what. She couldn't be falling but the discernment of time and space was more than she could process right now. Maybe it didn't matter, anyhow.

No, it wasn't Sissy sitting against the stacked tires. Maybe it was Deasely after all, because it was Bertie's face gleaming with sweat. Bertie's hands reaching out for something, the gleam of Bertie's gun in the glow of a flashlight, the short sharp dart of orange fire as Deets' gun went off. Bertie's hands stayed in the air for what seemed like years as a red wave flowed across her chest. Head and hands drooped down as Helen faded into the peace of a big blank nothing.

Chapter Fourteen

Light pierced Helen's eyes, knifing through her head and blurring her vision. She blinked a few times, trying to focus on whatever that tall shiny thing was standing next to the bed. Come to think of it, the bed felt unfamiliar, too. Oh, right. Hospital. And that tall shiny thing was an IV stand. Jesus, was it that bad? A glance down at her arms dissipated her fears — no tubes running from her veins, and no clear plastic bag holding some mysterious fluid hanging from the stand. She sighed with relief, even though the movement of her head had caused a fresh stab of pain, as though someone was throwing darts just beneath the surface of her forehead.

Helen closed her eyes and subsided against the flat pillows. Memories flooded her mind as soon as the pain had faded a bit. Memories she would far rather not have. The last time she'd been laid up like this was when someone had shot her in the abdomen. She felt her fingers stray across the covers, touching her own skin near her navel. The scar from that bullet was now just a thin ridge of flesh, a bump as familiar to her as her eyes and ears and nose. A part of who she was, the way Deasely was now imprinted on her bones like a deep scar. All those hours of therapy, both physical and mental, had boiled down to a pink slice of skin. Until now. She opened her eyes again. Last time, when she'd emerged from the coma, her old friend Father Hitchcock had been sitting by the bed, his face drawn with fatigue, his eyes lit with gladness as she croaked a bleary hello at him. Today, though, she was most definitely alone.

Someone in pale pink scrubs holding a clipboard walked in. "Good, you're awake." A doctor? No, maybe a nurse. Helen had a vague recollection of a skinny young man who looked like he'd just graduated junior high. He'd identified himself last night as Doctor Something or Other — she couldn't recall. And certainly this woman, with her plump round face and generous bosom, didn't look a thing like him.

Nurse E. Carmody — that's what her name tag read — checked Helen's pulse and temperature and fussed with a few other things while Helen lay very still, hoping to keep pain at bay. "How's your head?" E. Carmody asked as she made a few notes on her clipboard.

"It's definitely right here. Not too happy, I think," Helen said in a hoarse voice.

"Let's see if you can eat some breakfast before we try any medication." Helen struggled to sit up, hoping she wouldn't upchuck with the motion. The nurse assisted, expertly pushing pillows and movable tables around. "Maybe some toast?"

"Sure." Anything, just so she could sit still. The room stopped spinning as Nurse Carmody walked briskly from the room. The pain was a little better, too, now that she was upright. And maybe she did need some food, after all. Helen breathed in and out, deep and slow, trying to put her thoughts together. Too bad she'd been unable to question the cute friendly nurse about why the fuck she was in here. Tentatively Helen felt her body through the hospital gown and stiff white sheets. Nope, no real injuries. Just a broken head, it seemed. From that fall onto the concrete floor of —

Then it all came back in a sickening rush. Helen closed her eyes against the images, but it was no good. Like a movie it unfolded in technicolor, the almost-rape followed by a shootout with the local police. The three men whining in fear as their little party got interrupted and things didn't go as planned. The stench of dead cars and stagnant motor oil. Even the scurrying of tiny feet as some rat or raccoon or squirrel headed for the hills once the denouement was warming up.

And Bertie's body, slumped on the floor in front of a stack of tires, blood spreading a dark stain on her chest, her hands open and twitching on her lap as Deets lowered his own weapon. Great, now she really would throw up. Okay, concentrate on here and now, Helen lectured herself. I didn't get shot this time — that's good. Maybe a concussion? Maybe that's why they kept me overnight. She gingerly moved her legs under the sheets — no apparent problem there beyond some aching in her right leg. What the — oh, yeah, the little expedition to the church. Maybe, Helen mused, I should find a hobby soon. Knitting. Decopage. Something dull. As she let her mind rove over her body, taking in all the bumps and scrapes and dents, the final image of Bertie's dead body slouched forward, of Deets' meaty paw cradling his own gun, kept nagging at her like a tongue probing a sore tooth. What? Something there, something beyond the horror of watching the other woman die, something more than the fear that tasted like copper in her mouth. Damn, she'd lost it. And the irritation made her head worse. Fine. Enough of that. Time to get ready for toast.

Helen opened her eyes and tried to take in her surroundings. Tynedale didn't have its own hospital. Maybe this was Vicksburg? Possibly Jackson. She'd ask E. Carmody as soon as the nurse came back. Helen found herself hoping the round-faced smiling woman would come back soon. Okay, so she wasn't dead yet. Now that the pain in her head had receded a bit she let her gaze wander about the room. Nothing very interesting — the usual white-washed walls, an inoffensive Impressionist print of flowers and trees on one side, a television perched on a mount suspended from the ceiling. To Helen's left, a window spattered with raindrops displaying a gray sky and sodden rooftops. Beyond the buildings the thick brown Mississippi flowed sluggishly south, draining as it had for generations from the rich loam of the Delta and onward to the Gulf of Mexico. So it was Vicksburg Memorial, after all. She'd have to find some other reason to get E. Carmody to talk to her.

To Helen's right an empty hospital bed stretched out blank and vacant. It wasn't a private room, then, but she happened to be alone this morning. Thank God for that — she couldn't have handled anyone else around at the moment. Was it sheer luck, or had the police requested that Helen be alone? She glanced through the little square window of the door just opposite. Maybe a cop was posted just outside the hall, to make sure no one came in or out without official approval. Her heart sank, overwhelming any remaining sensation of pain or nausea. Maybe she'd blown everything in one night. Maybe this hospital visit was only the preliminary to getting locked up again. And Ludy would make sure it was for good, if he could manage it.

E. Carmody came in with a tray holding a plate of wheat toast and a plastic cup containing a tea bag. "Here we are," she said as she smacked the tray down in front of Helen. "Let's see if you can keep this down, okay?"

"Listen, are there — is there a cop guarding this room?"

The nurse's pleasant face crumpled in confusion. "A cop? You mean, like to guard the room?"

"Well, yeah. Look, I'm trying to find out if I'm in some kind of trouble."

The smile came back. "The only trouble you're in, sweetie, is that you got a pretty bad knock on the head last night. We kept you for observation to make sure you didn't have a concussion — kept you awake for a long time, in fact." She touched Helen's shoulder gently and peered into her face. "Do you remember last night, hon?"

Hon. Helen resisted the urge to bury her sore head on E.'s bosom — it was staring her right in the face, for Christ's sake — and settled for leaning back on the pillows. "I kind of remember the doctor. Tall and skinny and looked like he could be my grandchild."

"Doctor Belden," the nurse chuckled. "He was on duty last night in the ER. And yes, he's young. But he's the best, don't you worry."

"So I'm not under arrest, then?" She opened her eyes. The toast actually didn't look too bad. And that looked like two packages of strawberry jam on the plate. Things were looking up.

"Actually, you're kind of a local hero at the moment. Oh, maybe these folks can tell you about all that," and she turned away to greet Ludy and Deets. "Just for a few minutes, boys — like we agreed. Okay?"

Ludy, to Helen's astonishment, gave the nurse a wink and a grin. Deets smiled, too. It was sort of discouraging to see the way E. Carmody responded to the male attention, blushing and shaking her head as she hurried out of the room. Oh well. Helen took a bite of toast and chewed slowly, watching as the two men shuffled into the room. Maybe she should wait to eat until they'd left. Her appetite might get ruined at any moment.

Wait, E. had said she was a hero. She watched and chewed some more as Ludy arranged himself in the plastic chair beside her bed, while Deets perched his weighty frame on the

231

empty hospital bed, notebook in hand. Neither man spoke at first. Deets scribbled something in his notebook, eyes focused on the page. Ludy coughed, cleared his throat, fiddled with his hands as if longing for something to occupy them. Helen took another bite of toast, then a sip of tea, relishing Ludy's discomfort. Was it just hospitals that got to him so? Maybe. Maybe, though, it was the fact that he'd have to be obliged to Helen for something heroic, whatever the hell that meant. That would surely stick in his craw. Then as she swallowed down bread and jam Helen remembered their conversation in the church last night. For just a moment, between sips of tea, Helen saw the detective once again as she'd seen him in the church — overwhelmed by guilt and grief, his rage covering an enormous black hole of hurt.

Ludy jerked his head back toward the hall. "They say you're going to be fine," he said. "No concussion, just some ugly bruises."

Helen finished her tea and set the cup down. "Good. Then I can get out of here and go home?" She hadn't meant it to come out a question, but she wanted to be sure Ludy wasn't going to lock her up. Helen glanced down to see her fingers trembling on the bed tray, then flattened her hands so the shaking stilled. "I mean, if the doctor says it's okay."

"Your aunt will be around later this afternoon to take you home."

"Aunt Edna? Why?" The toast didn't look so good any longer, and Helen set it aside. "What about Mrs. Mapple?"

Deets and Ludy looked at each other. Helen felt her headache coming back. E. Carmody had it wrong — she wasn't a hero, not just yet. They just hadn't gotten enough yet to haul her off to the pokey. Ludy cleared his throat again and Deets shuffled through his notebook. "Under the circumstances, I think Mrs. Mapple just wants to be home alone with her boy."

"So Kyle is going home, then." Better be careful — she still didn't know what Kyle might have said to them about his own involvement with the little gang Bertie had put together. Or about the gun. She wasn't out of the woods yet.

"According to the three stooges we rounded up last night, he was pretty much just a hanger on. A wannabe. We don't think he was directly involved with any of the robberies." Ludy squirmed out of the chair and stood in front of the window, staring out at the rain. "At this point we think it's a case for the psychiatrists, not the police. That's one fucked up kid, you know? Maybe we got him in time — first offense — I don't think we'll have any problems with the judge on it." He turned around and looked directly at Helen, challenge in his eyes. "Unless you know some reason why things should go different. Something someone said last night."

"No, nothing about Kyle at all." Ludy stared at her a moment, decided she wasn't going to talk any more, then went on for a while about Bertie's small-town set up. How she'd latched onto these guys in the local bars, persuaded them by her feminine wiles and the promise of easy money to do a little pilfering from Smart-Save, how Bertie had been the brains of the little gang. And, thank god, they'd confirmed that Helen had nothing to do with any of it, despite Bertie's best efforts to draw her in.

"Apparently they had a lot to say," Helen commented when Ludy fell silent. Terrific. So why should Ludy believe anything they said? No doubt he was itching to find something, anything, to connect her to the crime wave in Tynedale. "Nothing new about Sissy?" she asked, desperate to talk about some subject besides herself.

"Just that they didn't do it, don't know anything about it."

"Really." Helen thought about Kyle's gun, glittering in the early morning sun as she tossed it into the river. She looked out the window past Ludy to the Mississippi, wondering if the gun would ever surface.

"And how do you fit into all this? What the hell were you doing there last night?" Ludy suddenly barked at her.

"I had left the church," Helen said with a glance at Deets. She wondered what Ludy had said to Deets about the church, but the older officer just scribbled away in his notebook, not even bothering to look up. "I'd left the church and decided to go by the park. Just one more time, you know. Kind of saying goodbye to Sissy. I saw lights in the alley. I thought that was kind of strange." Okay, he was just staring. Probably didn't buy it, but couldn't prove anything one way or another. "Then I saw what I thought was Bertie's car."

"Is that so. Interesting." Ludy sat down again. "Her car was parked around the other side of the shop. You couldn't see it from the alley."

"Well, right. I got out of my own car and looked around, you know? It just didn't seem right. That's when they heard me." Sort of. Not a complete lie, anyhow. Helen shifted uncomfortably in the bed beneath Ludy's level stare. "Then they — well, they might have killed me if you guys hadn't come along. How did that happen, anyhow? What made you come to the alley?" Shit. Hopefully Ludy wouldn't push this one. Just because no one was waiting with handcuffs didn't mean that she wasn't still under suspicion of being in cahoots with Bertie.

"Simple. I followed you." Ludy smiled — cold and hard, nothing like the flirtatious grin he'd given E. Carmody a few minutes ago. "From the church. I wanted to see what you were up to. I figured you'd gone this far, maybe you could lead me a little farther if I just sat back and watched. When I saw what was going down I called for backup." Right. That sounded almost as lame as her own explanation. "Guess we both did the right thing, then."

Okay. They were even now, Helen realized. Ludy wasn't going to give an inch with her, and although he knew Helen must be holding something back he couldn't really press it. Not when he'd added another feather in his crown in wrapping up the crime of the century in little ole Tynedale. Probably he figured by letting both Helen and Kyle go on their merry way they would lead him to Sissy's killer. Well, maybe he was right.

She glanced again at Deets. What did the older cop think of all this? His face gave nothing away. She wondered fleetingly how he'd looked when he shot Bertie — was it the same impassive round moon of a face, or did some different expression steal over his features as he watched her die? Again that little itch in her mind. What the hell was she trying so hard to remember?

Ludy opened his mouth, ready to probe Helen with more questions, but E. Carmody chose that moment to make another entrance. "Okay, boys, time to give her a break." A few moments of flirtatious comments — Helen still couldn't quite get over Ludy being charming and cute — and the two men vacated the room. E. left right behind them before Helen could ask about getting out of the hospital. Damn. The rain beat down on the window even harder, and Helen turned to look at the gray sky. The last thing she noticed before dozing off was lightning as it streaked across the river.

"Helen? Helen, can you hear me?" The voice broke into a weird dream about the auto shop, where Valerie and Bertie had somehow become the same person. Helen opened her eyes slowly, remembering the pain in her head from the morning. To her surprise there was only a dull ache on the side of her head where she'd hit the floor.

"They said I could come in." Aunt Edna perched where Ludy had recently sat. She was dressed in her Sunday best — beige suit with black piping, beige pumps, matching handbag, nails painted a soft coral — and wearing a faint trace of lipstick. A single strand of pearls lay on her throat. Helen realized she was looking at how her aunt was dressed so she couldn't see the older woman's face. Finally she steeled herself to meet Aunt Edna's gaze. Helen felt a sudden overwhelming urge to crawl into her aunt's lap and be comforted. Idiot. There was no such feeling between them any longer.

"The doctor says you'll be fine."

"Yes, they told me. They said I could go home." Helen bit her lip, not wanting to say that she didn't really have a home anymore. "I guess I can leave today."

"Well. That's why I'm here." Aunt Edna looked around the room, spotted the closet. "Your things are in here?"

"I guess so." Helen watched, confused, as her aunt took clothes off hangers and picked up the backpack from the floor. "Look, Aunt Edna, you don't have to —"

"Just hush, for once." Aunt Edna folded the dirty shirt and jeans into the backpack, then reached down for a plastic bag on the floor. "I brought you some clothes from the boarding house. Mrs. Mapple said it was all right for me to go in there and pack up your things."

"Aunt Edna —"

"Not that you had very much, Helen! Just your clothes, a couple of books. Even the sheets on your bed came from Mrs. Mapple." Now Aunt Edna was fussing over the shirt and slacks and socks she'd placed on the bed, straightening folds that didn't need straightening, arranging and rearranging, anything to keep from looking directly at her niece. "Everything fit in that one little suitcase you had, so I just packed it all away and put it in the trunk of the car."

"Listen, we should talk about this. About Bertie — I mean, Roberta —"

"No!" Aunt Edna's hands crumpled the clothes. She grimaced and turned away. "We're not going to talk about that — that person. Not in my presence. Ever again."

"But Bobby —"

"I said no!" The older woman took a deep breath and patted the clothes back into a neat pile, smoothing the wrinkles. "We'll just pretend none of it happened, Helen. Bobby will be told that his friend had to go away on a long trip."

"I really don't think —"

"That's how it will be, Helen." Edna had on her best smile. Her eyes glittered in the harsh light. She handed the clothes to Helen. "Now, then. As soon as you get dressed we'll be gone."

Helen reached for the clothes. Maybe it was just as well. It would be difficult enough to get used to life with the relatives. Denial had its good points, maybe.

"Oh, and your toothbrush and things are in there too. Now, let me see, there was something else." She put her finger to her lips and frowned in thought. "Oh, yes, Mrs. Mapple says you paid ahead in rent and she owes you some money."

"Aunt Edna!" Uh oh, she shouldn't have shouted. Helen winced and took a deep breath. At least it calmed the older woman down. Her aunt bit her lip and looked down at the bed. "Aunt Edna, please just sit down a minute." The older woman complied with a grimace. "Look. I appreciate what you're doing, but it's not necessary. I will find someplace else to stay, and —"

Helen stopped short as Aunt Edna wiped her eyes. Jesus, now she was crying. "I'm sorry. I just thought it would be better this way." God, I can't do anything right.

Her aunt rounded on her, shaking with anger — or maybe some other strong emotion. "Better for who? Better that you get almost killed and never tell me anything about it? I found out only because of the news last night, Helen!" She wiped her eyes and pulled a handkerchief from her pocket to dab at her nose. "My own flesh and blood, lying half dead in the hospital, not thinking I would be worried sick about her!"

"But — I thought —"

"You thought I didn't love you now, is that it? That I didn't care whether you lived or died." Edna gazed out the window, all her years now plainly visible on her face as she stared out into the rain. "Helen. We may disagree about a lot of things. We may not ever be able to talk the way you want to, baring our souls to each other. But don't you ever think you're not still my family. You and Bobby — you're all I got left on this earth now." She stopped as her voice broke, sobs shaking her thin shoulders.

Helen looked down at the sheet she'd twisted in her fingers. "Aunt Edna, I thought you would never want to see me again. Not after — after the way I spoke to you on Sunday."

But her aunt was shaking her head, a sad smile on her lips. "Helen, you were the one who left us to stay in that boarding house. I never wanted you to go away. And Bobby — it just about broke his heart. I think that's why he tried to make friends with that woman that they say — they say she was there last night."

"Look, Aunt Edna." Helen shoved her way out of the bed and sat near her aunt, taking the older woman's hands into her own. "You don't know how much it would mean to me to live with you and Bobby." And suddenly, sitting in that sterile hospital room, it was true. Helen wanted nothing more than to hide in something that resembled a family. A place to belong, even if it was only a facade. Just for a while. "But only if you're sure. I can't hide who I am. Not any longer."

Edna looked down at their hands, lying together on the bed. "I can only try, Helen. It's just my way, you know? All those years of living with your uncle and his lies, and knowing my only child would never grow up and be normal. I learned a long time ago to just keep things to myself. It was the only way I knew." She looked up at Helen. "It's the only thing that kept me going, all that time — keeping everything inside.

Helen almost backed away from the bleak emptiness that howled from her aunt's eyes. For a moment she had a vivid memory of how she'd felt light and free last night, at the exact instant she thought her life would end in the grimy auto shop. Had her aunt felt anything like that, once she'd faced up to the awful facts of her own life? That sense of surrender to the inevitable, accepting what she couldn't change? Staring into Aunt Edna's face, Helen felt her resistance crumble away.

She patted the older woman's hands. "If you're willing to take me in, I'm willing to give it a shot, too." The words tumbled out fast, before Helen could stop them. The answering light in Aunt Edna's eyes frightened her. Too late now. She'd find out soon enough if this was a big mistake.

Things happened fast after that. They were both uncomfortable with the emotional scene, so the interruption of doctors and Nurse E. Carmody was very welcome. A couple of hours after that Helen was dressed and sitting in Aunt Edna's car. The rain had stopped, and red-gold sunlight spilled out over the late afternoon. The silence in the car felt comfortable to Helen. She roused herself only long enough to ask about her car.

"Oh, that nice Officer Deets had one of his boys drive it over to my house. He sure is a nice man, isn't he? I guess he's been around forever in Tynedale. All the ladies at the church know him."

"Really?" If only they could stay in here forever, the gentle motion of the car on the highway lulling her to sleep. Thank god she didn't have to face Mrs. Mapple again. Or Kyle. Just her job. Tomorrow she'd try to go in for a bit. That would keep her from trying to get in touch with Valerie.

"Yes, I guess his wife used to be active in the Sunday school there until she died about fifteen years ago. He still comes himself once in a while." Her aunt's idle chatter added a pleasant drone to the background. Yes, just go back to sleep and not think about Valerie. That would be the best thing.

And she did fall asleep before they reached the house. No bizarre dreams this time — just blank silent oblivion until the car stopped. And her aunt was still talking. "I asked old Mrs. Carmichael from the church to sit with Bobby while I went to get you."

Great, Helen thought as she climbed up the steps, suitcase

in hand. Sure enough, old Mrs. Carmichael was standing in the foyer, bent and wrinkled and bright-eyed with curiosity about the convict niece of her sister in the Lord. Oh well.

"Well, here you are! You poor things, you must be exhausted! Hurry on inside before it starts to rain again!"

"Did Bobby behave for you? I surely hope he wasn't any trouble."

"Oh, he's just the sweetest old thing! He went upstairs to lie down after supper, and I haven't heard a peep out of him since."

All the while she spoke the elderly woman kept her bright little eyes fixed on Helen. Helen mumbled a few things under Mrs. Carmichael's piercing stare that missed nothing — not the bruises or the wrinkled clothes or the expression that would probably be described as "hardened." No doubt this meeting would be the subject of several hours of discussion amongst her aunt's "friends" at church.

"Well, Helen here should be getting to bed," Aunt Edna was saying. She patted Helen awkwardly on the shoulder. Helen realized with a start that she hadn't embraced her aunt once. Now was not the time to do anything about that, not with company looking on. She turned for the stairs but was stopped by Mrs. Carmichael.

"You had a message, dear."

"A message?" Maybe from work, although she didn't think anyone from SmartSave would know about her change of address. Helen hadn't even known until a few hours ago.

"That's right. A Valerie — Valerie Bosley? I wrote it down, now where did I put that piece of paper?"

"Never mind, ma'am. I know who it was."

"She gave me her number and everything. I thought I had it in my pocket." Mrs. Carmichael fussed at the foyer table, looked around confusedly. "Next thing you know I'll be losing my mind."

"That's okay. I know the number." Helen got one last longing stare from her before Aunt Edna steered her into the kitchen. Helen let the suitcase drop to the floor and went to the phone in the living room to return Valerie's call.

Valerie answered before the second ring. "Helen?"

"That's right. How did you know where to find me?" Shit, that came out so angry — not at all what she was feeling. "Is everything okay?"

"I should be asking you that question."

"I'm fine." Silence. "Really. I got the message that you called. What's up?"

"It's Sissy."

"What do you mean?" Helen sat down and braced herself.

"Mrs. Mapple told me you went back to your aunt's house. She gave me the number. I'm sorry, I wouldn't have called except that —"

"Valerie, just tell me. Please."

"Sissy's funeral is tomorrow. I thought you would want to be there. Helen? Are you still there?"

Now, that was a deep question. Was she, in fact, still here? Was she anywhere? "Yes. Just tell me when and where. I'll make it."

Chapter Fifteen

Clear blue skies and a warm breeze met the mourners at the cemetery the next morning. Having dashed over from the usual Wednesday morning staff meeting at the SmartSave warehouse, Helen tugged at the black slacks and dark blue blouse she'd hastily pulled on in the restroom. All her worries about why everyone at the warehouse was being so nice to her — letting her take so much time off, now to go to Sissy's funeral — faded as she stared at the gleaming wood of the casket. Helen squinted up at the bright sun hanging high over the birch trees at the edge of All Souls' Cemetery. Sissy's grave overlooked a gently sloping hill the rolled down toward a narrow stream flowing between rocks and flowering shrubs. Large mossy stones formed a niche of green and gray at the foot of the grave. The headstone, topped by a simpering angel, supported piles of flowers and scented wreaths that sent their sickening mingled fragrances out across the small crowd.

Helen looked away from the heap of floral tributes, away from the sentimental verse etched in gaudy script under the folded wings of the angel. From behind the safety of her sunglasses she took stock of the people gathered around her. On camp chairs, at the edge of the grave, the bereaved parents stared in a stupor at the glossy surface of the small casket, at the black-brown mud mounded around the narrow gash in the earth. Fortunately Nanette Greene had chosen a stoic silence as the best way to express her grief instead of the paroxysms of weeping and wailing, as Helen had feared. Come on, now, Helen chided herself as she studied the pale drawn face of Sissy's mother. The woman has lost her only child — cut her some slack. Helen fought to retain her charitable feelings when she saw Mrs. Greene make a moue of distaste as she noticed a smudge of mud on her shoes while dabbing at her eyes. Her husband stared out at nothing, his eyes glassy, a strange flush rising on his face. He sat rigid as a two-by-four on the chair. Helen stared hard. Drunk? Possibly. He was holding himself like he was afraid to relax, afraid that whatever held him up would fall apart at the least pressure.

Helen then turned her gaze to look at the rest of the crowd. A sweet-faced woman in her fifties, her features gray and saddened, stared down at the grave as tears streamed down her cheeks. Sissy's teacher, Valerie had murmured in the church. Grouped around her were a handful of kids from Sissy's class. Helen felt a tiny lightness open inside her at the thought that at least the girl had had a few friends. Given the fact that almost everyone in Tynedale belonged to some church or other, perhaps these kids had experienced funerals before. They stood in a knot, pale faces solemn with big staring eyes, unable to keep their stares away from the coffin. Some other folks, nondescript in black, sat on chairs behind Mr. and Mrs. Greene, their features showing varying levels of similarity to Nanette and Gary and revealing them to be members of the family.

All of this was opposite the side where Helen and Valerie and some assorted friends and neighbors stood. A couple of men wearing expensive tasteful suits lined up behind Valerie. Perhaps colleagues of Gary in his accounting firm? One of them had a very loud cell-phone that cut through the minister's words. Helen grit her teeth as the man pulled out the phone and started to murmur something about selling stocks into it. He had the belated manners to saunter off amongst the tombstones with his important deal as the minister intoned a final prayer.

To distract herself from the anger rising up at this intrusion into Sissy's farewell, Helen fixed her attention on the young preacher. She tried again, as she had all through the brief ceremony at All Souls' Episcopal Church, to place his origins. Small, lean, dark-skinned, no trace of southern accent. Perhaps south Asian, Indian or Pakistani. Maybe she could catch his name before it was all over. And although it was obvious he hadn't known the family or Sissy at all — most likely Gary or Nanette weren't regular churchgoers — Helen admired the way he'd quietly relied on a simple ceremony without a lot of words or flowery speeches, letting the graceful liturgy of the Church of England shape the services for a dead girl he'd never met.

Now he read closing comments from the Book of Common Prayer. Okay, okay, Helen told herself — you have to deal with this now, no more distractions. She looked down at the casket lowering into the ground with dry eyes. Maybe it was just the events of the past couple of days, the sheer exhaustion of it all. Or shock. Whatever the reason, Helen felt only a hollowness, a vacant blank opening up inside her as if the warm autumn breeze blowing across her face had also swept inside her through some unknown crevice.

"Ashes to ashes . . ." The words leavened the final moments of seeing the rich Mississippi loam piled over the deep rose colored wood of the coffin. Nanette did break into silent sobs at this point, faltering on her husband's arm as she stared down into the grave. Behind her Helen could hear sobs being choked back. Valerie. She forced herself to stare straight ahead, to resist the urge to reach over for the other woman's hand and draw her close.

Finally it was done, and Helen turned away with everyone else making a slow procession back to parked cars. Out of the corner of her eye she saw Deets and Ludy standing at a respectful distance next to a large granite mausoleum. Deets wore his uniform, and Ludy a brown raincoat. Official business, then. They knew she'd seen them, too — Ludy coughed and studied the ground, while Deets looked out over the cemetery toward the entrance gates. She had a fleeting memory of her own experiences as a cop in Berkeley, times when she'd had to be present at funerals or wakes or various other gatherings that mourned the dead, times when she'd felt that awkwardness they no doubt experienced today. It was always worse when a kid was involved, too. Only the hope of finding a killer could make anyone go through it.

"I see them, too." Valerie's voice at her shoulder startled Helen. With a small jump of surprise she looked at the other woman, concerned at the dark shadows ringing those deep blue eyes, the lack-luster fall of hair on her shoulders. "Guess it was to be expected." Valerie sighed deeply and matched her steps to Helen's as they made their way through tall grasses wet with dew and yesterday's rain. "Thank you for coming."

"I'm glad you called me. I wanted to be here." They walked in silence for a few seconds, making a steady progress to the parking lot. At the rear of the little group, Nanette Greene was now openly sobbing, held up on one side by Gary, on the other by the young pastor. Valerie sighed again, closed her eyes for a long moment. "Go ahead, I know they need you right now."

"Are you coming to the house? There's a kind of reception now at Gary and Nanette's place." Helen reluctantly agreed to follow Valerie's car out to the Greene house for a couple of hours. "Thanks — it would really be a help for me," she said as she went to her sister.

Helen sat in the Rambler watching people fill up cars and drive off, pondering Valerie's last comment. How the hell would her presence at this family ritual help Valerie? It didn't make a lot of sense. Unless Valerie just needed a sympathetic shoulder, a shoulder she had gotten to know rather intimately, at her disposal. Helen clamped down on her wish for something deeper with Valerie and started the engine when she saw Valerie slip behind the wheel of her rental car. The weather was still holding, but a knot of gray clouds bunched off to the east. They'd have rain before the day was out.

In fact, the first few raindrops pelted the Rambler's windshield as they passed Aunt Edna's house. She turned on the wiper blades and smeared dirt around the window as she peered out at Valerie's car ahead. To her surprise and relief Helen saw that the Greene residence was only two blocks away from her aunt's house. Helen let the engine idle while she surveyed the street for a parking spot. Nothing. The Rambler sputtered and coughed like an ailing old man, and Helen wondered if it would ever start up again once she'd turned it off. Valerie turned her own car into the driveway which looked like the last available space. Oh well — a little rain wouldn't hurt. Helen sped on past the house and turned back to Aunt Edna's. After parking there she dashed back through the light shower to Valerie and the wake.

"I thought you chickened out when I saw you drive off," Valerie said a couple of minutes later as she let Helen in.

"Not at all," Helen reassured her. "My aunt's place is right around the corner." She looked away from those blue eyes and tried to tidy her hair while looking at a mirror. Thank God the bruise on her cheek from the auto shop stayed tucked behind her hair. "I didn't think I'd melt if I walked here in the rain."

Valerie had a half smile on her face, her mouth open as if

about to make a teasing comment about melting, then thought better of it. "Let's go in. I'll get you a brandy."

"Thanks." Helen tried to take in details of the house as she waited for the offered drink. It was pretty much what she'd expected — a tasteful upper middle class suburban home, lots of tan and beige and off-white, inoffensive prints and understated luxury. A parson's table laden with small tea sandwiches and cakes stood unobtrusively against a wall facing the living room entrance. People clustered in clumsy groups, milling around with paper plates and napkins balanced in their hands, trying to think of things to say. The youthful Episcopalian minister was the only person who seemed at ease, sitting silently on the sofa beside Mrs. Green as he sipped tea. Gary was nowhere in sight but Nanette seemed to be holding court quite nicely on her own.

Helen took the brandy from Valerie, who then helped herself. "Did you do all this yourself?" she asked.

Valerie shook her head, gestured at the older woman Helen had noticed shepherding kids at the cemetery. "Miss Fletcher, Sissy's teacher. It was all her idea. We didn't have to lift a finger." Miss Fletcher spoke quietly to Sissy's classmates, who were grouped in the adjoining dining room with cakes and sodas. They listened to her with great seriousness, their gaze wandering now and then to Sissy's mother on the sofa.

Nanette at that moment was lifting her hand in a gesture of weary resignation to a couple who bent over her with whispered words of consolation. She leaned towards them with a regal air, inclining her head to listen. Helen stole a glance at Valerie, who watched her sister with a look of disgust. "You okay?" she asked.

Valerie shrugged and composed her face. "Nan's in her element right now — center of attention, the grieving mother, bravely bearing her loss. This is the first day she's been out of bed — the first day she's even tried to —" She gave an odd laugh. "Sorry, I'm just at the end of my patience. I'll just be glad when today is over. My head is splitting." The doorbell rang, and Valerie went to answer it, leaving Helen to her own devices for the moment.

She finished the brandy, looked for a safe place to set down her empty glass. To the side of the parson's table the entrance to the kitchen opened up into a vast white expanse of shiny appliances, butcher's block with pride of place in the center of the room, and two cavernous stoves. Helen rinsed out her glass at the sink. Gary certainly was doing well for himself. She had a brief moment of curiosity about where Nanette had surprised him in flagrante delicto — on the tasteful beige sofa in the living room, perhaps?

Thinking of Gary's profitable career reminded her of Earl Pemberton and his suicide a few days past. With a jolt she remembered that Gary had been Earl's accountant. A sordid little idea began to form in Helen's mind. Now that she was here in the Greene house, if Gary had an office here, she could maybe find something —

No. This was completely wrong. Helen stood at the sink, the murmur of distant voices in other rooms brushing against her own thoughts. There was simply no way she could allow herself to do such a thing, at such a time. But if it helped Sissy? Come on, now, you're just looking for a reason to play detective, she lectured herself, turning her empty glass around and around in her hands. This is fucking stupid. What if they caught you? She could just say she'd gotten lost looking for the bathroom. Idiot. She needed to go the bathroom, anyway. Why not look for it — and look for Gary's study at the same time? Didn't mean she would go in and poke around, right?

Right. She pushed herself away from the kitchen counter and went into the hallway. The living room was just to her right, and the hall led to other doors on the left. Helen could hear the sounds of muffled conversation, and she got a glimpse of Valerie in her dark blue dress leading newcomers over to the sofa. For a moment Helen paused, wondering why so many people were here. Had the Greenes been that popular in town? Maybe it was just morbid curiosity — people exercising their one chance to get a look at the home where so much horror had taken place. Actually by continuing to try deciphering what had happened to the girl Helen could be seen as doing them a favor, getting to the truth behind the murder. Uh huh. Just do what you're going to do, she lectured herself, quit trying to rationalize it. Resolutely she turned on her heel and went off to the left.

The bathroom door was ajar at the end of the hall. The door just before it opened into a small dark room overcrowded with heavy furnishings — mahogany desk, leather uphol-stered sofa, floor-to-ceiling bookcases housing weighty tomes on finance and accounting and statistics. Okay, this was it. Helen stood between the doors, hesitating one last time. What the hell could she hope to find that the police hadn't found already? This was fucking ridiculous.

"Uhhhhnn." She almost yelped at the noise coming from the study. Something moved on the sofa, squeaking against the upholstery. Its back faced Helen — all she had to go on was sound. Another groan. Helen ventured inside and found out where Gary Greene had gotten to. She peered down at his still form, straining to see in the half-dark created by the somber drapes pulled against the rainy day. Giving up she switched on the green-shaded light on the desk. It gave a sickly glow to Gary's sweating red face. He snuffed a couple of times and subsided back into drunken sleep.

Perfect. Helen straightened up and went back to the door, making sure it was only slightly ajar. Hopefully she could hear if anyone approached. If they did, she had her excuse ready — hearing strange noises from the study while on her way to the bathroom, coming in to investigate and finding Gary uncon-scious. But she'd have to be quick about it. She listened hard at the door for a few seconds, then went back to the desk.

Now. Where to start. Aside from writing checks off a business account for her long-defunct detective agency, Helen knew next to nothing about accounting. She'd hired someone for the task as soon as she could afford it, and up to that point her accounting methods had been basically to stay one step ahead of bill-collectors. She had, however, kept a ledger book of sorts. So perhaps Gary had kept ledgers for his customers. Or the virtual equivalent, Helen decided, turning on the computer monitor on the desk. Of course, she sighed, it probably requires some super secret password to get anywhere.

Sure enough, everything was password protected. Okay, now what? Helen stared cursing at the amber-glowing screen, then turned her glare to Gary. "Okay, what is it?" she hissed at him. "Can't you have a moment of weakness while your zonked out there and tell me your password?"

"Charlotte."

"I beg your pardon?" Yes, he'd said what sounded like a name, something like "Charlotte." Was that the password? Well, why not? Helen typed it in, got the expected negative response. Gary said it again, this time with a whine in his voice. And it came out louder, too.

"Hey, keep it down," Helen whispered, getting up from the desk to look at Gary. "Do you want all your neighbors in here?"

"Charlotte, baby, oh yes, just like that." He moaned and snuffled, turning over in his sleep. As he shifted on the sofa, something fell off the cushions and landed on Helen's foot.

Shit. He must be having dreams about the girl he'd ruined his marriage for. Or some other woman. At any rate, the name hadn't sounded a bit like Nanette. Helen reached down for whatever it was that he'd pushed off the sofa. Her hand closed around a plastic wrapped package of small firm squares. Computer disks? Helen took her find to the lamp. Yes, that's what it was. But why —

Then she saw the receipt wrapped around the disks. It was a flimsy carbon, a computer print-out, with the heading TYNEDALE POLICE DEPARTMENT in bold lettering on the top. Helen went back to the sofa, looked harder. The box of Sissy's belongings, also tagged by the police department, nestled above Gary's head. She gingerly looked through the items, taking care not to jostle the sofa's occupant. Jesus, her clothes, stained with mud and blood inside another plastic package. She replaced everything gently. Had Gary put them in here, hoping that his wife wouldn't stumble across them? No wonder the poor bastard had needed to get drunk.

Helen went with the disks back to the computer. Sure enough, they were labeled with Pemberton's name and a series of dates. The police must have asked for whatever records Gary had on the store owner, then returned them when Earl had made their job a lot easier by committing suicide in such a timely manner. No password on these, then.

It took only a few minutes to pull up Earl Pemberton's records, but Helen couldn't really make sense of them. Of course, the little "favors" Gary had asked Earl to perform wouldn't be anywhere in this, anyhow. And what the fuck was she looking for? Helen bit her lip in frustration while Gary snored. All she could make out was substantial withdrawals on a regular basis — not monthly, but every few months. Purchasing supplies for the store? And there wasn't much of an explanation to go with those entries. The others had all the things one would expect — payroll, office supplies, advertising — and they were on a regular monthly basis. Then there was the one marked "Church Fund." Whatever that meant. Gary had questioned it, too. Earl's secret, large sums of money, mysterious fund in the store's books — even her poor math skills could add it all up and make it equal blackmail.

Helen removed the disk and slipped it back into the plastic bag. She sat a few moments longer at the desk, lost in thought. What had Gary made of these entries? What could he say, in fact? She didn't really know all the rhyme and reason an accountant had to be responsible for. As long as laws were followed, bills taken care of and taxes paid, there might be no reason to question it. Certainly the police would have noted this, maybe were already investigating it. Blackmail? Maybe, given the suspicions Renee had expressed to her. And of course the police would know about that. Another reason for suicide, and one that made more sense if Earl's penchant was for boys instead of girls. Helen grimaced and stole a look at Gary. He'd shifted on the sofa so that she had a good look at his tear-stained face. What had he known about Earl? Surely not Earl Pemberton's sordid history — he wouldn't have engaged his unofficial services in that case. Would he?

Helen turned off the monitor and the room was plunged into darkness. Rain pounded down on the roof, coming down harder than when she'd first arrived. Gary slept silently on the sofa, whatever disturbing dreams that had caused him to cry out stilled for the moment. Something tugged at the back of Helen's mind, the same way something about Bertie's death continued to buzz around. Something she couldn't quite grasp. It was worse than having a tiny rock lodged in her shoe.

She stirred when muffled footsteps sounded on the hallway carpet. Someone appeared in the doorway just as she made it to the sofa, kneeling by Gary's side with her hands on the box of Sissy's things. The overhead light came on with a loud click, throwing the room's interior into high relief. "Helen?" Valerie's voice came from the doorway, pitched high in disbelief. "What on earth are you doing in here?" She came into the room and stared down at the scene. "Is everything okay?"

Gary moaned and tossed again as Helen stood up. "I think so," Helen whispered. "I was looking for the bathroom and heard something from in here. It — well, it sounded like someone was crying," she lied. They both looked at Gary as he snored. He looked oddly childlike, with one arm thrown up over his head, the other trailing on the floor. "Then I saw him." Helen gestured helplessly at the man on the sofa.

Valerie studied Helen's face. Was she buying this? "You were gone a long time, Helen. People are starting to leave, and I didn't know where you'd gone."

Damn. "Well, I wasn't sure what to do. I think, well, he's had a little too much to drink, and I wanted to make sure he wasn't going to be sick." Fucking lame, Helen knew. And Valerie had spied the box from the police department. She closed her eyes a moment and shuddered as she turned away. Helen followed her back into the living room, grateful that at least there was nothing specific Valerie could accuse her of. Thank God she'd left the desk before the other woman entered.

Valerie was talking in a low voice to Miss Fletcher as Helen stood uncertainly in the middle of the now empty living room. "Now, don't you worry, hon," the teacher was saying. "I'll take care of the kitchen and you just get your sister up to bed."

"Are you sure?"

"Absolutely." They all looked at Nanette, who was still sitting on the sofa, staring out the bay window at the rain. Miss Fletcher noticed Helen then and moved toward her. "You must be Sissy's friend, Helen," and she shook Helen's hand. "She talked about you several times."

"Really?" Helen wondered what she could have had to say.

"Maybe some other time we can talk, Helen." The older woman's warm brown eyes welled with tears as she looked long and hard at Helen. Something about the way she held herself, the set of her jaw, the firm handclasp — Helen was startled to feel a flicker of recognition. Miss Fletcher, huh? A woman in her fifties, unmarried, most definitely a "miss" and not a "ms" — and that direct gaze. Was Sissy's teacher trying to tell her something with that look that went past the surface? Trying to tell her that she recognized a member of the tribe in Helen? Maybe. "Yes, once things have settled down we'll have a good long talk," she said, a slow smile breaking the seriousness of her expression.

And to her amazement Helen found herself smiling back and returning the teacher's solid grip. "Yes, I'd like that a lot."

The older woman cleared her throat and walked purposefully off to the kitchen. Valerie managed to coax Nanette from the sofa as Helen busied herself helping Miss Fletcher carry empty glasses and plates into the kitchen. They worked for a few minutes in silence, then Valerie reappeared at the kitchen entrance.

Helen took in her gray face, eyes dimmed with exhaustion and grief, the way she leaned on the wall. "Helen, I'm going to take you home."

"Valerie, that's not necessary. It's only a couple of blocks —"

"Don't be silly. It's pouring outside. Emily, will you be okay for a few minutes?"

"Of course, hon." At least Helen knew her first name now. Emily Fletcher stood wiping her hands on a dishtowel, watching them both. "You gals take your time. I'll just let myself out when I'm finished, Valerie. Helen, we'll meet again."

"I hope so," Helen said — and meant it. A couple of minutes later she and Valerie had dashed out to Valerie's car and were making their way back to Aunt Edna's house. Helen sneaked a look at Valerie. She looked like shit. All the pressure, the grief, the strain of the past few days had taken their toll. Her skin had a papery texture, and the bruised shadows beneath her eyes appeared to go bone deep. Even her hands trembled on the wheel.

Helen looked away and gave directions. "Turn right here. It's the first house on this block, on the right. The yellow one." As Valerie stopped the car Helen wondered for a brief painful moment if she'd ever see her again. "Why don't you come inside for a while?"

Valerie drummed her fingers on the wheel, considering. "What about your aunt?"

"She said she was taking Bobby into Vicksburg today. He had some kind of party at the center where he takes lessons." Helen forced a laugh. "Actually, I think she wanted to get him away from me — she was afraid he'd ask questions about last night."

"Last night. Jesus, Helen." Valerie leaned her head against

the wheel. "You must think I'm terrible, not asking you what happened."

"Hush, none of that. Look, let's not do this out here. Let's get in the house where it's warm." Then her arms were around Valerie's shoulders, and her hands were stroking Valerie's hair.

"But Emily — I can't just leave her —"

"She said she'd be fine. Come on, it's getting cold. Just for a while." That was how Valerie ended up in Helen's arms, sitting on Aunt Edna's sofa, tears coming out in shuddering sobs. Helen held her close, her own grief quiet for now.

"God, I'm sorry, Helen." Valerie finally sat up and wiped at her eyes, digging in a pocket for tissue or handkerchief. "I haven't done that all day. Thought I wouldn't make it through the funeral."

"There's always one person, isn't there, who has to hold it together for everyone else?" Helen said, stroking Valerie's hair. "Looks like you were it today."

Valerie leaned into Helen's hand, turning the gesture into a caress, then a kiss on Helen's palm. Helen's breath caught in her throat. This wasn't why she'd asked Valerie in, she'd just wanted to offer comfort. "Thanks, Helen," she murmured, letting Helen's hand go. "I needed that."

"Anytime." Okay, the moment had passed. No harm done. No visible harm, anyhow. They were still holding hands when Aunt Edna walked in.

"Helen."

Shit. And Bobby was standing right behind her, peering curiously over his mother's shoulder.

Aunt Edna's voice cracked through the silence like breaking glass. "Aren't you going to introduce me to your friend?"

Chapter Sixteen

"So we'd like to offer Helen Black this bonus as a gesture of our thanks for her help. Helen, would you come up to the front here, please?"

Great. Helen could feel that her face burned as red as the stitching on her SmartSave shirt. Clambering over the legs of her fellow employees — some of whom deliberately kept their limbs sprawled in her path — Helen heard only a thin spattering of applause from the rows of seated workers. Her stomach knotted with anger so thick she thought she might lose her scanty breakfast right there on Bob's feet. Why the fuck were they doing this so publicly? As she looked at Bob's round doughy face beaming from behind his glasses, some of her rage melted. He certainly meant well, and his pride and pleasure were obvious. Even Marie, usually so taciturn and unapproachable, had a grin for Helen as she stepped by to receive the envelope.

The line of older men in suits, one of whom must be holding her prize, were another story altogether. Helen didn't recognize any of them, but from the way middle managers like Bob broke into a sweat whenever any of them so much as coughed, she felt safe in assuming these were corporate mucky-mucks shipped in for this little sideshow. From Jackson? Probably. The really important men, the ones who watched over not only SmartSave but all the subsidiaries domestic and foreign, would be in some high rise in New York.

"Now, what Helen is too modest to tell everyone is how she saved the company thousands of dollars with her efforts. Together with the local police, your co-worker here —" Bob clapped a meaty hand on her shoulder. She hadn't been expecting that, and she almost stumbled over her own feet with the recoil. Sniggers bubbled up from below as the audience enjoyed her discomfort.

Purgatory, pure and simple. The anger came churning back into her gut as Bob told a much-embellished version of how the missing shipment of computers and software had been located in a remote abandoned warehouse on the other side of town after Bertie's death. Only three days ago, Helen thought. The realization stunned her, obliterating Bob's speech and bringing Bertie's dying expression back into her mind. Only three days ago her life had changed. Again.

Uh oh. Bob was winding up. "So, we hope you'll accept this as a way of saying thanks for all your good work for the company." He glanced off to the line of suits perched uneasily on metal folding chairs. One of them stood up, straightened his tie, and put a stiff smile on his lips for the cameras' sake. Helen walked around Bob and Marie, not sure what she was supposed to do now. Bob made some kind of murmured introduction, and Helen forgot the man's name as soon as she heard it.

But she took the envelope, shook the dry pale hand offered to her, and made her way back to her seat through the deafening silence that had fallen over the cafeteria. She folded and stuffed the envelope, not bothering to open it in front of the others. At least they didn't ask me to make a speech, she consoled herself. Almost as soon as she'd relaxed into the chair, though, the gathering was over.

Helen shuffled out with the others, lingering long enough so that she was almost the last one out of the room. Bob and Marie were busy hobnobbing with the imported brass and didn't notice her slip out a side door to the parking lot. No way she was going to the planned reception with its obligatory cold cuts and soft drinks. She needed stronger fare. And fortunately management had timed this little soiree so that people could go right home afterwards. Thank God. The past two days since she'd come back to work had been sheer hell. Except for Marie and Bob, no one had been pleased to see her return. And why the hell should they be? Helen asked herself as she made her way through the parked cars under dimming sunlight.

"Don't you want to join the party?"

Helen spun around. This time it was the good looking kid with the bad teeth and bad breath who'd spoken. Usually it was the older guys, the ones with seniority who didn't have to worry too much about getting into trouble with management, who hassled her. At least that had been the rule for the last couple of days. She hadn't made it to lunch yet without some smart ass remark from one of them. Today obviously was no exception. And there they all were, lined up along a car and staring at her with cold blank eyes. No, not quite blank. They hated her. Literally. Fine. She sighed and walked the gauntlet past them.

She passed her own car, debated getting in and driving off — no, not yet. She needed to calm down and cool off before facing Aunt Edna and cousin Bobby.

Now — she thought she remembered a little corner where

she could hide — ah, yes. At the edge of the parking lot Helen found the little alley. It spread the length of the warehouse and ended up in an alcove close to the freeway. As the cold autumn wind bit through her thin workshirt, Helen wished she'd brought her jacket. What the hell. Instead she rounded the corner to the dumpsters, where a wall blocked out the worst of the wind. This isolated nook, redolent of everyone's fast food lunch remains for the past week, at least had the blessing of privacy. Just a few minutes, then, to calm down and think about the decision she'd made last night to leave SmartSave.

Now, where the hell was it? Helen patted her pockets for the cigarette and matches she knew she'd stashed away. Weird, she thought as she took her first delicious deep drag, how habits like this come and go and come again. Gray smoke curled up as she breathed out and leaned her back against the wall, facing the Dumpsters. Its acrid tang burned away some of the odors wafting up from the metal containers, and Helen watched it tuft away on the breeze. Putting the matches back into her pocket, her fingers crumpled the edges of the envelope she'd just received.

Okay, what the hell? With fingers stiffening from the cold Helen tore open the envelope and looked down at a figure with quite a number of zeros. She stared, not believing, trying to make sense of the fact that her lords and masters had just given her enough to live on for three months. She tipped ash onto the pavement, careful not to let it fall on the check, then folded the check back into her pocket. A thread of uncertainty wove into her thoughts as she finished the cigarette. Should she stay with SmartSave now? Was there any kind of future here with these people? Bob and Marie had certainly been very pleased for her, and that, Helen was sure, had been genuine.

And what the hell would she do, anyway? Helen stared down at the soiled pavement and scuffed her feet. Sure, it had sounded fine last night, lying in the comfort of a quiet room in her Aunt Edna's house — the idea of not putting on the ugly work shirt, of not looking at all the sullen faces that met hers every day in the warehouse, of not feeling that knot of tension between her shoulders whenever she heard whispers in the hallways at work. Last night it had just been wishful thinking, really. Now, with this money, it would be possible to give her aunt something while she looked for work elsewhere.

But then she remembered the line of pale blank faces arrayed on the platform, the men who had graciously descended for the occasion. For these guys it was all public relations. No doubt they'd be mildly pleased at the write-up they'd get from the local rag — Tynedale's version of mass media was thrilled to have something interesting to write about these days — and the value of this check was just so much lunch-money to men like them. They'd gotten out of this pretty cheaply, in fact. A check and a morning in the armpit of Mississippi, and that was that.

Helen smiled wryly to herself and pushed away from the wall. At least she'd wait until the check cleared before giving notice, she thought. And sleep on it for a couple of nights.

"What the fuck are you grinning about, bitch?"

She was in her early twenties — long curls the color of brass whipping in the wind, thick dark makeup ringing her hard blue eyes, and tight faded jeans outlining every curve of her ass and hips. Helen glanced past her at the sound of other footsteps. Yep, sure enough, she'd brought backup with her. Helen only vaguely recognized the faces of the three men lined up behind the woman. Two of them had quit working at the warehouse right after she'd started. The other man, a bit older than the rest, also looked faintly familiar. Maybe from her night at the tavern last week? At any rate, he was the only one who seemed nervous about whatever the hell was going on.

Helen's thoughtful gaze served only to irritate the redhead. "So what do you have to say for yourself?" she hissed at Helen. "Guess you're pretty proud of yourself now, aren't

you? Got all that money for fucking over someone else."
Helen's silence seemed to make things worse. The woman
flung her hair out of her eyes and came up close to Helen,
their faces just inches apart. Helen could smell the sickly
sweet scent of bubble gum on her breath. Then the woman
poked a finger into her sternum. Hard. "No one does that to
my man and gets away with it. You hear me, bitch?"

Realization dawned then. Jesus fucking Christ. "Dave's
girlfriend, right?" Now that they were so close Helen could
see the dark circles under the other woman's eyes, the reddened nose and swollen eyelids resulting from crying herself
to sleep for several nights. A brief stab of pity coursed through
Helen, and she raised both hands gingerly in the air in a
gesture of yielding. What was she supposed to say to her?

"Well? Don't got anything to say to me? Too chicken-shit
to talk?" She poked Helen again, harder this time. Helen
glanced over her shoulder at the three musketeers. The two
younger men grinned and shuffled their feet. Their eyes
gleamed with excitement at the prospect of watching a cat
fight. Their older companion — God knows how he'd gotten
dragged into this — squirmed in discomfort near the wall. He
kept looking over his shoulder, probably hoping others would
discover them and end this horrid little scene.

"Hey, bitch! I'm talking to you!" This time she slapped
Helen. Or made an attempt, at least. Her palm only grazed
Helen's cheek as Helen dodged easily.

"What's your name?"

"Huh?" The woman paused, her hand raised for another
blow, surprised at the question.

"I asked you what your name is." That's it, Helen encouraged herself. Talk to her, get her to talk about it instead
of hitting and shoving and slapping. Maybe get her to cry
again, then get the hell out of here.

"Doreen." She muttered the name, her brow wrinkled in
confusion.

"Doreen," Helen repeated as she took another step back

to find herself flat on the wall. Nice. "So you and Dave were together, huh?" Should she say she was sorry? Even though she was glad that good old Dave would probably spend a nice long time behind bars.

The confusion in Doreen's face deepened as Helen spoke. Helen was beginning to think she might get away without a fresh set of bruises when one of the two younger men spoke up. "You gonna let that cunt get away with it, Doreen?"

"Yeah," his buddy chimed in. "We brought you out here so you could fuck her up. You gonna do it, or do you want us to?"

That was all Doreen needed. She balled her plump be-ringed hands into childlike fists and tried to swing at Helen. With something like boredom Helen parried her blow and shoved her aside, grabbing her arm and twisting her around so that Doreen's elbow was locked into a very painful position. Doreen yelped in pain as she tried and failed to jerk herself away from Helen's grip. The woman — actually not much more than a girl, twenty-one at the most — felt like a brittle boned bird in her hands. Helen eased up on her hold. She really didn't want to hurt Doreen if she could help it.

Then Doreen started to cry, huge heaving sobs that rattled her whole body. "Y'all come on over here and help me! God-dammit, you said you was gonna kick her ass for me! Come on!"

They couldn't hold off their laughter any longer. Dave's two younger pals nearly doubled over with hilarity. Helen, sickened, let Doreen go. The girl tottered on her toes and nursed her sore arm. "Yeah, you got some really great friends there, Doreen," Helen murmured as she braced herself for God knows what kind of attack next. The guys quit laughing and glanced at each other. Some signal must have passed between them. The next thing Helen knew they were standing next to Doreen, wearing expressions of disgust.

"Get out of the way, Doreen," one of them ordered in a soft voice. "This bitch has got a lesson coming to her."

"Hey —" This came from the older man who was still

262

hovering in the background. He turned a worried face to them. "Cops just pulled up."

"What the fuck?" They all looked at Helen, then at their lookout. "How many?" one of the other guys wanted to know.

"Just the one car. It's old Deets."

"Shit." They turned heel and ran, pulling Doreen after them and ignoring the girl's whimpers.

"Good timing, wasn't it?" Helen said as the lookout walked by her.

"Yeah, someone must have made one of those anonymous calls," he said. He stalked off in a different direction from his buddies and he'd disappeared when Deets and another uniformed officer came back by the Dumpsters with Doreen and friends in tow.

"Someone reported a disturbance over here," Deets said as he herded the trio into the small paved area. "Said it sounded like a fight going on. Anybody here know anything about that?"

They all looked at Helen, who stared steadily at Deets. "Disturbance?" she said finally. "No, nothing like that. I was just having a conversation with these folks. Isn't that right, Doreen?"

Doreen refused to look at Helen but she managed a nod. She glared at her two useless knights, who stood by in mute tension. The two men had eyes only for the police.

"Well." Deets looked to his younger partner, who shrugged. "Guess that was a false alarm, then. Now, then — Doreen —" He touched Doreen's arm and tried to guide her away. Doreen brushed him off and stalked away with one final black glance at Helen. The men followed with furtive shamefaced looks at each other. Then it was just Helen and the cops. Again. How the hell did this keep happening to her? It seemed to be her fate forever, unplanned visitations from the Law.

"Mike, you go call this in for me, okay?" Deets shook his head and sighed as his partner went around the corner of the warehouse to the front of the building. Deets and Helen followed more slowly. Obviously the man had something to say to her, Helen decided. They finally moved away from the overpowering smell of garbage and emerged on the front lawn of the SmartSave building. The other cop talked on the radio in the black and white while Deets paused by the entrance, propping his foot on the low wall as he turned to Helen.

"So what was that all about?" Deets offered her a cigarette. Helen took one with a smile as she saw the brand. Somehow she'd known he wouldn't fuss with any low tar low nicotine shit. She took a grateful drag, watching the red tip glow in the growling twilight.

"You gonna tell me?"

Helen smiled. "Fuck if I know, officer," she said as she blew smoke out with a big sigh. "Someone put that poor girl up to a cat fight with me, I guess. I managed to talk my way out of it."

"This time." Deets looked at her seriously. In the fading light she could barely make out his face. It looked like a moon rising up over his shirt. "What about next time?"

"I know." Suddenly the taste went out of the cigarette. She dropped it to the sidewalk and crushed it under her shoes, sparing a quick glance at Deets' partner, who sat patiently in the car while Deets did his good neighbor thing. "I'm certainly not going to win the congeniality award in this place."

"Look, Ms. Black, today you got off easy. Next time you might not be so lucky. I might not have an old pal who gives me a call when he knows there's trouble about to happen."

Helen looked up, surprised. He sounded genuinely concerned. About her? Or about something else? "Don't worry about me, Deets. It's all under control. I'm well aware that these fuckers couldn't have gotten in here without someone from the warehouse opening the door for them. And that they probably won't stop with this. But I know how to watch my back."

"Yeah, maybe. That's how people get killed." He shifted off

the wall and stood with his hands on his hips, towering over Helen. "There's been too much of that going on around here."

Was he thinking of Bertie, or of Sissy? Still, he was in a talkative mood — maybe she could get a little information out of him. "Any more news about Sissy? Did those guys with Bertie the other night say anything about it?"

Deets shook his head and stared out toward the cars passing on the highway. "They swear up and down on their mama's graves that they don't know a thing about that. They steal stuff, they don't kill people."

"How about Ludy, does he buy that?"

Deets snorted. "What do you think?"

"Look, Deets, why are you really here talking to me? Is it because some old drinking buddy of yours gave you a jingle about some kind of brawl out here, or did Ludy set you on my trail? What are you, some kind of pet for Ludy? Does he toss you a biscuit now and then — like chasing me down here at my job?" Jesus, she was so fucking sick of this. How could they even imagine she'd chase a girl like Sissy to her death — but then, of course, they didn't know about the math sessions on the front porch swing. About the twist of pain Helen used to feel whenever Nanette screeched on her cell phone and ignored Sissy's misery. About the empty ache of knowing Sissy was never going to grow into the woman she could have been.

Deets just watched her as Helen struggled to gain control of herself. They both knew her words had been a big mistake. It only remained for Deets to make good use of it. "All we're doing is trying to get at the truth here," he finally said. His voice was calm and quiet. He knew he had the upper hand once again. "We just want to find out what happened."

"And you think I have some deep dark secret, Deets? Shit, you guys know everything there is to know about me already. You even know about the little shindig we had here today. What's left to know?" Helen felt a slender edge of hysteria creeping into her voice. "Why don't you spend some time finding out what happened to that little girl for a change? Quit wasting it on me."

"It's not a waste of time if we can find out who chased Sissy Greene to her death from that church."

"Well, you're not going to get any answers here, Deets. I'm all out of words." And she stayed silent as he lumbered across the SmartSave lawn to the waiting police car. As she watched him drive away Helen felt again that strange uneasiness nibbling at the edge of her mind. There was something happening here, something she almost had hold of that kept slipping away as soon as she focused attention on it. But what?

She stood for a while near the entrance of the warehouse, watching her co-workers file out to the parking lot. Should she go inside and punch out with the rest of them? Screw it. After her encounter with Deets she really didn't want to talk to anyone at all.

Well, almost anyone. A car wearing rental plates pulled up in front of the building and a familiar face appeared, looking through the windshield. "Need a ride?" Valerie asked her.

Chapter Seventeen

"What did your aunt say?"

Helen shrugged. "Nothing much." She decided to forego telling Valerie about the disapproval apparent in her aunt's tone of voice as Helen explained she wouldn't be coming home for dinner that evening. If Aunt Edna had had any glowing ideas of Helen settling down to a "normal" family life, she might as well get over the disillusionment immediately. Bobby, though — that was a different concern. He'd been worried about Helen going back to work today, hanging onto her as she left the breakfast table wearing her SmartSave uniform. Bobby apparently wasn't too sure these days that she'd come back whenever she left the house. Couldn't blame him, though. His wayward cousin Helen had a nasty little habit of disappearing for days — sometimes years — on end.

"Hey — earth to Helen. You okay over there?"

"Sorry." Helen managed a smile and picked up her fork. "It's been a long day." Should she tell her anything about the bonus? About the almost-fight that nearly ended her working day? No way, Helen decided as she viewed the food spread out before her. Valerie hadn't put together this elaborate farewell dinner so she could hear about more violence, more problems, more private stresses and strains.

And it was an elaborate dinner. Somehow, somewhere, Valerie had conjured up a romantic dinner and had it delivered to her hotel room. Romantic, Helen repeated to herself as she reached for her napkin. That's the catch. Even in this cheap hotel room, with its uncomfortable furniture and television screwed into the wall, even with the ever-present Gideon bible beside the bed, Valerie had set up a very special event. For Helen's sake, or her own?

"What did you tell her?" Valerie persisted. "Your aunt, I mean. She didn't seem to mind too much telling me where you worked, when I called this afternoon. Are you sure she's not angry?"

"She didn't say much, Valerie. And if she's mad at anyone, it's at me. Don't worry. It's okay, really." Helen looked at Valerie, hoping to distract herself from her own misgivings about spending yet another evening in the other woman's company. Even if it was the last evening they'd have together. "When do you have to take off?" she asked, raising her voice to be heard over the sudden burst of rain. The storm had broken just as Helen's Rambler had followed Valerie out of the SmartSave parking lot towards Tynedale. Even more romantic, she thought with some dismay as she listened to thunder pealing loud and deep in the distance. Maybe they could just talk about the weather for the duration of the dinner. Better that than going back to the one subject on both their minds at all times, of course.

But Sissy intruded on everything, just like it always did. Like it always would, Helen realized with a wave of sadness. The desultory remarks about travel and weather and aunts and cousins only pulled a thin sheet of decently veiled manners over the howling grief that threatened to burst through with every sentence.

Lost in these thoughts Helen barely heard the other woman's response. Valerie sipped at her glass of wine and stared back at Helen. "By check out time tomorrow — probably around noon. I should be back in New Orleans by dinnertime."

"I think there's supposed to be a storm tomorrow. Are you sure you'll be okay, driving back?" Wonderful, now we're going to have small talk, Helen despaired. I can't even bring myself to look at her.

Which was a lie, of course. How could she help looking at Valerie, when she was wearing that piercing blue shirt to match the color of her eyes? The way the neckline curved over her full breasts, the milky white skin of her neck, long thick black hair flowing across round shoulders — okay, enough already. Try to concentrate on this amazing meal she'd put together.

And for Tynedale it was a pretty impressive banquet. Penne pasta in a delicate herbed sauce, light on the oil and heavy on the flavor. A tart dish of dark leafy greens with a tangy dressing made of some mixture of fruit vinegars, she guessed. Rice and chicken in a delicate, understated blend of herbs. Thin strips of bread accompanied by garlic-flavored butter. And the dry white wine complemented all the tastes perfectly — just light enough to let the subtle melange speak for itself. "I can't get over this dinner. Where did you get all this?"

Valerie grinned and reached for the wine. "You'll never believe it. That diner downtown — Rosie's — the one you went to for breakfast."

"You've got to be kidding." Helen recalled her last visit

there — the basic southern breakfast of grits and bacon and fried eggs, certainly not the delightful and imaginative array spread out before them. "The menu I saw was your basic deep fried fare."

"It seems she caters on the side, and she jumped at the chance to put this together when I asked about it. And we're her guinea pigs tonight. That salad dressing is her latest invention."

Helen shook her head. "Amazing." Amazing, too, Helen thought, that Valerie went to all this trouble to get such a meal prepared and to serve it to Helen in her hotel room. She took a sip of wine and looked at Valerie over the edge of her glass. Helen knew she didn't really have to ask herself what was going on here. A private dinner in her hotel room felt like act one of another seduction scene. All they needed was a strolling violin player — although such a figure would have found it hard to stroll in these cramped quarters.

"Did you know there really is a Rosie? She owns the place."

"Huh, I didn't know that." Wonderful. The weather was starting to sound like a good topic. Then Helen heard the heavy sigh from across the table. Okay, now we get to process. Again.

"All right. What's the matter?" Valerie stared back, knife and fork laid down and wine forgotten. "You look unhappy."

Helen sighed. Shit, when was she ever going to have a simple conversation with this woman? Something ordinary and not convoluted, with both of them side-stepping a multitude of painful questions. Never, she realized. Not with the way things had started out. Helen gave up on trying to eat any more for the moment and leaned back in her chair. "It's just — well, I'm wondering what we're doing here, Valerie."

"I take it you don't mean in the cosmic sense." A chill had crept into Valerie's voice, and her blue eyes hardened.

Helen rubbed her hands over her forehead and looked down, noticing that her SmartSave shirt didn't really match the elaborate dinner very well. Neither did she herself, apparently. "Look, Valerie, the last thing I want to do is piss you off," she began. She tried not to notice Valerie's face turning into a steely mask as she forged ahead. "I was just very surprised at this invitation. I thought you'd never want to see me again, after all we've been through here. And I'm —" Helen stopped herself from admitting that she was tired. Tired of figuring out her own and other people's motives. Tired of the weight of guilt and grief that had been slung around her neck like the ancient mariner's albatross. Tired of the inner struggle between prison and freedom that still waged without respite.

"You're what? Sorry that you're here now?"

"No, that's not it. I just wanted things to be on different terms." This was not going well, not well at all. And now Valerie folded her arms across her breasts. Hurt and anger shone from her eyes, and for a moment Helen thought she might cry. "Valerie, I just can't seem to get any of this right. I'm not sure I ever will. What chance did we have, under the circumstances, anyhow?"

"You think I don't feel that way, Helen? You think I don't look at you and wish I could have met you some other way — that maybe you would have walked into my library one day, or I would have bumped into you at Rosie's diner when I was visiting my sister?" And now the tears did fall, silently, welling up out of her eyes and over her cheeks. "And you don't have to remind me about my own problems. I know them all too well, Helen. I know I get attracted to all the basket cases, and then —" The tears stopped as Valerie gasped in horror, realizing what she'd just said to Helen. "Jesus, that's not what I meant at all —"

Something inside Helen broke loose and flew up high and free. "Yeah, well, I guess I'm a little more exciting than your average alcoholic, like your ex, Julie. Must be a nice change for you."

Breathing heavily, her face flushed, Valerie stood up.

"That's how you think I get kicks? What about you, Helen? Take a look at yourself."

God. Suddenly she felt sick. Maybe she should go. "Valerie, please." Helen got up and walked around the table, kneeling beside the weeping woman. She took Valerie's hands in her own and spoke as gently as she knew how. "I want so badly to get it right, just for once. I want to build something the right way, with someone who wants the same things."

"And I want that too, Helen." Valerie's tears had stopped, and her voice was low and calm. She even managed a brief smile. "I guess it was silly, but I was just hoping for a nice evening with you. You know? A nice, normal, dull evening. A good meal, conversation. Maybe even turn on the tube over dessert, just like normal people do." She heaved a deep sigh and surveyed the remains of dinner spread out across the table. "Stupid, wasn't it?"

"No." Helen shook her head emphatically. "It wasn't stupid at all. Jesus, you think I don't want that, too? It's just that I don't know if you and I can have that. Ever." Okay, it was out there now. Encouraged by Valerie's silence — at least she wasn't kicking her out yet — Helen went on. "If it had only been at a different time, in a different place, there might be a chance for us."

"You're right, I know you are." Valerie stroked Helen's face and stood up with an awkward laugh. "I think I was just trying one last time for something more. Can you forgive me?"

Helen smiled sadly and sat on the edge of the bed. "There really isn't anything to forgive, Valerie. And there hasn't been anything else we could do." She reached for Valerie's hand and pulled her gently to the bed, where they sat side by side. "This dinner was really lovely and unexpected. Not to mention absolutely delicious. I'm the one who should be sorry for spoiling things."

Somehow her hold on Valerie's hand had become a caress, and their fingers intertwined. Helen could feel the heat through the other woman's palms, hear her quickened breathing. She tried to pull away but stopped at further pressure from Valerie's hand. "Helen, I know we both know there's not much going for us right now. But maybe — maybe this is enough." Valerie's lips brushed hers in a swift, soft kiss.

"Oh, God, Valerie, I don't know —"

But then she smelled Valerie's hair, felt her hands stroking and exploring. Helen made a half-hearted attempt to push herself away, only to feel Valerie come even closer. And it was easy, too — so much easier to just let it happen. To let Valerie make love to her one more time — most likely for the last time. To forget about all her own misgivings, for once. To just stop thinking.

And for most of the night it worked. First they undressed each other, both women lingering over the task as if they knew this was the last time it would ever happen. Helen couldn't get enough of Valerie's hair — its dark length and glossy shine, its rich scent of some enticing but unidentifiable spice, the way it contrasted the deep blue of her eyes. And the way it spilled like water over her shoulders and chest, draping across her heavy breasts as she mounted Helen, straddling Helen's face with her warm soft thighs.

Even when the lights went out, after a bright flash of lightning flared through the blinds, she could still see the gleam of Valerie's hair reflected in the pale moonlight that found a way through the storm and into the room. Valerie's faint cries of pleasure as she rode her climax, rocking over Helen's mouth as her thighs shuddered, were barely audible above the pounding of the rain. Her sighs marked the end of it, and Valerie slowly lifted herself off Helen to lie down, sweating and panting, on the rumpled sheets beside her.

"My turn," she murmured as her hand moved across Helen's naked belly to her crotch. Helen lay very still. Exhaustion took over, and Helen moved only to spread her legs a bit wider, allowing Valerie to do whatever she wanted without encouragement. And isn't this just easier? Helen asked herself. Isn't this better, to go through life reacting instead of acting. Taking it instead of doing anything about it. So what? I get some great sex and I don't have to deal with this woman again once she's gone. I let Ludy and Deets do their thing without me — finish my parole — take the money from the warehouse — stay at home with Bobby and Aunt Edna. That's it. I don't have to do anything but vegetate. Helen let these thoughts course through her mind as her body let Valerie demand a physical response. Nothing to it, she thought, as she felt her own climax build to bursting point. Piece of cake. Easy as pie.

Then, for a moment in the darkness, she saw Bertie's face. It wasn't Valerie who leaned over her, looking into her eyes, but Bertie who grinned and giggled at the way Helen's body twitched under her ministrations. The walls of the hotel room congealed into the blank gray concrete of Deasely, and the moon shining through the rain transformed into the corridor lights at the facility.

Helen jerked back from Valerie, nearly sliding off the bed in her efforts to get away. At that moment the lights came back on. Valerie huddled in a heap of sheets and pillows, looking up at Helen with alarm. "Are you all right?" Her blue eyes were alight with fear, and as if suddenly ashamed she clutched the blanket over her bare breasts. "Did I hurt you, Helen?"

Helen shivered. She was cold, standing stark naked in the middle of the room. Breathing hard, she tried to push down the images that had roused her from the bed. "No, not at all, Valerie. I'm okay."

"Like hell." Valerie kept watching her as she edged back on the bed, finally leaning against the headboard. "What was that all about?"

"I — I don't really know if I can tell you." And she didn't know. Helen took a tentative step forward, as if she were carefully skirting the edge of a precipice. As if a vast chasm lay just at her feet — a chasm she'd nearly stepped into with her eyes wide open. To think about Bertie when Valerie made love to her, to see Bertie's face when Valerie touched her and kissed her and brought her such pleasure — what did that mean? So close, so very close to giving up everything. Giving up on herself, on making any effort to have a real life. Giving up on Sissy.

"Talk to me, Helen. Tell me what happened just now." And Valerie looked scared, like a little kid, hunched in the corner. Like Sissy, Helen realized with a start. Maybe like Sissy if she'd had the chance to grow up.

Helen strode to the lamp and switched off the lights. Maybe this would be easier in the dark. Dammit, she'd have to try sometime to talk about this. Might as well be now. "I don't think you know how hard this is for me," she began carefully. "We have to be honest — we don't know each other well, and I've got a lot of scars you'd never imagine. Especially when it comes to sex."

"From prison." Valerie said the word carefully and precisely, as if forcing it out of her mouth.

"Yeah. Mostly. I just need to go really slow right now." Which sounded pretty ridiculous, considering they'd been fucking their brains out a lot lately. But the physical act wasn't the most important part. And how to have it make sense to a woman like Valerie? "This may sound a little odd right now, but maybe we could just hold each other?" Too bad if that sounded like something out of a soap opera. It was the truth.

And Valerie didn't protest when Helen gingerly curled up under the covers and shied away from her. "Sorry, Valerie. Jesus, that isn't nearly enough, is it? I can't get this right. I just know —" okay, here comes the hard part — "I just want to be here. With you. Here and now."

"You're sure?"

"Yeah." Helen lay sweating and struggling with her breath, every muscle rigid.

"Okay." After a few minutes of silence, Valerie sighed and snuggled down next to Helen. "You're not mad at me, are you?"

In answer Helen reached around and pulled Valerie close. The two women nestled like spoons. Helen let Valerie's arm rest across her waist and tried to think. Gradually she heard Valerie's breathing slow to a deep steady rhythm that meant she'd finally fallen asleep. Longing for a cigarette, Helen forced herself to stay still and quiet. The arm around her waist was no bigger than a child's, and once again Helen thought of Sissy. Unnerving, to have an image of that poor kid revolving around in her head right after having sex. Together with the eerie images of Bertie it was enough to send anyone to a monastery.

But the memory of Sissy persisted — perhaps aided by the childlike abandon displayed by Valerie cuddling up to her, as if seeking shelter from something. The memories shifted, though, into something less painful. In the strange half-alert state between sleep and consciousness Helen saw once again that plain heart-shaped face beneath the mousy brown hair. She saw Sissy's shy smile of gratitude that last morning on the porch swing. Already, she realized sadly, the picture of Sissy she carried in her mind was beginning to blur into indeterminate features. Inevitable, of course. This wouldn't be the first time Helen had experienced that melancholy loss of clear images that time imposed on memory.

Helen felt her own body slowly relax as the rain drummed a steady beat on the roof, drowning out the echo of her own thoughts. Maybe she could get some sleep, after all. Maybe this picture of Sissy running through the rain, running to mud and terror and death would go away —

Helen sat up suddenly. Valerie stirred and murmured beside her. Helen barely registered the other woman's presence as her mind, fully awake now, repeated it over and over. Sissy running from the church to her death. From the church. That was it. That was what had been eating at her for days.

"Helen? What is it now?" Valerie leaned on her elbow and reached for the bedside lamp. "Did you have a bad dream?"

But Helen was already up and looking for her clothes. "No, it's okay." Where the fuck were her shoes? Here, under the table. "Everything is fine. I just realized — I just need to get home, now." She sat heavily on the bed and pulled on socks and sneakers. Thank god the rain had let up a bit. Now if only the Rambler would start.

"You are angry at me, then." She turned around, buttoning her shirt, to see Valerie lying on her side staring at her. No tears this time, no emotion — just that flat statement of fact.

God. Helen moved around the bed and sat next to Valerie. What could she say to this woman that hadn't already been said? Maybe just goodbye. In the end Helen didn't even say that. Instead she gently took Valerie's face — a face she wasn't sure she'd ever see again — in her hands and bent over to kiss her. Not a passionate kiss, full of heat and urgency. A gentle touching of lips, this time, brief and sad. Helen leaned back and let her hands fall away from Valerie. "I hope I'll hear from you Valerie. I'd like to, but I think you should be the one to initiate things. Will you think about it?"

"You're not going to tell me what's going on are you?" Valerie sat up, the sheet falling from her breasts. "It's something to do with Sissy, isn't it? Then you have to tell me, Helen. You can't keep me locked out of it, not after what I've done for you."

She meant Kyle's gun, of course. "I just need to be alone now," Helen lied. "Thank you again for tonight. I mean it, Valerie." She shrugged into her jacket and left the room, with one final glance at Valerie over her shoulder as she went out into the chill drizzle. Thankfully the Rambler cooperated at the first try, rumbling into life with only a faint protesting cough of exhaust. As she left the hotel behind her, Helen tried to set aside her worries about Valerie. She hadn't meant to be cold and cruel — she was just too fucked up herself to get

277

further entangled. And she needed a clear head and heart right now, with what she'd figured out this evening.

As she'd feared, Aunt Edna was still up, watching some late night talk show. Helen briefly worried that her aunt would be able to tell she'd just had sex. Too fucking bad. If Helen was going to stay there, her aunt would have to get used to it. No chance, though, that she'd be able to escape up to her room without being noticed. "Did you and that Valerie have a nice time?" she heard called from the living room.

Helen detoured into the living room for just a moment to calm her aunt's fears and make explanations. After what seemed like an hour she got away to her own room, where she shed her clothes and put on warm dry sweats.

"Helen?"

Shit. Bobby was up. He stood like a big white lump in pajamas, leaning against the doorjamb. "You was gone a long time."

"Yeah, I know." Oh, Jesus. Helen's heart sank as she saw Bobby was cradling Bertie's gifts in his arms. What had Aunt Edna told him? "Come on in, Bobby."

He shuffled in and spread the books across Helen's bed. "You have the tapes, Helen," he said softly.

"I sure do. Here, let's get them out." She pulled them out of the bottom of her backpack and added them to the pile. "Do you know what happened to her, Bobby?"

He looked up, confused. "Momma said she won't be around any more. She won't bring me no presents."

"That's right. Well, I'll be around and I'll bring you lots of presents. Okay?"

"Okay. But how come she left, Helen?"

"Well, Bobby, she had to go away. She had some problems." Christ, what the hell was she supposed to say? And Bobby didn't get it at all.

His broad face wrinkled in puzzlement. "Momma says I should throw all these things out," he finally said. "But I don't want to. Look, it's broke." He pointed to the photo album. Its back cover was broken, the plastic peeling off the inside. "I want to keep it, Helen."

Helen glanced up at Bobby. She still hated having anything of Bertie's around her cousin, particularly photographs. "Maybe her daddy would like to have this back, Bobby," she ventured. "You think maybe you could give it to him?"

His face puckered again as he considered. "I borrowed it from her. I didn't steal it."

"I know, hon. It's okay." Not yet. Soon, though, she'd have to coax it off his hands.

"Can we fix the pictures? It's all busted."

"We'll take care of it. Why don't you go back to bed, now, Bobby? We'll get it all fixed up real soon." Still puzzled but somewhat satisfied, Bobby wandered off back to bed clutching the book of fairy tales to his chest. Helen stacked the books and tapes together after he was gone. The photo album, fat and oddly shaped, kept slipping off the pile. Helen crammed everything but the album onto the top shelf of her closet. She held the cheap plastic book. Her most important thing. That's how Bertie described it to Bobby. Had it just been to make Bobby believe he mattered?

Helen lay on her bed and looked at the photographs again. What had happened to the golden haired tot grinning over the birthday cake? She wondered briefly about Bertie's father, who had presumably taken a lot of these photographs. She couldn't imagine what it would be like, knowing that somehow this child had become Bertie Mullins on a cell block in Deasely.

Wait a minute. Why the hell would Bertie keep these around? Helen couldn't believe someone as far gone as Bertie would harbor any sentiment about youth and innocence. Weird. Helen looked more closely at the pathetic history encased in plastic. And she was looking for — what?

Then there were the blank pages at the back, where Bobby had hoped his own pictures would be displayed. Helen ran her fingers over the empty plastic pages. No pictures for Bobby.

He wasn't going to make an appearance in anyone's much loved photo album.

Helen was on the verge of throwing the thing across the room when she realized Bobby would look for it. With a sigh she lay back on the bed, photo album lying beside her. Thoughts of Bertie — of the last time Helen had seen her alive — kept floating through her mind. In the last foggy stages of waking, Helen drifted back to the auto shop. Her mind and body dredged up images. The cold concrete floor. The smell of oil. The flashing lights outside. Bertie's face, pale with fear.

Helen's eyes opened. Not just fear. Surprise. Astonishment. All of that. But — why surprise? Amazed that she'd reached the end? That it had finally come to this? And then there were Bertie's hands, flying up to her face.

Helen sat up. Of course. Bertie's hands. Both of them. Without a gun.

No way she could get back to sleep, now. Helen picked up the album again. Helen looked hard at every picture, then flipped through the end pages. This time the back cover came off in her hands, and Helen stared down at the photograph wedged inside the cover.

Her most important book, she'd said to Bobby. No wonder. This picture, a Polaroid, had been taken very recently. No sign of the sweet child smeared with birthday cake. This was a very grown up Bertie, breasts straining against halter top and butt pooched out in cheesecake for the camera. Posed in front of a sliding glass door, she pouted over her shoulder toward the photographer. And yes, Helen could make out a figure holding a camera, reflected in the glass door. Helen switched on the overhead light and stared down at the shadowy figure of Deets bent over the camera.

Chapter Eighteen

Wanda Wylie looked up from her desk and set her pen down to give Helen a closer look. This afternoon, Helen noted, she was wearing a lavender silk blouse. The delicate shade deepened the tone of her smooth dark skin. Helen tried not to think about how that color would look on Valerie as she met Wanda's gaze. She was suddenly very aware of how severe she looked in her SmartSave workshirt. Not to mention the stains from dirt and sweat obtained after a day of heaving boxes around in the warehouse. After yesterday's little melodrama with Doreen and Deets, Marie had contrived to keep her away from the other guys in the warehouse, ostensibly on a special project. That won't last long, Helen thought grimly as she let her gaze travel across Wanda's shoulders and neck.

Sooner or later she'd have to get out of the warehouse — and she didn't think Marie or Bob would object too much, if yesterday was a sample of how well she was going to fit in.

"And work? How's that going? I understand you had a little bit of trouble out there yesterday."

Shit. "It was nothing, really. One of the guys who got arrested the other night for the stolen property has a girlfriend who wasn't very happy with me. But it was no big deal, really." What if she were to tell Wanda it wasn't just yesterday, but every day? Every day that she got stares and hostility and little nasty jokes and jibes? Would she pat her on the hand and give her a lollipop?

Wanda grimaced. "Not according to Deets." She made another note. "Apparently you conducted yourself very well, though. And they'll be watching these people now. You might want to think about getting a different job, though."

Uh oh. Better watch myself, Helen thought. Wanda was still looking at her closely. Helen tried to relax her face and sit more at ease in the chair, hoping to keep Wanda off the scent. Anyhow, jobs weren't going to just appear wrapped up in a bow in front of someone like Helen Black. She'd already been given most of the week off, due to the kindness and forbearance of management — she couldn't push it much further, if she wanted to stay at SmartSave. Everyone had left her alone today, at least — just a lot of looks, a lot of the silent treatment. That was just fine with Helen.

"Are you sure you're okay, Helen?" Wanda tapped finger on the notes she'd been taking. "You've been through a terrible week. A lot of pressure."

Helen turned away and looked out the window. The storm had continued. Fat raindrops pelted the courthouse across the street, staining the white facade into something resembling gray dough. Flat, ugly, and devoid of life. It was just too easy to draw quick comparisons between the weather and her state of mind today. And she didn't have time to waste on that kind

282

of sentimental crap, not if she was going to get some answers. She wondered idly if Valerie had driven home in the rain, if she'd made it back to New Orleans safely. If it was raining there now, pounding on the library roof where Valerie worked. If there was any way in the world she'd ever get to see Valerie again.

"Helen?" Wanda was staring at her in alarm. Helen was touched to see what looked like genuine concern in her eyes. Well, maybe it was.

"Yes, I'm okay," Helen finally responded as she met her parole officer's gaze. "You're right, it has been tough."

"How are things at home with your aunt?" Wanda asked, folding her hands in her lap as she leaned back in her seat. "I know you were trying very hard to make a transition to real independence in the boarding house. I would expect going back to your aunt's place was tough."

And she wasn't taking notes — just asking Helen almost conversationally, like one friend to another. Hold it, that's a fucking slippery slope, Helen ordered herself. Let's not slide down that one yet. "I think it will only be a temporary solution," Helen answered. "As soon as I can get the money together I'll look for an apartment."

Wanda glanced back at the manila folder — the one with Helen's name on it — sitting on her desk. "You know, you're about half way through your parole. In all these weeks you haven't said a word about what you think you might do once that's over."

Jesus, why did this woman have to be so nice? Helen wondered as she fought to keep remote from Wanda. She just couldn't afford to like her, and that was that. Didn't matter if she had warm brown eyes and a deep soft voice and skin like dark honey. Didn't matter that she seemed to give a flying fuck about what happened to Helen. Didn't matter if she had a heart of gold. Giving in to this would just get in the way of what she had to do. "I'm just kind of taking it one day at a time, Wanda. Maybe in a couple more months, once I get my own place and things settle down — maybe then we can talk about it."

Good, that seemed to satisfy her. "Fair enough," she nodded, offering Helen one of those little smiles. "Oh, by the way —" Wanda fished in one of the desk drawers and came up with a business card. "This is a good friend of mine. If you need to talk about things, you might give her a call."

Wanda's therapist friend had an office just up the street. The card advertised sliding scales and evening hours, including some weekends. Helen resisted the urge to crumple the card into a tiny ball and toss it out to its destruction into the rain. Wanda meant well, that was obvious — no reason to give offense before she had to. What would this nice lady say if Helen started yelling about how her experience with therapy had so far been confined to re- covering from being gut shot and almost killed several years ago? That part of piecing her life together had been allowing a psychiatrist to poke around the Dumpster of her mind and heart, only to result in further despair?

When she realized Wanda was staring at her expectantly, Helen managed a stiff smile and tucked the card into her jeans pocket. "Thanks, I'll keep her in mind."

"Good." Wanda stood up with an air of dismissal, and minutes later Helen was walking outside, hunched in her jacket against the cold rain. It really wasn't coming down hard enough to justify digging her umbrella out of the Rambler. Besides, she had one other errand to run — this one with Ludy. Helen hurried up the main street to the police station and ducked inside just as a downpour let loose.

"I'm here to see Ludy," she told the bored young man who glanced up at the cold air from the door.

"Just take a seat over there," the desk sergeant said as he scribbled something in a notebook. He looked up only because she lingered at the desk. "Something else?"

"Is Deets in now?"

He shook his head. "Graveyard shift this week. Did you want —" But he pounced on the ringing phone and forbore finding out what she wanted with Deets.

Fortunately she didn't have a long wait for Ludy. She sat in one of the uncomfortable chairs ranged along the wall by the desk sergeant's counter, ignoring her own discomfort at the scrutiny of the uniformed officers milling around in the back office. Going back over Ludy's tone of voice in his phone call last night, Helen was certain it held no hint of anger or disgust or annoyance. Just a bland request, disguised as invitation, to come down to the station when she finished her appointment with Wanda. Still, Helen reminded herself, the fact that it was Ludy made it suspect. She realized she was clenching her fists in her jacket pockets, hunching in her chair like a scared rabbit. With an effort she flattened her palms against her legs and sat up straight.

Didn't matter — she still jumped when Ludy appeared and called her name. "Thanks for coming down," he said over his shoulder as he led her into his office. "Sit down." Helen complied as he shut the door against curious stares. Thank God the glass walls were clouded, providing a view of only vague shapes passing by in the corridor.

Helen glanced around Ludy's office as he rounded his desk and settled in the swivel chair facing her. She'd half expected to find walls papered with photographs, like something out of a television movie of the week — pictures of both Sissy and the children killed in New Orleans that haunted the detective's dreams. Maybe even a chalkboard with nice neat patterns and circle and lines connecting everything into a recognizable portrait of a killer. Or at least a map of Mississippi studded with different colored pins, tracing a murderous pattern across the state. Instead the room might have belonged to a monk. Neat, nearly empty desk, blank walls, not a plant or photograph in sight. A room stripped to the essentials — rather like Ludy himself, Helen thought.

"Just had a few things to clear up with you about Kyle

Mapple," he said, leaning back in the chair with a sigh. "Oh, you want some coffee? No? You sure? Okay," and with a careless gesture he tossed something swathed in a clear plastic evidence bag onto his desk.

Not for the first time Helen thanked the terrible gods of the prison system for schooling her in self-control. The gun had, of course, been cleaned and dried and no doubt test fired since they'd fished it up from the Mississippi River where she'd left it. And there were no prints to be found, hers or Kyle's, Helen was certain. No way they could connect her to this weapon except for Kyle Mapple's story. Helen also had a pretty good idea who had killed Sissy, and this gun didn't figure into it at all. So it was just a question of getting her heart to quit pounding and her palms to quit sweating, so Ludy wouldn't win this particular battle of the wills.

She looked up from the gun and met his gaze evenly, not speaking until she was sure she had her breathing under control. She raised her eyebrows. "Are you going to tell me what this is?"

Ludy smiled. Not a nice smile. A little grin of rage laced with mischief. Bad combo, in his case. "Early morning fisherman found it, over by a bridge south of Vicksburg. Kid who found it is convinced it was involved in every major crime that took place in the twentieth century. Kids," he said with a false chuckle, shaking his head indulgently.

Helen shrugged and tried to look unconcerned. Darn those early morning fishermen. "You wouldn't show me this without a reason, officer," she said mildly. "Want to let me in on it? Otherwise I should be getting home. They want me in early tomorrow morning at the warehouse."

"One kid in particular," Ludy went on, talking over her words. "Not the kid that found it. Another kid, one you know. Kyle Mapple."

Okay, let's try looking perplexed now. "I don't understand. This belonged to Kyle? Was it Bertie's?" Fuck, if only she knew exactly what Kyle had said. One more sentence out of either her mouth or Ludy's, and she'd have to try to get hold of a lawyer.

Ludy's face hadn't changed from the handsome stony mask he'd worn since she walked into the office. His eyes, though, seemed to light up with — what? Not anger. No, excitement. He smelled blood, and it showed. A smile continued to tease his lips, and Helen suddenly realized how attractive the man was. Dangerous, but definitely compelling. Which made him even more dangerous, of course. He picked up the gun, the plastic crackling beneath his strong hands, and held it up between them. "Kyle had a bunch of very strange stories about this gun," he said. "Something about you taking it from him the day he had the accident." When Helen didn't respond, Ludy went on, "He did say a lot of other things, too. About Bertie, about Dave and Chuck. Lot of ranting and raving. It's hard to know what really happened."

Helen shook her head. "Accidents will do that to you sometimes. Get you confused."

The light in Ludy's eyes went from a hot glow to dark ice. He placed the gun back on the desk. "Guess we'll never really know what happened to his gun, then. Or if this is the one. Especially since we're dropping all charges against him because he cooperated with us in rounding up Bertie's little nest of fuckers."

"Yeah, that's the way it happens sometimes," Helen said. "You never get all the answers."

"You're speaking from experience there, I expect." Ludy folded his arms behind his head and the smile crept back. "Me, I hate mysteries. I fucking hate 'em. Generally I don't let something like this go until I get an answer."

Helen stood up. Now or never. "Good luck, then." Ludy stayed silent as she slowly let herself out of his office. She never clearly remembered getting outside, but the next thing she knew she was walking through the rain back to her car. So what the hell was that all about? Some kind of warning, that he still didn't like her, didn't trust her, didn't believe that she was somehow connected with the whole fucking mess revolving around Sissy and Bertie and Kyle and any other plots being hatched on his turf. Helen barely felt the rain pelting her face as she pondered the meaning of that encounter with Ludy. He couldn't pin her down with anything yet, she thought as she finally reached the Rambler, but she had better watch her back. No false moves — he'd be waiting with a grin and a pair of handcuffs.

And what was she about to do now but take a very risky step, going to visit Kyle Mapple? If she could get past Mrs. Mapple, that is. Helen circled around the small grassy plot at the heart of Tynedale and headed uptown to Gramm Street.

Most of the way to the boarding house Helen considered turning around and telling Ludy what was sitting on the top shelf of her closet. She'd removed the picture from the album and put it in a plastic bag, safely tucked away behind old shoes and a moth-eaten sweater. But what would he say? He'd probably just ask her why she had the thing in the first place. And that would drag in Bobby and Aunt Edna — something Helen was determined not to do just yet. No. First, talk to Kyle. Try to put the pieces together a little better. Then maybe see if she could find out where the picture had been taken. On Deets' property, maybe?

Helen shook her head. She was sitting on a time bomb and she knew it. She just couldn't face Ludy without something further to go on, that's all. Ludy would probably figure Helen was trying to cover her own ass and came up with this vague outline of a man taking a picture to keep her own nose clean. Like those people who keep seeing shooters on the grassy knoll in Dallas in 1963. No, just a little bit more before she stepped back into the line of fire. It was still the word of an ex-con against a highly respected member of the community — a real Officer Friendly for the good folks of Tynedale. And Ludy most certainly wouldn't appreciate being the heavy in destroying a much loved member of the establishment here. Okay, then. Just until tomorrow, when she'd had a chance to think about it — just until tomorrow morning. Then she'd talk.

Her decision made, she realized she was almost there. Strange to be driving back down these familiar streets. The aging neighborhood, with its rows of small cramped houses, looked grim and gray and cold under the rain, presenting a sharp contrast to the newer bigger houses in her aunt's section of town. When she arrived at the boarding house she felt as if a chilly pall had settled over her mind and body, a dismal shroud that she couldn't ascribe to the rain. She approached the front porch with a deepening sense of depression. Maybe that's why she'd gravitated to this dead-end place to start with, avoiding the superficial warmth and physical comforts of her aunt's house. Maybe, she decided as she knocked on the door, it had felt as though she belonged in a place like this. A place without a future.

She knocked twice but heard only the rain pounding on the porch roof. She was about to turn away when the door cracked open and Mrs. Mapple's face peered out. "Oh, it's you." The older woman blinked as if unused to even the fading light of a rainy autumn afternoon. "What do you want?"

For a moment Helen stood stunned, unable to respond. From the neat, brisk, birdlike little old lady she remembered, in just days Mrs. Mapple had transformed into a shriveled wisp. Even in this dim light Helen could see her dry skin, the smudges under her little black eyes, the lackluster hair she didn't bother to pull back from her face now. With a shaky hand Mrs. Mapple pulled at her wrinkled dress. She stepped backward, her other hand poised to close the door. Gently Helen placed her hand flat on the door with just enough pressure to prevent its closure. "How are you, Mrs. Mapple?"

She got a tiny snort of something like laughter in response. "I was wondering how Kyle was doing. I heard all about the accident that night. He's at home now, right?" Mrs. Mapple offered no resistance as Helen kept talking, kept

289

moving forward into the house. "That must mean he's doing better."

"No thanks to those horrible men at the police station." The woman's voice rasped, as if she didn't use it much. Helen stood in the foyer, blinking her eyes to adjust them to the darkness of the house. Mrs. Mapple, barely visible in the gloom, brushed past Helen and led the way to the kitchen. "Kyle's asleep right now. He's still in a lot of pain, with his leg and all."

The kitchen was a little better than the rest of the house — at least there was still coffee on the stove, just like always. Helen took a sip of the bitter coffee as Mrs. Mapple talked, her animation returning as she told her story. It wasn't a pretty one, and the coffee threatened to turn into acid in Helen's guts as she listened. "That Ludy," Mrs. Mapple hissed, her fingers clenching into little knots of anger and despair as she placed her hands on the table. "As if Kylie, my little Kylie, could have anything to do with those awful people. He's just a child, Helen, you knew that," she whined with a pleading look. "They forced him to help them, threatened him with awful things. They're all going to burn in hell for their sins, and that horrible woman is already there now, staring Satan in the face. She corrupted my little Kylie."

Little Kylie. Helen didn't know whether to laugh or cry. Little Kylie would probably rather die a thousand deaths than hear his mother call him by such a cutesy childhood nickname. "How is he doing? What did the doctors say?"

Another snort. "They're no better than that nasty detective! Evil place, that hospital — full of godless atheists. And my Kylie has to go back there for months until he can walk again."

"I'm really sorry, Mrs. Mapple. Does — does that mean, though, that Kyle doesn't have any charges against him?"

It took a few more minutes to get her off the subject of secular humanists and back to what was happening with her son. Helen was able to breathe a sigh of relief at last. She drained the dregs of her coffee as Mrs. Mapple told her that Kyle's cooperation with the police had won his freedom. "Of course, he'll have to go to court for the trial of those sinful thieves."

Helen let her ramble a little longer, marveling at how much more alive she looked since she'd started her diatribe. Should she suggest that Mrs. Mapple take in boarders again? Not including Helen, perhaps — but maybe just to keep in touch with the world, to avoid drying up into the frightened old lady who'd greeted Helen at the door. "I'm so glad to have my baby boy back home safe, though," the older woman sighed, shaking her head. "At least we had that nice Tommy Deets there to help him."

Helen leaned forward, listening carefully. "You've known him a long time, haven't you? I guess he would naturally try to help you right now, with all these troubles."

She smiled, the first smile Helen had seen on her face today. "Oh, I am so grateful to the lord that Tommy Deets was there! He certainly kept a close eye on Kyle for me, the whole time that nasty detective kept hounding my boy."

Yeah, I'll bet, Helen thought. "I'm sure he did, since he's such an old friend. I think you said once you went to school together, didn't you?"

Mrs. Mapple was enjoying the chance to talk to someone. Helen watched as the words bubbled up and spilled out. "He made sure Detective Ludy didn't touch my boy, not one little hair. And he's been here so much, helping me out here at the house. Now that I'm all alone." Her face fell again. Helen felt a pang of sympathy. Mrs. Mapple certainly didn't have much left now. It would be very hard to come up with a whole new set of boarders — especially coming after all the notoriety garnered by Kyle, the Pembertons, Sissy, even Helen herself. "But we'll just keep praying, trying to go on and rebuild. Now that I have Kyle — and good friends like Tommy Deets. And — and you, too, Helen," she added shyly.

Helen tried to smile, tried to cover her guilt. Mrs. Mapple

291

didn't need to know why she was really here, having this conversation. She didn't need to know that sitting in that kitchen made her want to scream and run right back out into the rain. To get away from the dark depressing house, from the dark depressing life she lived here. Instead of letting all this out, Helen reached out and patted Mrs. Mapple on the hand. "That's so sweet of you," she managed to say. "As long as you have friends like Tommy Deets, you can't go wrong. I guess he lives close by, doesn't he? To be able to help you out so much, like he's doing right now."

"Not all that close, Helen — that's what makes it so special. He's got this cabin, way over on the other side of town, kind of off the road a bit. I think maybe he's lonely," she continued, her face wrinkling in sympathy. "All alone out there, no family — maybe he sort of sees my little Kylie like his own son, you know?" She wiped her eyes and sniffed. "He's taken Kylie out to his place a few times, too. He'll come pick him up and they'll spend all day together. I think Kyle really sees him as a father."

Helen bit her tongue on that one. No way she was going to burst that bubble right now. "Does Kyle talk a lot to him, then? About what happened?"

Tears escaped Mrs. Mapple's eyes and she grasped Helen's hand tightly. "Oh, they've spent hours and hours talking. It's good for Kylie, to have a man to talk to. He always seems a lot quieter after talking to his pal Tommy."

"That's really nice, Mrs. Mapple." They wandered off onto other subjects for a while, and Helen finally stood up as conversation dwindled. "Maybe I could take Kyle over to see Tommy one of these days. You know, just to give you a break once in a while. Maybe if Kyle is awake right now I could ask him about it?"

She finally talked Mrs. Mapple into taking her upstairs to Kyle's room. He lay like a pile of white sticks beneath the sheets, both legs encased in mounds of plaster, a pile of CDs and magazines splayed across the bed. With a flustered gesture Kyle swept the pornographic publications off the sheets. His mother didn't seem to notice.

"Look who's here to see you, Kyle!" She leaned over and gave him a smacking kiss on the cheek. Kyle visibly squirmed under his mother's affection and managed to send a glare Helen's way at the same time. Apparently Deets had protected Mrs. Mapple from understanding exactly what her son had done.

Helen leaned against the wall and regarded the boy, enjoying his discomfort. She'd put up with a lot for Mrs. Mapple, but it did her heart good to see Kyle miserable, awful though that sentiment was. "I hear you've been making friends with Officer Deets," Helen began.

"Can I get you anything, son? Do you want something to drink? How about another sandwich?" His mother picked and pulled at sheets and pillows, twisting the blanket until his pile of CDs clattered to the floor.

Kyle slapped her away. "Mom, please! Just leave it be," he whined. "All this fuss is giving me a headache."

But Mrs. Mapple remained oblivious to his irritation. "I'll just go get some cold water for you," and she scuttled back down the stairs.

Kyle sighed dramatically, rolling his eyes and slumping down under the blanket. "Jesus, she's gonna make me crazy. I can't get up and move with these fucking casts on me —"

Helen walked to the bed and leaned over. Kyle recoiled as a wave of fear fluttered across his pimply face. "We've only got a minute before she comes back. I need to know what you and Deets talked about on your little visits."

He sniffed and tried to sit up and look tough — not easy, given his plucked chicken appearance. "I didn't say nothin'! They don't know anything about you or the gun."

"Bullshit," Helen breathed. "Just tell me about the police. About what Deets is up to, hanging around so much."

"Fuck if I know." The sullen sneer came back. "That old fart is all over me, all over the place. Asking me all kinds of shit, trying to get me to tell him stuff instead of talking to that asshole Ludy." He snorted, sounding remarkably like his mother. "Like suddenly we're best friends, now. When he always used to look at me like I was a piece of gum on his shoe."

"And did you? Did you talk to him instead of Ludy, or a lawyer?"

"Hell, no. What do you think I am, a fucking idiot?"

Helen decided not to answer that one. "So he's just been here a lot, trying to talk to you. Or get you to talk." She spoke quietly, thinking hard. "Where's his house?"

His brow creased in puzzlement, making him look a lot older. Like Kyle the senior citizen. "Why do you want to know?"

"Listen, fuckhead —" She heard Mrs. Mapple on the stairs but took a couple of seconds to lean over and pull him up by the collar of his pajamas. "Ludy can still find out about the gun and about the shit you tried to pull with me the other day. Why don't you just tell me what I need to know and we'll let it go at that?"

"Okay, okay." He fell back when she dropped him, cowering away from her. "It's off Highway Twenty, take the Elton Road exit and follow it to the first turnoff. He's a mile or so in from there."

Later Helen couldn't even remember what she'd said to get out of the house and back into her car. The rain had stopped but a cold wind came up from the south. She shivered as the Rambler's heater coughed into life. By the time she reached the turnoff from Elton Road she'd calmed down enough to realize she was on a fool's errand. The only illumination came from pale starlight piercing the clouds. Long branches from the overarching trees lashed the windshield and scraped the sides of the Rambler. The road stretched on for maybe half a mile before opening out in front of a small one story building she could barely make out in the darkness.

Okay, fine, she told herself as the old car bumped and

rocked to a halt with the motor still running. I'll just see what it's like and then turn around. I won't do anything else at all tonight. What had made her take off like that, anyhow? She had only fragments — nothing solid. That and the memory of Sissy's face hovering like a distant planet in her mind. Thank God that cop at the station told me he was working graveyard shift now.

Then the cold air burst in on her and a big hand closed over her arm, yanking her out of the car. Deets smelled like rain and soil and trees — she could hear his heavy breathing as he pulled her away from the car. "I've been expecting something like this."

Chapter Nineteen

The handcuffs bit sharply into Helen's wrists. Last time she'd had to wear this kind of restraint they'd been the newer plastic kind. That had been the day the judge pronounced sentence on her for killing Victoria Mason. Deets apparently favored old fashioned methods, and the steel weighed heavy on her hands, tugging at her arms. He had her shackled so that her shoulders bent awkwardly, her arms pulled around the back of the chair. So how long had she been sitting there? Time had frozen when she'd felt the gun in her back. She could piece together the sequence of events — Deets marching her to this chair and cuffing her to it, then his disappearance into another part of the house. Helen figured maybe twenty minutes had elapsed when he came back to the dining room.

She stared at herself in the sliding glass door. The same door used as a backdrop to Bertie's taunting poses. How the hell had she persuaded Deets to do that? Helen looked away from herself. She had to start talking, even if all it did was get him mad. Anything would be better than this silence stretching out toward her own death.

Deets stood at the other end of the dining room table. It was polished to a high gloss, and reflected back the gray sheen of the gun he was loading. Helen considered coming up with some taunting remark, try to get him mad and off his guard. She thought better of it when she saw how deliberately and methodically he bent to his task, taking his time with great seriousness. This was a man who'd already stepped off the deep end and taken the plunge. Nothing she would say now could stop him. She'd have to come up with something else.

Okay, she just couldn't stand the silence any longer. "So why the fuck were you expecting me, Deets? I don't recall giving you a jingle to let you know I was on the way. Must have been your pal at the desk today. Did he tell you I'd been asking about you?"

His massive head lifted and she felt nausea at the sight of those blank mud toned eyes. "It wasn't only that. Yeah, he gave me a call this afternoon. But it's other things, too. I realized what I'd said to you at the warehouse. About Sissy running from the church. How would I have known about that if I hadn't been there myself?" He bent to his task again, breathing heavily through his nose. "And I know Bertie was hanging around your snatch. I figured you guys had started fucking, she'd shown you those pictures."

"Funny, I never thought of you as a stud, Deets."

Nope, that didn't get to him either. He just shrugged and continued loading the gun. "That was her idea. She thought she could get some people in the porno business interested if they saw what she had to offer." He smirked and set the gun down on the table. "She didn't know what a poor piece of cooze she was. Just to shut her up I took a few pictures.

Anyway, what could it hurt? The car business isn't what it used to be. I thought maybe I could branch out into home movies."

"I'm surprised you let those pictures out of your sight, Deets."

Again the smirk. "I thought I got 'em all. Guess I was wrong."

"Yeah, I guess you were."

"Don't matter." He sniffed and scratched his belly. "I figure you're going to tell me where they are pretty soon."

"Wrong again."

"We'll see." Which was worse, seeing herself reflected in the glass or seeing the smile on his face? Don't think about what he's going to do, she lectured herself — think about getting out of this place.

Helen could sense the beginning of tingling in her palms and fingers. Fucking wonderful, her arms were going to sleep now. She flexed her fingers, hoping to bring some life back into them, and was rewarded for her efforts with sharp stabs of pain. Fine. Think, dammit — think fucking hard. Deets never glanced at her as he sat down at the table. Okay, pay attention to the bastard, maybe he'll slip up and give me a chance to kick his balls in. The dining room light cast deep shadows over his end of the table. Helen could tell that he'd changed clothes but that was about all she could make out.

Helen knew she would scream if the quiet continued. "Aren't you taking a big chance, Deets, that you'll be missed at work tonight? People, especially other cops, might notice a thing like that."

This time he sighed, wearily, as if he were dealing with an exasperating child. "I don't start graveyard until tomorrow night. Now, just keep your mouth shut and let me finish this, will you?"

The silence in the room, except for the snick of bullets loaded into the gun's chambers, set Helen's teeth on edge. She was afraid she would literally start screaming if he didn't speak. Not that it would make much difference, stuck out here miles from the nearest neighbor. And just an hour ago Helen had been grateful for the remoteness of the house, grateful to have her illegal deeds masked by isolation from prying eyes.

"Deets —"

"Shut up." The complete transformation from kindly Officer Friendly to cold killer with steely eyes continued to rattle Helen so much that she could hardly breathe, let alone think. Deets regarded her from the other side of the room as if she were a new kind of beetle that had turned up under his boots. Helen complied with his command, her spine quivering into ice at the hollow voice. She'd seen that kind of look before — on the faces of men and women who had gone over the edge and into a dark chasm without boundaries. People who had nothing left to lose.

"What was it, the auto repair shop?" he asked.

Should she answer? Maybe it would buy her some time, give her some edge over him. "That, and some other things."

"Like what?" He sounded genuinely curious. She'd try to spin this out a while, she thought — hope swept through her at the tone of his voice. "You might as well tell me," he said with a weary sigh.

Because I'll be dead in a few minutes anyway, so telling him can't hurt. That's what he means, Helen thought. "The auto shop and the church, too."

"Yeah, I know. Ludy told me you'd been poking around in there."

"No, not from that."

"What do you mean?" He leaned forward on the table, his voice came out sounding puzzled. The gesture put his face and body into the light so that his expression, the way he carried himself, were clearly visible. It wasn't anger or fear or insanity she read in his heavy solid features. This was determination to get the job done, and get it done right. Immediately Helen wished he'd go back into the shadows so she could think her way through the panic. She tried not to

299

stare at his beefy arms, bulging through the workshirt and camouflage vest he wore. It wasn't fat, it was solid muscle. "I said, what do you mean?" he repeated in the same calm voice.

Okay, think of the thousand and one nights. Spin this out as long as you can. "Earl's church fund." Deet's face took on a blank look. "It was in Gary Greene's books. Lots of cash, initialed for a church fund."

Realization dawned, and he nodded. "Because we met on the church grounds."

"So when I put it together with the auto repair shop, I realized —" Helen stopped short, her mouth dropping open. Auto repair shop. "The car theft ring. The one Ludy broke up, right after he came to town. That was you."

Deets shrugged and went back to the fully loaded gun. He hefted its weight in his palm with a small smile that sent a shiver down Helen's spine. "That was close. He almost got me on that one."

"So why didn't he bust you about your connection to Bertie?"

At that one Deets actually laughed. "That fucking twat? He thought she was some dog shit on his shoe, never gave her a second thought. He was pretty surprised at the thought of Bertie controlling those assholes at the warehouse who were in on it." He shook his head, looking like a bemused bulldog. "Of course the twat was never meant to be a master criminal."

"But you were. Is that it? Is that what made you kill Sissy?"

A shadow crept over his face at the mention of the dead girl's name. For the first time he appeared angry, and Helen wondered for a brief terrified moment if she'd made a mistake mentioning Sissy. What did he feel about that? Grief? Regret? It looked more like anger — maybe anger at being reminded of what he'd done. But the anger didn't seem to be directed at Helen — more at the dead girl. "Hell, it was Earl's idea to go there when he paid me the money —"

"For keeping his little sins secret, right? He'd fork over cash and you'd make sure no one in Tynedale found out about his taste for boys."

"Hell, I didn't care where we took care of business. Some kind of guilt trip, I guess." Helen felt the seeds of anger bloom at Deets' casual tone. She tried to put together a mental image of Earl Pemberton — and came up only with a narrow face sporting a beak of a nose, a worried look drawing lines around the prissy mouth. She'd always assumed it was the stress of caring for his father. Now, at the thought of him eternally paying for his sins, doing penance in a ruined church by putting himself at the mercy of Deets, her disgust at both men rose like nausea in her stomach. "Anyway, he was about to crack. Any minute he was going to talk to Ludy, I could see that."

"So I guess you helped him solve his problems."

Deets shrugged and smiled again. Oddly enough he seemed to be enjoying himself. And why not? He never got to talk to anyone about all this, and the chance would probably never arise again. "No, that one he did all by himself. I just made sure there was a note."

"Practical. Guess killing a little girl wasn't so practical, though."

There, the anger again. Maybe she could use that to her advantage, keep baiting him until something snapped. Her gaze wavered to the gun. If she could just get him to set it down maybe she had a chance. "The little brat — how the hell was I supposed to know she'd be hiding in there? It was Earl's fault, though. When he saw her he just took to screaming like a banshee. Scared the hell out of both of us. I had to do something. She took off running and Earl pitched a fit."

For a few seconds rage at the girl's murder swept away fear. "So why'd you do it? Why'd you chase her down like you would a rabbit?"

But he was going on as if he hadn't heard her at all. "Fucking asshole, with his fucking God and guilt and sin.

Kept screaming and hollering. It was all I could do to keep the bastard quiet, get him out of there before the whole fucking neighborhood came in." Deets' massive jaw worked, as if the words hurt coming out. "Didn't even know it was a kid, for Christ's sake. All I know, someone was in that church and ran off. Didn't know it was her."

"So what went wrong?"

He got up and started pacing. Helen could smell his sweat as he walked by in his prowl. "That asshole just couldn't sit still, had to follow me into the bushes when I chased her. I wasn't going to shoot anyone, all right?" He grabbed Helen's chair, jerking it around so she faced him. She struggled to hide her pain at the sudden tightening of the cords around her wrists, struggled not to reveal her nausea at his face looming up into hers. "Hell, I thought it was Bertie, following me around, sticking her nose where it didn't belong."

Jesus. Bertie was small and lean, almost like a child. "You thought you were shooting at Bertie."

"Goddammit —" He slammed a fist into the table. "Son of a fucking bitch grabbed at my gun. He grabbed at my gun. It wasn't supposed to happen that way."

Helen closed her eyes. All one big stupid mistake. Sissy was dead for nothing. If Deets had known it was only a kid he'd probably have let the whole thing go. The toxic combination of Earl Pemberton's guilt and Deets' cold amorality had ended the girl's life. "So Sissy died for a couple of scum bags. For nothing."

"Listen, bitch." Spittle sprayed from his lips onto her cheeks. "I never meant to shoot her, even if it was Bertie. I did it to scare her. Stupid brat."

"Better to just leave her there, was that it? Wait for some dog or some kids in the park to do the dirty work."

Deets stood up. Confession seemed to have drained him of energy. Again his eyes glazed over with that muddy dull stare. "It started raining. Earl was half screaming, out there in the bushes. It was get him out of there or shoot him, too. Then

I'd have two bodies to worry about. Not to mention people in the neighborhood hearing us if he kept pitching a fit, howling about God and all that shit." He walked back around the table and picked up his gun.

Helen didn't know if she should be more scared of Deets calm than Deets mad. "Yeah, that's a tough problem. Getting rid of the body of a little girl. I'm not surprised you left her out there to rot."

"That's enough." His voice was flat, though, drained of all feeling. No, not flat — careful. Helen realized she must have touched a nerve with that one. But what? Maybe he'd been working hard at convincing himself the girl's death had been unavoidable, and Helen had just reminded him of his petty selfish motives for all this. Money, no more and no less.

That one made him put the gun down, all right — but only to come around the table and slap her hard. Helen held her breath until the sparkling colored lights cleared from her eyes. At least it was the cheek that hadn't landed on the cement floor of the auto shop — now she'd have a matched set of bruises.

"All right, you fucking cunt." Deets' face was only inches from her own. Helen smelled the acrid tang of his cigars on the breath that blew warm into her eyes. "All that crap — that's bullshit. I know you got more brains than Bertie ever had. Tell me what else you know." He jerked her collar in both his hands until she nearly left the chair.

"Bertie." She managed to get the word out and was gratified to see the puzzlement come back to his face. Deets dropped her back down with a jolt that jarred her shoulders. "When you shot her. You told Ludy she had a gun." Helen swallowed hard, not sure she could still talk. Her words came out in a hoarse croak. "She wasn't holding the gun. I wasn't out cold yet when you killed her. You didn't have to shoot her, Deets. She was unarmed. Her gun — it was just lying on the floor." Helen replayed the scene in her mind, Bertie with her hands flung up protectively over her face, the explosion from

Deets' gun, the blood spreading across her shirt. "You could have taken her, no problem. Instead you killed her."

Deets loosened his hold and stared over Helen's head. Now what? He looked down at her, seemed to reach some kind of conclusion. "Get up."

"What?" Helen jerked forward, banging the chair on the floor and her sore right knee against the table leg. She bit back an involuntary yelp of pain as Deets' expression turned into annoyance. He opened his mouth as if to order her again, then gave up and lumbered around the table. Helen cringed at the strength in his huge hands — he could snap her neck with one squeeze if he wanted to. He pulled her up, twisting both her arms even harder until they'd cleared the back of the chair. The sense of relief from having pressure taken off her shoulders dissipated in the terror that swept through her body as Deets propelled her forward.

God. Keep talking, keep trying. "Come on, Deets," she managed to say — even managing to sound angry. "Just tell my why, okay? Why did you do all this?"

He actually stopped at her question, jerked her around so he could see into her face. "Money. Why else?" He waved one hand around the room. "You think a two-bit cop could have all this? You think I could afford anything besides a trailer like a tin can stuck in some mobile home park on my pay?" He gazed around the cabin, a smile creeping over his big round face. "The good part is, I timed it all right after my wife died so everyone could think it was the insurance. Not that she ever left me a dime. Pretty sweet, huh?"

"So it's worth a couple of lives, is that it, Deets? So you can have your nice middle class house and pretend to be a human being, right?" Uh oh, he didn't like that. In answer he jerked her arms painfully. She bit her lip until it bled so she wouldn't cry out.

"Let's go." Helen stumbled through the living room, where just fifteen minutes ago she'd learned the truth. To her right stood the roll-top desk and the humidor with its incriminating papers, redolent of tobacco. To her left the heavy wood front door loomed, where Deets was headed. Helen bit down against making any sound — she'd be damned if she broke down in front of this fucker, the man who'd killed Sissy and Bertie and God knows who else — realizing too that any kind of whimper or whine would just infuriate him more. Deets paused in the foyer, massive head bent down, chewing at his lower lip in thought. After nodding to himself, he shoved her back down the hallway to another room she hadn't yet seen. "Just stand there," he muttered, letting go of her arm long enough to flick on the light switch.

Helen blinked at the sudden sharp light, then opened her eyes to see rows of guns lining the wall straight ahead. Deets pushed her unceremoniously onto a leather sofa next to the gun rack and surveyed his array of weapons. Helen felt sweat running in cold stinging rivulets into her eyes. There was nothing she could do but keep blinking, trying to clear her vision. Her whole body trembled as Deets set down his revolver and reached for a small locked case. Fear? Fatigue? Shock? All three, no doubt. One part of her mind rambled around the details of her condition while another larger part threatened to start screaming in terror. She almost did when Deets opened the case to reveal a wicked pair of hunting knives. They looked like the kind her uncles and cousins had used when skinning rabbits. Jesus fucking Christ.

Her mind raced over possibilities, none of them good. Deets continued his orderly review of the room once he'd pocketed the knife. His gaze seemed inward turned, however, almost as if he'd forgotten Helen's presence. Stupid hope. Helen looked around the room in desperation, trying to find something — anything — to distract Deets, trip him up, get him to take off the handcuffs. When she looked at him again he was regarding her calmly and seriously, his head cocked to one side, as if trying to figure out a math problem. Then, with a little nod of his head, he took out a small pistol from a battered cigar box under a pile of newspapers. He hefted the gun in his hand and smiled at her. "Know what this is?" When she didn't respond, his grin widened. "Sissy would recognize it."

Jesus. The same gun that killed Sissy. Helen's brain mapped it all out for her in fast forward. Deets would kill her with the same gun that had killed Sissy, making Helen's death look like suicide. Earl's death would just be a tragic circumstance, brought on by his past. More deaths than Shakespeare — but no one would ever look to Deets, even if they questioned Helen's convenient demise.

She must have made a sound then. Deets swiveled to look at her as he slipped one of the knives into the pocket of his vest. "Let's go."

This was it, then. Finally. Just like it had happened with Bertie in the auto repair shop, Helen felt an empty lightness flow through her, voiding her pain and terror as cleanly as if a wind had blown her apart. The only thing left for her now was to make sure someone would come after Deets for everything he'd done. Some way to leave evidence behind.

That thought kept her moving through the house, urged on by Deets pulling her by her sore arms. Outside the house the wind blew sharp and cold across her face. Helen wasn't surprised at the total silence surrounding Deets' house. No street lights, no neighbors, not even a fucking squirrel running up one of the huge oaks that fronted the place and kept it completely hidden from the highway. Helen stole a look overhead. The moon had dwindled to a crescent, barely visible through thin clouds. Maybe if she could just get the cuffs off the darkness would become her ally.

Deets halted at his car, propping Helen against the passenger door. Helen let out a cry and buckled over, playing up the pain with a huge — hopefully convincing — grimace. Deets gave her a glance and Helen turned on the tears, surprised at her own ability under pressure. "Can't you just take these things off?" Silence — but at least he hesitated at her plea. "Come on, you've got the gun, and the knife. You've got the whole thing going your way. What the hell could I do?" A couple of deep racking coughs, for effect. Deets isn't a torturer, she told herself, just a greedy fucker who's covering his ass.

Just a flat stare from Deets. He opened the door and pulled her by the arm again, preparing to shove her inside. This time Helen didn't have to fake her reaction. Her shoulders felt like raw meat wrenched from their joints. She made sure to yell out, risking another blow. Instead, Deets looked at her closely. With a sinking of relief that almost made her faint, Helen watched as Deets fished the tiny key for the handcuffs from one of the multiple pockets on his vest. As soon as the cuffs were off, Helen felt tears start in her eyes from the needles that shot through her fingers. Her arms tingled as blood and life flowed back through her veins, and the sensation distracted her from seeing Deet's hand poised to strike her again.

She reeled against the car and felt blood at the corner of her mouth. "Just a little reminder to keep quiet." He shoved her into the car where she landed on her side. As soon as she could see clearly she studied the car's interior. Shit, nothing helpful here. The car was spotless, not even a fucking paper clip on the floor. Something hissed and crackled on the dashboard. A car phone was nestled between the front seats. Helen looked at it longingly, realized she'd never have time to use it. And it was stupid to even think of making a dash for it, in this pitch blackness, through those thick trees. Deets might be older and slower, but she didn't really have a chance against the gun. And this was his turf — he'd probably planted those trees himself, knew every inch of the grounds.

Deets revved the engine and turned the car — not toward the highway, but facing the trees. The headlights picked out a narrow path leading into the forest, just big enough to accommodate the vehicle. Helen's heart sank as Deets drove swiftly along the path, maneuvering with ease through the maze of trees. The jolting motion hurt her right leg and she bit down on her lower lip. Deets knew exactly where he was going and what he was doing. He must have someplace in mind, she thought.

He did. The forest ended suddenly, opening into a clearing like a small valley with a lake in the center. No, not a lake. A big pond, really. Birch trees, their white trunks ghostly in the mist, lined the far edge of the pond. Something stirred in the water, rippling its surface into symmetric circles that spread out to lap at the muddy banks.

"Get out. Now." Deets prodded her with the gun until she obeyed. As she moved Helen tried to shut out the images of what Deets was about to do. Helen thought of the knife and felt her blood turn into ice. Now or never, she told herself. Just get clear of the car first, give yourself some room to run when the time comes.

"Okay. Now it's time to tell me where those pictures are."

Helen stayed silent.

Deets sighed. "You really want this? You sure about that? You know what this can do to you?" And something prodded at her breast.

Helen closed her eyes, forced the memory of Sissy's face into her mind. She could do this. "Fuck you," she said.

To her amazement Deets backed off. She opened her eyes and saw him staring at her. "It doesn't really matter," he said, quietly, as if talking to himself. "We'll be able to search your place later. I'll make it my personal responsibility."

Later. He means after I'm missing. Or found dead. And who would really care, the measly belongings of a murderer, an ex-con who just couldn't make it in the world.

"Come on. Let's get this done."

So it was back to damsel in distress. One look at his face in the dim moonlight told her that the act wouldn't wash anymore — she'd been lucky to work it well enough to get the cuffs off. But now she got a look at the eerie glint in his eyes, strangely similar to the one she'd seen in Bertie's the night

Deets killed her. The look that said they'd passed the point of no return. Time for different tactics.

Helen slipped on the mud, tried to stand up, then deliberately lost her footing again. She went down into the sticky soil as hard as she could, falling onto her back and making sure she coated her clothes with the stuff. Deets sighed and cursed, clutched at her slippery arm and yanked it hard. His grasp didn't hold. Helen felt a surge of hope spike through her body as she squirmed away from him, her hands clutching for something, anything in the mud.

"Bitch," he hissed at her. Helen scooped up as much mud as both hands could hold. She kept her hands close to her chest as Deets hauled her up by tugging at her armpits. Good. She was nearly eye to eye with him now, her feet dangling free above the ground. Deets gave her a long look, the strange light in his eyes fading into something like sorrow. "It didn't have to go like this," he muttered.

"What?"

"Why the hell did you have to come here?" He looked genuinely pained as he set her down gently on the ground. "Why couldn't you just stay the hell away from all this?"

Sissy, she almost said. Was it true? True enough, at any rate. "Because of a little girl that no one loved," she said, not knowing if she meant Sissy or herself.

Deets' face hardened back into a stony mask. Helen had figured out he was furious at having to look at his own actions. Keeping his eyes fixed on Helen Deets slowly pulled the knife from his pocket and slipped off its sheath. The blade glistened as he turned it over in his hand.

Helen thought of Sissy's face, already growing vague in her memory. Anger at that realization fueled her strength as she reached up with clenched fists and smeared thick clayey mud into Deet's eyes. When his mouth opened in shock she shoved mud there as well. Deets gagged, choked, stumbled backward and flailed his arms wildly. Deets staggered, barely keeping his balance. The knife clutched in his fist gleamed with a flat sheen as he spat and sneezed mud from his mouth.

That was all the time Helen needed. She balanced on her shaky right leg and kicked Deets in the balls as hard as she could. Still gagging, he landed on his ass at the water's edge. Helen kicked him again, and his mud-caked mouth opened in a silent roar of pain. She leaned over and felt the gun bulging at the front of his vest. Just as she put her hands on the weapon Deets grabbed her right ankle and pulled hard. The pain shot up through her knee and thigh and she nearly fell over on top of Deets.

"Fuck!" Her curse rang out over the pond. Blindly she fingered the gun again, squeezing her palm around its bulk as Deets twisted her leg out from under her. She fell backward, gun in hand, frantically scrambling away from the pond. As she scooted across the muddy grass she noticed a bulge in her right knee that shouldn't be there. Despite the pain she flexed her knee. Thank God it wasn't broken, just terribly twisted. Fearing that she might throw up, Helen forced herself to take deep breaths until the nausea passed. It hurt like hell, but she was sure she could get herself into the car. More important, she had the gun. She wiped her shaking hands on her thighs, finding a spot that wasn't already covered in mud, and took the safety off the gun. Jesus, Deets liked them big — this was sized to fit his huge paws. Helen cautiously rose up, careful not to jar her right knee any further, and aimed the weapon with both hands.

"Okay, Deets. It's finished now. We can go."

Deets had managed to get up. Still bent over his loins protectively, he turned his head to look at Helen. Mud slid off his forehead and plopped onto the pond as he moved. "Let's go, Deets. You know I'll use this thing if I have to."

Was he shaking his head? Helen squinted through tears and mud and took a jerky step forward. "I've had enough for one night," she started. Her words dried in her throat as once again she saw the hunting knife gleaming in his hand, drip-

310

ping as it flashed in the moonlight. Wonderful. Now she'd have to shoot him — maybe in his knee, to pay him back. That ought to hurt. "This is fucking stupid, Deets. Just get in the damn car and —"

There was no way she could have reached him in time, she told herself later. And Helen could have sworn he was smiling as he stuck the knife into his throat. He fell to his knees, blood spurting in gouts from his neck across his vest to form a puddle of red on the black mud. By the time Helen had made it to Deets he'd pitched forward, face down in the tall rough grass. Of course. He had been a hunter. He'd know exactly how to do this, she thought, exactly where to press the blade in.

Knee temporarily forgotten, Helen crouched down beside him as he died. She saw the light go out of his eyes, and his body convulsed in one heaving spasm as a bolus of blood spilled from his mouth. Silence fell across the pond as she placed the gun on the ground beside his body. She had no idea how long she sat there. She moved only when she realized her teeth were chattering from cold and shock.

Helen half-walked, half-crawled back to the car. Her hands shook so bad on the car phone that she could hardly dial 911. Helen closed the door and slid down into the driver's seat, hugging herself against the cold but too exhausted to look for a blanket. Her fingers trembled as she reached for the switch that operated the heater. She heard sirens approach as if from a great distance. And the next thing she knew, Ludy's face appeared at the car window, small and white and angry. "You again," Helen said before passing out.

Chapter Twenty

The window looked out over a narrow strip of grass lined with scraggly shrubs. Helen could see a couple of discarded bottles someone had tossed over the chain link fence caught in the thin stalks of green. Sunlight winked off the glass as it broke through scudding clouds in the chill winter breeze. Helen took a step closer to the window and peered out through the wire mesh. Off to the right, just within view, a pair of elderly ladies took slow steps along a paved path circling through beds of flowers — or what would be beds of flowers, perhaps, when spring arrived. Their coats flapped in the gusts of wind as they walked out of sight.

"Judge Pemberton?" Helen looked away from the bleak scene and turned back to the old man sitting on the edge of the bed. She wondered again where his briefcase had gone. Hopefully the attendants hadn't forced him to give it up. Maybe he'd discarded it himself, without pressure from anyone else. Maybe he'd realized that with his son dead it just didn't matter any longer. Helen stifled a sigh as she watched him. He did look a little healthier, she had to admit, than he had during his stint at the boarding house. Better fed, more rested. Miss Fletcher — Emily — had done some homework about this place, and so far what Helen could see checked out with the good reports Emily had received. But the judge still didn't look quite right. More than just the missing briefcase. Then Helen figured it out. She'd never seen him wearing anything but that rusty old suit with fraying hems. Today the old man wore a simple long sleeved shirt, buttoned up to the neck, and khaki slacks that rode low on his skinny hips. He no longer looked like a judge, she thought sadly. More like a scrawny plucked chicken ready for the pot.

Helen perched beside him, determined to give it one more try. "I just wanted to see if you were okay, if there was anything I could do for you or get you. Do you have everything you need here, sir?" No response, just vacant staring at the window. He probably didn't even know she was there.

"Maybe I could bring some toiletries or something next time," she went on doggedly. "I'll have to check with the nurse about what you might like. Or special treats. I bet she knows that. Would that be okay?" Who the fuck was she kidding? None of it was okay. None of it had been okay since he'd learned of his son's squalid desires years ago.

Helen looked out the window with him. The view was different from the bed. From here, she could see the clouds as they moved across the sky, dotted here and there with the circumflex of birds hurrying further south for warmer weather. "I don't know if I should have told you about how Earl really died," Helen said, breaking the heavy silence. "I guess I thought you should know the truth. Earl hadn't hurt anyone for years, and he had nothing to do with Sissy's death.

313

It was all Deets, all along. I thought — well, I thought it might make things better for you to hear this. And I didn't think anyone else had thought to come here."

Still no reaction. Helen forced herself to look long and hard into the wizened face, study the blank eyes and watch the trembling mouth for any kind of intelligent activity. A knot of frustration gathered inside her, only to be broken as she glanced down at his quivering hands, shaking gently on his thighs. It was better this way, Helen reasoned. Maybe if he understood everything he'd be a raving lunatic by now. He might be in so much pain over his horrible loss and the wasted life of his son that even this doubtful peace, the peace of oblivion, would be denied him.

Oh well. Helen stood up to go, moving slowly with the pain in her right leg. She was still pretty shaky whenever she tried to move fast on that leg. And they'd warned her about the pain she might feel. Along with their exclamations at how lucky she was to have escaped with so few injuries. Helen slowly let her weight settle evenly into both legs, testing her balance with small steps away from the bed. Okay, so she wasn't going to fall down this time. The pain eased as she flexed her knee.

Bending over she straightened the cheap blanket that had wrinkled under her. That was when a thin wrinkled hand closed over her fingers. The judge, still staring out the window, grasped her hand with surprising strength, giving the fingers a big squeeze. Then, just as suddenly, Judge Pemberton pulled away and folded his hands in his lap again.

Helen reached for her backpack, her eyes blurred and threatening to spill tears. When she could trust herself to speak, she said, "I'll check with the nurse and find out things I can bring you next time. Okay?" He gave no sign he'd heard her, and she softly closed the door behind her.

Two women wearing white uniforms sat in the nurses' station, staring at her as she walked up to them. "I've just been to visit Mr. Pemberton," Helen began. She took a pad

314

and pen out of her bag. "Are you able to tell me if anyone besides me has come to see him?" Perhaps someone else had been able to get through to the old man. And maybe there were relatives Helen could get in touch with. Just to make sure he wasn't totally forgotten.

The nurses looked at each other. One of them shrugged and said, "One guy did, a couple of weeks ago I think. Let's see, who was it?" She reached lazily for a clipboard and rifled through its pages.

"Wait, I know who it was," the other nurse said. "Remember, how I said I recognized him from the television news? That police detective?"

"Oh, right!" They both smiled widely, excited at the memory of their brush with local celebrity. "That good looking one, who found the little girl's killer. You know, the other cop."

Helen let them ramble on at each other while the fact sank in. Ludy. She didn't know how she felt about that. Relieved that the old man hadn't completely disappeared from sight, she supposed. Maybe even a little bit grateful that Ludy had troubled to make a call, official or not. Then she realized the nurses were looking at her expectantly. "Oh. I was just wondering if you could tell me what Mr. Pemberton needs. Or if you know of things he likes. Treats or foods or something."

One nurse looked away, bored, picked up a magazine. The other one grimaced. "Who can tell? I guess you could bring candy. They all like sweet stuff."

Emily Fletcher was waiting for her on the front porch. "How'd it go?" she asked as they got into her car. "Helen? That bad, huh? Damn, I knew I should have gone inside with you."

"No, no, it's okay," Helen said. From the side mirror she could see the front of the building recede into the distance, disappear as they rounded a bend in the road. "It was probably better for me to tell him all this with just the two of us. Thanks for stopping here with me."

"Well, it was on the way — no trouble at all. And I can

assure you that everything I've heard about this place has been positive." Emily went back through the information she'd gathered, and Helen tried to relax. First, though, she glanced over her shoulder at the covered casserole dish sitting on the floor of the car. She hadn't tried cooking anything since — well, since before Deasely. In fact, the last time she'd gone to a lesbian potluck everyone had been vegan. Except for her. She certainly hoped that Renee's crowd included people who'd be okay with bacon on their baked beans.

"Hey. Earth to Helen."

Helen gave Emily a smile, a real one. "Sorry. I was just wondering if I'd made enough. So, how many people will be there?" she asked for the third time.

"You can still back out if you want to."

Helen shook her head. Behind them, the sun was setting in an ocean of orange light. She turned around again and watched the road. "I'll be fine. It's just — well it's been a while. I don't know how to explain it. I guess I'm not used to the idea of having friends."

"You don't have to explain," Emily chuckled. "You should have seen me right after I divorced Sam, when I figured out I needed to be with women. It took me a long time to feel safe around people." She glanced at Helen. "But if this feels like rushing things —"

"Nope. I'm ready." And she was, too. Despite her nerves, she knew she was doing the right thing by accepting Renee's invitation. "Thanks for being my escort, Emily."

"Speaking of escorts, have you heard from Valerie?"

"Yes." The letter lay folded at the bottom of her backpack, safe from any eyes but her own. Later she'd take it out and re-read it, especially the part where Valerie had said something about making another visit to her sister next summer. It hadn't been a definite yes or no — just an open door for the future. Helen would answer soon, after giving her reply very careful thought. This time she didn't want to rush things, to let her loins dictate her behavior. This time she would go slow and careful. This time it would be better.

"Well? Or am I being just a nosy old lady?" Emily glanced at her expectantly.

"No, not nosy or old."

"A lady, then?"

"Always that. No, it's just that it's too soon to tell. I'll have to wait and see."

"Wait and see, huh? Well, that's usually the way with the important ones."

They drove in companionable silence. Helen began to relax, staring out at the stars just rising in the night sky. Then the lights of Tynedale glowed on the horizon, and her stomach began to clench. Hoping that Emily wouldn't notice, Helen began to take deep slow breaths. By the time they reached Renee's house she'd achieved a fragile calm again.

Emily rang the doorbell, holding a basket of bread, while Helen carefully clutched the casserole dish, favoring her sensitive right leg. As she stood up, carrying her offering in her hands, she saw Renee's wide grin over Emily's shoulder. Beyond Renee, in the foyer, she could make out women laughing and talking and moving around. Music — something she didn't recognize — welled out, warm and inviting as it spilled out across the lawn into the night.

"Hey! Helen! What are you waiting for?" Renee called to her, an undertone of laughter sending a different kind of warm invitation across the dark lawn between house and car.

Yeah, what am I waiting for? Helen held the dish with firm hands and went into the house.

About the Author

Pat Welch was born in Japan and grew up in small towns in the South. She has lived in the San Francisco Bay area since 1986. This is her second novel with Bella Books. *Moving Targets,* her first Bella novel, was nominated for a Lambda Literary Award.

Publications from
BELLA BOOKS, INC.
the best in contemporary lesbian fiction

P.O. Box 201007   Ferndale, MI 48220
Phone: 800-729-4992
www.bellabooks.com

A DAY TOO LONG: A Helen Black Mystery by Pat Welch. 328 pp. Helen puts her life back together.   ISBN 1-931513-22-8 $12.95

THE RED LINE OF YARMALD by Diana Rivers. 256 pp. A desperate coalition bands together to save the Hadra
ISBN 1-931513-23-6 $12.95

OUTSIDE THE FLOCK by Jackie Calhoun. 224 pp. Jo embraces her new love and life.   ISBN 1-931513-13-9 $12.95

LEGACY OF LOVE by Marianne K. Martin. 224 pp. Read the whole Sage Bristo story.   ISBN 1-931513-15-5 $12.95

STREET RULES: A Detective Franco Mystery by Baxter Clare. 304 pp. Gritty, fast-paced mystery with compelling Detective L.A. Franco   ISBN 1-931513-14-7 $12.95

RECOGNITION FACTOR: 4th Denise Cleever Thriller by Claire McNab. 176 pp. Denise Cleever tracks a notorious terrorist to America.   ISBN 1-931513-24-4 $12.95

NORA AND LIZ by Nancy Garden. 296 pp. Lesbian romance by the author of *Annie On My Mind*.   ISBN 1931513-20-1 $12.95

MIDAS TOUCH by Frankie J. Jones. 208 pp. Sandra had everything but love.   ISBN 1-931513-21-X $12.95

BEYOND ALL REASON by Peggy J. Herring. 240 pp. A romance hotter than Texas.   ISBN 1-9513-25-2 $12.95

ACCIDENTAL MURDER: 14th Detective Inspector Carol Ashton Mystery by Claire McNab. 208 pp.Carol Ashton tracks an elusive killer.   ISBN 1-931513-16-3 $12.95

SEEDS OF FIRE:Tunnel of Light Trilogy, Book 2 by Karin Kallmaker writing as Laura Adams. 274 pp. Intriguing sequel to *Sleight of Hand*.   ISBN 1-931513-19-8 $12.95

DRIFTING AT THE BOTTOM OF THE WORLD by Auden Bailey. 288 pp. Beautifully written first novel set in Antarctica.   ISBN 1-931513-17-1 $12.95

CLOUDS OF WAR by Diana Rivers. 288 pp. Women unite to defend Zelindar!   ISBN 1-931513-12-0 $12.95

OUTSIDE THE FLOCK by Jackie Calhoun. 220 pp. Searching for love, Jo finds temptation.   ISBN 1-931513-13-9 $12.95

WHEN GOOD GIRLS GO BAD: A Motor City Thriller by
Therese Szymanski. 230 pp. Brett, Randi, and Allie join
forces to stop a serial killer. ISBN 1-931513-11-2 $12.95

DEATHS OF JOCASTA: 2nd Micky Night Mystery by J.M.
Redmann. 408 pp. Sexy and intriguing Lambda Literary Award
nominated mystery. ISBN 1-931513-10-4 $12.95

LOVE IN THE BALANCE by Marianne K. Martin. 256 pp.
The classic lesbian love story, back in print!
ISBN 1-931513-08-2 $12.95

THE COMFORT OF STRANGERS by Peggy J. Herring.
272 pp. Lela's work was her passion . . . until now.
ISBN 1-931513-09-0 $12.95

CHICKEN by Paula Martinac. 208 pp. Lynn finds that the
only thing harder than being in a lesbian relationship is
ending one. ISBN 1-931513-07-4 $11.95

TAMARACK CREEK by Jackie Calhoun. 208 pp. An intriguing story of love and danger. ISBN 1-931513-06-6 $11.95

DEATH BY THE RIVERSIDE: 1st Micky Knight Mystery by
J.M. Redmann. 320 pp. Finally back in print, the book that
launched the Lambda Literary Award winning Micky Knight
mystery series. ISBN 1-931513-05-8 $11.95

EIGHTH DAY: A Cassidy James Mystery by Kate Calloway.
272 pp. In the eighth installment of the Cassidy James
mystery series, Cassidy goes undercover at a camp for
troubled teens. ISBN 1-931513-04-X $11.95

MIRRORS by Marianne K. Martin. 208 pp. Jean Carson and
Shayna Bradley fight for a future together.
ISBN 1-931513-02-3 $11.95

THE ULTIMATE EXIT STRATEGY: A Virginia Kelly
Mystery by Nikki Baker. 240 pp. The long-awaited return of
the wickedly observant Virginia Kelly. ISBN 1-931513-03-1 $11.95

FOREVER AND THE NIGHT by Laura DeHart Young.
224 pp. Desire and passion ignite the frozen Arctic in this
exciting sequel to the classic romantic adventure *Love on
the Line*. ISBN 0-931513-00-7 $11.95

WINGED ISIS by Jean Stewart. 240 pp. The long-awaited
sequel to *Warriors of Isis* and the fourth in the exciting
Isis series. ISBN 1-931513-01-5 $11.95

ROOM FOR LOVE by Frankie J. Jones. 192 pp. Jo and
Beth must overcome the past in order to have a future
together. ISBN 0-9677753-9-6 $11.95

THE QUESTION OF SABOTAGE by Bonnie J. Morris.
144 pp. A charming, sexy tale of romance, intrigue, and
coming of age. ISBN 0-9677753-8-8 $11.95

SLEIGHT OF HAND by Karin Kallmaker writing as
Laura Adams. 256 pp. A journey of passion, heartbreak

and triumph that reunites two women for a final chance
at their destiny.   ISBN 0-9677753-7-X $11.95

MOVING TARGETS: A Helen Black Mystery by Pat Welch.
240 pp. Helen must decide if getting to the bottom of a
mystery is worth hitting bottom.   ISBN 0-9677753-6-1 $11.95

CALM BEFORE THE STORM by Peggy J. Herring. 208
pp. Colonel Robicheaux retires from the military and
comes out of the closet.   ISBN 0-9677753-1-0 $12.95

OFF SEASON by Jackie Calhoun. 208 pp. Pam threatens
Jenny and Rita's fledgling relationship.   ISBN 0-9677753-0-2 $11.95

WHEN EVIL CHANGES FACE: A Motor City Thriller
by Therese Szymanski. 240 pp. Brett Higgins is back in
another heart-pounding thriller.   ISBN 0-9677753-3-7 $11.95

BOLD COAST LOVE by Diana Tremain Braund. 208 pp.
Jackie Claymont fights for her reputation and the right to
love the woman she chooses.   ISBN 0-9677753-2-9 $11.95

THE WILD ONE by Lyn Denison. 176 pp. Rachel never
expected that Quinn's wild yearnings would change her
life forever.   ISBN 0-9677753-4-5 $12.95

SWEET FIRE by Saxon Bennett. 224 pp. Welcome to
Heroy — the town with the most lesbians per capita than
any other place on the planet!   ISBN 0-9677753-5-3 $11.95

**Visit
Bella Books
at
www.bellabooks.com**